Vanished

Vanished

MEG CABOT

WRITING AS JENNY CARROLL

BOOK ONE & BOOK TWO

WHEN LIGHTNING STRIKES, CODE NAME CASSANDRA

SIMON AND SCHUSTER

A **pulse** book

First published in Great Britain in 2011 by Simon & Schuster UK Ltd,
1st Floor, 222 Gray's Inn Road, London WC1X 8HB
A CBS COMPANY

When Lightning Strikes Copyright © 2001 by Meg Cabot
Code Name Cassandra Copyright © 2001 by Meg Cabot

These titles were originally published individually by Simon & Schuster UK Ltd.
All rights reserved, including the right of reproduction in whole or in part in any form.

A CIP catalogue record for this book is available from the British Library
ISBN 978-0-85707-122-4

2 4 6 8 10 9 7 5 3 1

Printed and bound in Great Britain by Cox & Wyman Reading RG1 8EX

BOOK ONE
WHEN LIGHTNING STRIKES

CHAPTER

1

They want me to write it down. All of it. They're calling it my statement.

Right. My statement. About how it happened. From the beginning.

On TV, when people have to give a statement, there's usually someone sitting there who writes it down for them while they talk, and then all they have to do is just sign it after it's read back to them. Plus they get coffee and doughnuts and stuff. All I've got is a bunch of paper and this leaky pen. Not even so much as a diet Coke.

This is just further proof that everything you see on TV is a lie.

You want my statement? Okay, here's my statement:

It's all Ruth's fault.

Really. It is. It all started that afternoon in the

burger line in the cafeteria, when Jeff Day told Ruth that she was so fat, they were going to have to bury her in a piano case, just like Elvis.

Which is totally stupid, since—to the best of my knowledge—Elvis was not buried in a piano case. I don't care how fat he was when he died. I'm sure Priscilla Presley could have afforded a better casket for the King than a piano case.

And secondly, where does Jeff Day get off, saying this kind of thing to somebody, especially to my best friend?

So I did what any best friend would do under the same circumstances. I hauled off and slugged him.

It isn't like Jeff Day doesn't deserve to get slugged, and on a daily basis. The guy is an asshole.

And it's not even like I really hurt him. Okay, yeah, he staggered back and fell into the condiments. Big deal. There wasn't any blood. I didn't even get him in the face. He saw my fist coming, and at the last minute he ducked, so instead of punching him in the nose, like I intended, I ended up punching him in the neck.

I highly doubt it even left a bruise.

But don't you know, a second later this big, meaty paw lands on my shoulder, and Coach Albright swings me around to face him. It turned out he was behind me and Ruth in the burger line, buying a plate of curly fries. He'd seen the whole thing . . .

Only not the part about Jeff telling Ruth she was going to have to be buried in a piano case. Oh, no. Just the part where I punched his star tackle in the neck.

"Let's go, little lady," Coach Albright said. And he steered me out of the cafeteria and upstairs, to the counselors' offices.

My guidance counselor, Mr. Goodhart, was at his desk, eating out of a brown paper bag. Before you get to feeling sorry for him, though, that brown paper bag had golden arches on it. You could smell the fries all the way down the hall. Mr. Goodhart, in the two years that I've been coming to his office, has never seemed to worry a bit about his saturated-fat intake. He says he is fortunate in that his metabolism is naturally very high.

He looked up and smiled when Coach Albright said, "Goodhart," in this scary voice.

"Why, Frank," he said. "And Jessica! What a pleasant surprise. Fry?"

He held out a little bucket of fries. Mr. Goodhart had mega-sized his meal.

"Thanks," I said, and took a few.

Coach Albright didn't take any. He went, "Girl here punched my star tackle in the neck just now."

Mr. Goodhart looked at me disapprovingly. "Jessica," he said. "Is that true?"

I said, "I meant to get him in the face, but he ducked."

Mr. Goodhart shook his head. "Jessica," he said, "we've talked about this."

"I know," I said with a sigh. I have, according to Mr. Goodhart, some anger-management issues. "But I couldn't help it. The guy's an ass-hole."

This apparently wasn't what either Coach Albright or Mr. Goodhart wanted to hear. Mr. Goodhart rolled his eyes, but Coach Albright actually looked as if he might drop dead of a coronary right there in the guidance office.

"Okay," Mr. Goodhart said, real fast, I guess in an effort to stop the coach's heart from infarction. "Okay, then. Come in and sit down, Jessica. Thank you, Frank. I'll take care of it."

But Coach Albright just kept standing there with his face getting redder and redder, even after I'd sat down—in my favorite chair, the orange vinyl one by the window. The coach's fingers, thick as sausages, were all balled up into fists, like a little kid who was about to have a tantrum, and you could see this one vein throbbing in the middle of his forehead.

"She hurt his neck," Coach Albright said.

Mr. Goodhart blinked at Coach Albright. He said, carefully, as if Coach Albright were a bomb that needed defusing, "I'm sure his neck must hurt very much. I'm quite certain that a five-foot-two young woman could do a lot of damage to a six-foot-three, two-hundred-pound tackle."

"Yeah," Coach Albright said. Coach Albright is immune to sarcasm. "He's gonna hafta ice it."

"I'm certain it was very traumatic for him," Mr. Goodhart said. "And please don't worry about Jessica. She will be adequately chastened."

Coach Albright apparently didn't know what either adequately or chastened meant, since he went, "I don't want her touchin' no more of my boys! Keep 'er away from them!"

Mr. Goodhart put down his Quarter Pounder, stood up, and walked to the door. He laid a hand on the coach's arm and said, "I'll take care of it, Frank." Then he gently pushed Coach Albright out into the reception area, and shut the door.

"Whew," he said when we were alone, and sat back down to tackle his burger again.

"So," Mr. Goodhart said, chewing. There was ketchup at the corner of his mouth. "What happened to our decision not to pick fights with people who are bigger than we are?"

I stared at the ketchup. "I didn't pick this one," I said. "Jeff did."

"What was it this time?" Mr. Goodhart passed me the fries again. "Your brother?"

"No," I said. I took two fries and put them in my mouth. "Ruth."

"Ruth?" Mr. Goodhart took another bite of his burger. The splotch of ketchup got bigger. "What about Ruth?"

"Jeff said Ruth was so fat, they were going to have to bury her in a piano case, like Elvis."

Mr. Goodhart swallowed. "That's ridiculous. Elvis wasn't buried in a piano case."

"I know." I shrugged. "You see why I had no choice but to hit him."

"Well, to be honest with you, Jess, no, I can't say that I do. The problem, you see, with you going around hitting these boys is that, one of these days, they're going to hit you back, and then you're going to be very sorry."

I said, "They try to hit me back all the time. But I'm too fast for them."

"Yeah," Mr. Goodhart said. There was still ketchup at the corner of his mouth. "But one day, you're going to trip, or something, and then you're going to get pounded on."

"I don't think so," I said. "You see, lately, I've taken up kickboxing."

"Kickboxing," Mr. Goodhart said.

"Yes," I said. "I have a video."

"A video," Mr. Goodhart said. His telephone rang. He said, "Excuse me a minute, Jessica," and answered it.

While Mr. Goodhart talked on the phone to his wife, who was apparently having a problem with their new baby, Russell, I looked out the window. There wasn't a whole lot to see out of Mr. Goodhart's window. Just the teachers' parking lot, mostly, and a lot of sky. The town I live in is pretty flat, so you can always see a lot of sky. Right then, the sky was kind of gray and overcast. Over behind the car wash across the street from the high school, you could see this layer of dark gray clouds. It was probably raining in the next county over. You couldn't tell by looking at those clouds, though, whether or not the rain would come toward us. I was thinking it probably would.

"If he doesn't want to eat," Mr. Goodhart said into the phone, "then don't try to force him. . . . No, I didn't mean to say that you were forcing him. What I meant was, maybe he just isn't hungry right now. . . . Yes, I know we need to get him on a schedule, but—"

The car wash was empty. No one wants to bother washing a car when it's just going to rain. But the McDonald's next door, where Mr. Goodhart had picked up his burger and fries, was packed. Only seniors are allowed to leave campus at lunchtime, and they all crowd the McDonald's, and the Pizza Hut across the street.

"Okay," Mr. Goodhart said, hanging up the phone. "Now, where were we, Jess?"

I said, "You were telling me that I need to learn to control my temper."

Mr. Goodhart nodded. "Yes," he said. "Yes, you really do, Jessica."

"Or one of these days, I'm going to get hurt."

"That is an excellent point."

"And that I should count to ten before I do anything the next time I get angry."

Mr. Goodhart nodded again, even more enthusiastically. "Yes, that's true, too."

"And furthermore, if I want to learn to succeed in life, I need to understand that violence doesn't solve anything."

Mr. Goodhart clapped his hands together. "Exactly! You're getting it, Jessica. You're finally getting it."

I stood up to go. I'd been coming to Mr. Goodhart's office for almost two years now, and I'd gotten a pretty solid grasp on how things worked from his end. An added plus was that, having spent so much time in the reception area outside Mr. Goodhart's office, reading brochures while I waited to see him, I had pretty much ruled out a career in the armed services.

"Well," I said. "I think I get it, Mr. Goodhart. Thanks a lot. I'll try to do better next time."

I had almost made it out the door before he stopped me. "Oh, and Jess," he said, in his friendly way.

I looked over my shoulder at him. "Uh-huh?"

"That'll be another week of detention," he said, chewing on a fry. "Tacked on to the seven weeks you already have."

I smiled at him. "Mr. Goodhart?" I said.

"Yes, Jessica?"

"You have ketchup on your lip."

Okay, so it wasn't the best comeback. But, hey, he hadn't said he'd call my parents. If he'd said that, you'd have heard some pretty colorful stuff. But he hadn't. And what's another week of detention compared to that?

And, what the hell, I have so many weeks of detention, I've completely given up the idea of ever having a life. It's too bad, in fact, that detention doesn't count as an extracurricular activity. Otherwise, I'd be looking real good to a lot of colleges right about now.

Not that detention is so bad, really. You just sit there for an hour. You can do your homework if you want, or you can read a magazine. You just aren't allowed to talk. The worst part, I guess, is that you miss your bus, but who wants to ride the bus home anyway, with the freshmen and other social rejects? Since Ruth got her driver's license, she goes mental for any excuse to drive, so I've got an automatic ride home every night. My parents haven't even figured it out yet. I told them I joined the marching band.

Good thing they have way more important things to worry about than making sure they get to one of the games, or they might have noticed a general absence of me in the flute section.

Anyway, when Ruth came to pick me up after detention that day—the day this whole thing started, the day I punched Jeff Day in the neck—she was all apologetic, since I'd basically gotten in trouble because of her.

"Oh, my God, Jess," she said when we met up at four outside the auditorium doors. There are so many people on detention at Ernest Pyle High School that they had to start putting us all in the auditorium. This is somewhat annoying to the drama club, which meets on the auditorium stage every day at three, but we are supposed to leave them alone, and they pretty much return the favor, except when they need some of the bigger guys from the last row to move part of a set or something.

The plus side of this is I now know the play *Our Town* by heart.

The minus side is, who the hell wants to know the play *Our Town* by heart?

"Oh, my God, Jess," Ruth was gushing. "You should have seen it. Jeff was up to his elbows in condiments. After you punched him, I mean. He got mayo all over his shirt. You were so great. You totally didn't have to, but it was so great that you did."

"Yeah," I said. I was pretty stoked to head home. The thing about detention is, yeah, you can get all your homework done during it, but it's still a bit of a drag. Like school in general, pretty much. "Whatever. Let's motor."

But when we got out to the parking lot, Ruth's little red Cabriolet that she had bought with her bat mitzvah money wasn't there. I didn't want to say anything at first, since Ruth loves that car, and I sure didn't want to be the person to break it to her that it was gone. But after we'd stood there for a few seconds, with her rattling on about how great I was, and me watching all my fellow detainees climbing into their pickups or onto their motorcycles (most of the people in detention are either Grits or JDs—I am the only Townie), I was like, "Uh, Ruth. Where's your car?"

Ruth went, "Oh, I drove it home after school, then got Skip to bring me back and drop me off."

Skip is Ruth's twin brother. He bought a Trans Am with his bar mitzvah money. As if, even with a Trans Am, Skip is ever going to have a hope of getting laid.

"I thought," Ruth went on, "that it would be fun to walk home."

I looked at the clouds that earlier in the afternoon had been over the car wash. They were now almost directly overhead. I said, "Ruth. We live like two miles away."

Ruth said, all chipper, "Uh-huh, I know. We can burn a lot of calories if we walk fast."

"Ruth," I said. "It's going to pour."

Ruth squinted up at the sky. "No, it's not," she said.

I looked at her like she was demented. "Ruth, yes, it is. Are you on crack?"

Ruth started to look upset. It doesn't actually take all that much to upset Ruth. She was still upset, I could tell, over Jeff's piano-case statement. That's why she wanted to walk home. She was hoping to lose weight. She wouldn't, I knew, eat lunch for a week now, all because of what that asshole had said.

"I'm not on crack," Ruth said. "I just think it's time the two of us started trying to get into shape. Summer is coming, and I'm not spending another four months making up excuses about why I can't go to somebody's pool party."

I just started laughing.

"Ruth," I said. "Nobody ever invites us to their pool parties."

"Speak for yourself," Ruth said. "And walking is a completely viable form of exercise. You can burn as many calories walking two miles as you would burn running them."

I looked at her. "Ruth," I said. "That's bullshit. Who told you that?"

She said, "It is a fact. Now, are you coming?"

"I can't believe," I said, "that you even care what an asshole like Jeff Day has to say about anything."

Ruth went, "I don't care what Jeff Day says. This has nothing to do with what he said. I just think it's time the two of us got into shape."

I stood and looked at her some more. You should have seen her. Ruth's been my best friend since kindergarten, which was when she and her family moved into the house next door to mine. And the funny thing is, except for the fact that she has breasts now—pretty big ones, too, way bigger than I'll ever have, unless I get implants, which will so never happen—she looks exactly the same as she did the first day I met her: light-brown curly hair, huge blue eyes behind glasses with gold wire frames, a fairly sizable potbelly, and an IQ of 167 (a fact she informed me of five minutes into our first game of hopscotch).

But you wouldn't have known she was in all advanced-placement classes if you'd seen what she had on that day. Okay, in the first place, she was wearing black leggings, this great big EPHS sweatshirt, and jogging shoes. Not so bad, right? Wait.

She'd coupled this ensemble with sweatbands—I am not kidding—around her head and on her wrists. She also had this big bottle of water hanging in a net sling from one shoulder. I mean, you could tell she thought she looked like an Olympic athlete, but what she actually looked like was a lunatic housewife who'd just gotten *Get Fit With Oprah* from the Book-of-the-Month Club, or something.

While I was standing there staring at Ruth, wondering how I was going to break it to her about the sweatbands, one of the guys from detention pulled up on this completely cherried-out Indian.

May I just take this opportunity to point out that the one thing I have always wanted is a motorcycle? This one purred, too. I hate those guys who take the muffler off their bikes so they can gun it real loud while they try to jump the speed bumps in the teachers' parking lot. This guy had tuned his so it ran quiet as a kitten. Painted all black, with shiny chrome everywhere else, this was one choice bike. I mean *mint*.

And the guy riding it wasn't too hard on the eyes, either.

"Mastriani," he said, putting one booted foot on the curb. "Need a ride?"

If Ernest Pyle himself, famous Hoosier reporter, had risen from the grave and come up and started asking me for journalistic pointers, I would not have been more surprised than I was by this guy asking me if I wanted a ride.

I like to think I hid it pretty well, though.

I said, way calmly, "No, thanks. We're walking."

He looked up at the sky. "It's gonna pour," he said, in a tone that suggested I was a moron not to realize this.

I cocked my head in Ruth's direction, so he'd get the message. "We're *walking*," I said, again.

He shrugged his shoulders under his leather jacket. "Your funeral," he said, and drove away.

I watched him go, trying not to notice how nicely his jeans hugged his perfectly contoured butt.

His butt wasn't the only thing that was perfectly contoured, either.

Oh, calm down. I'm talking about his face, okay? It was a good one, not habitually slack-jawed, like the faces of most of the boys who go to my school. This guy's face had some intelligence in it, at least. So what if his nose looked as if it had been broken a few times?

And okay, maybe his mouth was a little crooked, and his curly dark hair was badly in need of a trim. These deficiencies were more than made up for by a pair of eyes so light blue they were really pale gray, and a set of shoulders so broad, I doubt I would have been able to see much of the road past them in the event I ever did end up behind them on the back of that bike.

Ruth, however, did not seem to have noticed any of these highly commendable qualities. She was staring at me as if she'd caught me talking to a cannibal or something.

"Oh, my God, Jess," she said. "Who *was* that?"

I said, "His name is Rob Wilkins."

She went, "A *Grit*. Oh, my God, Jess, that guy is a *Grit*. I can't believe you were even talking to him."

Don't worry. I will explain.

There are two types of people who attend Ernest Pyle High School: the kids who come from the rural parts of the county, or the "Grits," and the people who live in town, or the "Townies." The Grits and Townies do not mix. Period. The Townies think they are better than the Grits because they have more money, since most of the kids who live in town have doctors or lawyers or teachers for parents. The Grits think they are better than the Townies because they know how to do stuff the Townies don't know how to do, like fix up old motorcycles and birth calves and stuff. The Grits' parents are all factory workers or farmers.

There are subsets within these groups, like the JDs—juvenile delinquents—and the Jocks—the

popular kids, the athletes, and the cheerleaders—
but mostly the school is divided up into Grits
and Townies.

Ruth and I are Townies. Rob Wilkins, needless
to say, is a Grit. And for an added bonus, I am
pretty sure he is also a JD.

But then, as Mr. Goodhart is so fond of telling
me, so am I—or at least I will be, one of these days,
if I don't start taking his anger-management
advice more seriously.

"How do you even know that guy?" Ruth
wanted to know. "He can't be in any of your
classes. He is definitely not college-bound.
Prison-bound, maybe," she said with a sneer.
"But he's got to be a senior, for Christ's sake."

I know. She sounds prissy, doesn't she?

She's not really. Just scared. Guys—real guys,
not idiots like her brother Skip—scare Ruth. Even
with her 167 IQ, guys are something she's never
been able to figure out. Ruth just can't fathom the
fact that boys are just like us.

Well, with a few notable exceptions.

I said, "I met him in detention. Can we move,
please, before the rain starts? I've got my flute,
you know."

Ruth wouldn't let go of it, though.

"Would you seriously have accepted a ride
from that guy? A total stranger like that? Like, if I
weren't here?"

I said, "I don't know."

I didn't, either. I hope you're not getting the

impression that this was the first time a guy had ever asked me if I wanted a lift or anything. I mean, I'll admit I have a tendency to be a bit free with my fists, but I'm no dog. I might be a bit on the puny side—only five two, as Mr. Goodhart is fond of reminding me—and I'm not big into makeup or clothes or anything, but believe me, I do all right for myself.

Okay, yeah, I'm no supermodel: I keep my hair short so I don't have to mess with it, and I'm fine with it being brown—you won't catch me experimenting with highlights, like some people I could mention. Brown hair goes with my brown eyes which go with my brown skin—well, at least, that's what color my skin usually ends up being by the end of the summer.

But the only reason I'm sitting at home Saturday nights is because it's either that, or hanging out with guys like Jeff Day, or Ruth's brother Skip. They're the only kind of guys my mother will let me go out with.

Yeah, you're catching on. Townies. That's right. I'm only allowed to date "college-bound boys." Read, Townies.

Where was I? Oh, yeah.

So, in answer to your question, no, Rob Wilkins was not the first guy who'd ever pulled up to me and asked if I wanted a ride somewhere.

But Rob Wilkins *was* the first guy to whom I might have said yes.

"Yeah," I said to Ruth. "Probably I would have. Taken him up on his offer, I mean. If you weren't here and all."

"I can't believe you." Ruth started walking, but let me tell you, those clouds were right behind us. Unless we went about a hundred miles an hour, there was no way we were going to beat the rain. And the fastest Ruth goes is maybe about one mile an hour, tops. Physically fit she is not.

"I can't believe you," she said, again. "You can't go around getting on the back of Grits' bikes. I mean, who knows where you'd end up? Dead in a cornfield, no doubt."

Almost every girl in Indiana who disappears gets found, eventually, half-naked and decomposing in a cornfield. But then, you guys already know that, don't you?

"You are so weird," Ruth said. "Only you would make friends with the guys in detention."

I kept looking over my shoulder at the clouds. They were huge, like mountains. Only, unlike mountains, they weren't stationary.

"Well," I said, "I can't exactly *help* knowing them, you know. We've been sitting together for an hour every day for the past three or four months."

"But they're *Grits*," Ruth said. "My God, Jess. Do you actually *talk* to them?"

I said, "I don't know. I mean, we're not allowed to talk. But Miss Clemmings has to take attendance every day, so you learn people's names. You sort of can't help it."

Ruth shook her head. "Oh, my God," she said. "My dad would kill me—*kill* me—if I came home on the back of some Grit's motorcycle."

I didn't say anything. The chances of anybody asking Ruth to hop onto the back of his bike were like zero.

"Still," Ruth said, after we'd walked for a little while in silence, "he *was* kind of cute. For a Grit, I mean. What'd he do?"

"What do you mean? To get detention?" I shrugged. "How should I know? We're not allowed to talk."

Let me just tell you a little bit about where we were walking. Ernest Pyle High School is located on the imaginatively named High School Road. As you might have guessed, there isn't a whole lot of stuff on High School Road except, well, the high school. There's just two lanes and a bunch of farmland. The McDonald's and the car wash and stuff were down on the Pike. We weren't walking on the Pike. No one ever walks on the Pike, since this one girl got hit walking there last year.

So we'd made it about as far down High School Road as the football field when the rain started. Big, hard drops of rain.

"Ruth," I said, pretty calmly, as the first drop hit me.

"It'll blow over," Ruth said.

Another drop hit me. Plus a big flash of lightning cracked the sky and seemed to hit the water tower, a mile or so away. Then it thundered. Really loud. As loud as the jets over at Crane Military Base, when they break the sound barrier.

"Ruth," I said, less calmly.

Ruth said, "Perhaps we should seek shelter."

"Damned straight," I said.

But the only shelter we saw were the metal bleachers that surround the football field. And everyone knows, during a thunderstorm, you're not supposed to hide under anything metal.

That's when the first hailstone hit me.

If you've ever been hit by a hailstone, you'll know why it was Ruth and I ran under those bleachers. And if you've never been hit by a hailstone, all I can say is, lucky you. These particular hailstones were about as big as golf balls. I am not exaggerating, either. They were huge. And those mothers—pardon my French—hurt.

Ruth and I stood under these bleachers, hailstones popping all around us, like we were trapped inside this really big popcorn popper. Only at least the popcorn wasn't hitting us on the head anymore.

With the thunder and the sound of the hail hitting the metal seats above our heads, then ricocheting off them and smacking against the ground, it was kind of hard to hear anything, but that didn't bother Ruth. She shouted, "I'm sorry."

All I said was "Ow," because a real big chunk

of hail bounced off the ground and hit me in the calf.

"I mean it," Ruth shouted. "I'm really, really sorry."

"Stop apologizing," I said. "It isn't your fault."

At least that's what I thought *then*. I have since changed my mind on that. As you will note by rereading the first few lines of this *statement* of mine.

A big bolt of lightning lit up the sky. It broke into four or five branches. One of the branches hit the top of a corn crib I could see over the trees. Thunder sounded so loudly, it shook the bleachers.

"It is," Ruth said. She sounded like she was starting to cry. "It *is* my fault."

"Ruth," I said. "For God's sake, are you crying?"

"Yes," she said, with a sniffle.

"Why? It's just a stupid thunderstorm. We've been stuck in thunderstorms before." I leaned against one of the poles that held up the bleachers. "Remember that time in the fifth grade we got stuck in that thunderstorm, on the way home from your cello lesson?"

Ruth wiped her nose with the cuff of her sweatshirt. "And we had to duck for cover in your church?"

"Only you wouldn't go in farther than the awning," I said.

Ruth laughed through her tears. "Because I

thought God would strike me dead for setting foot in a goyim house of worship."

I was glad she was laughing, anyway. Ruth can be a pain in the butt, but she's been my best friend since kindergarten, and you can't exactly dump your best friend since kindergarten just because sometimes she puts on sweatbands or starts crying when it rains. Ruth is way more interesting than most of the girls who go to my school, since she reads a book a day—literally—and loves playing the cello as much as I love playing my flute, but will still watch cheesy television, in spite of her great genius.

And, most times, she's funny as hell.

Now was not one of those times, however.

"Oh, God," Ruth moaned as the wind picked up and started whipping hailstones at us beneath the bleachers. "This is tornado weather, isn't it?"

Southern Indiana is smack in the middle of Tornado Alley. We're number three on the list of states with the most twisters per year. I had sat out more than a few of them in my basement; Ruth, not so many, since she'd only spent the last decade in the Midwest. And they always seemed to happen around this time of year, too.

And, though I didn't want to say anything to upset Ruth any more than she already was, this gave all the signs of being twister weather. The sky was a funny yellow color, the temperature warm, but the wind really cold. Plus that wacked-out hail . . .

Just as I was opening my mouth to tell Ruth it was probably just a little spring storm, and not to worry, she screamed, "Jess, don't—"

But I didn't hear what she said after that, because right then there was this big explosion that drowned out everything else.

CHAPTER

2

It wasn't an explosion, I figured out later. What it was was lightning, hitting the metal bleachers. Then the bolt traveled down the metal pole I was leaning against.

So I guess you could say that, technically, I got hit by lightning.

It didn't hurt, though. It felt really weird, but it didn't hurt.

When I could hear again, after it happened, all I could hear was Ruth screaming. I wasn't standing in the same place I'd been a second before, either. I was standing about five feet away.

Oh, and I felt all tingly. You know when you're trying to plug something in and you're not really looking at what you're doing and you accidentally stick your finger in there instead of the plug?

That's how I felt, only about times three hundred.

"Jess," Ruth was screaming. She ran up and shook my arm. "Oh, my God, Jess, are you all right?"

I looked at her. She was still the same old Ruth. She still had on the sweatband.

But that was the start of me not being the same old Jess. That was when it started.

And it pretty much went downhill from there.

"Yeah," I said. "I'm fine."

And I really felt okay. I wasn't lying or anything. Not then. I just felt sort of tingly and all. But it wasn't a bad feeling. Actually, after the initial surprise of it, it kind of felt good. I felt sort of energized, you know?

"Hey," I said, looking out past the bleachers. "Look. The hail stopped."

"Jess," Ruth said, shaking me some more. "You got hit by lightning. Don't you understand? You got hit by lightning!"

I looked at her. She looked kind of funny in that headband. I started to laugh. Once, when I went to my Aunt Teresa's bridal shower, nobody was paying attention to how many glasses of pinot grigio the waiter poured me, and I felt the same way. Like laughing. A lot.

"You better lie down," Ruth said. "You better put your head between your knees."

"Why?" I asked her. "So I can kiss my butt good-bye?"

This cracked me up. I started laughing. It seemed hysterically funny to me.

Ruth didn't think it was so funny, though.

"No," she said. "Because you're white as a ghost. You might pass out. I'll go try to flag down a car. We need to take you to the hospital."

"Aw, geez," I said. "I don't need to go to any hospital. The storm's over. Let's go."

And I just walked out from underneath those bleachers like nothing had happened.

And, really, at the time I didn't think anything had. Happened, I mean. I felt fine. Better than fine, actually. Better than I'd felt in months. Better than I'd felt since my brother Douglas had come home from college.

Ruth chased after me, looking all concerned.

"Jess," she said. "Really. You shouldn't be trying to—"

"Hey," I said. The sky had gotten much lighter, and underneath my feet the hailstones were crunching, as if someone up there had accidentally overturned some kind of celestial ice cube tray.

"Hey, Ruth," I said, pointing down at the hailstones. "Look. It's like snow. Snow, in April!"

Ruth wouldn't look at the hailstones, though. Even though she was up to the swooshes of her Nikes in them, she wouldn't look. All she would do was look at me.

"Jessica," she said, taking my hand. "Jessica, listen to me." She dropped her voice so that it was almost a whisper. I could hear her fine, since the wind had died down and all the thunder and stuff had stopped. "Jessica, I'm telling you, you're not all right. I saw . . . I saw *lightning* come out of you."

"Really?" I grinned at her. "Neat."

Ruth dropped my hand and turned away in disgust.

"Fine," she said, starting back toward the road. "Don't go to the hospital. Drop dead of a heart attack. See if I care."

I followed her, kicking hailstones out of the way with my platform Pumas.

"Hey," I said. "Too bad lightning wasn't shooting out of me in the cafeteria today, huh? Jeff Day would've really been sorry, huh?"

Ruth didn't think this was funny. She just kept walking, huffing a little because she was going so fast. But fast for Ruth is normal for me, so I didn't have any trouble keeping up.

"Hey," I said. "Wouldn't it have been cool if I'd been able to shoot lightning at assembly this afternoon? You know, when Mrs. Bushey got up there and dared us to keep off drugs? I bet that would've shortened that speech of hers."

I kept up in that vein the whole way home. Ruth tried to stay mad at me, but she couldn't. Not because I am so charming or funny or anything, but because the storm had left some really cool damage in its wake. We saw all these tree branches that had been knocked down, and windshields that had been shattered by the hail, and a few traffic lights that had stopped working altogether. It was totally cool. A bunch of ambulances and fire engines went by, and when we finally got to the Kroger on the corner of High School Road and First Street, where we turned off for our houses, the KRO had been knocked out, so the sign just said, GER.

"Hey, Ruth, look," I said. "Ger is open, but Kro is closed."

Even Ruth had to laugh at that.

By the time we got to our houses—I mentioned we live next door to each other, right?— Ruth had gotten over being scared for me. At least, I thought she had. When I was about to run up the walk to my front porch, she heaved this real big sigh, and went, "Jessica, I really think you should say something to your mom and dad. About what happened, I mean."

Oh, yeah. Like I was going to tell them something as lame as the fact that I had been hit by lightning. They had way more important things to worry about.

I didn't say that, but Ruth must have read my thoughts, since the next thing she said was, "No, Jess. I mean it. You should tell them. I've read about people who've been struck by lightning the way you were. They felt perfectly fine, just like you do, and then, *wham!* Heart attack."

I said, "Ruth."

"I really think you should tell them. I know

how much they have on their minds, with Douglas and all. But—"

"Hey," I said. "Douglas is fine."

"I know." Ruth closed her eyes. Then she opened them again and said, "I know Douglas is fine. All right, look. Just promise me that if you start to feel . . . well, funny, you'll tell somebody?"

This sounded fair to me. I swore solemnly not to die of a heart attack. Then we parted on my front lawn with a mutual "See ya."

It wasn't until I was almost all the way into the house that I realized that the dogwood tree just off the driveway—the one that had been in full, glorious bloom that morning—was completely bare again, as if it were the middle of winter. The hail had knocked off every single leaf and every single blossom.

They talk all the time in my English class about symbolism and stuff. Like how the withered old oak tree in *Jane Eyre* portends doom and all of that. So I guess you could say that if this *statement* of mine were a work of fiction, that dogwood tree would symbolize the fact that everything was not going to turn out hunky-dory for me.

Only of course, just like Jane, I had no idea what lay in store for me. I mean, at the time, I totally missed the symbolism of the leafless dogwood. I was just like, "Wow, too bad. That tree was pretty before it got ruined by hail."

And then I went inside.

CHAPTER

3

I live—since it's probably important to give my address in this *statement* of mine—with my parents and two brothers in a big house on Lumley Lane. Our house is the nicest one on the street.

I am not saying that to brag. It's just true. It used to be a farmhouse, but a really fancy one, with stained-glass windows and stuff. Some people from the Indiana Historic Society came once and put a plaque on it, since it's the oldest house in our town.

But just because we live in an old house does not mean we are poor. My father owns three restaurants downtown, only eight or nine blocks from our house. The restaurants are: Mastriani's, which is expensive; Joe's, which is not; and a take-out place called Joe Junior's, which is the cheapest of all. I can eat at any of them anytime I want, for free. So can my friends.

You would think, because of this, that I would have more friends. But, besides Ruth, I only really hang out with a couple of people, most of whom I know from Orchestra. Ruth is first chair in the cello section. I am third chair in the flute section. I socialize with a couple of the other flutists—second and fifth chair, mostly—and a few people from the horn section, and one or two of the other cellists who've gotten Ruth's seal of approval, but other than that, I keep pretty much to myself.

Well, except for all the guys in detention.

My bedroom is on the third floor. My bedroom, and my bathroom, are the only rooms on the third floor. The third floor used to be the attic. It has low ceilings, and dormer windows. I used to be able to fit my whole body in one of the dormer windows, and I liked to sit up there and watch what was going on on Lumley Lane, which usually wasn't very much. I was up higher than anybody else on the street, though, and I always thought that was kind of neat. I used to pretend I was a lighthouse keeper and the dormer was my lighthouse, and I'd look out for boats about to crash on our front lawn, which I pretended was a treacherous beach.

Hey, come on. I was a little kid back then, okay?

And, in the words of Mr. Goodhart, even then I had issues.

Anyway, to get to the third floor, you have to

take the staircase that is right inside the front door, in what my mom calls, in this French accent, the foyer (She pronounces it *foi-yay*. She also calls Target, where we buy all our towels and stuff, *Tar-jay*. You know, as a joke. That's how my mom is). The problem is, right off the foyer is the living room, which has French doors that lead to the dining room, which has French doors that lead to the kitchen. And so the minute you open the front door, my mom can see you, all the way from the back of the house, through all those French doors, way before you have a chance of making it up those stairs without anybody noticing.

Which was, of course, what happened when I walked in that night. She saw me and yelled—since the kitchen is actually pretty far away—"Jessica! Get in here!"

Which, of course, meant I was in trouble.

Wondering what I could have done now—and hoping Mr. Goodhart hadn't gone ahead and called her anyway—I put down my backpack and my flute and everything on this little bench by the stairs and started the long walk through the living room and dining room, thinking up a good story for why I was so late, in case that was why she was mad.

"We had band practice," I started saying. By the time I got to the dining room table—which has this buzzer built into the floor beneath the chair at the head of the table, so the hostess can step on it and signal to the servants in the kitchen that it's time to bring out dessert, which, since we have no servants, is just this huge annoyance, especially when we were growing up, since it's impossible for little kids to keep from buzzing something like that all the time, which drove my mom, who was usually in the kitchen, postal—I was rolling with it.

"Yeah, band practice went long, Mom. On account of the hail. We all had to run and stand under the bleachers, and there was all this lightning, and—"

"Look at this."

My mom held a letter up to my nose. My brother Mike was sitting, kind of slumped, at the kitchen counter. He looked unhappy, but then, he had never looked happy a day in his life, as far as I can remember, except when my parents got him a Mac for Christmas. Then he looked happy.

I looked at the letter my mom was holding. I couldn't read it, since it was too close to my nose. But that was okay. My mom was going, "Do you know what this is, Jessica? Do you know what this is? It's a letter from Harvard. And what do you think it says?"

I said, "Oh, hey, Mikey. Congratulations."

Mike said, "Thanks," but he didn't sound very excited.

"My little boy." My mom took the letter and started waving it around. "My little Mikey! Going to Harvard! Oh, my God, I can hardly believe it!" She did a weird little dance.

My mom isn't normally so weird. Most of the time she's pretty much like other moms. She helps my dad out sometimes with the restaurants, like with the billing and payroll, but mostly she stays home and does stuff like regrout the tile in the bathrooms. My mom, like most moms, is totally into her kids, so Mike getting into Harvard—even though it's really no big surprise, seeing as how he got a perfect score on his SATs—was this really big deal to her.

"I already called your father," she said. "We're going to Mastriani's for lobster."

"Cool," I said. "Can I invite Ruth?"

My mom made a little waving gesture. "Sure, why not? When have we ever gone out for a family dinner and not brought along Ruth?" She was being sarcastic, but she didn't mean it. My mom likes Ruth. I think. "Michael, perhaps there is someone you'd like to invite?"

The way she said "someone," you could tell my mom, of course, meant a girl. But Mike has only ever liked one girl his entire life, and that's Claire Lippman, who lives two houses over, and Claire Lippman, who is a year younger than Mike and a year older than me, barely even knows Mike is alive, since she is too busy starring in all of our high school's plays and musicals to pay any attention to the geeky senior down the street who spies on her every time she lies out on her carport roof in her bikini, which she does every single day without fail starting as soon as school lets out for the summer. She doesn't go back inside, either, until Labor Day, or unless a cute guy in a car drives up and asks her if she wants to go swimming at one of the quarries.

Claire is either a slave to ultraviolet rays or a total exhibitionist. I haven't figured out which yet.

Anyway, there was no chance my brother was going to ask "someone" to go with us for dinner, since Claire Lippman would be like, "Now, who are you?" if he ever even got up the nerve to talk to her.

"No," Mike said, all embarrassed. He was turning bright red, and it was only me and Mom standing there. Could you imagine if Claire Lippman had actually been present? "There's nobody I want to ask."

"Faint heart never won fair lady," my mom said. My mom, besides frequently talking in a fake French accent, also goes around quoting from Shakespearean plays and Gilbert and Sullivan operettas.

On second thought, maybe she's not so much like other people's moms after all.

"I got it, Mom," Mike said through gritted teeth. "Not tonight, okay?"

My mom shrugged. "Fine. Jessica, if you're going, allow me to assure you you're not going in *that*." *That* was what I normally wear—T-shirt, jeans, and my Pumas. "Go put on the blue calico I made for Easter."

Okay. My mom has this thing about making us matching outfits. I am not even kidding. It was cute when I was six, but at sixteen, let me tell you, there is nothing cute about wearing a home-made dress that matches the one your mother has on. Especially since all the dresses my mom makes are of the Laura Ingalls variety.

You would think, considering the fact that I don't have any problem walking up to football tackles and punching them in the neck, that I wouldn't have any problem telling my mother to quit making me wear outfits that match hers. You would think that.

However, if your father promised you that if you wore them without complaining, he would buy you a Harley when you turned eighteen, you would wear them, too.

I said, "Okay," and started up the back stair-case, what used to be the servants' staircase, back at the turn of the century—the nineteenth into the twentieth, I mean—when our house was built. "I'll tell Douglas."

"Oh," I heard my mom say. "Jess?"

But I kept on going. I knew what she was going to say. She was going to say not to bother Douglas. That's what she always says.

Personally, I enjoy bothering Douglas. Also, I asked Mr. Goodhart about it, and he said it's probably good to bother Douglas. So I bother him a lot. What I do is, I go up to the door to his room, which has a big Keep Out sign on it, and I bang on it really hard. Then I yell, "Doug! It's me, Jess!"

Then I just walk in. Douglas isn't allowed to have a lock on his door anymore. Not since my dad and I had to knock it down last Christmas.

Douglas was lying on his bed reading a comic book. It had this Viking on the cover, with a girl with big boobs. All Douglas ever does, since he came home from college, is read comic books. And in all the comic books, the girls have big boobs.

"Guess what," I said, sitting down on Douglas's bed.

"Mikey got into Harvard," Douglas said. "I already heard. I expect the whole neighborhood heard."

"Nope," I said. "That's not it."

He looked at me over the top of the comic book. "I know Mom thinks she's taking us all to Mastriani's to celebrate, but I'm not going. She's going to have to learn to live with disappointment. And you better keep your hands off me. I'm not going, no matter how hard you hit me. And this time, I might just hit you back."

"That's not it, either," I said. "And I wasn't planning on hitting you. Much."

"What, then?"

I shrugged. "I got hit by lightning."

Douglas turned back to his comic book. "Right. Shut the door on your way out."

"I'm serious," I said. "Ruth and I were waiting

out the storm, underneath the bleachers at school—"

"Those bleachers," Douglas said, looking at me again, "are made of metal."

"Right. And I was leaning on one of the supports, and lightning struck the bleachers, and next thing I knew, I was standing like five feet from where I'd been, and I was tingly all over, and—"

"Bullshit," Douglas said. But he sat up. "That is bullshit, Jess."

"I swear it's true. You can ask Ruth."

"You did not get hit by lightning," Douglas said. "You would not be sitting here, talking to me, if you'd been hit by lightning."

"Douglas, I'm telling you, I was."

"Where's the entrance wound, then?" Douglas reached out and grabbed my right hand and flipped it over. "The exit wound? The bolt would have entered you one place, and left you in another. And there would be a star-shaped scar in both places."

As he'd been talking, he'd let go of my right hand and grabbed my left, and flipped it over, too. But there wasn't a star-shaped scar on either of my palms.

"See." He flung my hand away in disgust. Douglas knows about stuff like this because all he ever does is read, and sometimes he reads actual books, as opposed to comics. "You weren't struck by lightning. Don't go around saying stuff like that, Jess. You know, lightning kills hundreds of people a year. If you had been struck, you'd definitely be in a coma, at the very least."

He lay back down and picked his comic book up again. "Now, get out of here," he said, giving me a shove with his foot. "I'm busy."

I sighed and got up. "Okay," I said. "But you're going to be sorry. Mom says we're having lobster."

"We had lobster the night I got my acceptance letter to State," Douglas said to his comic book, "and look how that turned out."

I reached out and grabbed his big toe and squeezed it. "Okay, big baby. Just lie here like a big lump, with Captain Lars and his big-busted beauty, Helga."

Douglas looked at me from behind the comic book. "Her name," he said, "happens to be Oona."

Then he ducked back behind the comic book.

I left his room, closing the door behind me, and went up the stairs to my own room.

I'm not too worried about Douglas. I know I probably should be, but I'm not. I'm probably the only person in my family who isn't, except for maybe my dad. Douglas has always been weird. My whole life, it seems, I've been beating up people who called my older brother a retard, or a spaz, or a weirdo. I don't know why, but even though most of the time I'm way smaller than them, I feel obligated to punch them in the face for dissing my brother.

This freaks out my mom, but not my dad. My dad just taught me how to punch more effectively, by advising me to keep my thumb on the outside of my fist. When I was very little, I used to do it with my thumb on the inside. Consequently, I sprained it several times. My thumb, I mean.

Douglas used to get mad when I'd get into fights because of him, so after a while I learned to do it behind his back. And I guess it would be humiliating, having one's little sister constantly going around, beating up people on your behalf. But I don't think that contributed to what happened to Douglas later. You know, this past Christmas, when he tried to kill himself. I mean, you don't try to kill yourself because your little sister used to get into fights over you in junior high, or whatever.

Do you?

Anyway, once I was in my room, I called Ruth and invited her out to dinner with us. I knew that, even though today was the first day of what would be another one of her diets, thanks to Jeff Day, Ruth wasn't going to be able to resist. Not only was it lobster, but it was Michael. Ruth tries to pretend she doesn't like Michael, but between you and me, the girl has it bad for him. Don't ask me why. He's no prize, believe me.

And just like I knew she would, she said, "Well, I really shouldn't. Lobster is so fattening. Well, not the lobster, really, but all the butter . . .

but I guess it *is* a special occasion, what with Michael getting into Harvard and all. I guess I should go. Okay, I'll go."

"Come over," I said. "Give me ten minutes, though. I gotta change."

"Wait a minute." Ruth's voice grew suspicious. "Your mom's not making you wear one of those gay outfits, is she?" When I remained silent, Ruth said, "You know, I don't think a motorcycle is enough. Your dad should buy you a damned Maserati for what that woman puts you through."

Ruth thinks my mom is suffering from the oppression of a patriarchal society, consisting mainly of my dad. But that isn't true. My dad would totally love it if my mom got a job. It would keep her from obsessing about Douglas. Now that he's home again, though, she says she can't even think of working, since who would watch him and make sure he stays away from the razor blades the next time?

I told Ruth that, yes, I had to wear one of my mom's gay outfits, even though *gay* is the wrong word for it, because all the gay people I know are really cool and would sooner drop dead than wear something made out of gingham, except on Halloween. But whatever. I hung up and started undressing. I pretty much live in jeans and a T-shirt. In the winter, I'll put on a sweater, but seriously, I don't dress up for school like some girls. Sometimes I don't even shower in the morning. I mean, what is the point? There is no one there I want to impress.

Well, at least there *hadn't* been, until Rob Wilkins asked me if I wanted a ride home. Now *that* might be worth blow-drying for.

Only, of course, I couldn't let Ruth know. And she totally would, the minute she swung by to pick me up. She'd be like, "Mousse much?"

Although she'd probably approve—at least until she found out who I was moussing for.

Anyway, while I was undressing, it occurred to me that Douglas might have been wrong. There might have been a star-shaped scar somewhere else on my body, not necessarily on my palms. Say on the bottoms of my feet, or something.

But when I checked, my soles were just pink as usual. No scars. Not even any lint between my toes.

It was weird about Rob Wilkins asking me if I wanted a ride like that. I mean, I hardly knew the guy. We had detention together, and that was it. Well, that isn't strictly true. Last semester, he'd been in Health with me. You know, Coach Albright's class. You're supposed to take it as a sophomore, but for some reason—okay, probably because he'd flunked first time around—Rob had been taking it his senior year. He'd sat behind me. He was pretty quiet most of the time. Occasionally he'd have a conversation with the guy behind him, who was also a Grit. I'd eaves-drop, of course. These conversations generally revolved around bands—Grit bands, mostly heavy metal, or country—or cars.

Sometimes I couldn't help butting in. Like once I said that I really didn't think Steven Tyler was a musical genius. The artist formerly known as Prince was the only living musician I'd call a genius. And then, for about a week, we kind of dissected their lyrics, and Rob eventually agreed with me.

And once Rob was talking about motorcycles, and the guy behind him was going on and on about Kawasaki, and I was just like, "What are you, high? American, all the way," and Rob gave me a high five.

Coach Albright hadn't exactly been there in the classroom a lot. Football emergencies kept coming up, requiring him to leave us to work on the questions at the end of the chapter. You know the kind of questions. The spleen performs what function? The adult male generates how many sperm each day? The kind of questions you instantly forget the answers to as soon as you've passed the class.

I decided that, for school tomorrow, I might wear this Gap shirt Douglas had given me for Christmas. I'd never worn it to school before, because it had a scoop neck. Not exactly the kind of thing you want to wear while taking down a quarterback.

But, hey, if that's what it took to bag a ride on that Indian . . .

It wasn't until I was buttoning up my hideous lilac-colored Laura Ingalls dress that I glanced at my reflection in the mirror and saw it: this fist-sized red mark in the middle of my chest. It didn't hurt or anything. It was like I'd suddenly broken out in hives or something. Like someone had slipped a bad clam into my shells and sauce.

From the center of the red mark radiated these tendrils. In fact, looking at it in the mirror, I saw that the whole thing was . . .

Well, kind of shaped like a star.

CHAPTER

4

Ruth said, "I'm telling you, I don't see another one. There's just the one."

"Are you sure?"

I was standing, stark naked, in the middle of my bedroom. It was after dinner, which I guess had been delicious. I wouldn't know, having been unable to taste anything, what with my excitement over having been really and truly struck by lightning. The star-shaped burn proved it. It was the entrance wound Douglas had been talking about.

The only problem was, I couldn't find an exit wound. I'd made Ruth come over after dinner and help me look. Only she wasn't being much help.

"I had no idea," she said from my bed, where she was lying, flipping through a copy of *Critical*

Theory Since Plato—you know, just a little light reading—she'd brought over, "you'd actually grown breasts. I mean it. You aren't an A cup anymore. When did that happen?"

"Ruth," I said, "what about on my back? Do you see one on my back?"

"No. What are you now, a B?"

"How should I know? You know I never wear a bra. How about on my butt? Anything on my butt?"

"No. Is there something between a B and a C? Because I think that's what you are now. And you really should start wearing one, you know. You could start to sag, like those women in *National Geographic*."

"You," I said to her, "are no help."

"Well, what do you expect me to do, Jess?" Ruth turned grumpily back to her book. "I mean, it's a little weird, having your best friend ask you to check her body for entrance and exit wounds, don't you think? I mean, it's a bit *gay*."

I went, "I don't want you to feel me up, you moron. I just wanted you to tell me if you saw an exit wound." I pulled on a pair of sweats. "Get over yourself."

"I can't believe," Ruth said, ignoring me, "that Michael's going to Harvard. I mean, *Harvard*. He is so smart. How can someone so smart fall for Claire Lippman?"

I pulled a sweatshirt over my head. "Claire's not so bad," I said. I knew her pretty well, see, from detention. Not that she ever got detention, but they held detention in the auditorium, and Claire always had the lead in whatever play the drama club was putting on, so I'd watched most of her rehearsals when she played Emily in *Our Town*, Maria in *West Side Story*, and, of course, Juliet in *Romeo and Juliet*.

"She's a really good actress," I said.

"I highly doubt," Ruth said, "that Michael admires her for her *talent*."

Ruth always calls Mike Michael, even though everyone else calls him Mike. She says Mike is a Grit name.

"Well," I said, "you got to admit, she does look good in a bathing suit."

Ruth snorted. "That slut. I can't believe she does that. Every summer. I mean, it was one thing back before she hit puberty. But now . . . what's she trying to do? Cause a traffic accident?"

"I'm hungry," I said, because I was. "You want something?"

Ruth said, "I'm not surprised. You hardly touched your lobster."

"I was too excited to eat then," I said. "I mean, come on. I got electrocuted today."

"I wish," Ruth said, to the book, "you'd go to a doctor. You could be hemorrhaging internally, you know."

I said, "I'm going downstairs. You want anything?"

She yawned. "No. I gotta go. I'll just stop by Michael's room to say congratulations one more time, and good night."

I thought it would be best to leave the two of them alone, you know, in case there was a romantic interlude, so I went downstairs to forage for food. The chances of Mikey ever even looking twice in Ruth's direction are like nil, but hope springs eternal, even in the heart of a fat girl. Not that Ruth is that fat. She's just twice the size of Claire Lippman. Not that Claire is so skinny—she's pretty hippy, actually. But boys seem to like that, I've noticed. In magazines, they make out if you're not Kate Moss, your life is over, but in real life, boys—like my brothers—wouldn't look twice at Kate Moss. Claire Lippman, though, who's gotta be thirty-four, twenty-four, thirty-eight or so, they drool over. I think a lot of it is how you project yourself, and Claire Lippman projects herself like she's got it on, you know?

Ruth doesn't. Project herself with any confidence, I mean. Ruth's problem is that she's just, you know, a big girl. All the crash diets in the world aren't going to change that. She just needs to accept that and accept herself and calm down. Then she'll get a boyfriend. Guaranteed.

But probably not Mike.

I was thinking about how weird bodies are while I poured myself a bowl of cereal. I wondered if the star-shaped scar was going to stay on my chest. I mean, who needed that? And where was that exit wound, anyway?

Maybe, I thought, as I poured milk over my Total with raisins, the lightning was still inside of me. That would have been weird, huh? Maybe I was walking around with it buzzing inside of me. And maybe, like Ruth said, I could send it shooting at people. Like Jeff Day. He so deserved it. I thought about shooting bolts of lightning at Jeff Day while I read the back of the milk carton. Man, would that put a crimp in his football career.

When I got back upstairs, Ruth was gone. Mike's door was closed, but I knew she wasn't in there, because I heard him typing furiously on his computer. Probably sending E-mail to all his dweeby Internet buddies. Hey, guys, I got into Harvard! Just like Bill Gates.

Only maybe, unlike Bill Gates, Mike would actually graduate. Not that that had mattered, at least in Bill's case.

The door to Douglas's room was closed, too, and no light spilled out from under it. But that didn't stop me. Douglas was at his window, a pair of binoculars to his head, when I came barging in.

He turned around and went, "One of these days, you're going to do that and you're going to end up seeing something you really never wanted to see."

"Already saw it," I said. "Mom used to make us take baths together when we were little, remember?"

He said, "Go away. I'm busy."

"What are you looking at, anyway?" I asked, going to sit on his bed in the darkness. Douglas's room smelled like Douglas. Not a bad smell, really. Just a boy smell. Like old sneakers mingled with Old Spice. "Claire Lippman?"

"Orion," he said, but I knew he was lying. His room has a view straight into Claire Lippman's, two houses away. Claire, exhibitionist that she is, never pulls down her blinds. I doubt she even has blinds.

But I didn't mind Douglas spying on her, even though it was sexist and a violation of her privacy and all. It meant he was normal. Well, for him, anyway.

"Not to tear you away from your lady love," I said, "but I found an entrance wound."

"She's not my lady love," Douglas said. "Merely the object of my lust."

"Well, whatever," I said. I pulled on the neck of my sweatshirt. "Take a look at this."

He turned on his reading lamp and swiveled it in my direction. When he saw the scar, he got real quiet.

"Jesus Christ," he said after a while.

"Told you," I said.

He said, "Jesus Christ," again.

"There's no exit wound," I said. "I had Ruth check me, all over. Nothing. Do you think the lightning is still inside me?"

"Lightning," he said, "does not just stay inside

you. Maybe this is the exit wound, and the bolt came in through the top of your head. Only that isn't possible," he said, to himself, I guess, "because then her hair would be scorched."

It was possible, though, that he wasn't speaking to himself. He could have been speaking to the voices. He hears voices sometimes. They were the ones who told him to kill himself last Christmas.

"Well," I said, letting my sweatshirt snap back into place. "That's all. I just wanted to show you."

"Wait a minute." I had gotten up, but Douglas pulled me back down onto his bed again. "Jess," he said. "Did you *really* get struck by lightning?"

"*Yes*," I said. "I *told* you I did."

Douglas looked serious. But then, Douglas was always serious. "You should tell Dad."

"No way."

"I mean it, Jess. Go tell Dad, right now. Not Mom, either. Just Dad."

"Aw, Douglas . . ."

"Go." He pulled me up and pushed me toward the door. "Either you do it, or I will."

"Aw, hell," I said.

But he started to look funny, all pinch-faced and stuff. So I dragged myself downstairs and found my dad where he usually was when he wasn't at one of the restaurants—at the dining room table, going over the books, with the TV in the kitchen turned to the sports channel. He couldn't see the TV from where he sat, but he could hear it. Even though he looked totally absorbed in the numbers in front of him, if you switched the channel, he'd totally freak out.

"What," he said when I came in. But not in an unfriendly way.

"Hey, Dad," I said. "Douglas says I have to tell you I got hit by lightning today."

My dad looked up. He had his reading glasses on. He looked at me over the tops of them.

"Is Douglas having an episode?" he asked. That's what the shrinks call it when Douglas's voices get the better of him. An episode.

"No," I said. "It's really true. I did get struck by lightning today."

He looked at me some more. "Why didn't you mention this at dinner?"

"Because, you know," I said, "it was a celebration. But Douglas said I have to tell you. Ruth, too. She says I could have a heart attack in my sleep. See, look."

I stretched out the neck of my sweatshirt again. It was okay, because the scar was way above my boobs, up by my collarbone. My dad's been kind of weird about my boobs, ever since I got some. I think he's afraid they'll get in the way of my swing when I haul off a right hook at somebody.

He looked at the scar and went, "Were you and Skip playing with firecrackers again?"

I think I mentioned before that Skip is Ruth's

twin brother. He and I used to have a thing about firecrackers.

"No, Dad," I said. "Jeez. I'm way over fire-crackers." Not to mention Skip. "That's from the lightning."

I told him what had happened. He listened with this very serious look on his face. Then he went, "I wouldn't worry about it."

That's what he always used to say when I'd wake up in what seemed like the middle of the night—but was probably only about eleven—when I was a very little kid, and I'd come down and tell him my leg, or my arm, or my neck hurt.

"Growing pains," he'd say, and give me a glass of milk. "I wouldn't worry about it."

"Okay," I said. I was just as relieved as I'd been back then, when I was little. "I just thought I should tell you. You know, in case I don't wake up tomorrow morning."

He said, "You don't wake up tomorrow, your mother will kill you. Now go to bed. And if I hear anything about you seeking shelter under metal again during a thunderstorm, I'll wear you out."

He didn't mean it, of course. My dad doesn't believe in spanking. That's because his older brother, my uncle Rick, used to beat the tar out of him, my mom says. Which is why we never go to visit Uncle Rick. I think that's also why my dad taught me how to punch. My dad thinks you have to learn to defend yourself from all the Uncle Ricks of the world.

I went back upstairs and practiced my flute for an hour. I always try to play my best when I practice ever since this one morning, back before Ruth got her car and we used to take the bus to school, Claire Lippman saw me with my flute case, and went, "Oh, you're the one," in this meaningful voice. When I asked her what she meant, she said, "Oh, nothing. Just that we always hear someone playing the flute around ten o'clock every night, and we never knew who it was." So I was totally mortified and turned bright red, which she must have seen, since she went, in this nice voice—Claire, in spite of being an exhibitionist, is really pretty nice—"No, no, it's not bad. I like it. It's like a free concert every night."

Anyway, once I heard that, I started treating my practice hour like a performance. First I warm up with scales, but I do them really fast to get them over with, and kind of jazzy, so that they don't sound boring. Then I work on whatever we're doing in Orchestra, but at double-time, also to get it over with. Then I do some cool medieval pieces I dug up last time I went to the library, some really ancient versions of *Greensleeves* and some Celtic stuff. Then, when I'm totally warmed up, I do some Billy Joel, since that's Douglas's favorite, though he'd deny it if you asked him. Then I do some Gershwin, for my dad, who loves Gershwin, and finish up with some Bach, because who doesn't love Bach?

Sometimes Ruth and I will practice together on the few pieces we've found for flute and cello. But we don't practice from the same house. What we do is, we open our bedroom windows and play from there. Like a little mini-concert for the neighborhood. That's pretty cool. Ruth says if some conductor walked by our houses, he'd be like, "Who are those incredible musicians? I need them in my orchestra immediately!" She's probably right.

The thing is, I play much better at home than I do at school. Like, if I played as well at school as I do at home, I'd definitely be first chair, instead of third. But I mess up a lot at school on purpose, because, frankly, I don't want to be first chair. First chair is way too much pressure. I get enough grief as it is from people trying to challenge me for third.

Karen Sue Hanky, for instance. She's fourth chair. She's challenged me ten times already this year. If you don't like your chair, you can challenge the person ahead of you, and move up if you win. Karen Sue started out as ninth chair, and challenged her way up to fourth. But she's been stuck at fourth all year, because one thing I won't do is let her win. I like third chair. I'm always third chair. Third chair, third kid. You get it? I'm comfortable being third.

But no way am I going to be fourth. So whenever Karen Sue challenges me, I play my best, like I do at home. Our conductor, Mr. Vine, always gives me this lecture afterward, when Karen Sue's gone off in a huff, which she always does, because I always win. Then Mr. Vine goes, "You know, Jessica, you could be first chair, if you'd just challenge Audrey. You could blow Audrey away, if you just tried."

But I have no desire to blow anybody away. I don't want to be first chair, or even second chair.

But I'll be damned before I let anybody take third chair away from me.

Anyway, when I was done practicing, I took a shower, and then went to bed. Before I turned out the light, though, I felt the place on my chest where the scar was. I couldn't really feel it. It wasn't raised, or anything. But I could still see it, when I'd looked in the mirror coming out of the shower. I hoped it wouldn't still be there the next day. How else was I going to wear my scoop-necked T-shirt?

CHAPTER

5

When I woke up the next morning, I knew two things right away. One, I had not died of a heart attack in the night. And two, Sean Patrick O'Hanahan was in Paoli, while Olivia Marie D'Amato was in New Jersey.

That's three things, I guess. But the second two were totally random. Who the hell was Sean Patrick O'Hanahan, and how did I know he was in Paoli? Ditto the stuff about Olivia Marie D'Amato.

Crazy dreams. I'd been having some crazy dreams, that was all. I got up and took another shower, since the red mark was still there, and I couldn't wear the scoop neck. I decided to go for clean hair instead. Who knew? Maybe Rob Wilkins would offer me another ride, and when we were at a stop sign or something, he'd turn his head and smell me.

It could happen.

It wasn't until I was eating breakfast that I realized who Sean Patrick O'Hanahan and Olivia Marie D'Amato were. They were the kids on the back of the milk carton. You know, the missing ones. Only they weren't missing. Not anymore. Because I knew where they were.

"You don't think you're actually wearing those jeans to school, do you, Jessica?"

My mom was way disenchanted with my ensemble, which I had put together very carefully, with Rob Wilkins in mind.

"Yeah, really," Mike said. "What do you think this is? The eighties?"

"Like," I said, "you know anything about fashion, science boy. Where's your pocket protector, anyway?"

"You cannot," my mother said, "wear those jeans to school, Jessica. You'll shame the family."

"There's nothing wrong with my jeans," I said. 1-800-WHERE-R-YOU. That was the number you were supposed to call if you knew where Sean Patrick O'Hanahan or Olivia Marie D'Amato were. I'm not kidding. 1-800-WHERE-R-YOU. Cute. Very cute.

"The knees have given out," my mother went on. "There's a hole starting at the crotch. You can't wear those jeans. They're falling apart."

That was the point, see. I couldn't expose my chest area, so I'd decided to go for my knees. I have pretty nice knees. So, when I was riding behind Rob Wilkins on his motorcycle, he'd look down and see these totally sexy knees sticking out of my jeans. I'd shaved my legs and everything. I was way ready.

The one thing I hadn't figured out was how I was going to get a ride home if he didn't ask. Call Ruth, I guess. But Ruth was going to be mad at me if I asked her not to come in the first place. She was bound to be all, "Why? Who's taking you home? Not that Grit, I hope."

Being best friends with someone like Ruth is hard sometimes.

"Go upstairs and change, young lady," my mom said.

"No way." My mouth was filled with cereal.

"What do you mean, no way? You cannot go to school dressed like that."

"Watch me," I said.

My dad came in then. My mom went, "Joe, look what she's wearing."

"What?" I said. "They're just jeans."

My dad looked at my jeans. Then he looked at my mom. "They're just jeans, Toni," he said.

My mom's name is Antonia. Everyone calls her Toni.

"They're slut jeans," my mother said. "She's dressing in slut jeans. It's because she reads that slut magazine." That's what my mom calls *Cosmo*. It sort of *is* a slut magazine, but still.

"She doesn't look like a slut," my dad said. "She just looks like what she is." We all looked at

60

him questioningly, wondering what I was. Then he went, "Well, you know. A tomboy."

Fortunately, at that moment, Ruth honked outside.

"Okay," I said, getting up. "I gotta go."

"Not in those jeans, you're not," my mom said.

I grabbed my flute and my backpack. "Bye," I said, and left by the back door.

I ran all the way around to the front of the house to meet Ruth, who was waiting in the street in her Cabriolet. It was a nice morning, so she had the top down.

"Nice jeans," she said sarcastically, as I climbed into the passenger seat.

"Just drive," I said.

"Really," she said, shifting. "You don't look like Jennifer Beals, or anything. Hey, are you a welder by day and a stripper by night, by any chance?"

"Yes," I said. "But I'm saving all my money to pay for ballet school."

We were almost to school when Ruth asked, suddenly, "Hey, what's with you? You haven't been this quiet since Douglas tried to . . . you know."

I shook myself. I hadn't been aware of vegging, but that's exactly what I'd done. The thing was, I couldn't get this picture of Sean Patrick O'Hanahan out of my head. He was older in my dream than in the picture on the milk carton.

Maybe he was one of those kids who'd been kidnapped so long ago, he didn't remember his real family.

Then again, maybe it had just been a dream.

"Huh," I said. "I don't know. I was just thinking, is all."

"That's a first," Ruth said. She pulled into the student parking lot. "Hey, do you want to walk home again tonight? I'll have Skip drop me off again at four, when you get out of detention. You know, I weighed myself this morning, and I already lost a pound."

I think she probably lost the pound from not eating any dinner the night before, being way too busy staring dreamily at Mike to consume anything. But all I said was, "Sure, I guess. Except . . ."

"Except what?"

"Well, you know how I feel about motorcycles."

Ruth looked heavenward. "Not Rob Wilkins again."

"Yes, Rob Wilkins again. I can't help it, Ruth. He's got that really big—"

"I don't want to hear it," Ruth said, holding up her hand.

"—Indian," I finished. "What did you think I was going to say?"

"I don't know." Ruth pushed a button, and the roof started going up. "Some of those Grits wear pretty tight jeans."

"Gross," I said, as if this had never occurred to me. "Really, Ruth."

She undid her seatbelt primly. "Well, it's not like I'm blind or anything."

"Look," I said. "If he offers me a ride, I'm taking it."

"It's your life," Ruth said. "But don't expect me to sit by the phone waiting for you to call if he doesn't ask."

"If he doesn't ask," I said, "I'll just call my mom."

"Fine," Ruth said. She sounded mad.

"What?"

"Nothing," she said.

"No, not nothing. What's wrong?"

"Nothing's wrong." Ruth got out of the car. "God, you're such a weirdo."

Ruth is always calling me a weirdo, so I didn't take offense. I don't think she even means anything by it anymore. Anything much, anyway.

I got out of the car, too. It was a beautiful day, the sky a robin's-egg blue overhead, the temperature hovering around sixty, and it was only eight in the morning. The afternoon would probably be roasting. Not the kind of day to spend indoors. The perfect kind of day for a ride in a convertible . . . or, even better, on the back of a bike.

Which reminded me. Paoli was only about twenty miles from where I was standing. It was the next town over, actually. I couldn't help wondering how Ruth—or Rob Wilkins—would feel about taking a little trip over there after detention. You know, just to check it out. I wouldn't tell either of them about my dream or anything. But I was pretty sure I knew exactly where that little brick house was . . . even though I was equally sure I'd never been there before.

Which was the main reason, actually, that I wanted to check it out. I mean, who goes around having dreams about kids on the back of milk cartons? Not that my ordinary dreams are all that exciting. Just the usual ones, about showing up to school naked, or sucking face with Brendan Fraser.

"Hello?"

I blinked. Ruth was standing in front of me, waving a hand in my face.

"God," she said, putting her hand down. "What is the matter with you? Are you sure you're all right?"

"Fine," I said automatically.

And the funny thing was, I really thought I was fine.

Then.

6

Detention at Ernie Pyle High is traditionally run by the staff member with the least seniority. This year, it was Miss Clemmings, the new art teacher. Now, I don't mean to be sexist, but they had to be kidding. Miss Clemmings is barely as tall as me, and can't weigh more than I do, like a hundred pounds or so.

And yet, unlike me, Miss Clemmings is hardly an expert kickboxer—or even a mediocre one. But there she was, supposed to keep these giant football players from fighting with one another. I mean, it was ridiculous. Coach Albright I could see. Coach Albright would be able to establish some control. But all Miss Clemmings could do was threaten to report these guys when they acted up. And all that happened when they got reported was that they got longer detentions.

Miss Clemmings had to keep them from fighting that much longer. It was kind of retarded.

So I wasn't super-surprised when Miss Clemmings, at the start of detention at the end of the day, called me up to the front of the auditorium and said, in her wispy little-girl voice, "Jessica, I need to talk to you."

I couldn't imagine what Miss Clemmings wanted. Oh, all right, I'll admit it: a part of me thought she was going to let me off for the rest of the semester, on account of my good behavior. Because I really am a little angel . . . during detention, anyway. That was more than could be said for any of my fellow detainees.

Which was, in a way, what she wanted to talk to me about.

"It's the Ws," she whispered.

I looked at her uncomprehendingly. "The Ws, Miss Clemmings?"

She went, "Yes, in the back row?" And then she pointed at the auditorium seats.

It was only then that I caught on. Of course. The Ws. We're seated alphabetically for detention, and the guys in the last row—the Ws—have a tendency to get a little rambunctious. They'd been restless during rehearsals for *West Side Story*, rowdy during *Romeo and Juliet*, and downright rude during *Our Town*. Now the drama club was putting on *Endgame*, and Miss Clemmings was afraid a riot might break out.

"I hate to ask this of you, Jessica," she said,

looking at me with her big blue eyes, "but you are the only girl here, and I've often found that placing a strong female influence in amongst a predominantly testosterone-driven group has a tendency to diffuse some of the—"

"Okay," I said, real fast.

Miss Clemmings looked surprised. Then she looked relieved. "Really? Really, Jessica? You wouldn't mind?"

Was she kidding? "No," I said. "I wouldn't mind. Not at all."

"Oh," she said, placing a hand to her heart. "Oh, I'm so glad. If you could, then, just sit between Robert Wilkins and the Wendell boy—"

I couldn't believe it. Some days, you know, you wake up, and okay, maybe you had some wacked-out dreams, but then, suddenly, things just start going your way. Just like that.

I went back to my seat in the *Ms*, picked up my backpack and my flute, and shoved my way down the *W* row until I'd gotten to the seat between Rob and Hank. There were a lot of cat-calls while I did this—enough so that the drama coach turned around and shushed us—and a few of the guys wouldn't pick up their stupid feet and let me by. I got them back, however, by kicking them really hard in the shins. That got them moving, all right.

We have to sit one seat apart from one another, so that necessitated everyone from Rob Wilkins down moving one seat over. Only Rob didn't

seem to mind. He picked up his leather jacket—
he had nothing else, no books, no bag, nothing,
except a paperback spy novel he kept in the back
pocket of his jeans—and sat down again, his blue
eyes on me as I arranged my stuff under my seat.

"Welcome to hell," he said to me when I
straightened up.

I flashed him my best smile. The guy on the
other side of him saw it, and grabbed his crotch.
Rob noticed, looked at him, and said, "You're
dead, Wylie."

"Shhh," Miss Clemmings hissed, clapping her
hands at us. "If I hear another word back there,
you're all getting an extra week."

We shut up. I took out my geometry book and
started doing the homework we'd been assigned
for the weekend. I tried not to notice that Rob
wasn't doing anything. He was just sitting there,
watching the play rehearsal. The guy to my left,
Hank Wendell, was making one of those paper
footballs. He was using spit instead of tape to
hold the paper together.

None of the guys in the Ws seemed particularly impressed—or cowed—by my presence.

Then suddenly Rob leaned over and grabbed
my notebook and pen out of my hands. He
looked at my homework, nodded, and turned the
page. Then he wrote something down, and
passed the notebook and the pen back to me. I
looked at what he had written. It was:

So did you get caught in the rain yesterday?

I looked down at Miss Clemmings. I'm not sure whether or not you're allowed to pass notes in detention. I'd never heard of anybody trying it before.

But Miss Clemmings wasn't even paying attention. She was watching Claire Lippman perform this really boring monologue from inside a big Rubbermaid trash can.

I wrote, *Yes*, and passed the notebook back to him.

Not exactly scintillating, or anything. But what else was I supposed to say?

He wrote something down and passed the notebook back. He'd written: *Told you so. Why don't you ditch the fat girl and come for a ride with me after this?*

Jesus Christ. He was asking me out. Sort of.

And he was also dissing my best friend.

Are you mentally impaired or something? I wrote. *That fat girl happens to be my best friend.*

He seemed to like that. He wrote for a long time. When I got the notebook back, this is what he'd put down: *Jesus, sorry. I had no idea you were so sensitive. Let me rephrase. Why don't you tell your gravitationally challenged friend to take a hike, and come for a ride with me after this?*

I wrote: *It's Friday night, you loser. What do you think, I don't already have plans? I happen to have a boyfriend, you know.*

I thought the boyfriend part might be stretching it a little, but he seemed to eat it up. He wrote: *Yeah? Well, I bet your boyfriend isn't rebuilding a '64 Harley in his barn.*

A '64 Harley? My fingers were trembling so hard I could barely write. *My boyfriend doesn't have a barn. His dad*—as long as I was making up a boyfriend, I figured I'd give him an impressive lineage—*is a lawyer.*

Rob wrote: *So? Dump him. Come for a ride.*

It was right then that Hank Wendell leaned over and went, "Wylie. Wylie?"

On the other side of Rob, Greg Wylie leaned over and went, "Suck on this, Wendell."

"Both of you," I hissed through gritted teeth, "shut the hell up before Clemmings looks over here."

Hank sent his paper football flying in Wylie's direction. But Rob stuck out his hand and caught it before it got to where it was supposed to.

"You heard the lady," he said, in this dangerous voice. "Knock it off."

Both Wylie and Wendell simmered down. Boy. Miss Clemmings had been right. It was amazing what a little estrogen could do.

Okay, I wrote. *On one condition.*

He wrote, *No conditions* and underlined it heavily.

I wrote, in big block letters, *Then I can't go.*

He'd seen what I was writing before I finished it. He snatched the notebook from me, looking annoyed, and wrote, *All right. What?*

Which was how, an hour later, we were headed for Paoli.

CHAPTER

7

Okay. Okay, so I'll admit it. Right here, on paper, in my official *statement*. You want a confession? You want me to tell the truth?

Okay. Here it is:

I like to go fast.

I mean, *really* fast.

I don't know what it is. I've just never been scared of speed. On road trips, like when we'd drive up to Chicago to see Grandma, and my dad would go eighty or so, trying to pass a semi, everyone in the car would be like, "Slow down! Slow down!"

Not me. I was always, "Faster! Faster!"

It's been that way ever since I was a little girl. I remember back when we used go to the county fair (before it was determined to be too "Gritty"), I always had to go on all the fast rides—the

Whip, the Super Himalaya—by myself, because everyone else in my family was too scared of them. Just me, by myself, going sixty, seventy, eighty miles an hour.

And that still wasn't fast enough. Not for me.

But here's the thing I found out that day I went for a ride with Rob: Rob liked going fast, too.

He was safe about it and everything. Like he made me wear a spare helmet he had in the storage container on the back of the bike. And he obeyed all traffic laws, while we were still within city limits. But as soon as we were out of them . . .

I have to tell you, I was in heaven. I mean it.

Of course, part of it might have been because I had my arms wrapped around this totally buff guy. I mean, Rob had abs that were hard as rock. I know, because I was holding on pretty tight, and all he was wearing beneath that leather jacket was a T-shirt.

Rob was my kind of guy. He liked taking risks.

It wasn't like there were any other cars on the road. I mean, we're talking country lanes here, surrounded by corn fields. I don't think we passed another car all night, except when we finally made the turn into Paoli.

Paoli.

What can I tell you about Paoli? What do you want to know? You want to know how it started? I guess you do. Okay, I'll tell you. It started in Paoli.

Paoli, Indiana. Paoli's just like any other small town in Southern Indiana. There was a town square with a courthouse on it, one movie theater, a bridal shop, a library. I guess there was probably an elementary school, too, and a high school, and a rubber tire factory, though I didn't see them.

I do know there were about ten churches. I made Rob turn left at one of the churches—don't even ask me how I knew it was the right one— and suddenly we were on the same tree-lined street from my dream. Two blocks later, and we were in front of this very familiar-looking little brick house. I tapped Rob on the shoulder, and he pulled over to the curb and cut the engine off.

Then we sat there, and I looked.

It was the house from my dream. The exact same house. It had the same crabgrassy lawn, the same black mailbox with just numbers, no name on it, the same windows with all the blinds down. The more I looked at it, the more I suspected that, in the backyard, there'd be a rusty old swing set, and one of those kiddie wading pools, cracked and dirty from having sat outside all winter.

It was a nice house. Small, but nice. In a modest but nice neighborhood. Someone who lived nearby had gotten out the barbecue and was grilling burgers for dinner. In the distance, I could hear the voices of children shouting as they played.

"Well," Rob said, after a minute. "This the boyfriend's place, then?"

"Shhh," I said to him. That's because someone was coming toward us on the sidewalk. Someone short, dragging a jean jacket behind him. Someone who, when he got close enough, suddenly veered off the sidewalk and onto the lawn of the little brick house I was staring at.

I pulled off the helmet Rob had lent me.

No, my eyes weren't playing tricks on me. It was Sean Patrick O'Hanahan, all right. Older than he'd been in the picture on the back of the milk carton by about five or six years. But it was him. I just knew it.

I don't know what made me do it. I'd never done anything like it before. But I got down from Rob's bike, crossed the street, and said, "Sean."

Just like that. I didn't yell it or anything. I just said his name.

He turned. Then he went pale. Before he even saw me, he went pale. I swear it.

He was probably about twelve. Small for his age, but still only a few inches shorter than me. Red hair beneath a Yankees cap. Freckles stood out starkly against his nose, now that he'd gone so pale.

His eyes were blue. They narrowed as his gaze flicked first over me, then behind me, toward Rob.

"I don't know what you're talking about," he said. He didn't shout it, any more than I'd shouted his name. Still, I heard the undercurrent of fear in his little-boy voice.

I got as far as the sidewalk before I thought I'd better stop. He looked ready to bolt.

"Oh, yeah?" I said. "Your name's not Sean?"

"No," the kid said, in that snotty way kids talk when they're scared, only they don't want it to show. "My name's Sam."

I shook my head slowly. "No, it isn't," I said. "Your name's Sean. Sean Patrick O'Hanahan. It's okay, Sean. You can trust me. I'm here to help you. I'm here to help get you home."

What happened next was this:

The kid went, if such a thing is possible, even whiter. At the same time, his body seemed to turn into Jell-O, or something. He dropped the jean jacket as if it weighed too much for him to hold on to anymore, and I could see his fingers shaking.

Then he rushed me.

I don't know what I thought he was going to do. Hug me, I guess. I thought maybe he was so happy and grateful at being found, he was going to throw himself into my arms and give me a great big kiss for having come to his rescue.

That was so not what he did.

What he did instead was reach out and grab me by the wrist—quite painfully, I might add—and hiss, *"Don't you tell anyone. Don't you ever tell anyone you saw me, understand?"*

This was not exactly the kind of reaction I'd

been expecting. I mean, it would have been one thing if we'd gotten to Paoli and I had found out the house I'd dreamed about didn't exist. But it did exist. And what's more, in front of that house was the kid from the milk carton. I'd have staked my life on it.

Only, for some reason, the kid was claiming he was someone else.

"I am not Sean Patrick O'Hanahan," he whispered in a voice that was as filled with anger as it was with fear. "So you can just go away, do you hear? You can just go away. *And don't ever come back.*"

It was at this point that the front door to the little house opened, and a woman's voice called, sharply, "Sam!"

The kid let go of me at once.

"Coming," he said, his voice shaking as badly as his fingers were.

He threw me just one more furious, frightened look as he stooped to pick his jean jacket up off the lawn. Then he ran inside and slammed the door behind him without glancing in my direction again.

Standing out on the sidewalk, I stared at that closed door. I listened to the sounds of the birds, of the children I could hear playing somewhere nearby. I could still smell the burgers grilling, and something else: fresh-cut grass. Someone had taken advantage of the unseasonable warmth and mowed their lawn.

Nothing inside the house in front of me stirred. Not a blind was lifted. Nothing.

But everything—everything I had ever known—was different now.

Because that kid *was* Sean Patrick O'Hanahan. I knew it as well as I knew my name, my brothers' names. That kid was Sean Patrick O'Hanahan.

And he was in trouble.

"Kid's a little young for you," I heard a voice behind me point out, "don't you think?"

I turned around. Rob was still straddling the motorcycle. He'd taken his helmet off, and was observing me with a perfectly impassive expression on his good-looking face.

"Takes all kinds, I guess," he said with a shrug. "Still, I didn't have you pegged for having a Boy Scout fixation."

I probably should have told him. I probably should have said right then, *Look, I saw that kid on the back of a milk carton. Let's go get the police.*

But I didn't. I didn't say anything. I didn't know what to say. I didn't know what to do.

I didn't understand what was happening to me.

"Well," Rob said. "We could stand around out here all night, if you want to. But the smell of those burgers is making me hungry. What do you say we go try to find some of our own?"

I gave the little brick house one last look. *Sean, I thought to myself, I know that's you in there. What did they do to you? What did they do to you, to make you so afraid to admit your own name?*

"Mastriani," Rob said.

I turned around and got back onto the bike.

He didn't ask me a single question. He just handed me my helmet, put his own on, waited until I said I was ready, and then he hit the gas.

We left Paoli.

It wasn't until we were doing ninety again that I perked up. It's hard to keep a speed freak down when she's doing ninety. Okay, I reasoned to myself as we cruised. You know what you have to do. You know what you have to do.

So after we'd pulled up to the burger place Rob had in mind—a Hell's Angels hangout called Chick's that I'd always wanted to go to, since we drove past it every January 5 on our way to the dump to get rid of the Christmas tree, only Mom would never let me—I did it.

I went to the pay phone by the ladies' room and dialed.

"1-800-WHERE-R-YOU," a woman's voice said after it had only rung twice. "This is Rosemary. How may I help you?"

I had to stick a finger in my other ear, the jukebox was pumping John Cougar Mellencamp so loudly.

"Hi, Rosemary," I shouted. "This is Jess."

"Hi, Jess," Rosemary said. She sounded like she might be black. I don't happen to know any black people—there aren't any in my town—but I have seen them in movies, and on TV and stuff. So that's how I knew. Rosemary sounded like an older black lady. "I can barely hear you."

"Yeah," I said. "Sorry about that. I'm in a . . . well, I'm in a bar."

Rosemary didn't sound too shaken to hear that. On the other hand, she had no way of knowing that I am only sixteen.

"What can I do for you today, Jess?" Rosemary asked.

"Well," I said. I took a deep breath.

"Listen, Rosemary," I said. "This is going to sound kind of weird, but there's this kid, Sean Patrick O'Hanahan. You guys have him on a milk carton. Anyway, I know where he is." And then I told her.

Rosemary kept going, "Uh-huh. Uh-huh. Uh-huh." And then she said, "Honey, are you—"

Rob shouted my name. I looked toward him, and he held up two red plastic baskets. Our burgers were up.

I went, "Rosemary, I gotta go. But real quick. That Olivia Marie D'Amato? You guys'll be able to find her at—" And then I gave her a street address, a city in New Jersey, and a zip code, for good measure. "Okay? I gotta go. Bye!"

I hung up.

It was funny, but I felt relieved. Like I had gotten something off my chest. Isn't that weird? I mean, I know Sean had told me not to tell anyone. *Told* me not to tell? He'd *begged* me.

But he had also looked so scared at being

found out that I couldn't imagine whoever he was with could be any good for him. Not if they were making him lie about his name and stuff. What about his parents? He had to know they were missing him. He had to know they would protect him from whoever these people were who had him.

I had done the right thing, calling. I had to have. Otherwise, why would I have felt so good?

I ended up having a good time. Rob, it turned out, had quite a few friends at Chick's. All of them were guys who were way older than he was, and, for the most part, they had really long hair and were heavily tattooed. Their tattoos said things like *1/31/68*, which I remembered from World Civ was the day of the Tet Offensive in the Vietnam war. Rob's friends seemed strangely astonished to see me—although they were very nice—which led me to believe that either:

a) Rob had never brought a girl to Chick's before (unlikely), or
b) the girls he'd brought there had looked more like the girls who were hanging around the Hell's Angels—i.e., tall, blond, excessively made-up, named Teri or Charleen, and who probably never wore gingham in their lives (more likely).

Which might be why, every time I opened my mouth, the guys would all look at one another, until finally one of them said to Rob, "Where'd you *get* her?" to which I replied, because it was such a stupid question, "The girlfriend store."

Everybody but Teri and Charleen laughed at that one.

So, overall, when I got home that night, I was one happy camper. I had saved a kid's life—maybe even two kids' lives, although there was no way I was going all the way to Jersey to check Olivia D'Amato's situation. And I had spent the afternoon and part of the evening with a totally hot guy who liked going fast, and who, if I wasn't mistaken, seemed to like me, too. What could be better than that?

Not having my parents find out about it, that's what.

And there was no chance they were going to, either. Because the minute I walked in the door, around nine or so—I made Rob drop me off way down the street, so my folks wouldn't hear his bike—I saw that they hadn't even noticed I was gone. I had called, of course, from Chick's, and said band rehearsal was running long, but nobody had picked up. When I walked in, I saw why. My mom and dad were having a huge fight. Over Douglas. As usual.

"He's not ready!" my mom was screaming.

"The longer he waits," my dad said, "the harder it's going to be for him. He's got to start now."

"Do you want him to try it again?" my mom wanted to know. "Is that what you want, Joe?"

"Of course not," my dad said. "But it's different now. He's on the medication. Look, Toni, I think it would be good for him. He needs to get out of the house. All he does is lie up there, reading comic books."

"And you think slaving away in a hot restaurant kitchen is the cure for that?" My mom sounded very sarcastic.

"He needs to get out," my dad said. "And he needs to start earning his keep."

"He's sick!" my mom insisted.

"He's always going to be sick, Toni," my dad said. "But at least he's being treated now. And the treatments are working. The doctors said as long as he was taking his medication, there's no reason why he can't—" My dad broke off because he saw me in the doorway. "What do you want?" he asked, not rudely.

"Cereal," I said. "Sorry I missed dinner."

My dad waved at me. A *whatever* wave. I got down a box of Raisin Bran and a bowl.

"He's not ready," my mother said.

"Toni," my dad said. "He can't stay up there in his room forever. I mean, he's twenty years old, for Christ's sake. He's got to start getting out, seeing people his own age—"

"Oh, and back in the kitchen at Mastriani's, that's what he'll be doing. Getting out." My mom was being sarcastic again.

"Yes," my dad said. "With kids his own age. You know the crew back there. They'll be good for him."

My mother snorted. I ate my cereal, pretending to be very interested in the back of the milk carton, but really listening to their conversation.

"Next thing, you'll probably want to send him to one of those halfway houses," my mother said.

"Well, Toni," my dad said, "it might not be such a bad idea. He could meet other kids with his same problem, learn he's not alone in this—"

"I don't like it," my mother said. "I'm telling you, I don't like it."

My dad threw his hands in the air. "Of course you don't like it, Toni," he said. "You want to keep the kid wrapped up in cotton wool. But you can't do it, Toni. You can't protect him forever. And you can't watch him forever. He's going to find a way to do it again, whether you're keeping an eye on him or not."

"Dad's right," I said with my mouth full.

My mother glared at me. "Don't you have some place to be, young lady?"

I didn't, but I decided to go to my room to practice. Nobody bothered asking me why I was practicing after I'd just—supposedly—been at band practice for like six hours or something. That's just the way my family is.

Claire Lippman's not the only one who can hear me practicing. Ruth can hear me, too. As soon as I was done, the phone rang. It was Ruth, wanting to know all about my bike ride.

"It was okay," I said as I ran a cloth through

the inside of my flute with this metal stick to clean out all the spit.

"*Okay?*" Ruth echoed. "*Okay?* What'd you do? Where did you go?"

"Just for a ride," I said. Don't ask me why, but I couldn't bring myself to tell Ruth about Sean. I hadn't even been able to tell Rob about Sean. In answer to his persistent questioning, I'd finally said, "He's my loan shark, okay?" which had gotten a hoot from Rob's friends.

"You went for a ride?" Ruth's voice rose incredulously. "To where? Chicago?"

"No. Just around. And then we went to Chick's."

"Chick's?" Ruth sounded close to spontaneous combustion. "That's a *bar*. A *biker* bar."

"Yeah," I said.

"And you didn't get carded?"

"No," I said. We didn't get carded because Rob knew the bartender.

"Did you *drink?*"

"Of course not," I said.

"Did he?"

"Duh, Ruth. Do you think I really would have gotten onto a bike with a guy who was drinking? We just had sodas."

"Oh. Well, did he kiss you?"

I didn't say anything. I was taking my flute apart, putting it into the little velvet compartments inside my case.

"Jeez," Ruth breathed. "He did. I can't believe he kissed you. Was there tongue?"

"Regrettably, no."

"Oh, my God," Ruth said. "Well, that's probably better. You shouldn't let him tongue you on a first date. He might think you're easy. So, are you going out again?"

"Maybe next weekend," I said, vaguely. He hadn't mentioned a thing, I realized now, about seeing me again. What did *that* mean? Did he not like me? Or was it just that it was my turn to ask him? Never having dated before, I was not sure how these things worked.

And there was no use asking Ruth. She was even more clueless than I was.

"I still can't believe," she was saying, "that you're seeing a Grit."

"You're such a snob," I said. "What does it matter? He's totally cool. And he knows everything about bikes."

"But he's not going to college, right? After he graduates?"

"No. He's going to work in his uncle's garage."

"Jeez," Ruth said. "Well, I guess it's okay if you just use him for sex and free bike rides."

"I'm hanging up now, Ruth," I said.

"Okay. You working tomorrow?"

"Is the Pope Catholic?"

"Okay. Wow. I can't believe he kissed you."

Actually, I couldn't, either. But I didn't tell

Ruth that. Or about how, when he'd done it, I'd practically fallen off the back of his bike, I'd been so surprised. Just because I'm in detention a lot doesn't mean I'm experienced.

I hope it didn't show.

Every Saturday, and most Sundays after church, I have to work at one of my dad's restaurants. So does Michael. So did Douglas, before he went away to college, and got sick. I guess all kids whose parents own restaurants have to work in them at some point. It's supposed to teach us to have a work ethic, so we don't go around thinking everything just gets handed to you on a platter. Instead, we're the ones handling the platter. And the dishes. And the steam table. And the cash register. And the reservation book.

You name it, and if it has to do with food service, I've done it.

That particular Saturday, though, I was kind of spacing it with the cash register, so Pat, the manager, stuck me on busing. Hey, I had a lot on my mind. And no, it wasn't Rob Wilkins. It was the fact that, when I'd woken up that morning, I knew where Hadley Grant and Timothy Jonas Mills were.

My mom had thrown out the old milk carton, the one with Sean Patrick and Olivia Marie, and bought a new one. And I knew where the missing kids on the new one were, too.

It was freaking me out a little. I mean, where were these dreams coming from? It was so random to just wake up with all this information about a couple of total strangers in my head.

I wasn't going to call again. Once had been bad enough. But twice—well, that was pushing it. I mean, I didn't even know whether or not the information I'd given Rosemary had been accurate. What if it turned out to be totally bogus? What if, by some fluke, that really *hadn't* been Sean Patrick O'Hanahan? What if it had just been some random kid, and I'd totally freaked him out. . . .

No. It *had* been him. I remembered the way he'd gone so pale beneath those freckles. It had been Sean, all right.

And if I'd been right about Sean . . .

The first break I got, I was on the pay phone by the ladies' room, on hold with 1-800-WHERE-R-YOU. I couldn't believe they'd put me on hold. How many people could be calling in on a Saturday afternoon? Jeesh. I only got a five-minute break, and I hadn't even gone to the bathroom yet. The minutes were ticking by, and a family had come in and sat down at one of the tables I hadn't bused yet. They were sitting there, pushing all the empty glasses and used plates into this big, precarious pile. I swear to God, people do not know how to act.

Finally, this woman picked up and asked how she could help me. I went, "Rosemary?"

"No," the woman said. She was white and Southern, I could tell. "Rosemary's not in today. This is Judith. How may I help you?"

I said, "Oh, well, I think I know where these two kids are. Um, Hadley Grant and Timothy Jonas Mills?"

Judith went, "Oh?" in this way suspicious voice.

"Yeah," I said. The family at the table I still hadn't bused was starting to look around in an angry way. One of their kids had tried to drink the leftover ice in one of the used glasses. "Look, Hadley's at—" And I gave her the exact address, which happened to be in Florida. "—and Timothy's in Kansas." I gave her the street address. "Did you get all that?"

"Excuse me, miss," Judith said. "Are you the—"

I said, "Sorry, gotta go," and hung up, mostly because the family was starting to pile the dirty plates on a table that had just opened up beside theirs, but also because I thought Judith had been about to yell at me about Sean and Olivia, and that I did not need.

But after I hung up, I felt better. Just like yesterday. I felt like a weight had been lifted off me.

At least until Pat told me I couldn't bus anymore, and sent me in the back to wash dishes.

The rest of the weekend passed pretty much without incident. On Saturday night, Ruth came over, and this time she actually brought her cello. We played a concerto, then watched some videos she'd rented. Mike came down for a little while and teased us about our taste in movies. Ruth only likes movies that have a beauty makeover in them. Like *Pretty Woman*, when Julia Roberts gets all the clothes. I tend to like movies with explosions. There's only a few movies that have both. *Point of No Return*, with Bridget Fonda, is about the only one. We've seen that movie nine times.

Douglas popped in, too, for a few minutes, on his way to the kitchen to dump off some cereal bowls that had been in his room for a few weeks. He watched the movie for a little while, but then my mom caught him, and started asking if he felt all right. So he had to run back upstairs and hide.

Around eleven o'clock, I could have sworn I heard the purr of Rob Wilkins's Indian outside our house. But when I looked out the window, there was no one there. Wishful thinking, I guess. He was probably totally freaked-out by what an inexperienced kisser I am, and would never ask me out again.

Oh, well. His loss.

Sunday, after church, my dad dumped us off

at Mastriani's to help with the brunch crowd. Well, me and Mike, anyway. Douglas doesn't have to go to church anymore. Instead, he stays home and reads comic books. I know Douglas is sick and all, but I wouldn't mind staying home on Sunday morning and reading comic books. Or watching TV, even. But I never tried to kill myself, so I have to go to church. And I have to go in a dress that matches my mother's.

It's enough to make a girl think there might not actually be a God.

The only thing that happened on Sunday was that we ran out of milk, and my mom sent me and Mike to the store to buy some. Mike let me drive on the way there, but then, on the way back, he totally wouldn't let me near the wheel. But you know, I think speed limits are really just suggestions. If there's nobody else on the road, you should be able to go as fast as you want. Unfortunately, Mike—and your friends at the Department of Motor Vehicles, who keep refusing to give me a license—disagree.

At the grocery store, I picked out a milk carton that had some kids on it I hadn't seen already, just as a kind of experiment. It was slotted to expire in two days, but the way Douglas chows, I knew we'd need more by tomorrow, anyway. Douglas can eat an entire family-size box of Cheerios in one sitting. It's a wonder he isn't fat. But he's always had a very high metabolism, like Mr. Goodhart.

Also at the grocery store, we ran into Claire Lippman. She was standing by the magazine rack, reading *Cosmo,* while her mom was rooting through the corn in the vegetable section. Mike stared at her longingly for a while. Finally I got sick of it, and poked him and said, "Just go *talk* to her, for God's sake."

Mike went, "Oh, right. About what?"

"Tell her you can't wait to see her in *Endgame.*"

"What's that?"

"It's a play. She's in it. She plays Nell. She has to sit in a plastic trash can all during the show."

Mike looked at me. "How do you know? Since when are you in the drama club?"

I realized I had made a mistake. I said, "God, never mind. Come on, let's go."

Only Mike wouldn't go. He just kept staring at Claire. "I mean," he said, "it's not like she'd go with me. If I asked her. Why would she go with me? I don't even have a car."

"You could have bought a car," I said, "with all the money you earned working at the restaurant. But, no. You had to buy that stupid scanner."

"And a printer," Mike said. "And a Zip drive. And—"

"Oh, my God," I said. "Whatever. You can always borrow Dad's car."

"Yeah," Mike said. "A Volvo station wagon. Right. Come on. Let's go."

God. I can't believe boys. It's a wonder any-body gets married at all.

Nothing else much happened on Sunday, except that that night, while I was practicing, I thought I heard a motorcycle going down our street again. And this time, when I looked out my window, the one I can see the whole street on, I saw one set of tail lights, way down Lumley Lane, making the turn off onto Hunter.

Hey, it could have been Rob. You never know.

I went to bed all happy, thinking maybe a boy liked me. It's stupid that that's all it takes, some-times, to make you happy. Thinking that some-one likes you, I mean. It's especially stupid in light of what happened the next day. I had way bigger problems, it turned out, than whether or not a boy liked me.

Way bigger.

CHAPTER

9

What happened was, the next day, Ruth drove me to school as usual. All during the drive, I couldn't get those kids out of my head. The kids on the side of the milk carton I'd bought the night before, I mean. Once again, I'd wakened with this feeling that I knew exactly where they were, down to the street address. It was getting creepy, let me tell you.

But just like on Friday and Saturday, I couldn't stop thinking about them. So, as soon as we got to school, and I managed to ditch Ruth, I gave old 1-800-WHERE-R-YOU a call. This time Rosemary answered.

"Hey, Rosemary," I said. "It's me, Jess. From Friday, remember?"

Rosemary sucked in her breath. "Jess!" she said. Actually, she practically screamed it in my ear. "Honey, where are you?"

I thought it was kind of funny that somebody who worked for 1-800-WHERE-R-YOU would be asking where *I* was. I went, "Well, right now I'm at school."

"People are looking for you, hon," Rosemary said. "Did you call here on Saturday?"

"Yeah," I said. "Why?"

"Hold on," Rosemary said. "I have to get my supervisor. I promised I would if you called back."

The late bell rang. I went, "Wait, Rosemary. I don't have time. I have to tell you about Jennie Lee Peters and Samantha Travers—"

"Jess," Rosemary said. "Honey, I don't think you understand. Haven't you looked at a newspaper? They found them. They found Sean and Olivia, exactly where you said they'd be. And the children you called about on Saturday—they found them, too. People here want to talk to you, honey. They want to know how you knew—"

So it had been Sean. It had been Sean, after all. Why had he told me his name was Sam? Why had he looked so scared when it was clear I was there to try to help him?

I said, in reply to Rosemary's question, "I don't know how I knew. Look, Rosemary, I'm gonna be late. Just let me tell you—"

"Here's my supervisor, Larry Barnes," Rosemary said. "Larry, it's her. It's Jess."

This man's voice came on over the phone. "Jess?" he said. "Is this Jess?"

"Look," I said. I was getting kind of scared. I mean, I just wanted to help out some missing kids. I didn't want to have to talk to Larry the supervisor. "Jennie Lee Peters is in Escondido, California." I rattled off the address really fast. "And Samantha Travers, it's kind of weird about her, but if you go down Rural Route 4, just outside of Wilmington, Alabama, you'll find her by this tree, this tree with a big rock next to it—"

"Jess," Larry said. "It's Jessica, isn't it? May I have your last name, Jess? And where you're calling from?"

I saw Mrs. Pitt, the Home Ec teacher, wadding toward me. Mrs. Pitt totally hates me because of the time I poured a soufflé over another kid's head in her class, even though he deserved it for asking me how it felt to have a retard for a brother. Mrs. Pitt would not hesitate to write me up.

"Gotta go," I said, and hung up.

But it didn't matter. Mrs. Pitt was like, "Jessica Mastriani, what are you doing out of class?" And then she wrote me up.

Thanks a lot, Mrs. Pitt. I'd like to record my gratitude for your caring and understanding right here in my *statement*, which, I understand, will be made public someday, so that everyone in the whole world will know just how fine a teacher you are.

At lunch, I went to see Mr. Goodhart about

being written up. He said all the usual stuff about how I need to start applying myself more, and how I'm never going to get into college at this rate, etc. After he gave me another week's detention for my own good, I asked him if he had any newspapers, because I had to do a current event for U.S. History.

This was a total lie, of course. I just wanted to see if Rosemary was right.

Mr. Goodhart gave me a copy of *USA Today*. I sat down in the waiting area and looked all through it. There were many entertaining stories about celebrities doing foolish things that distracted me, but finally I found it, this story in the "Nation" section, about an anonymous caller who had contacted 1-800-WHERE-R-YOU and told them the exact location of four children, one of whom had been missing from his home for seven years.

Sean.

I stared at the article. *Me*, I kept thinking. *I* was the anonymous caller. *I* was in the newspaper. A *national* newspaper.

The National Organization for Missing Children wanted to know who I was, so they could extend their thanks.

There was also, it turned out, a substantial reward for finding Olivia Marie D'Amato. Ten thousand bucks, to be exact.

Ten thousand bucks. You could get a heck of a motorcycle for ten thousand bucks.

But then, on the heels of that thought came another: I can't take *money* for doing what I'd done. I mean, I never paid much attention in church, but one thing that had managed to sink in was the fact that you're *supposed* to do nice things for people. You don't do them because you expect to get paid for them. You do it because it's the right thing to do. Like punching Jeff Day, for instance. That had been the right thing to do. Accepting reward money for doing the right thing . . . well, that just seemed wrong to me.

Since I didn't want any lousy reward—and since I didn't want my picture in *USA Today*—I decided not to call NOMC. I mean, it wasn't as if I really wanted anyone to know about this thing I could do. I was enough of a reject at school already. If people found out about this, I'd end up like Carrie, or something, with pig blood all over me. Who needed the hassle?

Besides, the last thing my family could survive was another crisis. My mother hadn't even begun to get over what had happened to Douglas. Although I suspect finding out your kid is psychic is better than finding out he's schizophrenic, it still adds up to one thing: Not Normal. All my mother has ever wanted was to have a normal family.

Though what's so normal about two women wearing the same homemade dress, I cannot begin to imagine.

But still. I did not need the added pressure. I had enough of my own.

So I didn't call 1-800-WHERE-R-YOU back. I didn't call anybody. I just went along, doing my normal thing. At lunch, Ruth teased me about dating a Grit in front of some of our other friends from Orchestra, so they started teasing me, too. I didn't mind, though. I knew they were just jealous. And they had every right to be. Rob Wilkins was hot. When I strolled into detention after school that day, I have to admit, my heart kind of skipped a beat when I saw him. The guy is good-looking.

We didn't have a chance to speak before Miss Clemmings cracked the whip. But after she did, and I took out my notebook and started doing my homework, Rob didn't lean over and grab it and start writing cute little notes to me, like he had on Friday. Instead he just sat there, reading his spy novel. It was a different spy novel from the one he'd had last week, and I suppose it was pretty engrossing and all, but come on. He could at least have said hi.

The fact that he didn't made me cranky. I suppose other girls would have gotten the message, but I had no experience in that department. I couldn't figure out what I had done. Was it the way I'd reacted when he'd kissed me? You know, almost falling off the back of his bike like that? I'll admit, that was pretty juvenile, but give me a break: it was my first kiss.

Maybe it was the girlfriend-store remark. Or

the fact that I so obviously didn't fit in with Teri and Charleen. The fact that I didn't know made me even more cranky.

Which would probably explain why, when Hank Wendell leaned over and whispered, "Hey, Mastriani, what's this I hear about Wilkins slipping you the sausage last Friday?" I elbowed him in the throat.

Not hard enough to crush his larynx and cause him to lose consciousness (unfortunately), but hard enough to make him really, really mad.

But before Hank's fist could connect with my face (I was fully prepared to roll with the punch, as my father had taught me), this hand shot out, and Hank's arm was twisted up and out of my line of vision.

"I thought we agreed you were going to leave her alone." Rob had to lean over me to keep his grip on Hank. Consequently, his belt buckle was level with my nose. Not exactly a very dignified position.

It made me mad. Almost as mad as Hank's remark.

"Have you been going around telling people we had *sex*?" I demanded, craning my neck to see Rob's face.

Over on the stage, rehearsal had stopped dead. All the cast members of *Endgame* were staring at us. Miss Clemmings was going, "What's happening back there? Mr. Wilkins, release Mr. Wendell and sit down at once!"

"Jesus, Wilkins," Hank said in a strangled voice. Maybe I'd gotten him harder than I thought. "You're breaking my goddamned arm."

"I'll snap it off," Rob said, in this very scary voice I had never heard him use before, "if you don't leave her alone."

"Jesus, all right," Hank said, and Rob let him go.

Hank collapsed back into his seat. Rob retired to his. And Miss Clemmings, who'd been halfway up the aisle, paused and said, "That's better," in this very satisfied voice, as if the fight had broken up on account of something she'd done.

Right.

I was furious.

"What did he mean?" I hissed at Rob as soon as Miss Clemmings's back was turned. "What was he talking about?"

"Nothing," Rob said. He buried his face back in his book. "He's an asshole. Just cool it, will you?"

Okay, I might as well let you know now that one thing I really hate is when people tell me to cool it. For instance, people often make cracks about Douglas, and then tell me to cool it when I get mad. And I can't. I can't cool it.

"No, I will not cool it," I snarled. "I want to know what he was talking about. What the hell is going on? Did you tell your friends we *did it*?"

Rob looked up from his book then. He had

absolutely no expression on his face as he said, "First of all, Wendell is not my friend."

On my left, Hank, still massaging his wrist, grunted. "You got that right."

"Secondly," Rob went on, "I didn't tell anybody anything about you, okay? So just calm down."

I hate it when people tell me to calm down, too.

"Look," I said. "I don't know what's going on here. But if I find out you've been telling people stuff about me behind my back, I will pound you. Understand?"

For the first time all day, he smiled at me. It was like he didn't want to, but he couldn't help it.

And Rob, well, he has one of *those* smiles. You know the kind.

Then again, maybe you don't. I forgot who I was writing this for.

Anyway, he went, *"You're* going to pound *me?"* in this very amused voice. Which just made me madder.

"Don't, man," Hank warned him. "She hits really hard, for a girl."

"Yeah," I said. "So you better watch it."

I don't know what—if anything—Rob would have replied, since Miss Clemmings went "Shhh," just then, in this way I suppose she meant to be threatening. Rob, looking as expressionless as ever, buried his head back in his book.

I had no choice but to turn back to my homework.

But inside, I was fuming.

I was fuming even harder when, after Miss Clemmings let us go for the day, I walked outside and found that I had no ride home. Like an idiot, I had told Ruth not to bother picking me up. I had assumed Rob would give me a ride home.

Great. Just great.

I could have called my mom, I guess. But I was too wound up to stand around and wait for her. I felt like, if I didn't hit somebody, I would lose it. And when I feel like that, it's better not to be around people. Especially my mom.

So I just started walking. I didn't care about the two miles. I couldn't even feel my feet, I was that mad. It was nice out, not a cloud in the sky. No worrying about being struck by lightning today. Not that I cared. A thousand bolts of lightning could come down out of the sky and I wouldn't even notice.

How could I have been so stupid? How could I have been so *dumb?*

I was walking parallel to the bleachers—scene of the crime—when I heard the purr of Rob's bike. He was coasting along by the curb.

"Jess," he said. "Come on."

I didn't even look at him. "Get lost," I said. I really meant it, too.

"What are you going to do, walk all the way home? Come on, I'll give you a ride."

I told him where he could stick his ride.

"Look," he said. "I'm sorry. I made a mistake, all right?"

I thought he was talking about having ignored me in detention.

"You better believe it," I said.

"I just thought you were older, okay?"

That stopped me right in my tracks. I turned around and looked at him.

"What do you mean, you thought I was *older?*" I demanded.

He didn't have his helmet on, so I could see his face. He looked uncomfortable.

"I didn't know you were only sixteen, okay? I mean, you don't act like a sixteen-year-old. You seem a lot more mature. Well, except for the whole punching-guys-who-are-a-lot-bigger-than-you-are thing."

I was having trouble making sense of this.

"What the hell does it matter," I demanded, "how old I am?"

"It matters," he said.

"I don't see why."

"It just does," he said.

I shook my head. "I still don't see why."

"Because I'm eighteen." He wasn't looking at me. He was looking at the road beneath his boots. "And I'm on probation."

Probation? I had been out with a *felon?* My mom was going to die if she ever found out.

"What'd you do?" I asked.

"Nothing."

A Volkswagen went by, honking its horn. Rob was pulled way off to the side of the road, so I couldn't see what the problem was. Then the driver waved. It was Miss Clemmings. Toot-toot. Buh-bye, kids. See you in detention tomorrow.

"No, seriously," I said. "What'd you do?"

"Look," Rob said. "It was stupid, all right?"

"I want to know."

"Well, I'm not going to tell you, so you'd better just forget about it."

My imagination was working overtime. What had he done? Robbed a bank? No, you don't get probation for that. You go to jail. Ditto if he'd killed someone. What could he have done?

"So, I don't think it's such a good idea," he went on. "Us going out, I mean. Unless . . . When's your birthday?"

"Just had it last month," I said.

He said a word that I will refrain from recording here.

"Look," I said. "I don't care that you're on probation."

"Yeah, but your parents will."

"No, they're cool."

He laughed. "Right, Jess. That's why you made me drop you off at the end of the street the other night, instead of in front of your house. Because your parents are so cool. They're so cool, you didn't want them to know anything about

me. And you didn't even know about the probation thing then. Admit it."

He had me there.

"Well," I said. "They're just going through sort
of a hard time right now, and I don't want to
cause them any more stress. But look, there's no
reason they have to know."

"Word gets around, Jess. Look at Wendell.
It's only a matter of time before your parents—
and my probation officer—get wind of what's
going on."

Well, I wasn't going to stand there and beg
him to go out with me. The guy was hot and
everything, but a girl has her pride. So I just
shrugged and said, "Whatever."

Then I turned around and started walking
again.

"Mastriani," he said, in a tired voice. "Look,
just get on the bike, will ya? I'll take you home.
Or to your street corner, I guess."

"I don't know," I said, looking back at him
and fluttering my eyelashes. "I mean, Miss
Clemmings already saw us together. Supposing
she goes running to the cops—"

He looked annoyed. "Just get on the bike,
Mastriani."

I can tell what you're thinking.

You're thinking that, in spite of the whole
jailbait thing, Rob and I went on to have this
totally hot and steamy relationship, and that I'm
going to go into all the lurid details right here in

my *statement*, and that you're going to get to read all about it.

Well, sorry to disappoint you, but that is so not going to happen. In the first place, my love life is my own business, and the only reason I mention it here is that it becomes pertinent later on.

And in the second place, Rob didn't lay a finger on me.

Much to my chagrin.

No, he dropped me off, as promised, on the corner, and I walked the rest of the way home, cursing the fact that I have to live in this backward state with its backward laws. I mean, a sixteen-year-old girl can't date an eighteen-year-old boy in the state of Indiana, but it's perfectly okay for first cousins to marry at any age.

I'm serious. Look it up if you don't believe me.

As usual when I got home that night, there was a commotion going on in the kitchen. This one involved my mom and dad and Douglas (big surprise). Douglas was standing there, looking down at the floor, while my mom yelled at my dad.

"I told you he wasn't ready!" she was screaming. My mom has a pretty healthy set of lungs on her. "I told you! But did you listen? Oh, no. Big Joe Mastriani always knows what's best."

"The kid did great," my dad said. "Really great. Okay, so he dropped a tray and broke some stuff. Big deal. Trays get dropped every day. It doesn't mean—"

"He's not ready," my mom yelled.

Douglas saw me in the doorway. I rolled my eyes at him. He just looked back down at the floor again. There are kids, back at school, who say things to me about my "psycho" brother, about how he's been voted most likely to be a serial killer, and that kind of thing. That's one of the reasons I have detention from now until the foreseeable future. Because I've had to slug so many people for talking dirt about Douglas. But I don't think Douglas could ever be a serial killer. He's way too shy. That Ted Bundy guy, he was pretty outgoing, from what I heard.

My dad noticed me in the doorway and went, "Where have you been?" only not in a mean way.

"Band practice," I said.

"Oh," my dad said. Then he started yelling at my mom some more.

I grabbed a bowl of cereal—checking the milk carton, of course. As I'd suspected, my mom had seen the expired date and run out to buy a new one. I studied the faces of the kids on this particular box. I wondered if, in the morning, I would know where they lived. I had a feeling I would. After all, the mark on my chest, where the lightning had struck me, was still there. It hadn't faded hardly at all.

I wondered how Sean was doing. By now he'd probably been joyfully reunited with his family. He owed me, I thought, one heck of a big thank you. And an apology for acting like such a little headcase that day outside his house.

I went upstairs, but before I got to my room, Mike scared the bejesus out of me by tearing open, not his bedroom door, but Douglas's, and going, "All right. Who the hell is he?"

I had slammed back against the hallway wall in my surprise at seeing him come out of nowhere like that. I went, "Who the hell is who? And what were you doing in Douglas's room?"

Then I saw the binoculars in his hand, and I knew.

"Okay," I said. "It's not what you think."

"Oh, yeah?" Mike glared at me through the lenses of his glasses. "What I think is that you are slutting around with some Hell's Angel. That's what I think."

"You are so lame," I said. "He isn't a Hell's Angel, and I am not slutting around with anybody."

"Then who is he?"

"God, he's in your class, all right? He's a senior. His name is Rob Wilkins."

"Rob Wilkins?" Mike glared down at me some more. "I don't know any senior named Rob Wilkins."

"Color me surprised," I said. "You don't know anyone whose name isn't followed by an *A* in a little circle and the words *AOL dot com.*"

He wasn't letting me off the hook though, no matter how hard I dissed him.

"What is he?" Mike demanded. "A dropout?"

"No," I said. "Not that it's any business of yours."

"Well, then, how come I don't know him?" Then Mike's jaw dropped. "Oh, my God. Is he a *Grit?*"

"Gosh, Mike," I said. "That is so PC of you. I bet your new friends at Harvard are just going to love your open-minded attitude."

Mike shook his head. "Mom is going to *kill* you."

"No, she isn't, because you aren't going to tell her."

"Like fun I'm not," Mike declared. "I don't want my little sister going out with a Grit."

"We aren't going out," I said. "And if you don't tell Mom, I'll . . . I'll take your shift at the restaurant this weekend."

He brightened up, his protectiveness for his little sister forgotten. Hey, why not? More time on the Internet for him.

"Really?" he asked. "The Sunday night one, too?"

I sighed, like this was a big sacrifice, when really, I would have worked *all* his shifts for the rest of my natural life if he'd asked me to, in order to keep Mom from finding out about Rob.

"Sunday night, too, I guess," I said.

Mike looked triumphant. Then he seemed to remember he was my older brother, and he was supposed to look out for me and stuff, because he said, "Don't you think a senior is a little old for you? I mean, after all, you're just a sophomore."

I said, "Don't worry, Mikey. I can handle myself."

He still looked worried, though. "I know, but what if this guy . . . you know. Tries something?"

It was my fondest wish that he would. Unfortunately, it did not look like this was going to happen.

"Look," I said. "Don't worry about it. Seriously, Mike. You just keep on spying on Claire Lippman, and let me do the actual making out, okay?"

Mike turned kind of red, but I didn't feel sorry for him. He was blackmailing me, after all.

That night, after I'd gone to bed, my mind was too filled with the whole Rob problem to think about what was going on, you know, with the psychic thing. I mean, the missing-kid stuff just didn't seem that important.

Of course, that changed completely, the next day.

CHAPTER

10

Rosemary sounded strange when I called her the next morning. Maybe it was because someone else had answered at first, and I had been all, "Is Rosemary there?" The man who had answered had said, "One moment, please," and then I'd heard a click, and then Rosemary came on.

"Hey," I said. "It's me, Jess."

"Hi, Jess," she said. But she didn't sound as excited as she had the day before. "How are you doing, honey?"

I said, "Fine. I got some more addresses for you."

She didn't sound like she was any too eager to take them down, though. She said, "I don't suppose you saw the paper, did you, hon?"

"About the reward, you mean?" I scraped at

the words *Fuck You,* which someone had carved into the metal door over the change slot of the pay phone I was using. "Yeah, I saw about the reward. But that seems kind of wrong to me. Collecting a reward, for something any decent human being would do for free. Know what I mean?"

Rosemary said, "Oh, I know what you mean, honey. But that isn't what I was talking about. I was talking about the little girl you called about yesterday. You told Larry they'd find her by a tree."

"Oh," I said. I was keeping an eagle eye out for Mrs. Pitt. I was determined not to let her catch me this time. All I saw, however, was a black car that had pulled up in the teachers' parking lot. Two men in suits got out of it. Undercover cops, I thought. Somebody had obviously narked on somebody. "Yeah. I thought that was kind of strange. What was she doing by that tree, anyway?"

Rosemary said, "She wasn't by the tree, honey. She was under it. She was dead. Somebody murdered her and buried the body where you said they'd find it." Then Rosemary said, "Honey? Jess? Are you still there?"

I went, "Yeah. Yeah, I'm here." Dead? Little Whatever-Her-Name-Had-Been? Dead?

This wasn't so fun anymore.

And then it *really* wasn't fun. Because I noticed that the two undercover cops were walking toward *me.* I thought they'd been going into the administrative offices, which would have made sense, but instead, they walked right up to *me.*

Up close, I could see that they both had very short hair, and that they were both wearing suits. One of them reached into his breast pocket. When his hand came out again, it was holding a small wallet, which he flipped open and held out toward me.

"Hello, there," he said in a pleasant voice. "I'm Special Agent Chet Davies, and this is my partner, Special Agent Allan Johnson. We're with the FBI. We have some questions we'd like to ask you, Jess. Will you hang up the phone and come with us, please?"

In my ear, I could hear Rosemary saying, "Jess, honey, I'm so sorry, I didn't want to have anything to do with it, but they made me."

Special Agent Chet Davies took me by the arm. He said, "Come on, sweetheart. Hang up the phone."

I don't know what made me do it. To this day, I don't know what made me do it. But instead of hanging up the phone, like the agent asked, I punched him in the face with the receiver as hard as I could.

And then I ran.

I didn't go very far, though. I mean, once I started running, I realized how stupid I was being. Where was I going to go? I had no car. How far was I going to get on foot? This was the

FBI. It wasn't our Podunk town cops, who are so fat they couldn't chase a cow, let alone a sixteen-year-old girl who'd won the two-hundred-yard dash in P.E. every year since she was ten.

No offense, guys.

But it was like I went mental or something. And when I go mental, I usually end up in the same place. So I decided to cut to the chase and go where I'd probably end up anyway. I ran into the counseling office, threw open Mr. Goodhart's door, and collapsed into the orange vinyl chair by the window.

Mr. Goodhart was eating a cheese Danish. He looked at me over it and said, "Why, Jess, what a pleasant surprise. What brings you here so bright and early?"

I was panting a little. I said, "Two FBI guys just tried to pull me into their car for questioning, but I punched one of them in the face and came here instead."

Mr. Goodhart picked up a coffee mug that had Snoopy on it and took a sip from it. Then he said, "Okay, Jess, let's try that again. I say, 'What brings you here so bright and early,' and you say something like, 'Oh, I don't know, Mr. Goodhart. I just thought I'd drop in to talk about the fact that I'm doing poorly in English again, and I was wondering if you could help convince Miss Kovax to give me some extra credit.'"

Then Mr. Goodhart's secretary, Helen,

appeared in the doorway. She looked flustered. "Paul," she said. "There're two men here—"

But she didn't get to finish, because Special Agent Chet Davies pushed her out of the way. He was holding a handkerchief to his nose, from which blood was streaming. He waved his badge at Mr. Goodhart, but his gaze, which was blazing, was on me.

"That was pretty slick," he said, sounding a bit nasal, which wasn't surprising, since I guess I'd broken some cartilage or something. "But assaulting a federal agent happens to be a felony, little lady. Get up. We're going for a drive."

I didn't get up. But just as Special Agent Davies was reaching for me, Mr. Goodhart went, "Excuse me."

That's all. Just, "Excuse me."

But Special Agent Davies pulled his hand away from me as if I'd been on fire or something. Then he threw Mr. Goodhart this very guilty look.

"Oh," he said. He groped for his badge. "Special Agent Chet Davies. I'm taking this girl in for questioning."

Mr. Goodhart actually picked up his Danish, took a bite, and put it down again before he said, "Not without her parents, you're not. She's a minor."

Special Agent Allan Johnson showed up then. He flashed his badge, introduced himself, and said, "Sir, I don't know if you're aware of the fact that this young lady is wanted for questioning in several kidnapping cases, as well as a murder."

Mr. Goodhart looked at me with his eyebrows raised.

"You've been busy, haven't you, Jess?"

I said, in a croaky voice, because suddenly I was as close to crying as I'd ever been, "I was just talking on the phone, and then these two men I've never seen before told me I had to get into a car with them. Well, my mother told me never to get into cars with strangers, and even though they said they were FBI agents and they had those badges and all, how was I supposed to know they were real? I've never seen an FBI badge before. And that's why I hit him, and, Mr. Goodhart—I'm afraid I'm going to cry."

Mr. Goodhart said, in his teasing way, "You aren't going to cry, Jess. You weren't really afraid of these two clowns, were you?"

"Yes," I said with a sob. "I really was. Mr. Goodhart, I don't want to go to jail!"

By the end of all that, I'm embarrassed to say I wasn't close to crying anymore. I *was* crying. I was practically bawling.

But, come on. You would have been scared, too, if the FBI wanted to question you.

While I was sniffling and wiping my eyes and blaming Ruth in my head for this whole mess, Mr. Goodhart looked at the FBI guys and said, in a voice that wasn't teasing at all, "You two go and have a seat in the outer office. She isn't going anywhere until her parents—and their lawyer—get here."

You could tell by Mr. Goodhart's face that he meant it, too. I had never felt such a wave of affection for him as I did at that moment. I mean, he may have doled out the detentions pretty strictly, but he was a stand-up kind of guy when you needed him.

The two FBI guys seemed to realize this. Special Agent Davies swore loudly. His partner looked a little embarrassed for him. He said to me, "Look, we didn't mean to scare you, Miss. We just wanted to ask you a few questions, that's all. Maybe we could find someplace quiet where we could just straighten out this mess."

"Sure you can," Mr. Goodhart said. "After her parents get here."

Special Agent Johnson knew when he'd been beat. He nodded and went into the outer office, sat down, and picked up a copy of *Seventeen* and started to flip through it. Special Agent Davies, on the other hand, said another swear word and began pacing up and down in the outer office, while Helen, the secretary, watched him nervously.

Mr. Goodhart didn't look nervous at all. He took another sip of coffee, then picked up the phone. "Okay, Jess," he said. "Who's it going to be—your mother, or your father?"

I was still crying pretty hard. I said, "M-my dad. Oh, please, my dad."

Mr. Goodhart called my dad at Mastriani's, where he was working that morning. Since neither of my parents had ever been called to school on account of me—in spite of all the fights I'd been in—I could hear urgency in my dad's voice as he asked Mr. Goodhart if I was all right. Mr. Goodhart assured him that I was, but that he might want to call his lawyer, if he had one. My dad, God bless him, hung up with a brisk, "We'll be there in five minutes." He never once even asked why.

After Mr. Goodhart hung up, he looked over at me, then reached for some tissues he kept in a box for the losers who sat in his office and cried all day about their unsatisfactory family life, or whatever.

I'm one of those losers now, I thought, as I dejectedly blew my nose.

"Tell me about it," Mr. Goodhart said.

And so, with a nervous glance at the FBI guys, to make sure they couldn't overhear, I did. I told Mr. Goodhart everything, from getting hit by the lightning all the way up until that morning, when Special Agent Davies flashed his badge. The only stuff I left out was the parts about Rob. I didn't figure Mr. Goodhart needed to know that.

By the time I got done telling Mr. Goodhart, my dad had arrived with our lawyer, who also happened to be Ruth's dad, Mr. Abramowitz. Special Agent Davies had recovered himself by then, and he acted like nothing had happened.

Like he hadn't tried to grab me, and like I hadn't hit him in the face with a phone receiver.

Oh, no. Nothing of the sort. He was way professional as he told my dad and Mr. Abramowitz about how the FBI was very interested in the person who'd been making calls to the National Organization of Missing Children from the pay phone at which they'd found me. Apparently, at 1-800-WHERE-R-YOU, they had caller-ID phones, so Rosemary had known from the very first day I'd been calling from Indiana. All they needed to do was track down where in Indiana, then actually catch me making the call.

Then, *voilà*, as my mom would say, they had me.

Of course, the big question was what, now that they had me, were they going to do with me? As far as I knew, I hadn't actually broken any laws—well, except for striking a federal agent, and Special Agent Davies didn't seem all that anxious to bring that up again.

All the excitement—having two FBI agents, a father, and a lawyer in his counseling offices—had dragged out the principal, Mr. Feeney. Mr. Feeney rarely came out of his office, except sometimes during assembly to remind us not to drink and drive. Now he offered us the use of his private conference room, where we sat, the seven of us—me, my dad, Ruth's dad, the two special agents, Mr. Goodhart, and Mr. Feeney—while I repeated the story I'd just told Mr. Goodhart.

I guess you could say that, when I finished, they looked . . . well, skeptical. And it was kind of hard to believe. I mean, how had it happened? How was it that I just woke up every morning, knowing this totally random stuff about these kids? Yeah, the lightning had probably done it . . . but how? And why?

Nobody knew. My guess was, nobody would ever know.

But Special Agent Johnson, it turned out, really wanted to. Know, I mean. He asked me a ton of questions. Some of them were really weird, too. Like, had I experienced bleeding from my palms or my feet. I said, "Uh, no," and looked at him like he was crazy.

"If this is true," he began, after I thought he'd exhausted all the questions anyone could possibly ask somebody.

"*If* this is true?" my dad interrupted. My dad's not the world's most even-tempered guy. Not that he gets mad a lot. He hardly ever gets mad. But when he does, watch out. One time, this guy at the municipal swimming pool was following Douglas around, calling him a retard—this was when Douglas was like eleven or twelve years old. The guy was in his twenties, at least, and probably not too swift upstairs himself. But that didn't matter to my dad. He hauled off and slugged the guy, and *then* he held his face underwater for a while, until the lifeguard made him stop.

It was way cool.

"*If?*" my dad repeated. "Are you doubting the word of my little girl here?"

Special Agent Johnson probably hadn't heard the story of the guy at the swimming pool, but he looked scared, just the same. Because you could tell my dad was really proud of me. Not just because I hadn't cried this time while I was telling my side of things, but because, when you think about it, what I had done was pretty nifty. I had found a bunch of missing kids. Granted, one of them had been dead, but, hey, we'd never have known that if it hadn't been for me. And considering that he had one kid who was a schizo, and another who was basically a social leper, even if he had gotten into Harvard, well, I guess my dad was kind of stoked that at least one of his kids was making good, you know?

Special Agent Johnson held up a hand and said, "No, sir. Don't misunderstand me. I believe Miss Mastriani's story wholeheartedly. I'm only saying that, if it's true, well, then she's a very special young lady, and deserves some very special treatment."

I thought he might be talking about a ticker-tape parade in New York City, like the one they had for the Yankees that time they won the World Series. I wouldn't mind riding on a float, if it didn't go too slow.

But my dad right away suspected he was talking about something else.

"Like what kind of treatment?" he said, suspiciously.

"Well, usually, in cases like these—and I will have you know that we at the FBI respect those with extrasensory perception like Miss Mastriani's very highly. In fact, we often seek out advice from psychics when we find ourselves at a dead end in an investigation."

"I bet. What does that have to do with Jess?" My dad still sounded suspicious.

"Well, we'd like to invite Miss Mastriani—with your permission, of course, sir—to one of our research facilities, so that we can learn more about this astonishing ability of hers."

I immediately flashed back on one of my favorite videos when I'd been a kid, *Escape to Witch Mountain*. If you've seen that movie, you will recall that the kids in it, who have ESP—or extrasensory perception, as Special Agent Johnson called it—get sent to a special "research facility," where, even though they get their own soda fountain in their room—by which I'd been particularly impressed, since my mother wouldn't even let me have an E-Z Bake Oven for fear I'd burn down the house—they were still, basically, held prisoner.

"Um," I said loudly. Since no one had really been talking to me, everyone turned their heads to look at me. "No, thank you."

Mr. Goodhart, who obviously hadn't seen *Escape to Witch Mountain*, said, "Now, hold on a second, Jess. Let's hear Special Agent Johnson out. It isn't every day that someone with your special ability comes along. It's important that we try to learn as much as possible about what's happened to you, so that we can better understand the extraordinary ways in which the human mind works."

I glared at Mr. Goodhart. What a traitor! I couldn't believe it.

"I am not," I said, in a voice that was still too loud for Mr. Feeney's conference room, "going to any special research facility in Washington, D.C."

Special Agent Johnson said, "Oh, but this one is right here in Indiana. Only an hour away, at Crane Military Base, as a matter of fact. There we can adequately study Miss Mastriani's extraordinary talent. Maybe she could even help us find more missing people. When you were calling the Missing Children's Organization this morning, Miss Mastriani, it was because you had the location of yet another missing child, was it not?"

I scowled at him. "Yes," I said. "Not like I ever got the chance to tell them that, though. You two guys made me completely forget the addresses."

This was a complete and utter lie, but I was feeling grumpy. I didn't want to go to Crane Military Base. I didn't want to go anywhere. I wanted to stay where I was. I wanted to go to detention after school today and sit by Rob. When else was I ever going to get to see him?

And what about Karen Sue Hanky? She had

challenged me again. I had to kick her butt one more time. I *needed* to kick her butt one more time. *That* was my special ability. Not this freaky thing that had been happening lately. . . .

"There are many, many more people missing in the world, Miss Mastriani," Special Agent Johnson said, "than are pictured on the back of milk cartons. With your help, we could find missing prisoners of war, for whose safe return their families have been praying for twenty, even thirty years. We could locate deadbeat dads, and make them pay back the money their children so badly need. We could track down vicious serial killers, catch them before they can kill again. The FBI does offer significant cash rewards for information leading to the arrest of individuals for whom it has issued warrants of arrest."

I could tell my dad was totally falling for this. I even caught myself falling for it, a little. I mean, it would be totally cool to reunite families with their missing loved ones, or to catch bad guys, and see that they got what they deserved.

But why did I have to go and do it from an army base?

So I asked him that. And I added, "I mean, it might not even work. What if I can only find these people from my own bed, in my own house? Why would I have to do it from Crane Military Base? Why couldn't you just let me do it from Lumley Lane?"

Special Agent Johnson and Special Agent

Davies looked at one another. Everyone else looked at them, too, with *Yeah, why couldn't she?* expressions on their faces.

Finally, Special Agent Johnson said, "Well, you could, Jessica." I noticed he wasn't calling me Miss Mastriani anymore. "Of course you could. But our researchers would dearly love to run some tests. And the fact that all of this seems to have stemmed from being struck by lightning— well, I don't want to sound like an alarmist, but I would think you would welcome those tests. Because we have found in the past that, in cases like yours, there has sometimes been damage to vital internal organs that goes undetected for months, and then . . ."

My dad leaned forward. "And then what?"

"Well, often the individual simply drops dead, Mr. Mastriani, from a heart attack—being struck by lightning puts an incredible strain on the heart. Or of an embolism, aneurism—any number of complications can and often do arise. A thorough medical exam—"

"Which I could have right here," I said, not liking the sound of this. "In Dr. Hinkle's office." Dr. Hinkle had been our family doctor my whole life. He had, of course, misdiagnosed Douglas's schizophrenia as ADD, but hey, we can't all be perfect.

"Certainly," Special Agent Johnson said. "Certainly. Although the general practitioner is not often trained to detect the subtle changes that occur in a system that has been violated in the manner yours has."

"About these cash rewards," Mr. Feeney said suddenly.

I glared at him. What an asshole. I could tell he was totally trying to think up some angle whereby he could get his hands on the reward money, and design a new trophy cabinet for the main hallway, so he could display all of our stupid state championship cups, or whatever. God, I hated school.

That was it. I had had enough. I stood up, pushing back my chair—which was way nicer than any chair in any of the classrooms: it had wheels on it, and was made of some plush, squishy material that surely couldn't have been real leather, or Mr. Feeney would have gotten in trouble with the school board for overspending—and said, "Well, okay, if you're not going to arrest me, I think I'd like to go home now."

Special Agent Johnson said, "We're not through here, Jess."

Then an extraordinary thing happened. My lower lip started to jut out a little—I think I was still feeling a little emotional from that whole they're-gonna-arrest-me scare—and my dad, who noticed, stood up and said, "No."

No. Just like that. No.

"You've intimidated my daughter enough for one day. I'm taking her home to her mother."

Special Agents Johnson and Davies exchanged

glances. They did not want to let me go. But my dad was already walking over to me, picking up my backpack and flute, and laying a hand on my shoulder.

"Come on, Jess," he said. "We're going."

Ruth's dad, meanwhile, was reaching into his pocket. He took out some business cards and dropped them on Mr. Feeney's conference table.

"If you gentlemen need to contact the Mastrianis," he said to the agents, "you can do so through my offices. Have a nice day."

Special Agent Johnson looked disappointed, but all he said was that I should call him the minute I changed my mind about Crane Military Base. Then he gave me his card. Special Agent Davies, as he was leaving the conference room, made a gun out of his index finger and thumb and shot me. I thought this was a little alarming, considering the fact that his nostrils were all crusted over with blood, and a purply bruise was starting to show across the bridge of his nose. . . .

Mr. Feeney was pretty nice about giving me the rest of the day off from class. He never even mentioned a thing about me making up detention, and then I realized that was because he didn't even know I had detention from now until the end of school in May. Mr. Feeney doesn't pay a whole lot of attention to the students.

But Mr. Goodhart, who does, didn't mention making up the detention day either. That's because I had begged him a long time ago not to pester my parents about anything, what with Douglas and all. He stuck to his word, though he did say he wished I would rethink the Crane Military Base thing. I said I would, even though I hadn't the slightest intention of doing so.

My dad drove me home. On the way home, we stopped at a Wendy's, and he bought me a Frosty. This was sort of a joke, because he used to buy me a Frosty every day on our way home from the county hospital, back when I'd had out-patient treatments for a third-degree burn I'd gotten on my calf from the exhaust pipe of our neighbor's Harley. Dr. Feingold, the neurologist, had bought a completely cherried-out mint-green Harley-Davidson for his fiftieth birthday, and when I was a little kid, I used to beg him for rides, and he'd take me, more often than not, probably just to shut me up. He warned me about the exhaust pipe a million times, but I forgot one day, and wham! Third-degree burn the size of a fist. I still had the scar, though the burn ward had worked diligently, every day for three months, to remove all the infected skin.

The way they removed it was worse than the burn itself, though. With tweezers. I used to pass out every time. Then, to cheer me up, my dad would take me to Wendy's for a Frosty. So, you can see that this gesture of his was deeply moving, even though it may not sound like much to you guys. It was all about sharing this bonding moment from our past. Mr. Goodhart would have eaten it up.

Anyway, on the way home, my dad agreed to break the news to Mom, but not tell anybody else—I made him swear—and I agreed not to keep any more secrets from him. I still didn't tell him about Rob, though, because that was a secret I strongly suspected the FBI didn't have a lead on, so I probably wasn't going to almost get arrested for it.

Plus I was way more worried about my mom's reaction to finding out about Rob than the story of me and the milk-carton kids.

CHAPTER

11

In the end, of course, it turned out that my dad wasn't the one I ought to have sworn to secrecy.

It was Mr. Feeney.

I don't know if he thought he could get his hands on that reward money somehow, or if he'd decided that spilling the beans would make his school district stand out from all the others in Indiana—like, since it was his school's bleachers I'd gotten electrocuted under, that somehow made Ernest Pyle High School special—or what.

But anyway, when the town paper hit our front porch that afternoon—the town paper came out at three in the afternoon every day, instead of seven in the morning, so the reporters and everybody don't have to get up too early—there was this giant picture of me on the front of it: my very flattering sophomore yearbook picture, in fact, the one in which my mom had made me wear one of her hideous homemade dresses, under a headline that read, TOUCHED BY THE FINGER OF GOD.

Have I pointed out that there are more churches in our town than there are fast-food restaurants? Southern Indiana is way religious.

Anyway, the article went on to describe how I had saved all these kids after being touched by the finger of God, or lightning, as it is called by the secular community. It went on to say that I was just an average student who played third-chair flute in the school orchestra, and that on weekends I helped my dad out in his restaurants, which they listed. I knew all this stuff couldn't have come from Mr. Feeney, since he didn't know me all that well. I figured Mr. Goodhart must have had something to do with it.

And let me tell you, that kind of hurt, you know? I mean, even though he hadn't mentioned anything about the trouble with Douglas, or my detentions, he sure had mentioned everything else he knew. Isn't there some sort of confidentiality thing with school counselors? I mean, can't they get in trouble for that?

But when my dad called Mr. Abramowitz and asked him, he was like, "You can't prove the information came from the counselor. It came from someone at the school, most definitely. But you can't prove it was the counselor."

Still, Ruth's dad started putting together a

lawsuit, aimed at hitting Ernest Pyle High School for slipping the town paper my school photo. That, Mr. Abramowitz said, was an invasion of privacy. He sounded really happy about it. Ruth's dad doesn't get that many interesting cases. Mostly, he just does divorces.

My mother was happy about it, too. Don't ask me why, but the whole story totally delighted her. She was in hog heaven. She wanted me to have a press conference in the main dining room at Mastriani's. She kept going on about how much money it would bring in to the restaurant, feeding all those out-of-town reporters. She even started picking out dress patterns, right then and there, for what she wanted me to wear at this press conference. I'm telling you, she went mental. I had kind of thought she'd be all weird about it, you know? I mean, considering her *I just want us to be a normal family* mentality. But that went right out the window when she heard about the rewards.

"How much?" she wanted to know. "How much per child?"

We were eating dinner at that point—fettucine with a mushroom cream sauce. My dad went, "Toni, the rewards are not the point. The point is, Jessica is a young girl, and I do not want her exposed to the media at such a young—"

"But is it ten thousand dollars per child?" my mother wanted to know. "Or just for that one child?"

"Toni—"

"Joe, I'm just saying, ten thousand dollars is nothing to sneeze at. It could buy a new steam table and then some over at Joe Junior's—"

"We will raise the money for a new steam table over at Joe Junior's the old-fashioned way," my father said. "We will take out a loan for it."

"Not when we're already going to have to take out a loan for Michael's tuition." Michael—whose sole reaction to the news about my new-found psychic ability had been to ask me if I knew where the man in the blue turban, whom Nostradamus had predicted would start World War III, was hanging out these days—rolled his eyes.

"Don't you roll your eyes at me, young man," my mother said. "Harvard was very generous with the scholarship money, but it's still not enough—"

"Especially not," my dad said, dipping his semolina into the cream sauce left on his plate, "if Dougie's going back to State."

That did it. My mom dropped her fork with a clatter. "Douglas," she said, "is not going back to that school. Not ever."

My dad looked tired. "Toni," he said. "The boy's going to have to get an education. He can't sit in that room up there and read comic books for the rest of his life. People are already starting to call him Boo Radley."

Boo Radley, I remembered from freshman

English, was the guy in *To Kill a Mockingbird* who never left his house, just sat around cutting up newspapers all day, which is what people did before there was TV. It was a good thing Douglas had refused to come downstairs for dinner, or he might have heard that and been offended. For a guy who tried to kill himself, Douglas is very sensitive about being called strange.

"Why not?" my mother demanded. "Why can't he sit in his room for the rest of his life? If that's what he wants to do, why can't you just let him?"

"Because nobody gets to do what they want to do, Toni. I want to lie in the backyard in a hammock all day," my dad said, jerking a thumb at his chest. "Jess over there wants to cruise the countryside on the back of a hog. And Mikey—" He looked at Michael, who was busy chewing. "Well, I don't know what the hell Mikey wants to do—"

"Screw Claire Lippman," I suggested, causing Michael to kick me very hard beneath the table.

My dad shot me a warning look, and continued. "But whatever it is, Toni, he doesn't get to do it. Nobody gets to do what they want to do, Toni. What they get to do is what they *should* do, and what Dougie *should* do is go back to college."

Relieved to have some of the heat off me, I excused myself and cleared my place at the table. I hadn't talked to Ruth all day. I was eager to see what she thought of this whole thing. I mean, it isn't every day your best friend ends up on the front page of the local rag.

But I never got to find out what Ruth thought of the whole thing. Because when I stepped outside onto the porch, preparing to jump over the hedge that separated our two houses, I was confronted by what looked like an army of reporters, all of them parked in front of our house and waving cameras and microphones.

"There she is!" One of them, a newscaster I recognized from Channel Four, came stumbling across my lawn, her high heels sinking into the grass. "Jessica! Jessica! How does it feel to be a national heroine?"

I stared down at the fuzzy microphone blankly. Then about a million other microphones appeared in my face. Everyone started asking questions at once. It was my mother's press conference, only all I had on was jeans and a T-shirt. I hadn't even thought to comb my hair.

"Um," I said into the microphones.

Then my dad was there, yanking me back into the house, and yelling at all the reporters to get off his property. No one listened—at least, not until the cops came. Then we got to see how all those free lunches my dad had given the guys on the force paid off. You never saw people as mad as those cops were when they turned down Lumley Lane and couldn't even find a place to park, there were so many news vans blocking the way. There are so few crimes in our neck of the woods that when one did happen, our boys in blue go to town on the offender.

When they saw all the reporters on our lawn, they went mental, only in a different way than my mom had. They called back to the station, and, next thing you knew, they had brought out all their fanciest equipment, riot gear and drug-sniffing dogs and flash grenades. You name it, they brought it over, and looked pretty intent on using it on the reporters, some of whom were from pretty big networks.

I have to say, I was way impressed. Mike and I watched the whole thing from my dormer window. Mike even went on the Internet and ran a search for my name, and said there were already two hundred and seventy sites that mentioned Jessica Mastriani. Nobody had taken my face and superimposed it over a Playboy bunny's naked body, but Mike said it was only a matter of time.

Then the phone started ringing.

The first few calls were from reporters standing outside, using their cell phones. They wanted me to come out and make a statement, just one. Then they promised to leave. My dad hung up on them.

Then people who weren't reporters, but whom we still didn't know, started calling, asking if I was available to help them find a missing relative, a child, a husband, a father. At first my dad was nice to them, and told them that it didn't work that way, that I had to see a picture of the missing person. Then they started saying they'd fax a picture, or e-mail it. Some of them said they were coming right on over with one, they'd be there in a few hours.

That's when my dad disconnected the phone.

I was a celebrity. Or a prisoner in my own house. Whichever you prefer.

I still hadn't gotten to talk to Ruth, and I really wanted to. But since I couldn't go outside or call her, my only resource was to instant-message her from Michael's computer. He was feeling sorry for me, so, in spite of my crack about Claire Lippman, he let me.

Ruth, however, wasn't too pleased to hear from me.

Ruth: Why the HELL didn't you tell me about any of this?

Me: Look, Ruth, I didn't tell *anybody*, okay? It was all just too weird.

Ruth: But I'm supposed to be your best friend.

Me: You *are* my best friend.

Ruth: Well, I bet you told Rob Wilkins.

Me: I swear I didn't.

Ruth: Oh, right. You don't tell the guy you're boffing that you're psychic. I really believe that one.

Me: First of all, I am not boffing Rob Wilkins. Second of all, do you really think I wanted anyone to know about this? It's totally freaky. You know I like to keep a low profile.

Ruth: It was totally uncool of you not to tell me. Do you know people from school have been calling, asking me if I knew, and I've had to pretend like I did, just to save face? You are the worst best friend I've ever had.

Me: I'm the *only* best friend you've ever had. And you don't have any right to be mad, since it's all your fault anyway, for making me walk in that stupid thunderstorm.

Ruth: What are you going to do with the reward money? You know, I could really use a new stereo for the Cabriolet. And Skip says to tell you he wants the new Tomb Raider.

Me: Tell Skip I said I'm not buying him anything until he apologizes for that whole strapping-my-Barbie-to-the-bottle-rocket business.

Ruth: You know, I don't see how any of us are going to be able to get to school tomorrow. The street is totally blocked. It looks like a scene out of *Red Dawn* down there.

The truth was, Ruth was right. With the cops forming this protective shield in front of my house, and our driveway all blockaded, it sort of did look like the Russians were coming or something. No one could get up or down our street without flashing an ID that proved they lived there to the cops. For instance, if Rob wanted to cruise by on his Indian—not that he would want to, but let's say he took a wrong turn, or whatever—he totally couldn't. The cops wouldn't let him through.

I tried not to let this bother me. I logged off with Ruth, after assuring her that, though I hadn't told her, I hadn't told anyone else, either, which seemed to placate her somewhat, especially after I told her, if she wanted to, she could tell everyone she'd already known—I certainly didn't care. This made her very happy, and I suppose after she logged off with me, she logged on with Muffy and Buffy and all of the pathetic popular kids whose friendship she so assiduously courts, for reasons I had never been able to fathom.

I took out my flute and practiced for a while, but to tell you the truth, I didn't really put my heart into it. Not because I was thinking about the whole psychic thing. Please. That would make sense.

No, in spite of my resolve not to allow them to, my thoughts kept creeping back to Rob. Had he wondered where I was when I didn't show up for detention that afternoon? If he tried calling to find out where I was, he wouldn't be able to get through, since my dad had disconnected the phone. He had to have seen the paper, right? I mean, you would think, now that he knew I'd been touched by the finger of God, he might want to talk to me, right?

You would think that. But I guess not. Because

even though I listened for it, I never did hear the purr of that Indian.

And I don't think it was because the cops wouldn't let him through the blockade. I think he didn't even try.

So much for unrequited love. What is *wrong* with guys, anyway?

CHAPTER

12

When I woke up the next morning, I was kind of cranky, on account of Rob preferring not to have to go to jail rather than spend time in my company. But I perked up a little when I remembered I didn't have to slink around anymore, looking for a pay phone in order to call 1-800-WHERE-R-YOU. Hell, I could just call them from my own house. So I got up, reconnected the phone, and dialed.

Rosemary didn't answer, so I asked to speak to her. The lady who answered went, "Is this Jess?" and I said, "Yes, it is," and she said, "Hold on."

Only instead of connecting me with Rosemary, she connected me to Rosemary's butt-head supervisor, Larry, who I'd spoken to the day before. He went, "Jessica! What a pleasure. Thank you so much for calling. Do you have some more addresses for us today? I'm afraid we were cut off yesterday—"

"Yes, we were, Larry," I said, "thanks to your phoning in the Feds. Now, connect me with Rosemary, or I'm hanging up."

Larry sounded kind of taken aback. "Well, now, Jess," he said. "We didn't mean to upset you. Only, you have to understand, when we get a call like yours, we're obligated to investigate—"

"Larry," I said, "I understand perfectly. Now put Rosemary on the phone."

Larry made all these indignant noises, but, eventually, he transferred me to Rosemary. She sounded really upset.

"Oh, Jess," she said. "I am so sorry, honey. I wish I could have said something, warned you somehow. But you know, they trace all the calls—"

"That's okay, Rosemary," I said. "No harm done. I mean, what girl doesn't want a news crew from *Dateline* in her front yard?"

Rosemary said, "Well, at least you can joke about it. I don't know if I could."

"Water under the bridge," I said. At the time I really meant it, too. "So, look, here's the two kids from yesterday, and I have two more, if you're ready."

Rosemary was ready. She took down the information I gave her, said, "God bless you, sweetheart," and hung up. Then I hung up, too, and started getting ready for school.

Of course, that was easier said than done.

Outside our house it was a zoo again. There were more vans than ever before, some with these giant satellite dishes on top of them. There were reporters standing in front of them, and when I turned on the TV, it was sort of surreal, because on almost every channel, you could see my house, with someone standing there in front of it going, "I'm here in front of this quaint Indiana home, a home that has been declared a historic landmark by the county, but which has reached international fame by being home to heroine Jessica Mastriani, whose extraordinary psychic powers have led to the recovery of a half dozen missing children. . . ."

The cops were there, too. By the time I got downstairs, my mom was already bringing them seconds of coffee and biscotti. They were gulping them down almost as fast as she could bring them out.

And, of course, the minute I had put the phone down, it started ringing. When my dad picked it up, and someone asked to speak to me but wouldn't give his name, he disconnected it again.

It was, in other words, a mess.

None of us realized how bad a mess, however, until Douglas wandered into the kitchen, looking a little wild-eyed.

"They're after me," he said.

I nearly choked on my corn flakes. Because the only time Douglas ever starts talking about "them" is when he is having an episode.

My dad knew something was wrong, too. He put down his coffee and stared at Douglas worriedly.

Only my mom was oblivious. She was loading more biscotti onto a plate. She said, "Don't be ridiculous, Dougie. They're after Jessica, not you."

"No," Douglas said. He shook his head. "It's me they want. You see those dishes? Those satellite dishes on top of their vans? They're scanning my thought waves. They're using those satellite dishes to scan my thought waves."

I dropped my spoon. My dad went, gently, "Doug, did you take your medicine yesterday?"

"Don't you see?" Douglas, quick as a flash, yanked the biscotti out of my mom's hands and flung the plate to the floor. "Are you all blind? It's me they want! It's me!"

My dad jumped up and put his arms around Douglas. I pushed away my cereal bowl and said, "I better go. Maybe if I go, they'll follow me—"

"Go," my dad said.

I went. I got up, grabbed my flute and my backpack, and headed for the door.

They followed me. Or, I should say, they followed Ruth, who'd managed to convince the cops to let her out of her driveway and into mine. I jumped into the front seat, and we took off. If I hadn't been so worried about Douglas, I would have enjoyed watching all the reporters trying to scramble into their vans and follow us. But I was concerned. Douglas had been doing so well. What had happened?

"Well," Ruth said. "You have to admit, it's a lot to take."

"What is?"

Ruth reached up to adjust her rearview mirror. "Um," she said, staring pointedly into it. "That."

I looked behind us. We had a police escort, a bunch of the motorcycle cops rolling along beside us in an attempt to keep the hordes of news vans from bearing down on us too hard. But there were a lot more news vans than I would have thought. And they were all coming right at us. It wasn't going to be very funny when we tried to get out of the car.

"Maybe they won't let them onto school property," I said, hopefully.

"Yeah, right. Feeney's going to be standing there with a big welcome banner. Are you kidding?"

I said, "Well, maybe if I just talked to them . . ."

Which was how, just before the start of first period, I found myself standing on the school steps, fielding questions from these news reporters I'd been watching on TV my whole life.

"No," I said, in reply to one question, "it didn't hurt, really. It just felt sort of tingly."

"Yes," I said to someone else, "I do think the government should be doing more to find these children."

"No," I replied to another question, "I don't know where Elvis is."

Mr. Feeney, just as Ruth had predicted, was there all right. He was there with a little flock of reporters all his own. He and Mr. Goodhart stood on either side of me as I answered the reporters' questions. Mr. Goodhart looked uncomfortable, but Mr. Feeney, you could tell, was having the time of his life. He kept on saying to anyone who would listen how Ernest Pyle High School had won the state basketball championship in 1997. Like anyone cared.

And then, in the middle of this lame little impromptu press conference, something happened. Something happened that changed everything, even more than Douglas's episode had.

"Miss Mastriani," someone in the middle of the horde of reporters cried, "do you feel any guilt whatsoever over the fact that Sean Patrick O'Hanahan claims that, when his mother kidnapped him five years ago, it was in order to protect him from his abusive father?"

I blinked. It was another beautiful spring day, with the temperature already climbing into the seventies. But, suddenly, I felt cold.

"*What?*" I said, scanning the crowd, trying to figure out who was talking.

"And that your revealing Sean's whereabouts to the authorities," the voice went on, "has not only endangered his life, but put his mother's freedom in jeopardy?"

And then, instead of there being a sea of faces in front of me, there was only one face. I couldn't even tell if I was really seeing it, or if it was just in my mind's eye. But there it was, Sean's face, as I'd seen it that day in front of the little brick house in Paoli. A small face, white as paper, the freckles on it standing out like hives. His fingers, clinging to me, had shaken like leaves.

"Don't you tell anyone," he'd hissed at me. *"Don't you ever tell anyone you saw me, understand?"*

He had begged me not to tell. He had clung to me and begged me not to tell.

And I had told anyway. Because I had thought—I had honestly thought—he was being held against his will, by people of whom he was deathly afraid. He had certainly acted as if he were afraid.

And that was because he *had* been afraid. Of me.

I had truly thought I was doing the right thing. But I hadn't been doing the right thing. I hadn't done the right thing at all.

The reporters were still yelling questions at me. I heard them, but it was as if they were yelling them from very far away.

"Jessica?" Mr. Goodhart was looking down at me. "Are you all right?"

"I am not Sean Patrick O'Hanahan." That's what Sean had said to me that day outside his house. *"So you can just go away, do you hear? You can just go away."*

"And don't ever come back."

"Okay." Mr. Goodhart put his arm around me and started steering me back into the school. "That's enough for one day."

"Wait," I said. "Who said that? Who said that about Sean?"

But, unfortunately, as soon as they saw I was leaving, all the reporters started screaming questions at once, and I couldn't figure out who had asked me about Sean Patrick O'Hanahan.

"Is it true?" I asked Mr. Goodhart as he hustled me back inside the school.

"Is what true?"

"Is it true what that reporter said?" My lips felt funny, like I'd been to the dentist and gotten novocaine. "About Sean Patrick O'Hanahan not having been kidnapped at all?"

"I don't know, Jessica."

"Could his mom really go to jail?"

"I don't know, Jessica. But if it is, it isn't your fault."

"Why isn't it my fault?" He was walking me to my homeroom. For once I was late and nobody gave a damn. "How do you know it isn't my fault?"

"No court in the land," Mr. Goodhart said, "is going to award custody of a child to an abusive parent. The mother's probably just brainwashed the kid into thinking his father abused him."

"But how do you know?" I repeated. "How can anyone know? How am *I* supposed to know if what I'm doing, revealing these kids' locations to the authorities, is really in the best interest of the kids? I mean, maybe some of them don't want to be found. How am I supposed to know the difference?"

"You can't know," Mr. Goodhart said. We'd reached my classroom by then. "Jess, you can't know. You just have to assume that if someone loved them enough to report them missing, that person deserves to know where they are. Don't you think?"

No. That was the problem. I hadn't thought. I hadn't thought about anything at all. Once I'd figured out that my dream was true—that Sean Patrick O'Hanahan really was alive and well and living in that little brick house in Paoli—I had acted, without the slightest bit of further consideration.

And now, because of it, a little kid was in more trouble than ever.

Oh, yeah. I'd been touched by the finger of God, all right.

The question was, which finger?

13

It wasn't all bad news.

The good news was, I no longer had detention.

Pretty impressive, right? Girl gets psychic powers, girl gets punishment lifted. Just like that. I wonder how Coach Albright would feel if he knew. Essentially, I'd pretty much gotten away with punching his star tackle. That's gotta be a kick in the pants, right?

In the midst of beating myself up over the whole Sean Patrick O'Hanahan thing, I spared a thought, every once in a while, for Miss Clemmings and the Ws. How was she going to handle Hank and Greg without my help? And what about Rob? Would he miss me? Would he even notice I was gone?

I got my answer after lunch. Ruth and I were

making our way toward our lockers, when suddenly she elbowed me, hard. I grabbed my side and was like, "What are you trying to do, give me a splenectomy? What is with you?"

She pointed. I looked. And then I knew.

Rob Wilkins was standing by my locker.

Ruth made a hasty and completely obvious retreat. I squared my shoulders and kept going. There was nothing to be nervous about. Rob and I were just friends, as he'd made only too clear.

"Hey," he said when I walked up.

"Hey," I said. I ducked my head, working my combination. Twenty-one, the age I'd like to be. Sixteen, the age I am. Thirty-five, the age I'll be before Rob Wilkins decides I am mature enough for him to go out with.

"So," he said. "Were you ever going to tell me?"

I got out my geometry book. "Actually," I said, "I wasn't planning on telling anyone."

"That's what I figured. And the kid?"

"What kid?" But I knew. I knew.

"The kid in Paoli. That was the first one?"

"Yep," I said. And all of a sudden I felt like crying.

Really. And I never cry.

Well, except for that time with the FBI agents in Mr. Goodhart's office.

"You could have told me," he said.

"I could have." I took out my geometry notebook. "Would you have believed me?"

"Yeah," he said. "Yeah, I would have."

I think he would have, too. Or maybe I just wanted to think he would have. He looked so . . . I don't know. Nice, I guess, standing there, leaning against the locker next door to mine. He didn't have any books or anything, just that ubiquitous paperback in the back pocket of his jeans, those jeans that were butter-soft from constant wear, and faded in spots, like at the knees and other, more interesting, places.

He had on a long-sleeved T-shirt, dark green, but he'd pushed up the sleeves so his forearms, tanned from all the riding he does, showed, and . . .

See how pathetic I am?

I slammed my locker door closed.

"Well," I said. "I gotta go."

"Jess," he called after me, as I was turning to walk away.

I looked back.

I changed my mind. That's what I was hoping he was going to say. *I changed my mind. Want to go to the prom with me?*

What he actually said was, "I heard. About the kid. Sean." He looked uncomfortable, like he wasn't used to having these kinds of conversations in the middle of the school hallway, under the unnatural glow of the fluorescent overheads.

But he went on anyway.

"It wasn't your fault, Jess. The way he acted that day, outside his house . . . well, I thought there was something weird going on with him, too. You couldn't have known. That's all." He nodded, like he was satisfied he'd made every point he'd meant to. "You did the right thing."

I shook my head. I could feel tears pricking my eyes. Dammit, I was standing there, with about a thousand people streaming around me, trying not to cry in front of this guy I had a total crush on. Could there possibly be anything more humiliating?

"No," I said. "I didn't."

And then I turned around and walked away.

And this time, he didn't try to stop me.

Since I didn't have detention anymore, Ruth and I came home together after school. We decided we'd practice together. She said she'd found a new concerto for flute and cello. It was modern, but we'd take a stab at it.

But when she pulled onto Lumley Lane, I saw right away something was wrong. All the reporters had been herded down to the far end of the street, where they were standing behind police barricades. When they saw Ruth's car, they started yelling and frantically taking pictures. . . .

But the cops wouldn't let them near our house.

When Ruth pulled into my driveway, and I saw the blood on the sidewalk, I knew why.

Not just on the sidewalk either, but little drops of it, leading all the way up to the front porch.

Ruth saw them, too. She went, "Uh-oh."

Then the screen door opened, and my dad and Mikey came out. My dad held up both his hands and said, "It's not as bad as it looks. This afternoon, Dougie attacked one of the reporters who'd stayed behind to try and interview the neighbors. They're both all right. Don't get upset."

I guess it might have sounded funny, my brother attacking a reporter. If it had been Mike who'd done it, it would have been very funny. But since it was Doug, it wasn't funny. It wasn't funny at all.

"Look," my dad said, sitting down on the porch steps. Ruth had switched off the ignition, and we both got out of the car. I went and sat down beside my dad, careful not to look at—or touch—any of the spots of blood all around us. Ruth went to sit with Mike on the porch swing. It creaked ominously under both their weights. Plus Mike looked annoyed at having to share it, only Ruth didn't notice.

"It's not your fault, Jess," my dad went on, "but the reporters, and the news vans, and the police and everything. It was all just a little too much for Dougie. Things started going a little haywire in his head. After you left this morning, we thought we'd calmed him down. We got him to take his medicine, and it seemed like he was okay. But the doctor says stress can sometimes—"

I groaned and laid my head upon my knees.

"What do you mean, it isn't my fault?" I wailed. "Of course it's my fault. Everything is my fault. If I'd never called that stupid number—"

"You had to call that stupid number," my dad said patiently. "If you hadn't called that stupid number, those kids' parents would still be wondering what happened to their little son or daughter—"

"Yeah," I said. "And Sean Patrick O'Hanahan wouldn't be being sent back to his abusive father. And his mother wouldn't be in trouble. And—"

"You did the right thing, Jess," my dad said again. "You can't know everything. And Douglas will be all right. It would just be better if he could be somewhere a little quieter—"

"Yeah, but where?" I demanded. "The hospital? Dougie has to go back to the hospital because of me? Nuh-uh. No, thanks, Dad. It's clear what the problem is here. The problem isn't Douglas." I took a deep breath. The air was thick and humid. Soon, I knew, it would be summer. It had grown steadily hotter all day, and now the late afternoon sun beat down on the porch.

Beat down on me.

"It's me," I said. "If I weren't here, Douglas would be all right."

"Now, honey," my dad said.

"No, I'm serious. If I weren't here, you wouldn't have reporters dropping Powerbar wrappers all over the lawn, and Mom wouldn't be baking biscotti twenty-four seven, and Douglas wouldn't be in the hospital—"

"Just what are you suggesting, Jessica?"

"You know what I'm suggesting. I think tomorrow I'd better do what Special Agent Johnson said, and go off to Crane for a while."

Both Ruth and Mike looked at me like I was nuts, but my dad said, after a moment's silence, "You have to do what you think is right, honey."

I said, "Well, I don't think it's right that this family should have to suffer because of me. And that's what we're doing, suffering. If I went away for a while, all those reporters and everything would go away. And then things could get back to normal. Maybe even Doug could come home."

Mike said softly, "Yeah, and maybe Claire would open her blinds back up. She's been so freaked by all the cameras—"

When Ruth and I turned to stare at him, he realized what he'd said, and clamped his mouth shut.

Ruth was the only person who voiced a note of dissent.

"I don't think that's a very good idea," she said. "Your going to Crane, I mean. I don't think that's a very good idea at all."

"Ruth," I said, surprised. "Come on. They just want to do some tests—"

"Oh, great," Ruth said. "So now you're a human guinea pig? Jess, Crane is an *Army* base. Get it? We're talking about the *military.*"

"Jeez, Ruth," I said. "Be a little paranoid, won't you? It'll be all right."

Ruth stuck out her chin. I don't know what it was. Maybe she'd just seen *Point of No Return* one too many times. Maybe she just didn't want to have to face the halls of Ernest Pyle High School on her own.

Or maybe she suspected something that I, even with my brand-new powers, couldn't sense. Ruth is smarter than most people . . . about some things, anyway.

"And what," she asked quietly, "if they want you to find more kids?"

My dad said, "Well, of course they'll want her to find more kids. That's what this is all about, I'm sure."

"Does Jess *want* to find more kids?" Ruth asked, her eyebrows raised.

They say that intelligence quotient tests only measure a certain kind of knowledge. Those of us who don't test well—for instance, me—comfort ourselves with the fact that, yeah, okay, Ruth has an IQ of 167, but she knows nothing about boys. Or yeah, Mike's 153, but again, what kind of people skills does the guy have? Nada.

But with that single question, Ruth proved there wasn't anything wrong with her people skills—at least, not where I was concerned. She'd hit the nail straight on the head.

Because there was no way I was finding any more missing kids. Not after Sean. Not unless I could be convinced the kids I was finding really wanted to be found.

Unlike Sean.

Mike went, "It doesn't matter what she wants. She has a moral obligation to the community to share this . . . whatever it is."

Ruth backed down at once. How could she take a stand against her beloved?

"You're right, Michael," she said, blinking at him shyly from behind her glasses.

So much for those people skills I mentioned.

"They're not going to make Jess do anything she doesn't want to," my dad said. "We're talking about the U.S. Government, here. Jessica is a citizen of the United States. Her constitutional rights are guaranteed. Everything will be all right."

And the sad thing is, at the time I really thought he was right.

I really and truly did.

CHAPTER

14

Crane Military Base, located about an hour's drive from my hometown, had been one of the many Army bases closed by the government during the eighties. At least, it was supposed to have closed. But, somehow, it never did—at least not all the way, in spite of all those stories in my hometown paper about all the locals who worked there as maintenance men and cooks who ended up losing their jobs. The military jets—the ones that were constantly breaking the sound barrier—never quite disappeared, and we still had uniformed officers showing up for lunch and dinner in all three of my dad's restaurants long after the base was said to have been shut down.

Douglas, when he was at his most paranoid, had insisted that Crane was like Area 51, that place where the Army swears there's no base, but over which people always see these flashing lights late at night.

But when I arrived at Crane, it certainly didn't look as if anyone was trying to keep the fact that it was still open a secret. And it didn't look as if it had been neglected, either. The place was pretty clean, the lawns neatly mowed, everything looking like it was in its place. I didn't see any giant hangars where spacecraft might have been hidden, but then again, they could have been keeping those underground, like in the movie *Independence Day*.

The first thing Special Agent Johnson did—after introducing me to Special Agent Smith, a lady officer with pretty pearl earrings who had apparently replaced his former partner, Special Agent Davies (out on disability . . . oops, my bad)—was show me and my dad the room in which I'd be staying—a nice room, actually, like a hotel room, with a TV and a phone and stuff. No soda fountain, I was relieved to see.

Then he and Special Agent Smith took us to a different building, where we met some Army guys, this one colonel who squeezed my hand too hard, and this pimply-faced lieutenant who kept looking at my jeans like they were thigh-high boots or something. Then the colonel introduced us to a bunch of doctors in a different building, who acted really excited to see me, and assured my dad I was in the best of hands. My dad, even though I knew he was itching to get back to his restaurants, wouldn't leave, in spite of the doctors' assurances. He kept saying stuff like, was Special Agent Smith going to be on call in case I needed something in the middle of the night, and who was going to make sure I got enough to eat? It was kind of embarrassing.

Finally, one of the doctors, whose nametag said Helen Shifton, told my dad they were ready for me, and that I'd call him as soon as I was back in my room. After that, it was sort of obvious that they wanted him gone, so my dad left, saying he'd be back to pick me up next week. By then, we hoped that all the hoopla with the reporters and everything would have died down, and I could come back home.

He hugged me right in front of everyone, and kissed the top of my head. I pretended not to like it, but after he left, I couldn't help feeling a little bit . . .

Well, scared.

I didn't tell that to Dr. Helen Shifton, though. When she asked how I was feeling, I said I was fine.

I guess she didn't believe me, though, since she and a nurse gave me this complete physical, and I mean complete, with blood drawn and stuff poked into me—the whole thing. They checked my blood pressure, my cholesterol, my heart, my throat, my ears, my eyes, the bottoms of my feet. They wanted to do a gynecological exam, so I let them, and while they were down there, I asked them about birth control and stuff . . . you know, because I might need some, someday, when I'm like forty.

Dr. Shifton was totally cool about it, unlike my family doctor would have been, and answered all my questions, and told me everything looked normal. She even examined my scar, the one the lightning had left, and said it looked as if it was fading, and that someday, it would probably go away altogether.

"When the scar goes, do the superpowers go, too?" I asked her, a little hopefully. Having superpowers was turning out to be more of a responsibility than I liked.

She said she didn't know.

After that, Dr. Shifton made me lie down in this big tube and keep really still while she took photographs of my brain. She told me not to think about anything, but I thought about Rob. I guess the pictures turned out okay anyway, since after that Dr. Shifton made me get dressed, and then she left and this little bald man came in and asked me a lot of really boring questions, like about my dreams and my sex life and stuff. Although my sex life had, in recent days, shown signs of improving—albeit all too briefly—I didn't really have anything to tell him, and my dreams were all pretty boring, too, mostly about forgetting how to play the flute right before my challenge with Karen Sue Hanky.

It wasn't until the little bald man started asking me a bunch of stuff about Douglas that I got annoyed. I mean, how did the U.S. Government know about Douglas's suicide attempt?

But they did, and when they asked me about it, I got defensive, and the little bald man wanted to know why.

So I said, "Wouldn't you be defensive if someone you didn't know started asking you stuff about your schizophrenic brother?" But he said no, he wouldn't—not unless he had something to hide.

So then I said the only thing I had to hide was the fact that I wanted to give him a big old knuckle sandwich, and he asked if I always felt so much aggression when discussing my family, and that's when I got up and left his office and told Dr. Shifton that I wanted to go home now.

You could tell Dr. Shifton was totally mad at the little bald man, but she couldn't show it, since she's a professional and all. She said to him that she thought we'd talked long enough, and he slunk away, giving me all these dirty looks, like I'd ruined his day or something. Then Dr. Shifton told me not to worry about him, that he was just a Freudian, and nobody thought much of him anyway.

After that, it was time for lunch. Special Agent Smith took me to the cafeteria, which was in yet another building. The food wasn't bad, better than at school. I had fried chicken and mashed potatoes. I noticed the little bald man eating there, too. He looked at what I was eating and wrote it down in a little book. I pointed this out to Special Agent Smith, and she told me to ignore him, he probably had a complex.

Since there was no one my age to sit with, I sat with Special Agent Smith, and asked her how she came to be an FBI agent. She was pretty cool, answering my questions. She said she was a distinguished expert in marksmanship, which I guess meant she was a good shot, but she'd never killed anyone. She'd pulled her gun on people plenty of times, though. She even took it out of the holster and showed it to me. It was cool, really heavy. I want one, but I'll wait until I'm eighteen.

Another thing I have to wait for until I'm eighteen.

After lunch, Dr. Shifton sent me into this other doctor's office, and we spent a boring half hour with him holding up playing cards with the backs facing me and asking me what suit they were. I was like, "I don't know. You're holding them away from me," and he told me to guess. I guessed right only about ten percent of the time. He said that was normal. I could tell he was disappointed, though.

Then this weird skinny lady tried to get me to move stuff with my mind. I felt so sorry for her; I really tried, but of course I failed miserably at that, too. Then she took me into a room that was like our language lab at school, and I got to wear headphones and I was kind of excited, thinking there'd be a movie.

But the doctor in charge, a very nervous-looking man, said there'd be no movie, just some photos. I was supposed to look at the photos, and that was all.

"Am I supposed to remember what these people look like?" I asked, after the doctor got the ball rolling and the photos started flashing up onto the screen in front of me. "Like is there going to be a quiz?"

He went, "No, no quiz."

"Then I don't see the point." I was already bored with looking at the pictures. The pictures were totally uninteresting. Just men, mostly white, some faintly Arab-looking. A few black. A few Asian. Some Hispanic. No names underneath, nothing. It was almost as boring as detention. Through the headphones came some piped-in Mozart—not very well-played, I might add. At least the flutist sucked. No life, you know?

After a while I took the headphones off and was like, "Can I take a break?"

Then the doctor got way nervous and asked if I had to go to the bathroom or something, and I wanted to be like, "No, this just blows," but I didn't want to insult his experiment, so I said, "I guess not," and I went back to looking at the photos.

Middle-aged white guy. Middle-aged white guy. Middle-aged Asian guy. Kind of hot-looking Arab guy, like that dude from *The Mummy*, only no facial tattoos. Middle-aged white guy. Middle-aged white guy. I wonder what they're serving for dinner. Old white guy. Serial-killer-looking kind of guy. Middle-aged white guy. Middle-aged white guy. Middle-aged white guy.

Finally, after what seemed like a year, Dr. Shifton came out and told me I'd done great, and that I could take the rest of the day off.

Actually, after that, there wasn't a whole lot of day left. It was around three o'clock. Back home, I'd just be going into detention. I felt a wave of homesickness. Can you believe that? I actually missed detention, Miss Clemmings, the Ws . . . and Rob, of course.

But when Special Agent Smith took me back to my room, and asked if I had a swimsuit, I forgot all about Rob, because it turned out there was a pool on the base. Since I hadn't brought a swimsuit, Special Agent Smith took me to a nearby mall, and I bought a kick-ass suit and a Sony PlayStation on the government's tab, and went back to the base and went swimming.

It was plenty hot out, and the sun was still coming down hard, even though it was so late in the day. I lounged around on a deck chair and watched the other people at the pool. It was mostly women with young children . . . the wives, I guessed, of the men who worked on the base.

Some of the older kids were playing Marco Polo. I leaned back on my deck chair and closed my eyes, feeling the sun burning my skin. It was a nice feeling. I started to relax.

Maybe, I told myself, everything would be all right after all. The smell of chlorine was tangy and pleasant in my nose. It smelled clean and sharp.

Things usually work out for the best.

The sound of the children shouting filled my ears. "Marco!" Then a splash.

"Polo!" Then another splash.

"Marco!" Splash.

"Polo!" Splash. Laughter.

"Marco!" Splash.

"Polo!" Splash. Screaming. Hysterical laughter.

I guess I must have fallen asleep, because I had a weird dream. In it, I was standing in an enormous body of water. All around me were kids. Hundreds and thousands of kids. Big kids. Little kids. Fat kids. Skinny kids. White kids. Black kids. Kids of every describable kind.

And they were all of them screaming "Polo," at me.

"Polo!" Splash. Scream.

"Polo!" Splash. Scream.

And I was swimming around, trying to catch them. Only in my dream, it wasn't just a game. I wasn't Marco. In my dream, if I didn't catch these kids, they would be swept away by these rapids, and tossed over the side of this like two-hundred-foot waterfall, and fall screaming to their deaths. Seriously.

So I was swimming and swimming, snatching up kid after kid, and moving them to safety, only to have them get caught in the current and get sucked away from me again. It was horrible. Kids were slipping past my fingertips, plunging to their deaths. And they weren't shouting "Polo" anymore, either. They were screaming my name. They were screaming my name as they died.

"Jess. Jess. Jessica, wake up."

I opened my eyes. Special Agent Smith was looking down at me. I was lying in a deck chair by the pool, but something was wrong. I was the only one there. All the mothers and their kids had gone home. And the sun was almost down. Just a last few rays lit the pool deck. And it had gotten quite a few degrees cooler outside.

"You fell asleep," Special Agent Smith said. "It looked like you were having a pretty bad dream. Are you okay?"

I said, "Yeah." I sat up.

Special Agent Smith handed me my T-shirt. "Ooo," she said, wincing. "You're all burnt. We should have gotten you some sunscreen."

I looked down at myself. I was the color of a mulberry.

"It'll turn to tan by tomorrow," I said.

"That must have been some dream. Do you want to tell me about it?"

"Not particularly."

After that, I went to my room and practiced my flute. I did the usual warm-up, then I practiced the piece Karen Sue Hanky had declared she was going to challenge me on. It was so damned easy, I started doing some improv, adding some trills here and there to jazz it up a little. When I got through, you could hardly recognize it was the same song. It sounded much better.

Poor Karen Sue. She's going to be stuck in fourth chair forever.

Then I did a little Billy Joel—"Big Shot," in honor of Douglas. He won't admit it, but it's his favorite.

I was cleaning my flute when someone tapped on the door. "Come in," I said, hoping it was room service. I was starved.

It wasn't, though. Room service, I mean. It was that colonel guy I'd met at the beginning of the day. Special Agents Smith and Johnson were with him, along with the nervous little doctor who'd made me look at all those pictures of middle-aged guys. He looked, for some reason, more nervous than ever.

"Hi," I said, when they'd all come in and were standing around, staring down at my flute like it was an AK-47 I was assembling or something. "Is it time for dinner?"

"Sure," Special Agent Johnson said. "Just let us know what you want."

I thought about it. Why not, I thought, ask for the best? "Surf and turf would be good," I said.

"Done," the colonel said, and he nodded at Special Agent Smith. She took out her cell phone and punched some numbers, then spoke softly into it. God, I thought. How sexist. Here Special Agent Smith is, an FBI agent, who put herself through school and is a distinguished expert markswoman and all, and she still has to take the food orders.

Remind me not to be an FBI agent when I grow up.

"Now," the colonel said. "I was told you had a little nap today."

I was bending over, putting the different pieces of my flute in their individual sections in the velvet-lined case. But something in the colonel's voice made me look up at him.

He, like all the guys in the photos, was middle-aged, and he was white. He had what they call in the books we are forced to read in English class "ruddy features," meaning he looked as if he spent a lot of time outdoors. Not tan, like me, but sun-damaged and wrinkly. He had bright blue eyes, however. He squinted down at me and went, "You wouldn't, during your little nap, happen to have dreamed about any of those men whose photos you saw today in Dr. Leonard's office, now, did you, Miss Mastriani?"

I blinked. What was going on here?

I looked at Special Agent Smith. She had hung

up her cell phone, and now she looked at me expectantly.

"You remember, Jessica," she said. "You told me you had a bad dream."

"Yeah," I said, slowly. I think I was starting to catch on. "So?"

"So I mentioned it to Colonel Jenkins," Special Agent Smith said. "And he was just wondering if you happened to dream about any of the men whose photos you saw this afternoon."

I said, "No."

Dr. Leonard nodded and said to the colonel, "It's just as we suspected. REM-stage sleep is necessary for the phenomenon to occur, Colonel. Nappers rarely achieve the level of deep sleep necessary for REM."

Colonel Jenkins frowned down at me. "So you think tomorrow morning then, Leonard?" he rumbled. He looked very forbidding in his uniform, with all its medals and pins. He must, I thought, have fought in some pretty important battles.

"Oh, definitely, sir," Dr. Leonard said. Then he looked down at me and went, in his nervous little voice, "You tend only to have these, er, dreams about the missing children after a complete night of rest, am I correct, Miss Mastriani?"

I went, "Uh. Yeah. I mean, yes."

Dr. Leonard nodded. "Then we should check back with her tomorrow morning, sir."

Colonel Jenkins said, "I don't like it," so loudly that I jumped. "Smith?"

"Sir?" Special Agent Smith snapped to attention.

"Bring the photos," he said. "Bring them for her to look at tonight, before she goes to sleep. So they'll be fresh in her memory."

"Yes, sir," Special Agent Smith said. Then she got back on the cell phone and started murmuring things into it again.

Colonel Jenkins looked down at me. "We have high hopes for you, young lady," he told me.

I went, "You do?"

"We do, indeed. There are hundreds of men—traitors to this great nation—who have been running from the law for far too long. But now that we have you, they don't stand a chance. Do they?"

I didn't know what to say.

"Do they?" he barked.

I jumped and said, "No, sir."

Colonel Jenkins seemed to like the sound of that. He left, along with Dr. Leonard and Special Agents Smith and Johnson. A little while later, this guy in a chef's uniform delivered shrimp scampi and a perfectly grilled steak to my door.

I wasn't fooled. There may not have been a soda fountain in my room, but I knew what was going on. The book of photos arrived shortly after the food did. I flipped through it while I ate, just for the hell of it. Traitors, Colonel Jenkins had said. Were these men spies? Murderers? What? Some of them looked pretty scary. Others didn't.

What if they weren't murderers or spies? What if they were just people who, like Sean, had gotten into some trouble through no fault of their own? Was it really *my* responsibility to find them?

I didn't know. I thought I'd better talk to somebody who might.

So I called my house. My mom answered. She told me that Dougie had been released from the hospital, and that he was doing so much better now that he was back in his own room and "all the excitement had died down."

All the excitement, I knew, had moved to the gates outside of Crane, where all the news vans and stuff had gone as soon as they learned I'd been brought there. Even so, my mom kept complaining about how the whole thing had been triggered by Dad making Dougie work in the restaurant, until finally I couldn't stand it anymore, and I said, "That's bullshit, Mom, it was because of me and all the reporters," and then she got mad at me for swearing, so I hung up without having talked to my dad—which was who I'd called to talk to in the first place.

To cheer myself up, I started flipping around the channels on my big TV. I watched *The Simpsons*, and then a movie about some boys who do a beauty makeover on this girl who looked just fine before they got their mitts on her. This movie was so boring—although Ruth would have liked it, because of the beauty makeover thing—that I started flipping again. . . .

And then froze when I got to CNN . . .

Because they were showing a picture of me.

It wasn't my dorky school picture. It was a picture one of the reporters must have taken when I wasn't looking. In the picture, I was laughing. I wondered what I'd been laughing at. I couldn't remember laughing too much these past few days.

Then my picture was replaced by another one I recognized. Sean. A picture of Sean Patrick O'Hanahan, looking much as I'd last seen him, baseball cap turned around backwards, his freckles standing out starkly from his face.

I turned up the volume.

"—irony is that the boy appears to be missing *again*," the reporter said. "Authorities say Sean disappeared from his father's Chicago home yesterday before dawn, and he hasn't been seen, or heard from, since. It is believed that the boy left of his own volition, and that he is heading back to Paoli, Indiana, where his mother is being held without bail on charges of kidnapping and endangering the welfare of a minor—"

Oh, my God. They'd *arrested* Sean's mom. They'd arrested Sean's mom, because of *me*. Because of what *I'd* done.

And now the kid was on the lam. And it was all my fault. I'd been lounging around a pool while Sean was God knew where, going through God knew what, trying to get back to his incarcerated mother. And just what, I wondered, did he think he was going to do when he got back to Paoli? Bust her out of jail?

The kid was alone and hopeless, because of me.

Well, all that was going to change, I decided, switching off the TV. He may have been alone for now, but come tomorrow, he wouldn't be. Want to know why?

Because I was going to find him again.

I had done it once. I could do it again.

And this time, I was going to do it right.

CHAPTER

15

When they came for me the next morning, I was already gone.

Oh, don't get your panties in a wad. I left a note. It went like this:

> To Whom It May Concern,
> I had to run out to do an errand. I'll be right back.
>   Sincerely,
>   Jessica Mastriani

I mean, I didn't want anyone to worry.

What happened was, I woke up early. And when I woke up, I knew where Sean was. Again.

So I showered and got dressed, and then I went out into the hallway, down some stairs, and out a door.

No one tried to stop me. No one was even around,

except some soldiers, who were practicing drills or something in the yard. They just ignored me.

Which suited me fine.

Yesterday, when I'd been coming back from the pool, I'd noticed a little minibus that had pulled up to a stop outside the base's family housing units, where the officers with spouses and children lived. I walked over there now. Again, nobody tried to stop me. After all, it wasn't like I was a prisoner, or anything.

The minibus, the people at the stop said, went into the nearest town, where I'd bought my swimsuit and Sony PlayStation . . . and where I happened to know there was a bus station.

So I waited with all the other people, and when the minibus finally pulled up, I got on it. It chugged away, right in front of all the news vans and reporters and stuff. It rolled right along past them and the soldiers guarding the entrance to the base, keeping the reporters out.

And as simple as that, I left Crane Military Base.

The town outside of Crane isn't exactly this booming metropolis, but I still had trouble finding the bus station. I had to ask three people. First the minibus driver, who gave me the lamest directions on earth, then the kid behind the cash register of a convenience mart, and finally an old guy sitting outside a barber shop. In the end, I located it thanks to the fact that there was a bus sitting outside of it.

I bought my round-trip ticket—seventeen dollars—with the money my dad had given me before he'd left. "In case of an emergency," he'd said, and slipped me a hundred bucks.

Well, this was an emergency. Sort of.

I had breakfast at the bus stop. I got two chocolate fudge Pop-Tarts and a Sprite from the vending machines. Another dollar seventy-five.

I figured I might be bored during my ride, so I bought a book to read. It was the same book I'd noticed in Rob's back pocket the last time I'd seen him. I thought reading the same book might somehow bring us closer together.

Okay, I admit it: that's not true. It was the only book on the rack that looked the least bit interesting.

My bus pulled up at nine o'clock. I was the only person who got on it. I got a window seat. Have you ever noticed that things always look better when you look at them out of one of those tinted bus windows? I'm serious. Then you get off the bus and everything's all bright and you can see the dirt and you just think, "Ugh."

That's what I think, anyway.

It took us more than an hour to get to Paoli. I spent most of it looking out the window. There's not a lot to see in Indiana, except cornfields. I'm sure that's true of most states, however.

When we got to Paoli, I got off the bus and went into the station. It was bigger than the one outside of Crane. There were rows of plastic chairs for people to sit in, and a bank of pay phones. Still, I could pick out the undercover cops easy. There was one sitting by the vending machines, and another sitting near the men's room. Every time a bus came in, they'd stand up and go outside, and pretend to be waiting for someone. Then, when Sean didn't get off the bus, they'd go back and sit down again.

I observed them for over an hour, so I know what I'm talking about. There was also an unmarked police car parked across the street from the bus station, and another one in front of the bowling alley, a little ways away.

When it came time for Sean's bus to arrive, I knew I had to set up a diversion so the cops wouldn't snatch Sean before I had a chance to talk to him. So this is what I did:

I started a fire.

I know. People could have been killed. But listen, I made sure no one was in there first. I just lit this match I got from a pack I found, and threw it into the trash can in the ladies' room, after first checking to make sure all the stalls were empty. Then I went and stood by the pay phones, like I was expecting a call. Nobody noticed me. Nobody ever notices me. Short girls like me, we don't exactly stand out, you know?

After a few minutes, the smoke was billowing out really good. One of the ticket sellers noticed it first. She went, "Oh, my God! Fire! Fire!" and pointed toward the ladies' room door.

The other clerks totally freaked out. They started screaming for everyone to get out. Somebody shouted, "Dial 911!" One of the undercover cops asked if there was a fire extinguisher anywhere. The other got on his cell phone. He was telling the guys waiting outside in the unmarked cars to radio the fire department.

And right then the eleven-fifteen from Indianapolis pulled up outside. I sauntered out to meet it.

Sean was the fifth person to get off. He had on a disguise—or what he thought was one, anyway. What he'd done was, he'd dyed his hair brown. Big deal. You could still see his freckles from a mile away. Plus he still had on that stupid Yankees cap. At least he'd tried to pull it down low over his face.

But, I'm sorry, a twelve-year-old kid, who was small for his age anyway, getting off a Greyhound by himself, in the middle of a school day? Talk about conspicuous.

Fortunately, my little fire was really plugging away. I don't know if you've ever smelled burning plastic trash can before, but let me tell you, it isn't pleasant. And the smoke? Pretty black. Everyone who got off the bus looked, in a startled way, toward the station. Thick, acrid smoke was really pouring out of it now. All the ticket-takers were standing around outside, talking in shrill voices. You could tell this was the most exciting thing that had happened in the Paoli bus station for a while. The undercover cops were rushing around, trying to make sure everybody had gotten out. And then the fire engines showed up, sirens on full blast.

While all this was going on, I stepped up to Sean, took him by the arm, and said, "Keep moving," and started steering him down this alley by the station, as fast as I could.

He didn't want to come with me at first. It was kind of hard to hear what he said, since the fire engine's siren was so loud. I shouted into his ear, "Well, if you'd prefer to go with them, they're over there waiting for you," and I guess he got the message, because he stopped struggling after that.

When we'd gotten far enough away from the station that the sound of the sirens could no longer drown out our voices, Sean snatched his arm out of my grasp and demanded, in a very rude voice, "What are *you* doing here?"

"Saving your butt," I said. "What were you thinking, coming back here? This is the first place anybody with brains would look for you, you know."

Sean's blue eyes flashed at me from beneath the brim of his baseball cap. "Yeah? Well, where else am I supposed to go? My mom's in the city lockup," he said. "Thanks to *you*."

"If you had leveled with me that day," I said, "instead of acting like such a little head-case, none of this would be happening."

"No," Sean shot back. "If you weren't a *nark*, none of this would be happening."

"Nark?" That got me mad. Everyone had been going on about what a wonderful "gift" I had. How it was a miracle, a blessing, blah, blah, blah.

No one had ever called me a *nark*.

Little brat, I thought. Why am I even wasting my time? I should just leave him here. . . .

But I couldn't. I knew I couldn't.

I walked on without saying a word. It wasn't very pleasant, the alley we were in. There were Dumpsters brimming with trash on either side of us, and broken glass beneath our feet. Even worse, in about five yards, the alley ended, and I could see there was a busy street up ahead. If I was going to make sure Sean wasn't caught, I had to keep him from being seen.

"Anyway," Sean said, in the same snotty voice, "if anybody with a brain knew I'd be coming here, how come none of them found me?"

"Because I'm the only one who knew which bus you'd be coming in on," I said.

"How'd you know that?"

I gave him a bored look. He said, in a very sarcastic way, "You *dreamed* I'd be on the eleven-fifteen from Indianapolis?"

"Hey. Nobody said my dreams were interesting."

"Well, so what was all that about back there? You said *they* were waiting for me. Who's *they*?"

"Bunch of undercover cops posted in the bus

station, waiting for you. They must have suspected that was how you'd try to get here. By
bus, I mean. I had to create a diversion."

His blue eyes grew wide. *"You* started that
fire?"

"Yeah." We were almost to the street. I put my
arm out and stopped him. "Look, we have to
talk. Where can we go around here where we
can . . . you know, blend?"

"I don't want to talk to you," he said. He
sounded like he meant it, too.

"Yeah, well, you're going to. Somebody has to
get you out of this mess."

"And you think *you're* going to do it?" he
asked with a sneer.

"Like it or not, Junior," I said, "I'm all you've
got."

That earned me an eye-roll. Well, it was
progress, anyway.

We ended up going where everybody goes
when they don't know where else to go.

That's right: the mall.

The mall in Paoli, Indiana, is no Mall of
America, let me tell you. It was two stories, all
right, but there were only about twenty stores,
and the food court consisted of a Pizza Hut and
an Orange Julius. Still, beggars can't be choosers.
And since it was lunchtime, at least we weren't
the only kids around. Apparently, the sole place
in Paoli where it was possible to get a pitcher and
a pie was the Pizza Hut in the mall, so the place

was jammed with high school kids, trying to squeeze a meal into the fifty minutes they had before they had to get back to campus.

I told Sean to try to sit up tall in his seat. I was hoping he could pass, maybe, for a scrawny freshman.

And that I could pass for a loser who'd date a freshman.

"Whoa," I said, as I watched him attack his pizza. "Slow down. What, is that the first thing you've eaten all day?"

"Two days," he said, with his mouth full.

"What is wrong with you? You didn't think to steal any money from your dad before you took off?"

He said, chugging down a few swallows of Pepsi, "A credit card."

"Oh, a credit card. Smart. It's easy to buy stuff at McDonald's with a credit card."

"I just needed the bus ticket from Chicago," he said defensively.

"Oh, right." So that was how the cops knew he'd be there. "But no food."

"I forgot about food," he said. "Besides." He gave me this look. I can't really describe it. I guess it was the kind of look you would call reproachful. "I was too worried about my mom to eat."

I'll admit it. I fell for it. I got all weepy for him, and kicked myself for like the hundredth time.

Then I saw the size of the bite he took out of his last piece of pizza.

"Oh, cut the crap," I said. "I said I was sorry."

"No, you didn't."

"I didn't?" I blinked at him. "Okay, well, I'm sorry. That's why I'm here. I want to help you."

Sean shoved his empty plate at me. "Help me to another pizza," he said. "This time, no vegetables."

I sat there and watched him down a second individual pizza. I was only having a soda. I can't eat Pizza Hut. Not because it's gross or anything. I'm sure it's very good. Only we've never been allowed to eat pizza from anywhere but our own restaurants. Both my parents treat it like this huge betrayal if you even *think* about Little Caesar's, or Dominos, or whatever. It was a pie from Mastriani's, or nothing.

So I was having nothing. It's not easy, having parents in the restaurant business.

"So," I said, when Sean seemed well enough into the second pie for conversation. "What, exactly, were you planning on doing when you got here?"

He looked at me darkly. "What do you think?"

"Busting your mother out of jail? Oh, sure. Good plan."

His dark look turned into a glower. "You did it," he pointed out, and there was admiration in his voice. Grudging, but there just the same. "With the fire in the bus station. I could do something like that."

"Oh, yeah. And all the guards would come

rushing outside, and leave all the jail cells open, and you could just sneak in and grab your mom and go."

"Well," he said. "I didn't say I actually had a plan. Yet. But I'll come up with something. I always do."

"Well," I said. "I think I have one."

He just looked at me. "One what?"

"A plan."

"Aw, Jesus," he said, and reached for his Pepsi.

"Hey," I said. "Don't swear."

He looked at me very sarcastically. "You do it."

"I do not. And, besides, I'm sixteen."

He rolled his eyes again. "Yeah, that makes you an adult, I guess. Do you even have a driver's license?"

I fiddled with my straw. He had me there. I had my learner's permit, of course, but I had sort of accidentally flunked my first try at the driving test. It wasn't my fault, of course. Something weird seems to happen when I get behind a wheel. It all goes back to that speed thing. If no one else is on the road, why should you only go thirty-five?

"Not yet," I said. "But I'm working on it."

"Jesus." Sean flopped his eighty-pound body against the back of the booth. "Look, you are not exactly trustworthy, you know? You busted me once already, remember?"

"That was a mistake," I said. "I said I was

sorry. I bought you pizza. I told you I have a plan to make things right again. What more do you want?"

"What more do I want?" Sean leaned forward so that the cheerleaders at the next table wouldn't overhear him. "What I want is for things to go back the way they were before you came along and severely messed them up."

"Oh, yeah? Well, no offense, Sean, but I don't think things were exactly swell before. I mean, what's going to happen when one of your teachers, or your friends' moms, or your Boy Scout leader, goes to the grocery store and sees your face on the back of a milk carton, huh? Are you and your mom going to pick up and run every time someone recognizes you? Are the two of you going to keep running until you're eighteen? Is that the plan?"

Sean eyed me angrily from beneath the brim of his baseball cap. "What else are we supposed to do?" he demanded. "You don't know . . . My dad, he's got friends. That's why the judge ruled the way he did. My dad got his friends to put the squeeze on the guy. He knew exactly what kind of guy my dad is. But he awarded him custody anyway. My mom didn't have a chance. So, yeah, we'll keep running. No one can help us."

"You're wrong," I said. "I can."

Sean leaned forward and said, very deliberately, "You . . . can't . . . even . . . drive."

"I know that. But I can help you. Listen to me.

My best friend's dad is a lawyer, a good one. Once, when I was over at their house, I heard him talking about this case where a kid sued to be emancipated—"

"This," Sean said, shoving his empty plate away, "is bullshit. I don't know why I'm even listening to you."

"Because I'm all you've got. Now, listen—"

"No," Sean said, shaking his head. "Don't you get it? I've heard about you."

I blinked at him. "What are you talking about?"

"I saw on the news how they've got you up at that place, that military base."

"Yeah? So?"

"You're so stupid," Sean said. "You don't know anything. I bet you don't even know why they got you there. Do you?"

I shifted uncomfortably in my seat. "Sure, I do. They're doing some experiments on me. You know, to figure out how it is I know where people like you are. That's all."

"That isn't *all*. They've got you lookin' for people, don't they?"

I thought about those photos, all those middle-aged men it had seemed so important to the colonel for me to look at.

"Maybe . . ."

"So, don't you get it? You're not helping anybody. You don't know who those guys were. Some of those people they want you to find might be on the run for a reason, like me and my mom. Some of them might actually be innocent. And you're servin' 'em up to the cops like big old plates of chocolate-glazed donuts."

I don't like to hear the police disparaged, especially by someone so young. After all, the police provide a vital service for our society, for little pay and even less glory. I said, my voice sounding lame even to my own ears, "I am sure that if someone is wanted by the U.S. Government, he must be guilty of something. . . ."

But the truth was, he wasn't saying anything I hadn't already thought of myself. For some reason, he reminded me of my dream. *Marco. Polo. Marco. Polo.* So many people, so many voices.

And I couldn't reach a single one of them.

Sean's face was white beneath his freckles. "What about *The Fugitive*, huh? He hadn't done anything. It was that one-armed man. For all you know, one of those people they want you to find for them might be just like Harrison Ford in that movie. And you're Tommy Lee Jones." He shook his head disgustedly. "You really are a nark, you know that?"

Nark? Me? I wanted to wring the little twerp's neck. I was totally regretting having come after him like this.

Marco.

"Nark's not even the word for it," he said. "You know what you are? A dolphin."

I gaped at him. Was he kidding? Dolphins were friendly, intelligent animals. If he was trying to insult me, he'd have to try a little harder.

"You know what the government used to do?" Sean was on a roll. "They used to train dolphins to swim up to boats and tap them with their noses. Then, when World War I started, they strapped bombs to the dolphins' backs, and made them swim up to enemy boats and touch them with their noses. But this time when they did it, what do you think happened? The bombs went off, and the enemy ships—and the dolphins—were blown to smithereens. Oh, sure, everybody says, 'Think how many people would have been killed by that boat, if it hadn't been blown up. The dolphin gave its life for a worthy cause.' But I bet the *dolphin* didn't feel that way. The dolphin didn't start the war. The dolphin had nothing to do with it."

He narrowed his eyes at me. "Do you know what, Jess?" he said. "You're the dolphin now. And it's just a matter of time before they blow you up."

I narrowed my eyes right back at him, but I had to admit, the story about the dolphins gave me the chills.

Polo.

"I'm no dolphin," I said. I was beginning to regret having found Sean Patrick O'Hanahan. And I definitely regretted having bought him two individual pizzas and a large Pepsi.

Unfortunately, though, the more I thought

about it, sitting there in the restaurant, with the Paoli High cheerleaders giggling in the next booth, and the mall Muzac playing softly around us, the more I realized that was exactly what I was . . . or rather, what I'd almost let myself become. *I'll be right back.* That's what I'd said in the note I'd left that morning. Had I really meant that? Had I really meant to come back?

Or had I actually meant hasta la vista, baby, this tuna is dolphin-free?

Marco.

"Look," I said to Sean. "We aren't here to discuss my problems. We're here to discuss yours."

He eyed me. "Fine," he said. "What am I supposed to do?"

"In the first place," I said, "stop using your dad's credit card. Here." I dug around in my pocket, then pushed what was left of my dad's hundred dollars at him. "Take this. Then we're going to get you into a cab."

"A cab?"

"Yeah, a cab. You can't go back to the bus station, and we've got to get you out of Paoli. I want you to go to my school—" I'd reached into my backpack and brought out a pen. I was scrawling the address of Ernest Pyle High School on a Pizza Hut napkin. "Ask for Mr. Goodhart. Tell him I sent you. He'll help you. Tell him he needs to call Ruth's dad, Mr. Abramowitz. Here, I'm writing it down for you. Quit grabbing my hand, I'm writing it down for you."

But Sean kept on pawing at my hand. I didn't know what the kid wanted. The pen? What did he want the pen for?

"Cool it, would you?" I said, looking up at him. "I'm writing as fast as I can."

But then I got a look at his face. He wasn't even looking at me. He was looking just past me, at the door to the restaurant.

I turned around, just in time to make eye contact with Colonel Jenkins. When he saw me, his big hands balled up into fists, and I was reminded, inexplicably, of Coach Albright.

And that wasn't all. Marching behind him was a whole pack of meaty-fisted guys in army fatigues and crew cuts, who just happened to be armed.

Polo.

"Shit," I said.

The colonel nodded at me. "There she is," he said.

Sean may only have been twelve, but he sure wasn't stupid. He whispered, "Run!"

And even though he was only twelve, that sounded like pretty good advice to me.

CHAPTER

16

Colonel Jenkins and his men were blocking the doorway, but that was okay. There was a side door that had the word *Exit* over it. We dove through it, and found ourselves right in front of JCPenney.

"Wait," I said to Sean as he was preparing to flee. I had had the presence of mind to hang on to the napkin I'd written on. I reached out and grabbed him by his shirt collar, then shoved the napkin in the front pocket of his jeans. He looked a little surprised.

"Now go," I said, and shoved him.

We split up. We didn't discuss it or anything. It just happened. Sean took off toward the Photo Hut. I headed for the escalators.

Back when I'd first started having to defend Douglas at school, and I hadn't known too much about fighting, my dad had taken me aside and given me a few pointers. One of the best pieces of advice he gave me—besides showing me how to hit—was that if I ever found myself in a situation where I was outnumbered, the best thing to do was run. And, specifically, run downhill. Never, my father said, go uphill—or stairs, or whatever—during a chase. Because if you go up, and the people after you block the only way down, you have no way of getting out—except by jumping.

But I had Sean to think about. Seriously. Thanks to me, there were armed men chasing us, for Christ's sake. I was not going to let them get hold of a little twelve-year-old kid, a kid who'd only gotten involved in this in the first place through my own fault.

So I knew that I was going to have to let myself get caught in the end . . . but, in the meantime, I had to make this chase last as long as possible, in order to give Sean a solid chance at escaping. I was going to have to create another diversion. . . .

And so I headed for those escalators.

And, by God, they followed me right up them.

It was still lunchtime so, except for the food court, the mall wasn't that crowded. But what few people there were I managed to weave around pretty good. The soldiers chasing after me weren't quite so nimble: I heard people screaming as they tried to get out of the way, and things like a vending cart called the Earring Tree, which I whizzed by with no problem, crashed to the floor as the soldiers stumbled into it.

I knew better than to dive into any stores in my efforts to ditch these guys. They'd just corner me there. I kept to the main corridor, which had plenty of stuff to dodge around—a big fountain, cookie vendors, and, best of all, a giant traveling diorama, featuring life-size robotic dinosaurs, meant to teach kids and their parents about pre-historic earth.

I am not kidding. Well, okay, maybe about the life-size part. The tallest dinosaur was only about twenty feet tall, and that was the *T. Rex*. But they were all crowded into this hundred-foot space, jammed in there with fake ferns and palm trees and jungly-type stuff. Weird jungle sounds, like shrieking monkeys and birds, played over these speakers designed to look like rocks. There was even, in one area, a volcano from which actual fake lava was spewing—or made to look like it was spewing, anyway.

I looked behind me. My pursuers had untangled themselves from the mess by the Earring Tree, and were now gaining on me. I glanced to my side, over the balustrade that looked out across the main floor, a story below me. I saw Sean dodging past Baskin-Robbins, Colonel Jenkins close at his heels.

"Hey," I yelled.

Heads everywhere whipped around as people turned to stare at me, including Colonel Jenkins.

"Here I am!" I shouted. "Your new dolphin! Come and get me!"

Colonel Jenkins, as I had hoped, stopped chasing Sean and headed for the escalator.

I, of course, headed for the dinosaur diorama.

I hurdled across the velvet rope separating the display from the rest of the mall, followed closely by a half dozen of Colonel Jenkins's men. As my sneakered feet sank into the brown foamy stuff they'd sprayed on the mall floor to look like dirt, I was assaulted by the sound of jungle drums— apparently the makers of the diorama were unaware that dinosaurs predated man (and drums) by several hundred thousand years. There was a lonely wail, which sounded mysteriously like a peacock to me. Then a roar—distinctly lion—and steam sprayed from the *T. Rex*'s nostrils, two dozen feet above my head.

I dodged behind a couple of velociraptors, who were feasting on the bloody carcass of a saber-toothed tiger. No good. Jenkins's men were on my heels. I decided to really screw with them, and leapt into the shallow water they'd set up to look like a lake, out of which both the fake volcano and the head of a brachiosaurus reared. I sank into the artificially blue water, the water hitting me about mid-shin, soaking my sneakers and the bottoms of my jeans.

Then I started wading.

Jenkins's men, apparently thinking that catching me was not exactly worth getting their feet wet, halted on the rim of the artificial lake.

Okay, so I knew they were going to catch me eventually. I mean, come on. Even if I got out of the mall, where was I going to go? Home?

Not.

But I didn't have to make it easy on them. So, when I saw them elbow each other and split up to opposite sides of the lake, ready to catch me wherever I tried to come ashore, I did the only thing I could think of:

I climbed the volcano.

Okay, my sneakers were kind of squelchy. And okay, the volcano wasn't all that sturdy, and groaned beneath my weight. But hey, I had to do something.

And when I reached the top of the volcano, it was just in time for it to start spewing again. I stood up there—some fifteen feet in the air—and looked down at everyone, as all around me steam hissed out, and the lava, made of scarlet plastic with a bunch of little lights inside it, started to glow. The diorama's bogus sound track made a noise like the earth splitting, and then a thunderous rumble shook the so-called lake.

"Be careful!" shouted an old lady in jogging shoes, who'd watched from the velvet rope as I'd climbed.

"Don't slip in those wet shoes, dear," cried her friend.

The soldiers looked at them almost as disgustedly as I did.

From my perch, I could see down to the mall's main floor. As I watched, another six soldiers stormed by—and as soon as they passed, Sean darted out from between some racks of clothes in the Gap and headed, a streak of blue jeans and badly dyed brown hair, toward the Cineplex.

I knew a secondary diversion was necessary. So I teetered on the rim of the volcano and shouted, "Don't come any closer, or I'll jump!"

Both the old ladies gasped. The soldiers looked more disgusted than ever. In the first place, they'd clearly had no intention of coming any closer. In the second, even if I did jump, that fall wouldn't exactly be fatal: I wasn't all that high up.

Still, I suppose it looked very dramatic. There I was, this young virgin (unfortunately), poised on the edge of a volcano. Too bad my hair was so short, and I wasn't dressed in flowing white. Jeans spoiled the effect, in my opinion.

Then Colonel Jenkins strode up, pointing at me and bleating at his soldiers in a manner that more than ever put me in mind of Coach Albright.

"What's she doin' up there?" he demanded. "Get her down right now."

I glanced down at the Cineplex. I could still see Sean, cowering behind a life-size cardboard cutout of Arnold Schwarzenegger. The soldiers were milling around, trying to figure out where he'd disappeared to.

Hoping to get their attention long enough for Sean to be able to make another run for it, I shouted, "I really mean it! If anyone comes near me, I'll do it! I'll jump!"

Bingo. The soldiers looked up. Sean slithered out from behind the cardboard Arnold and made a break for the concession stand.

"All right, Miss Mastriani," Colonel Albright called out to me. "Fun's over. You come down here right now before you hurt yourself."

"No," I said.

Colonel Jenkins sighed. Then he flicked a finger, and four of his men climbed over the velvet rope and began wading toward me.

"Get back," I cried warningly. Sean, I could see, had only to duck past the ticket-taker, and he'd be in. "I mean it!"

"Miss Mastriani," Colonel Jenkins said, in a tone of voice that suggested to me that he was trying very hard to be reasonable. "Have we done something to offend you? Have you been mistreated in any way since your father left you in our care?"

"No," I said. The soldiers were coming closer.

"Isn't it true, in fact, that Dr. Shifton and Special Agent Smith and everyone else at Crane have gone out of their way to make you feel comfortable and welcome?"

"Yes," I said. Below, the ticket-taker caught

Sean trying to sneak into the theater. She grabbed him by his shirt collar, and said something I couldn't hear.

"Well, then, let's be rational. You come on back to Crane, and we'll talk this out."

The ticket-taker raised her voice. The six soldiers watching me started to turn their heads, distracted by the commotion at the Cineplex.

I looked at the two old ladies. "Call the police," I shouted. "I'm about to be taken against my will back to Crane Military Base."

"Crane," the old lady in the jogging shoes said. "Oh, but that's closed."

"Goddammit," Colonel Jenkins said, apparently forgetting his audience. "Come down from there right now, or I'll pull you down myself!"

Both of the old ladies gasped. But the soldiers had spied Sean. They began jogging toward him.

And the soldiers Colonel Jenkins had sicced on me were almost at the base of my volcano.

"Oh, nuts," I said as I watched Sean get nabbed. That was it. It was over.

But there was no reason to make it easy on them.

"Let the kid go," I threatened, "or I'll jump!"

"Don't do it, honey," one of the old ladies shouted. They had been joined now by some of the high school kids, who'd come out to see what all the commotion was.

The high school kids yelled at me to jump.

I looked beneath me, down into the center of

the volcano. I could see a circle of bare mall floor there, ringed by bars of metal scaffolding, which was holding the volcano up. They'd drag me out, of course. But it would take them a while.

I looked up again. Colonel Jenkins's men were still struggling to climb up the side of the volcano. They were hampered by the fact that their wet boots couldn't gain much traction on the slick plastic surface.

Down below, Sean was being dragged, kicking and screaming, from the Cineplex.

I unfolded my arms, perching on the edge of the volcano.

"No!" Colonel Jenkins cried.

But it was too late. I jumped.

CHAPTER

17

It took them almost half an hour to get me out.
The hole in the top of the volcano wasn't that
wide. None of the soldiers, let alone Colonel
Jenkins, could reach me through it. All my jump-
ing into it accomplished was that it made Colonel
Jenkins really mad.

It was worth it.

I sat down there, pretty much comfortably,
while they tried to figure out ways to get to me.
Finally, someone went over to Sears and bought a
power saw, and they cut a big hole in the side of
the volcano. They dragged me out, and the people who'd stuck around to watch applauded, like
it had all been some big stunt for their benefit.

Special Agents Johnson and Smith were there
when they finally dragged me out. They both
acted like it was this big personal affront, my tak-

ing off the way I had. I did my best to defend myself.

"But I left a note," I insisted as we took off in the carefully nondescript black government vehicle (with tinted windows) that was going to drive us back to Crane, Special Agents Johnson and Smith in the front seat, Sean and I in the back.

"Yes," Special Agent Smith said, "but you took several things with you that led us to believe you weren't coming back."

I demanded to know what those things were. In reply, Special Agent Smith held up the book of photos Colonel Jenkins had left in my room, in hopes of my discovering the whereabouts of a few of its subjects. She'd fished it out of my backpack, which they'd confiscated from me as soon as they'd dug me out of the volcano.

"I was just going to show that to somebody," I said, truthfully. Somewhere in the back of my mind, I'd had this idea—way before Sean had ever called me a dolphin—of taking the book of photos to my brother Michael. I had hoped that, with all his computer skills, he might have been able to find out who the men in it were, using the Internet, or something. I wanted to make sure they were really wanted criminals and not innocent lawyers, like Will Smith in *Enemy of the State*, or something.

Dumb idea, maybe, but then, I'd learned a lesson or two since that morning I'd woken up knowing where Sean was.

"I was going to bring it back," I said.

"Were you?" Special Agent Smith turned to look at me. She seemed particularly disappointed. You could tell she no longer thought I'd be good Bureau material. "If you were planning on coming back, then why'd you take this with you?"

And she pulled my flute, in its wooden case, from my backpack, which she had with her in the front seat.

She had me there, and she knew it.

"When I saw this was missing," she said, illustrating some of the cognitive abilities that had earned her special agent status, "I knew you weren't planning on returning, despite your note and the fact that that bus ticket you bought was for a round-trip."

"Is that how you figured out I was in Paoli?" I asked. I was genuinely interested in learning what my mistakes had been. You know, just in case there was a next time. "The bus ticket?"

"Yes. Clerk at the bus station back by Crane recognized you." Special Agent Johnson, much to my disappointment, drove at exactly the speed limit. It was sickening. All these semis were passing us. With the exception of the band of cars behind us, carrying Colonel Jenkins and his men, ours was the slowest car on the highway. "You aren't exactly an anonymous citizen anymore, Miss Mastriani. Not when you've had your photo on the cover of *Time* magazine."

"Oh," I said. I nodded toward the convoy behind us. "All that firepower, just for little ol' me?"

"You were carrying highly classified data," Special Agent Johnson said, indicating the book of photos. "We just wanted to make sure we got it back."

"But now that you have it back," I said, "you're going to let me go, right?"

"That isn't up to us to decide," Special Agent Johnson said.

"Well, who's it up to?"

"Our superiors."

"The smoking man?"

The agents looked at one another. "Who?" Special Agent Johnson asked.

"Never mind," I said. "Look, can you just tell your superiors that I quit?"

Special Agent Smith looked back at me. She was wearing diamond stud earrings today.

"Jess," she said, "you can't quit."

"Why not?"

"Because you have an extraordinary gift. You have a responsibility to share it with the world." Special Agent Smith shook her head. "I just don't understand where all of this is coming from," she said. "You seemed perfectly happy yesterday, Jess. Why is it that, suddenly, you want to quit?"

I shrugged. Claire Lippman would have been jealous of my acting, I swear. "I guess I'm just homesick."

"Hmmm," Special Agent Johnson said. "I thought the whole reason you changed your mind about coming up here was that you were concerned about your family, that you felt they were being tormented by the media. I thought you felt that leaving them was the only way to give them back some of the privacy they so craved."

I swallowed. "Yeah," I said. "But that was before I got so homesick."

Special Agent Smith shook her head. "Your brother, Douglas. I think they only just released him from the hospital. Seems like, if you went back now, he might just end up there again. All those cameras, flashbulbs going off everywhere—that really shook him up."

That was a low blow. My eyes filled up with tears, and I began seriously to consider flinging myself out the car door—we were certainly going slowly enough that I wouldn't be badly hurt—and making a run for it.

The only problem was that the doors were locked, and the button to unlock them didn't work. The controls were all up in the front seat, by Special Agent Johnson.

And, anyway, I had Sean to think of.

Special Agent Smith was still going on about my responsibility to the world, now that I had this extraordinary gift.

"So I'm supposed to help evil men be brought to justice?" I asked, just to make sure I was clear on things.

"Well, yes," Special Agent Smith said. "And reunite people like Sean here with their loved ones."

Sean and I exchanged glances.

"Hello," Sean said. "Don't you guys read the papers? My dad's a jerk."

"You never really got a chance to know him, now, did you, Sean?" Special Agent Smith said in a soothing voice. "I understand your mother took you from him when you were only six."

"Yeah," Sean said. "Because he'd broken my arm when I didn't put all my toys away one night."

"Jeez," I said, looking at Sean. "Who's your dad, anyway? Darth Vader?"

Sean nodded. "Only not as nice."

"Oh, good job," I said to Special Agents Johnson and Smith. "You two must be real proud of yourselves, reuniting this little boy with a dark lord of the Sith."

"Hey," Sean said, looking appalled. "I'm not little."

"Mr. O'Hanahan," Special Agent Smith said in a tight little voice, "has been declared a fit parent and Sean's rightful guardian by the Illinois state court."

"It used to be legal to have slaves in Illinois, too," Sean said. "But that didn't make it right."

"Courts make mistakes," I said.

"Big ones," Sean said.

I was the only one in the car, I was pretty sure,

who heard his voice shake. I reached out and took his hand. I held it the rest of the way, too, even though it got a little sweaty. Hey, the whole thing was my fault, right? What else was I supposed to do?

They split us up when we got to Crane. Sean had already given everyone the slip once, and I guess they wanted to make extra sure he didn't do it again, so, since his dad wasn't due to pick him up until sometime the next day, they locked him in the infirmary.

I'm not kidding.

I suppose they picked the infirmary, and not, say, the brig, where I think they locked naughty soldiers, because later, they could say he wasn't being held against his will at all . . . after all, they'd given him the run of the infirmary, hadn't they? They'd probably say they locked him in for his own safety.

But even though it wasn't exactly a jail cell, it might as well have been. The windows—there were four of them—were all barred from the outside, I guess to keep people from breaking in and stealing drugs, since the infirmary was on the first floor. And I happened to know, from having been in there the day before for my physical, that all the cabinets with the cool stuff in them, like stethoscopes and hypodermic needles, were locked, and the magazines and stuff were way out of date. Sean wasn't going to have much to keep his mind off his dad's impending arrival.

Me, they locked back into my old room. Seriously. I was right back where I'd started from that morning, with one difference: the door was locked from the outside, and the phone, strangely enough, no longer worked.

I don't know what they thought I was going to do—call the police or something?

"Officer, officer, I'm being held against my will at Crane Military Base!"

"Crane Military Base? What are you talking about? That place closed down years ago!"

No phone privileges for me. And no more trips to the pool, either. My door was very firmly locked.

Marco Polo is locked down for the night. Repeat. Marco Polo is locked down.

Or so they must have thought. But here's the thing:

When you take a kid—who is basically a good kid, but maybe a little quick with her fists—and you make her sit for an hour every day after school with a lot of not-so-good kids, even if she isn't allowed to talk to them during that hour, the fact is, she's going to pick up some things.

And maybe the things she's going to pick up are the kind of things you don't necessarily want a good kid to know. Like, for instance, how to start a really smoky fire in a bus station ladies' room.

Or how to pick a lock. It's pretty easy, actually, depending on the lock. The one to my room wasn't very tough. I managed to do it with the ink cartridge from a ballpoint pen.

Look, you just pick these things up, all right?

They caught me right away. Boy, was Colonel Jenkins mad. But not as mad as Special Agent Johnson. He'd been viewing me as a thorn in his side since the day I'd broken his last partner's nose. You could tell I'd really done it this time.

Which was why they threw the book at me. They'd really had it. They intended to shut me up for good this time.

Dr. Shifton did some pleading on my behalf. I overheard her insisting that I obviously have issues with authority figures, and that they were going about this all wrong. I would come around, she said, when they made it seem like it was my idea.

Colonel Jenkins didn't like the sound of that. He went, "Dammit, Helen, she knows the location of every single one of those men whose photos we showed her. I can see it in her eyes. What are we supposed to do, just wait around until she's in the mood to tell us?"

"Yes," Dr. Shifton said. "That's exactly what we do."

I liked Dr. Shifton for that. And, anyway, I did not know where every single one of those men were.

Just most of them.

I happened to overhear all this because Dr. Shifton's office is right next to the infirmary, and that's where they put me after I escaped that second time: in the infirmary, with Sean. . . .

Exactly as I'd wanted them to.

Don't start thinking that I had any sort of plan or anything. I totally didn't. I just figured the kid needed me, is all.

That he didn't happen to agree is really beside the point.

"What are *you* doing here?" he asked, looking up from the bed he was stretched out on. His tone implied he was not pleased to see me.

"Slumming," I said.

"My dad's going to be here first thing in the morning, they said." His face was pinched and white. Well, except for the freckles. "He couldn't make it tonight because of some board meeting. But he gets a police escort tomorrow morning, as soon as he's ready to leave." He shook his head. "That's my dad. Work always comes first. And if you get in the way of that, look out."

I said, gently, "Sean, I said I was going to make it up to you, and I meant it."

Sean looked pointedly at the locked door. "And how are you going to do that?"

"I don't know," I said. "But I will. I swear it."

Sean just shook his head. "Sure," he said. "Sure you will, Jess."

The fact that he didn't believe me just made me more determined.

Hours slid by, and no one came near the infirmary—not even Dr. Shifton. We passed the time trying to figure out ways to escape, listening to talk radio, and doing old *People* magazine crosswords.

Finally, around six o'clock, the door opened, and Special Agent Smith came in, holding a couple of McDonald's bags. I guess my days of surf and turf were over. I didn't care, though. The smell of those fries set my stomach, which I hadn't noticed up until then was quite empty, rumbling noisily.

"Hi," Special Agent Smith said, with a rueful smile. "I brought you guys dinner. You guys okay?"

"Except for the fact that our constitutional rights are being violated," I said, "we're fine."

Special Agent Smith's smile went from rueful to forced. She spread our dinner out on one of the beds: double cheeseburger meals. Not my favorite, but at least she'd super-sized it.

Sean practically inhaled his first burger. I admit to stuffing far more fries into my mouth than was probably good for me. As I stuffed, Special Agent Smith tried her hand at reasoning with me. I guess Dr. Shifton had been coaching her.

"You have a really special gift, Jess," she said. She was practically ignoring Sean. "And it would be a shame to waste it. We need your help so desperately. Don't you want to make this world a safer, better place for kids like yourself?"

"Sure," I said, swallowing. "But I don't want to be a dolphin, either."

Special Agent Smith knit her pretty brow. "A what?"

I told her about the dolphins, while Sean looked on, silently chewing. I'd given him one of my cheeseburgers, but even after three of them, he didn't seem satisfied. He could put away an alarming amount of food for such a small boy.

Special Agent Smith shook her head, still looking perplexed. "I never heard that one before. I know they used German shepherds for similar missions in World War I—"

"German shepherds, dolphins, whatever." I stuck out my chin. "I don't want to be used."

"Jess," Special Agent Smith said. "Your gift—"

"Don't," I said, holding up a single hand. "Seriously. Don't say it. I don't want to hear about it anymore. This 'gift' you keep talking about has caused me nothing but trouble. It sent my brother over the edge, when he'd been doing really well, and it put this little boy's mother in jail—"

"Hey," Sean said indignantly. I'd forgotten about his objections to my use of the word "little" as it related to him.

"Jess." Special Agent Smith balled up the empty bags from my meal. "Be reasonable. It's very sad about Sean's mother, but the fact is, she broke the law. And as for your brother, you can't drop the ball just because of one little setback. Try to keep things in perspective—"

" 'Keep things in perspective'?" I leaned forward and enunciated very carefully so she would be sure to understand me. "Excuse me, Special Agent Smith, but I got struck by lightning. Now, when I go to sleep, I dream about missing people, and it just so happens that when I wake up, I know where those missing people are. Suddenly, the U.S. Government wants to use me as some sort of secret weapon against fugitives from justice, and you think I should *keep things in perspective?*"

Special Agent Smith looked annoyed. "I think you should try to remember," she said, "that what you call a dolphin, most Americans would call a hero."

She turned to throw my empty McDonald's wrappers in the garbage.

"I really didn't come in here," she said, when she turned around again, "to argue with you, Jess. I just thought you might like this back."

She handed me my backpack. The book of photos was gone from it, of course, but my flute was there. I grasped it tightly to my chest.

"Thanks," I said. I was oddly touched by the gesture. Don't ask me why. I mean, it was my flute, after all. I hoped I wasn't beginning to suffer from that thing hostages get, when they start sympathizing with their captors.

"I like you, Jess," Special Agent Smith said. "I really hope that while you're in here tonight, you'll think about what I said. Because you know, I think you'd make a fine federal agent someday."

"Really?" I asked, like I thought this was an enormous compliment.

"I do." She went to the door. "I'll see you two later," she said.

Sean, over on his bed, just grunted. I said, "Sure. Later."

She left. I heard the door lock behind her. The lock on the infirmary door was one that even I, with my extensive knowledge of such things, could not penetrate.

But that didn't matter. Because Special Agent Smith had been right when she'd said I'd make a fine federal agent:

While she'd been throwing out the trash from my meal, I'd reached over and swiped her cell phone from her purse.

I held it up for Sean to see.

"Oh, yeah," I said. "I'm good. *Real* good."

18

It took us a while to figure out how Special Agent Smith's cell phone worked. Of course there was a password you had to use to get a dial tone. That's what took the longest, figuring out her password. But most passwords, I knew from Michael—who gets his thrills figuring out this kind of thing—are four to six digits or numbers long. Special Agent Smith's first name was Jill. I pressed 5455, and, *voilà,* as my mom would say: we were in.

Sean wanted me to call Channel 11 News.

"Seriously," he said. "They're right outside the gates. I saw them as we drove in. Tell them what's going on."

I said, "Calm down, squirt. I'm not calling Channel 11 News."

He quit bouncing and said, "You know, I'm

getting sick of you calling me squirt and talking about how little I am. I'm almost as tall as you are. And I'll be thirteen in nine months."

"Quiet," I said as I dialed. "We don't have much time before she notices it's gone."

I called my house. My mom picked up. They were eating dinner, Douglas's first since he'd gotten out of the hospital. My mom went, "Honey, how are you? Are they treating you all right?"

I said, "Uh, not exactly. Can I talk to Dad?"

My mom said, "What do you mean, not exactly? Daddy said they had a lovely room for you, with a big TV and your own bathroom. You don't like it?"

"It's okay," I said. "Look, is Dad there?"

"Of course he's here. Where else would he be? And he's as proud of you as I am."

I had been gone only forty-eight hours, but apparently, during the interim, my mother had lost her mind.

"Proud of me?" I said. "What for?"

"The reward money!" my mom cried. "It came today! A check in the amount of ten thousand dollars, made out to you, honey. And that's just the beginning, sweetie."

Man, she had really gone round the bend. "Beginning of what?"

"The kind of income you'll be generating from all of this," my mom said. "Honey, Pepsi called. They want to know if you'd be willing to endorse a new brand of soda they've come up with. It has gingko biloba in it, you know, for brain power."

"You have got," I said, my throat suddenly dry, "to be kidding me."

"No. It's quite good; they left a case here. Jessie, they're offering you a hundred thousand dollars just to stand in front of a camera and say that there are easier ways to expand your brain power than getting struck by lightning—"

In the background I heard my dad say, "Toni." He sounded stern. "She's not doing it."

"Let her make up her own mind, Joe," my mother said. "She might like it. And I think she'll be good at it. Jess is certainly prettier than a lot of those girls I see on the TV—"

My throat was starting to hurt, but there was nothing I could do about it, because all the drugs in the infirmary, even the mouthwash, were locked up.

"Mom," I said. "Can I please talk to Dad?"

"In a minute, honey. I just want to tell you how well Dougie is doing. You're not the only hero in the family, you know. Dougie's doing great, just great. But, of course, he misses his Jess."

"That's great, Mom." I swallowed hard. "That's . . . So, he isn't hearing voices?"

"Not a one. Not since you left and took all those nasty reporters with you. We miss you, sweetie, but we sure don't miss all those news vans. The neighbors were starting to complain. Well, you know the Abramowitzes. They're so fussy about their yard."

I didn't say anything. I don't think I could have spoken if I'd wanted to.

"Do you want to say hi to Dougie, honey? He wants to say hi to you. We're having Dougie's favorite, on account of his being home. Manicotti. I feel bad making it when you aren't here. I know it's your favorite, too. You want me to save you some? Are they feeding you all right up there? I mean, is it just army food?"

"Yeah," I said. "Mom, can I please talk to—"

But my mother had passed the phone to my brother. Douglas's voice, deep but shaky as ever, came on.

"Hey," he said. "How you doing?"

I turned so that I was sitting with my back to Sean, so he wouldn't see me wipe my eyes. "Fine," I said.

"Yeah? You sure? You don't sound fine."

I held the phone away from my face and cleared my throat. "I'm sure," I said, when I thought I could speak without sounding like I'd been crying. "How are you doing?"

"Okay," he said. "They upped my meds again. I've got dry mouth like you wouldn't believe."

"I'm sorry," I said. "Doug, I'm really sorry."

He sounded kind of surprised. "What are you sorry about? It's not your fault."

I said, "Well, yeah. It kind of is. I mean, all those people in our front yard were there on account of me. It stressed you out, having all those people there. And that was my fault."

"That's bull," Douglas said.

But it wasn't. I knew it wasn't. I liked to think that Douglas was a lot saner than my mom gave him credit for being, but the truth was, he was still pretty fragile. Accidentally dumping a tray of plates in a restaurant wasn't going to set off one of his episodes. But waking up to find a whole bunch of strangers with film equipment in his front yard definitely was.

And that's when I knew that, much as I wanted to, I couldn't go home. Not yet. Not if I wanted Douglas to be okay.

"So, are they treating you all right?" Douglas wanted to know.

I stared out between the bars across the windows. Outside, the sun was setting, the last rays of the day slanting across the neatly trimmed lawn. In the distance, I could see a small runway, with a helicopter sitting near it. No helicopters had taken off or landed since I'd been watching. There were no UFOs at Crane. There was no nothing at Crane.

"Sure," I said.

"Really? Because you sound kind of upset."

"No," I said. "I'm okay."

"So. How are you going to spend that reward money?"

"Oh, I don't know. How do you think I should spend it?"

Douglas thought about it. He said, "Well, Dad could use a new set of clubs. Not that he ever gets a chance to play."

"I don't want golf clubs," I heard my dad yelling. "We're putting that money away for Jess's college."

"I want a car!" I heard Michael yell.

I laughed a little. I said, "He just wants a car so he can drive Claire Lippman to the quarries."

Doug said, "You know that's true. And I think Mom would love a new sewing machine."

"So she can make us some more matching outfits." I smiled. "Of course. What about you?"

"Me?" Douglas was beginning to sound even farther away than ever. "I just want you home, and everything back to normal."

I coughed. I had to, in order to cover up the fact that I was crying again.

"Well," I said. "I'll be home soon. And then you'll wish I wasn't, since I'll be barging in on you all the time again."

"I miss you barging in on me," Douglas said.

This was more than I could take. I said, "I . . . I have to go."

Douglas said, "Wait a minute. Dad wants to say—"

But I had hung up. Suddenly, I knew. I couldn't talk to my dad. What was he going to do for me anyway? He couldn't get me out of this.

And even if he could, where was I going to go? I couldn't go home. Not with reporters and

Pepsi representatives following me everywhere I went. Douglas would completely lose whatever fragile grip he had on sanity at the moment.

"Jess?"

I started. I had almost forgotten Sean was in the room with me. I threw him a startled glance.

"What?" I said.

"Are you . . ." He raised his eyebrows. "You are."

"I'm what?"

"Crying," he said. Then his eyebrows met in a rush over the bridge of his freckled nose. He scowled at me. "What are you crying for?"

"Nothing," I said. I reached up and wiped my eyes with the back of my wrist. "I'm not crying."

"You're a damned liar," he said.

"Hey. Don't swear." I began hitting buttons on the phone again.

"Why not? You do it. Who are you calling now?"

"Someone who's going to get us the hell out of here," I said.

CHAPTER

19

It was a little after midnight when I heard it: the same motorcycle engine that I'd been straining my ears to hear on and off for the past couple of weeks. Only this time, it wasn't roaring down Lumley Lane, the way it had in my dreams.

No, it was roaring through the empty parking lots of Crane Military Base.

I leapt up off the bed where I'd been dozing and rushed to the window. I had to cup my fingers over my eyes in order to make out what was going on outside. In a circle of light thrown by one of the security lamps, I saw Rob. He was riding around, his face—hidden by the shield of his motorcycle helmet—turning right and left, trying to figure out which building I was in.

I pounded on the windowpane, and called his name.

Sean, curled up on the bed beside mine, sat bolt upright, as fully awake as he'd been soundly asleep just a second before.

"It's my dad," he said in a choked voice.

"No, it's not your dad," I said. "Stand back while I break this window. He can't hear me."

I knew I only had a few seconds before he thundered past the infirmary. I had to act fast. I grabbed the nearest thing I could find—a metal trash can—and heaved it at the window.

It did the trick. Glass went flying everywhere, including back over me, since a lot of the shards ricocheted off the metal grate. I could feel tiny slivers of glass in my hair and on my shirt.

I didn't care. I yelled, "Rob!"

He threw out a foot and skidded to a halt. A second later, his foot was up again, and he was tearing through the grass toward me. It was only then that I noticed that behind him were about a half dozen other bikers, big guys on Harleys.

"Hey," Rob said when he'd thrown down his kickstand and yanked his helmet off. He got off the bike and came toward me. "You okay?"

I nodded. I can't even tell you how good it felt to see him. It felt even better when he reached through the metal grate, wrapped his fingers around the front of my shirt, dragged me forward, and kissed me through the bars.

When he let go of me, it was so abrupt that I knew he hadn't meant to kiss me at all. It had just sort of happened.

"Sorry," he said—only not looking too sorry, if you know what I mean.

"That's okay," I said. Okay? It was the best kiss I'd ever had—even better than the first one. "Are you sure you don't mind doing this?"

"Piece of cake."

Then he went to work.

Sean, who'd observed the whole thing, said in a very indignant voice, "Who's *that?*"

"Rob Wilkins," I said.

I must have said it a little too happily, however, since Sean asked, suspiciously, "Is he your boyfriend?"

"No," I said. I wish.

Sean was appalled. "And you're just going to let him get away with kissing you like that?"

"He was just glad to see me," I said.

A particularly hairy face had replaced Rob's in the window. I recognized his friend from Chick's, the one with the Tet Offensive tattoo. He snaked a chain through the grate, then secured the other end to the back of one of the bikes.

"Stand back, y'all," he said to us. "This here's gonna make a helluva racket."

The face disappeared. Sean looked up at me.

"These are friends of yours?" he asked, in a disapproving voice.

"Sort of," I said. "Now stand back, will you? I don't want you to get hurt."

"Jesus," Sean muttered. "I am not a baby, all right?"

But when the biker gunned his engine, and the chain rattled, then went taut, Sean clapped his hands over his ears. "We are so busted," he moaned with his eyes closed.

I had a bad feeling Sean was right. The grate was making ominous groaning noises, but not budging so much as an inch. Meanwhile, the motorcycle engine was whining shrilly, its wheels kicking up a ton of dirt, throwing it and bits of grass back through the grate and into the room, already carpeted with glass.

For a minute, I didn't think it was going to work—or that, if it did, the noise would rouse Colonel Jenkins and his men, and they'd be after us in a heartbeat. The grate was simply too deeply embedded into the concrete window frame. I didn't want to say anything, of course—Rob was trying as best he could—but it looked like a hopeless cause. Especially when Sean dug his fingers into my arm and hissed, "Listen. . . ."

Then I heard it. Above the shriek of the motorcycle's engine, the sound of keys rattling outside the infirmary door.

That was it. We were busted.

What was worse, I'd probably gotten our rescuers busted, too. How long would Rob end up in jail because of me? What was the mandatory sentence for trying to break a psychic free from a military compound?

And then, with a sound like a thousand fingernails on a mile-wide chalkboard, the entire grate popped out from the sill and was dragged a few feet until the biker slammed on the brakes.

"Come on," Rob said, reaching for me over the crumbling sill.

I shoved Sean forward. "Him first," I said.

"No, you." Sean, in an effort to be chivalrous, tried to force me through the window first, but Rob got hold of him and hauled him through.

Which gave me a chance to grab my backpack—which Special Agent Smith had so graciously brought me—then vault over the window sill behind them, just as the dead bolt on the infirmary door slid back.

Outside, it was a humid spring night, silent and still . . . except for the thunder of motorcycle engines. I was astonished to see that, in addition to Rob's friends from Chick's, Greg Wylie and Hank Wendell, from the back row of detention, were also there, on majorly cherried-out hogs. I have to admit, I got a little teary-eyed at the sight of them: I had no idea I was so well-liked by my fellow juvenile delinquents.

Sean, however, was not so impressed.

"You have got to be kidding me," he said when he got his first good look at his rescuers.

"Look," I said to him as I pulled on the helmet Rob handed to me. "It's these guys or your dad. Take your pick."

"Boy," Sean said, shaking his head. "You drive a hard bargain."

Hank Wendell shoved a helmet at him. "Here

ya go, kid," he said. He made room on his seat for Sean's eighty-pound frame, then gave his engine a rev. "Hop on."

I don't know if Sean would have gotten on if, at that moment, an eardrum-piercing siren hadn't begun to wail.

One of the guys from Chick's—Frankie, who had a tattoo of a baby on his bicep—called out, "Here they come."

A second later, some military types came running up to the barless window, shouting for us to stop. Headlights lit up the parking lot.

"Hang on," Rob said as I swung onto the seat behind him and wrapped my arms around him.

"Halt," a man's voice bellowed. I glanced over my shoulder. There was a military jeep coming toward us, with a man standing up in the back, shouting through a megaphone. Behind him, I could see lights turning on in the buildings all across the base, and people running outside, trying to see what was going on.

"This is U.S. Government property," the guy with the megaphone declared. "You are trespassing. Turn off your engines now."

And then the night air was ripped apart by an earth-shaking explosion. I saw a ball of flame rise up in the air over by the airstrip. Everyone ducked—

Except Frankie and the guy with the Tet Offensive tattoo, who high-fived one another.

"Oh, yeah," Frankie said. "We still got it."

"What was *that?*" I shouted as Rob accelerated.

"A helicopter," Rob shouted back. "Just a little diversionary tactic, to confuse the enemy."

"You'll blow up a helicopter," I said, "but you won't go out with me?" I couldn't believe it. "What is wrong with you?"

I didn't have a chance to complain for long, however, because Rob sped up, and suddenly we were whipping through the darkened lots that made up Crane, heading for the front gates. The night sky behind us was now filled with an orange glow from the burning helicopter. New sirens, evidently from fire engines sent to put out the flames, sliced through the night, and searchlights arced against the low-lying clouds.

All this, I thought, to bust a small boy and a psychic out of an infirmary.

We hadn't managed to ditch the guy in the jeep. He was right behind us, still shouting through his megaphone for us to stop.

But Rob and his friends didn't stop. In fact, if anything, they sped up.

Okay, I'll admit it: I loved every minute of it. Finally, *finally*, I was going fast enough.

Then, a hundred yards from the front gates, Rob threw his foot out, and we skidded to a halt. His friends followed suit.

For a moment, we sat there, all six bikers, Rob, Sean, and me, engines roaring, staring straight ahead of us. The glow from the fire on the airstrip clearly lit the long road leading to the base's front gates. There were guards there, I remembered from when I'd gone by them on the bus to the mall. Guards with rifles. I had no idea how Rob and the others had gotten past these armed sentries to get onto the base, and I had no idea how we were going to get past them getting off of it. All I could think was, over and over in my head, "Oh, my God, they blew up a helicopter. *They blew up a helicopter.*"

But maybe it was a good thing they did. Because there was no one blocking our path. Everyone was heading toward the airstrip to help put out the fire.

Except for the guy in the jeep behind us.

"Turn off your engines and put your hands up," the guy said.

Instead, Rob lifted up his foot and we lurched forward, heading straight for the gates.

Which were down.

Then someone in a bathrobe came striding across the road, until he stood right in front of the gates. It was someone I recognized. He lifted a megaphone.

"Halt," Colonel Jenkins's voice boomed through the night, louder than the motorcycle engines, louder than the sirens. "You are under arrest. Turn off your engines now."

He was standing directly in front of the gates. His robe had fallen open, and I could see he had on pale blue pajamas.

Rob didn't slow down. If anything, he sped up.

"Turn off your engines," Colonel Jenkins commanded us. "Do you hear me? You are under arrest. Turn off your engines now."

The gatehouse guards appeared with their rifles. They didn't point them at us, but they stood their ground on either side of Colonel Jenkins.

No one turned off their engines. In fact, Greg and Hank let out whoops and started racing even faster toward the gates. I had no idea what they thought was going to happen when they reached the men standing there. It wasn't as if they were simply going to move out of the way and let us by. This was no ordinary game of chicken. Not when the other guy was holding a high-powered rifle.

I guess Colonel Jenkins figured out that nobody was going to turn off his engine, since suddenly he put down the megaphone and nodded to the two guards. I tightened my grip on Rob's waist, and ducked my head, afraid to look. They were only, I was sure, going to shoot into the air, to get our attention. Surely he couldn't mean to—

But then I never did find out whether or not they would have shot at us, because Rob gave the front of the bike a violent jerk. . . .

And then we were sailing off the base. Not through the front gates, but through a wide section of the chain-link fence that had been care-

232

fully peeled back to one side of the gates. This was how Rob and his friends had gotten past the sentries. All it had taken was a little determination, a pair of wire cutters, and some experience in breaking-and-entering.

Once we were off the base, the only light we had to see by were the bikes' headlights. That was all right, though. I looked behind me, and saw that the jeep was still behind us, intent on stopping us somehow.

But when I told Rob this, he only laughed. The road that led to Crane was little used, except for traffic to and from the base. All around it were cornfields, and beyond the fields, wooded hills. It was toward these hills Rob plunged, the other bikers following him, veering off the road and into the corn, which this early in spring was only ankle-high.

The jeep bounced along behind us, but it was rough going. The colonel must have gotten the message out, since that single jeep was soon joined by some SUVs. It didn't matter, though. We were darting between them like fireflies. No one could have kept up, except maybe the helicopter, and, well, that wasn't happening, for obvious reasons.

And then we lost them. I don't know if they simply gave up, or were called back to the base, or what. But suddenly, we were on our own.

We had done it.

Still, we stuck to back roads, just to be safe.

I'm pretty sure we weren't followed, though. We stopped several times to check, in sleepy little towns along the way, where there was one gas pump attached to a mom-and-pop general store, and where the noise from the hogs' engines caused bedroom lights to turn on, and dogs chained up in yards to bark.

But there was nothing behind us, nothing except long, empty stretches of road, winding like rivers beneath the heavy sky.

Marco.

Polo.

We were free.

20

Rob took us to his house.

Not Greg and Hank and those guys. I have no idea where they went. Well, actually, that's not true. I have a pretty good idea. I think they went to Chick's to pound back a few, and to celebrate their successful penetration of a government facility thought by many to be as impenetrable as Area 51.

Obviously those who thought that had never met anybody from the last row of detention at Ernest Pyle High School.

Sean and I, however, did not join in the festivities. We went to Rob's.

I was surprised when I saw Rob's house. It was a farmhouse, not big—though it was kind of hard to tell in the dark—but built at around the same time as my house on Lumley Lane.

Only, because it was on the wrong side of town, no one had come and put a plaque on it, declaring it a historic landmark.

Still, it was a sweet little house, with a porch out front and a barn out back. Rob lived there with just one other person, his mom. I don't know what happened to his dad, and I didn't want to ask.

We crept into the house very quietly, so as not to wake Mrs. Wilkins, who had recently been laid off from the local plastics factory. Rob showed me his room, and said I could sleep there. Then he gathered up a bunch of blankets and stuff, so that he and Sean could go sleep in the barn.

Sean didn't look particularly happy about this, but then, he was so tired, he could hardly keep his eyes open. He followed Rob around like a little zombie.

I was a little zombie-like myself. I couldn't quite believe what we had done. After I'd gotten undressed, I lay there in Rob's bed, thinking about it. We had destroyed government property. We had defied the orders of a colonel in the United States Army. We had blown up a helicopter.

We were going to be in big trouble in the morning.

Still, I was so sleepy, it was kind of hard to worry about that. Instead, all I could think about was how weird it was to be in a boy's room. At least, a boy who wasn't my brother. I'd been in

Skip's room—you know, over at Ruth's—plenty of times, but it was nothing like Rob's. In the first place, Rob didn't have any posters of Trans Ams up on his walls. Nor did he have any *Playboys* under the bed (I checked). Still, it was pretty alarmingly manly. I mean, he had plaid sheets and stuff.

But his pillow smelled like him, and that was nice, very comforting. I can't tell you what it smelled like, exactly, because that would be too hard to describe, but whatever it was, it was good.

I didn't have a whole lot of opportunity to lie there and enjoy it, though. Because almost as soon as I'd crawled into bed, I fell asleep.

And I didn't wake up again for a long, long time.

When I finally did wake up, it was about noon. It took me a minute to figure out where I was. Then I remembered:

I was in Rob's room, at his house.

And I was wanted by the FBI.

Not just the FBI, either, but the United States Army.

And I wouldn't have been surprised if the Secret Service, the Bureau of Alcohol, Tobacco and Firearms, and the Indiana State Highway Patrol wanted a piece of me, too.

And, interestingly, from the moment I woke up, I knew exactly what I was going to do about it.

It's not every day a girl wakes up knowing

she's wanted by the federal law enforcement agency of the most powerful country in the world. I thought about lying around, relishing it, but I was kind of worried about the impression that would make on Mrs. Wilkins, who could, if I played my cards right, be my mother-in-law someday. I didn't want her thinking I was this big slacker or something, so instead I got up, got dressed, and went downstairs.

Sean and Rob were already there, sitting at the kitchen table. In front of them was one heck of a lot of food. There was toast, and eggs, and bacon, and cereal, and a bowl of some white stuff I could not identify. The plate in front of Rob was empty—he was apparently through eating. But Sean was still putting it away. I don't think he'll ever be through eating. At least, not until after he's done going through puberty.

"Hi, Jess," he said when I walked into the kitchen. He sounded—and looked—a good deal perkier than he had during the last twenty-four hours I'd spent with him.

"Hi," I said.

A plump woman standing by the stove turned and smiled at me. She had a lot of red hair piled up on top of her head with a barrette, and didn't look a thing like her son Rob.

Until a shaft of sunlight, coming through the window above the sink, lit her face, and I saw that she had his eyes, so light blue they were the color of fog.

"You must be Jess," she said. "Pull up a chair and sit yourself down. How do you like your eggs?"

"Um," I said, awkwardly. "Scrambled is fine, thank you, ma'am."

"The eggs are fresh," Sean informed me as I sat down. "From the henhouse out back. I helped gather them."

"Your friend Sean's turning into a real farmhand," Mrs. Wilkins said. "We'll have him milking, next."

Sean giggled. I blinked at him. He'd actually *giggled*.

That was when I realized, with a shock, that I had never seen him happy before.

"There you go," Mrs. Wilkins said, setting a plate down in front of me. "Now you eat up. You look as if you could use a good hearty country breakfast."

I had never had fresh eggs before, and I was kind of worried they'd have some half-formed chicken fetus in them, but they didn't. They were really delicious, and when Mrs. Wilkins offered seconds, I gladly took them. I was pretty hungry, I discovered. I even ate some of the white stuff Mrs. Wilkins glopped onto my plate. It tasted like the Cream of Wheat my father always made us eat before school on really cold days when we were little.

But it wasn't Cream of Wheat. It was, Rob informed me with a little smile, grits.

If Ruth could only see me now, I thought.

After I'd helped Mrs. Wilkins wash the break-fast dishes, however, the fun was over. It was time to get down to business.

"I need to use a phone," I announced, and Mrs. Wilkins pointed to hers, hanging on the wall by the refrigerator.

"You can use that one," she said.

"No," I said. "For this particular call, I think I better use a pay phone."

Rob eyed me suspiciously. "What's up?" he wanted to know.

"Nothing," I said, innocently. "I just need to make a call. Is there a pay phone around here?"

Mrs. Wilkins looked thoughtful. "There's the one down the road, over by the IGA," she said.

"Perfect." To Rob, I said, "Can you drive me over there?"

He said he could, and we got up to go. . . .

And so did Sean.

"Nuh-uh," I said. "No way. You stay here."

Sean's jaw dropped. "What do you mean?"

"I mean there are probably cops crawling all over the place, looking for a sixteen-year-old girl in the company of a twelve-year-old boy. They'll be on to us in a second. You stay here until I get back."

"But that's not fair," Sean declared, his voice breaking.

I felt of bubble of impatience well up inside me. But instead of snapping at him, I grabbed

Sean by the arm and steered him out onto the back porch.

"Look," I said softly, so Rob and his mother wouldn't hear. "You said you wanted things back the way they were, didn't you? You and your mom, together, without your dad breathing down your necks?"

"Yes," Sean admitted, sullenly.

"Well, then let me do what I have to do. Which is something I have to do alone."

Sean was right about one thing: He was small for his age, but he really wasn't little. He wasn't even all that shorter than me. Which was how he was able to look me straight in the eye and say, accusingly, "That guy really is your boyfriend, isn't he?"

Where had *that* come from?

"No, Sean," I said. "I told you. We're just friends."

Sean brightened considerably. He said, "Okay," and went back inside.

Men. I swear I just don't get it.

Ten minutes later, I was standing in front of a little general store, the handset to an ancient pay phone pressed to my ear. I dialed carefully.

1-800-WHERE-R-YOU.

I asked for Rosemary, and when she came on, I said, "Hey, it's me. Jess."

"Jess?" Rosemary's voice dropped to a whisper. "Oh, my goodness. Is that really you?"

"Sure," I said. "Why?"

"Honey, I've been hearing all sorts of things on the news about you."

"Really?" I looked over at Rob. He was refilling the Indian's tank from the single pump in front of the store. We hadn't watched the news yet, and Mrs. Wilkins didn't get any newspapers, so I was eager to hear what they were saying about me. "What kind of stuff?"

"Well, about how last night, a group of Hell's Angels tore up Crane Military Base and kidnapped you and little Sean O'Hanahan off of it, of course."

"WHAT?" I yelled, so loud that Rob looked over at me. "That's not how it happened at all. Those guys were helping us to escape. Sean and I were being held against our will."

Rosemary said, "Well, that's not how that fellow—what's his name? Johnson, I think. That's not how Special Agent Johnson is telling it. There's a reward out for your safe return, you know."

This sounded interesting. "How much?"

"Twenty thousand dollars."

"Each?"

"No, that's just for you. Sean's father posted a hundred thousand dollar reward for his return."

I nearly hung up, I was so disgusted. "Twenty thousand dollars? Twenty piddling thousand dollars? That's all I'm worth to them? That loser. That's it. This is war."

Rosemary said, "I'd look out if I were you,

honey. There's APBs out all over the state of Indiana. Folks are looking for you."

"Oh, yeah, I bet. Listen, Rosemary," I said, "I want you to do me a favor."

Rosemary said, "Anything, hon."

"Give Agent Johnson a message for me. . . ."

Then I carefully stated the message I wanted Rosemary to relay.

"Okay," she said, when I was through. "You got it, honey. And, Jess?"

I had been about to hang up. "Yes?"

"You hang in there, honey. We're all behind you."

I hung up and told Rob about Special Agent Johnson's bogus kidnapping story—not to mention the crummy reward out for my capture. Rob was as mad as I was. Now that we knew there was an APB out on me, and that Hell's Angels were being blamed for what had happened at Crane, we agreed it wasn't a good idea for me to be seen tooling around on the back of Rob's bike. So we hurried back to his mom's place—but not until after I'd made one last call, this one from a pay phone outside a 7-Eleven on the turnpike.

My dad was where he usually is at lunchtime: Joe's. They get quite a noon crowd from the courthouse.

"Dad," I said. "It's me."

He nearly choked on his rigatoni, or whatever the special for the day was. My dad always taste-tests.

"Jess?" he cried. "Are you all right? Where are you?"

"Of course I'm all right," I said. "Now, anyway. Look, Dad, I need you to do me a favor."

"What are you talking about?" my dad demanded. *"Where are you?* Your mother and I have been worried sick. The folks up at Crane are saying—"

"Yeah, I know. That a bunch of Hell's Angels kidnapped Sean and me. But that's bogus, Dad. Those guys were rescuing us. Do you know what they were trying to do, Special Agents Johnson and Smith, that Colonel Jenkins guy? They were trying to make me into a dolphin."

My dad sounded like he was choking some more. "A *what?"*

Rob poked me hard in the back. I turned around to see what he wanted, and was horrified when an Indiana State Police patrol car eased into the parking lot of the convenience store.

"Look, Dad," I said, quickly ducking my head. "I gotta go. I just need you to do this one thing for me."

And I told him what the one thing was.

My dad wasn't too thrilled about it, to say the least.

He went, "Have you lost your mind? You listen here, Jessica—"

Nobody in my family ever calls me Jessica, except when they are really peeved at me.

"Just do it, please, Dad?" I begged. "It's really

important. I'll explain everything later. Right
now, I gotta go."

"Jessica, don't you—"

I hung up.

Rob had drifted away from me, distancing
himself and his bike from the teenage girl at the
pay phone, in case the cops made a connection.
But it didn't look as if they had. One of them
even nodded to me as he went into the store.

"Nice day," he said.

As soon as they were inside, Rob and I made a
mad dash for his bike. We were already at the
turnpike by the time they realized what they'd
missed and came hurtling out of the store. I
looked back over my shoulder and saw their
mouths moving as we tore away. A few seconds
later, they were in their car, sirens blaring.

I hung onto Rob more tightly. "We've got company," I said.

"Not for long," Rob said.

And suddenly we were off-road, brambles
and sticks tearing at our clothing as we plunged
down a ravine. Seconds later, we were splashing
through a creekbed, the Indian's front wheel
kicking up thick streams of water on either side
of it. Above us, I could see the patrol car following along as best it could. . . .

But then the creek made a bend away from the
road, and soon the cop car disappeared from
view. Soon I couldn't even hear its siren anymore.

When Rob finally pulled out of the creekbed and back up the ravine, I was wet from the waist down, and the Indian's engine was sounding kind of funny.

But we were safe.

"You all right?" Rob asked me, as I was wringing out the bottom of my T-shirt.

"Peachy," I said. "Listen, I'm sorry."

He was squatting beside the bike's front wheel, pulling out sticks and weeds that had wound into the spokes during our flight down the ravine. "Sorry about what?"

"Getting you involved in all this. I mean, I know you're on probation and all. The last thing you need is to be harboring a couple of fugitives. What if you get caught? They'll probably lock you up and throw away the key. I mean, depending on whatever it is you did to get on probation in the first place."

Rob had moved to the back tire. He squinted up at me, the afternoon sun bringing out the strong planes in his face. "Are you through?"

"Through what?"

"Through trying to trick me into telling you what I'm on probation for."

I put my hands on my hips. "I am not trying to trick you into doing anything. I am merely trying to let you know that I am aware of the great personal sacrifice you are making in helping Sean and me, and I appreciate it."

"You do, huh?"

He straightened. One of the sticks he'd wrenched from the wheel had flicked drops of water up onto his face, so he pulled the bottom of his T-shirt out from the waistband of his jeans and scrubbed at them. When he did this, I happened to get a look at his bare stomach. The sight of it, all tightly muscled, with a thin band of dark hair down the center, did something to me.

I don't know what came over me, but suddenly, I was on my tiptoes, planting this big wet one on him. I have seriously never done anything like that before, but I just couldn't help it.

Rob seemed a little surprised at first, but he got over it pretty quickly. He kissed me back for a while, and it was just like in *Snow White* when all the woodland animals come out and start singing, and Prince Charming puts her up on the horse. For about a minute it was like that. I mean, my heart was singing just like one of those damned squirrels.

Then Rob reached up and started untangling my arms from around his neck.

"Jesus, Mastriani," he said. "What are you trying to do?"

That broke the spell pretty quick, let me tell you. I mean, Prince Charming would never have said something like that. I would have been mad if I hadn't heard the way his voice shook.

"Nothing," I said, very innocently.

"Well, you better cut it out," he said. "We've got a lot do. There's no time for any distractions."

I mentioned that I happened to like that particular distraction.

Rob went, "I'm in enough trouble right now without you adding to it, thanks." He picked up one of the helmets and shoved it down over my head. "And don't even think about trying something like that in front of the kid."

"What kid? What are you talking about?"

"The kid. O'Hanahan. What are you, blind, Mastriani? He's got it bad for you."

I tilted the helmet back and squinted at him. "*Sean? For me?*"

But all of a sudden, all the questions he'd been asking about Rob made sense.

I let the helmet drop back over my face. "Oh, God," I said.

"You got that right. He thinks you are one dope girl, Mastriani."

"He said that? He sure doesn't act like he thinks that. He really said I was dope?"

"Well." Rob swung onto his seat and gave the accelerator a kick. "I might be allowing my own feelings to cloud the matter a little."

Suddenly, all the birds and squirrels were singing again.

"You think I'm dope?" I asked dreamily.

He reached out and flicked my helmet. It made a hollow echoing sound inside my head, and brought me right out of my reverie.

"Get on the bike, Mastriani," he said.

When we got back to Rob's, Sean and Mrs.

Wilkins were shelling peas and watching Ricki Lake.

"Jess," he said when I walked in. "Where have you been? You totally missed this guy. He weighed four hundred pounds and got stuck in a bathtub for over forty-eight hours! If you'd been here sooner, you could have seen it."

It was love. I could totally tell.

This was going to be harder than I thought.

CHAPTER

21

The marching band was playing "Louie, Louie."

And not very well, I might add.

Still, Sean and I stayed where we were, sitting on the same metal bleachers that a week or so before I'd been electrocuted under. Before us stretched the football field, a sea of luscious green, upon which marched a herd of musicians playing for all they were worth, even though it was only an after-school rehearsal, and not the real thing. Football season was long over, but graduation was coming up, and the band would play at commencement.

Just not "Louie, Louie," hopefully.

"I don't get it," Sean said. "What are we doing here?"

"Wait," I said. "You'll see."

We weren't the only spectators in the stands. There was one other guy, way, way up at the top behind us.

But that was it. I wasn't sure if Rosemary had failed to get my message to Special Agent Johnson, or if he'd chosen merely to ignore it. If he was ignoring it, he was making a grave mistake. The guy up in the stands would make sure of that.

"Why won't you tell me what we're doing here?" Sean demanded. "I think I have a right to know."

"Drink your Big Gulp," I said. It was hot out. The late afternoon sun was beating down on us. I didn't have any sunglasses or a hat, and I was dying. I was worried Sean might be getting dehydrated.

"I don't want my stupid Big Gulp," Sean said. "I want to know what we're doing here."

"Watch the band," I said.

"The band sucks." Sean glared at me. Most of the brown had washed out of his hair when he'd showered at Rob's. It was a good thing he'd let Mrs. Wilkins give him a trim, or the bits of red sticking out of the back of his baseball cap would have been a dead giveaway.

"What are we doing here?" he wanted to know. "And why is Jed waiting down there?"

Jed turned out to be the name of Rob's friend from Chick's, the one who'd been in Vietnam. He was sitting in a pickup not far from us, parked over behind the bleachers . . . almost exactly, in fact, in the place where I'd been struck by lightning. It was shady where he was. He probably didn't feel sweat prickling all along his hairline, the way I did.

"Just cool it, will you?" I said to Sean.

"No, I will not cool it, Jess. I think I deserve an explanation. Are you going to give me one or not?"

Something caught the sunlight and winked at me. I shaded my eyes and looked toward the parking lot. A black, nondescript sedan had pulled up.

"Louie, Louie" ended. The band started a spirited rendition of Robert Palmer's "Simply Irresistible."

"How come you aren't in Band?" Sean wanted to know. "I mean, you play the flute and all. How come you're not in Band?"

The car pulled up to a halt. The two front doors opened, and a man and a woman got out. Then a back door opened, and another woman got out.

"Because I'm in Orchestra," I said.

"What's the difference?"

"In Orchestra, you play sitting down."

"That's it?"

The man and woman from the front seats moved until they stood on either side of the woman who'd gotten out of the backseat. Then they started walking across the football field, toward Sean and me.

"The Orchestra doesn't play at school events," I said. "Like games and stuff."

Sean digested this. "Where do you play, then?"

"Nowhere. We just have concerts every once in a while."

"What's the fun in that?" Sean wanted to know.

"I don't know," I said. "I couldn't be in Band, anyway. I'm always in detention when they practice."

"Why are you always in detention?"

"Because I do a lot of bad stuff."

The trio moving across the football field had gotten close enough for me to see that they were who I was expecting. Rosemary had gotten my message across, all right.

"What kind of bad stuff?" Sean wanted to know.

"I hit people." I reached into the back pocket of my jeans.

"So?" Sean looked indignant. "They probably deserve it."

"I like to think so," I said. "Look, Sean, I want you to take this. It's for you and your mom. Jed's going to drive you to the airport. I want you guys to get on a plane—any plane—and take off. Don't make any calls. Don't stop for anything. You can buy whatever you need when you get to where you're going. Understand?"

Sean looked down at the envelope I was holding out to him. Then he looked up at me.

"What are you talking about?" he asked.

"Your mom," I said. "You two are going to have to start over, somewhere else. Somewhere far away, I hope, where your dad won't be able to find you. This will help you get started." I tucked the envelope into the front pocket of his jean jacket.

Sean shook his head. His face was tight with emotion. Conflicting emotions, from the looks of it. "Jess. My mom's in jail. Remember?"

"Not anymore," I said. And then I pointed.

The three people approaching us were close enough now that I could make out their features. Special Agent Johnson, Special Agent Smith, and between them, a slim woman in blue jeans. Sean's mother.

He looked. I heard him inhale sharply.

Then he turned to stare at me. The conflicting emotions on his face weren't so hard to make out now. There was joy, mingled with concern.

"What did you do?" he whispered. "Jess. What did you do?"

"I cut a little deal," I said. "Don't worry about it. Just go get her, and then go and get into the pickup with Jed. He'll take you to the airport."

Even as I sat there, looking down at him, his blue eyes filled with tears.

He said, "You did it. You said you'd do it. And you did it."

"Of course," I said, as if I was shocked he could ever have thought otherwise.

And then his mother saw him and broke away from her escorts. She called Sean's name as she ran toward him.

Sean leapt up and began hurtling down the bleachers. I stayed where I was. Sean had left his Big Gulp behind. I reached over and took a sip. My throat really hurt, for some reason.

They met at the bottom of the bleachers. Sean flung himself into Mrs. O'Hanahan's arms. She swung him around. Special Agents Johnson and Smith stopped where they were, and looked up at me. I waved. They didn't wave back.

Then Sean said something to his mother, and she nodded. The next thing I knew, he was running back toward me.

This had not been part of the plan. I stood up, alarmed.

"Jess," Sean cried, panting, as he hurried to my side.

"What are you doing here?" I asked, more sharply than I should have. "Go back to her. I told you to take her to the pickup. Hurry up, you don't have much time—"

"I just . . ." He was breathing so hard, he had to fight to get the words out. "I wanted . . . to say . . . thank you."

And then he threw his arms around my neck.

I didn't know what to do at first. I was pretty surprised. I looked down at the football field. The agents were still standing there, looking up at me. The band launched into a new song. The Beatles' "Hard Day's Night."

I hugged Sean back. My throat hurt even worse, and my eyes stung.

Allergies, I thought.

"When am I going to see you again?" Sean wanted to know.

"You're not," I said. "Not unless things change. You know, with your dad. Don't you dare call me otherwise. They'll probably be tapping my phone forever."

"What about—" He broke away from me and looked at me. His eyes were streaming as badly as mine. "What about when I'm thirty? You'll be thirty-three. It wouldn't be so weird, would it, a thirty-year-old going out with a thirty-three-year-old?"

"No," I said, giving the brim of his baseball cap a tap. "Except when you're thirty, I'll be thirty-four. You're only twelve, remember?"

"Just for nine more months."

I kissed him on his wet cheek. "Get out of here," I said.

He managed a watery smile. Then he turned around and ran away again. This time when he got to his mother's side, he took her hand and started dragging her around the side of the bleachers, to where Jed waited.

Only after I heard the engine start up and the truck pull away did I make my own way down the bleachers—making sure I'd wiped my eyes first.

Special Agent Johnson looked hot in his suit and tie. Special Agent Smith seemed a bit cooler in her skirt and silk blouse, but not by much. Standing there together like that, in their sunglasses and nice clothes, they made kind of a cute couple.

"Hey," I said as I sauntered up to them. "Do you two have an *X-Files* thing going?"

Special Agent Smith looked down at me. She had on her pearl earrings today. "I beg your pardon?" she said.

"You know. One of those Scully/Mulder things. Do you burn for one another with a passion that must be denied?"

Special Agent Johnson looked at Special Agent Smith. "I'm married, Jessica," he said.

"Yes," Special Agent Smith said. "And I'm seeing someone."

"Oh." I felt strangely let-down. "Too bad."

"Well." Special Agent Johnson peered at me expectantly. "Do you have the list?"

I nodded. "Yeah, I've got it. Do I have your word that nobody is going to try to stop Sean and his mother at the airport?"

Special Agent Smith looked offended. "Of course."

"Or when they get to where they're going?"

Special Agent Johnson said, impatiently, "Jessica, nobody cares about the child and his mother. It's the list we want."

I gave him a very mean look. "*I* care about

them," I said. "And I'm sure Mr. O'Hanahan isn't going to be too happy when he finds out."

"Mr. O'Hanahan," Special Agent Smith said, "is our problem, not yours. The list, please, Jessica."

"And nobody's going to press any charges?" I asked, just to make sure. "About the whole Crane thing? Against me or anybody else?"

"No," Agent Johnson said.

"Even about the helicopter?"

"Even," Agent Johnson said, and I could tell his teeth were gritted, "about the helicopter."

"The list, Jessica," Special Agent Smith said, again. And this time she held out her hand.

I sighed, and dug into my back pocket. The band launched into a particularly corny version of "We're the Kids in America."

"Here you go," I said, and surrendered a crumpled sheet of paper into the agent's hand.

Special Agent Smith unfolded the paper and scanned it. She looked down at me disapprovingly.

"There are only four addresses on here," she said, handing the paper to her partner.

I stuck out my chin. "What do you think?" I demanded. "I'm not a machine. I'm just a kid. There'll be more where those came from, don't worry."

Special Agent Johnson folded the sheet of paper back up and stuck it in his pocket.

"All right," he said. "What now?"

"You two go back to your car and drive away," I said.

"And you?" Special Agent Smith asked.

"I'll be in touch," I said.

Special Agent Smith chewed her lower lip. Then she said, as if she couldn't help it, "You know, it didn't have to be this way, Jess."

I looked at her. I couldn't read her eyes behind her dark glasses.

"No, it didn't," I said. "Did it?"

She and Special Agent Smith exchanged glances. Then they turned around and started the long walk back to their car.

"You know," I called after them. "No offense to Mrs. Johnson and all, but you two really do make a cute couple."

They just kept walking.

"That was pushing it, don't you think?" Rob asked, as he crawled out from underneath the bleachers, where he'd been stationed the whole time.

"I'm just messing with them," I said.

Rob brushed dust off his jeans. "Yeah," he said. "I noticed. You do that a lot. So are you going to tell me what was in that envelope?"

"The one I gave to Sean?"

"The one you gave to Sean after you made me pick it up from your dad. Who, by the way, hates me."

I noticed there was some dust on his black T-shirt, too. This gave me a good excuse to touch his chest as I brushed it off.

"My dad can't possibly hate you," I said. "He doesn't even know you."

"He sure looked like he hated me."

"That's just because of what was in the envelope."

"Which was?"

"The ten grand I got as a reward for finding Olivia Marie D'Amato."

Rob whistled, low and long. "You gave that kid ten grand? In *cash?*"

"Well, him and his mother. I mean, they have to have something to live on while she finds a new job and everything."

Rob shook his head. "You are one piece of work, Mastriani," he said. "Okay. So that's what was in the envelope. What was on that sheet of paper you handed to the Feds?"

"Oh," I said. "Just the addresses of some of America's most wanted. I said I'd give them up in return for the charges against Mrs. O'Hanahan being dropped."

"Really?" Rob seemed surprised. "I thought you didn't want to get involved in all of that."

"I don't. That's why I only gave them the addresses of the guys from that book of theirs who happen to be deceased."

A slow smile crept over Rob's face. "Wait a minute. You—"

"I didn't lie or anything. They really will find those guys where I said they'd be. Well, what's left of them, anyway." I wrinkled my nose. "I have a feeling it's not going to be pretty."

Rob shook his head again. Then he reached

out and put an arm around my shoulders. "Jess," he said, "you make me proud to have sat by you in detention. Did you know that?"

I smiled sunnily at him. "Thanks," I said. Then I looked up at the lone figure still sitting in the bleachers, high above our heads.

"Come on," I said, taking Rob's hand. "There's still one more thing I have to do."

Rob looked up at the guy in the stands. "Who's that?" he asked.

"Who, him? Oh, that's the guy who's going to set me free."

CHAPTER

22

I probably don't have to tell you the rest. I mean, I'm sure you've already read about it, or seen it on the news, or something.

But just in case, here goes:

The story came out the next day. It was on the front page of the *Indianapolis Star*. Rob and I had to pick up a copy from the Denny's down the highway from his mother's house. Then we ordered a Grand Slam breakfast and ate while we read.

Lightning Girl Claims to Have Run Out of Juice, the headline ran. Then there was a story all about me, and how I had tragically lost my power to find people.

Just like that, I'd told the reporter that day in the bleachers. He'd been so excited about his scoop, he'd eaten up every word, hardly even asking a single question.

I just woke up, I said, and it was gone. I'm a normal girl again.

End of story.

Well, it wasn't quite the end, of course. Because the reporter asked me a lot of searching questions about what had happened at Crane. I assured him that the whole thing had been a misunderstanding, that the alleged Hell's Angels were actually my friends, and that after my special power had disappeared, I had gotten homesick, so I'd called them, and they'd come to pick me up. I had no idea why that helicopter had blown up. But it was a good thing nobody had been in it at the time, wasn't it?

And the O'Hanahan boy? the reporter had asked. What had happened to him?

I said I had no idea. I'd heard, just as the reporter had, about Sean's mother being mistakenly released from jail. Yes, I could imagine Mr. O'Hanahan had been plenty mad about that.

But wherever Sean and his mother were, I told the reporter, I wished them well.

The reporter didn't look as if he believed this, but he was so excited to be breaking the story, he didn't care. The only conditions I gave him were that he didn't mention Rob's or his mother's names.

The reporter didn't let me down. He got the story exactly the way I wanted it, and even put in some quotes from the people at Crane, whom he'd called after interviewing me. Dr. Shifton he reported as being relieved I was all right. It wasn't at all unusual, she said, that my mysterious power had vanished just as suddenly as it had appeared. It often worked that way with lightning-strike victims.

Colonel Jenkins wasn't quoted anywhere in the article, but Special Agent Johnson was, and he said some nice things about me, and about how I had used my special gift to help others, which was admirable, and how he hoped that if my powers ever came back I'd call him.

Ha. As if.

Finally, the reporter interviewed my parents, who sounded bewildered, but happy to know I was all right. "We just can't wait," my mother said, "to have our baby back home, and everything back to normal again."

You'd be surprised how fast everything did go back to normal. The *Star* broke the story, and by later that night, every newscast mentioned something about the "lightning girl" and how she'd lost her special missing-child finding skill.

By the next day, the story had moved to the "Lifestyle" section of most papers, in the form of reflections on the part of columnists on the hidden powers of the brain and how all of us have the potential to be a "lightning girl," if we just pay attention to what our subconscious is trying to tell us.

Yeah, right.

By the day after that, the reporters in front of

my house had packed up and left. It was safe. I could go home.

And so I did.

Well, that's pretty much my "statement." My hand is really tired. I hope this "statement" is long enough. But if it isn't, I don't really care. I'm hungry, and I want dinner. Mom promised to make manicotti, which is Douglas's favorite, and mine, too. Also, I have to practice. Monday after school I have to defend my chair in Orchestra from Karen Sue Hanky.

My one regret about all this is that there are only a few weeks of school left, and since detention is the only place I'll ever see Rob, this is a problem. In spite of everything, I still haven't been able to convince him that going out with me would not be a crime.

I haven't given up, though. I can be very persuasive when I put my mind to it.

Now that I've read back over this statement, I'm not so sure anymore that all of this is Ruth's fault. The fact that I got struck by lightning, maybe. On the other hand, Ruth never would have wanted to walk home that day if it hadn't been for Jeff telling her she was as fat as Elvis. So maybe it's all Jeff's fault.

Yeah, I think it is. Jeff Day's fault, I mean.

Signed:

Jessica Antonia Mastriani

INTERNAL MEMORANDUM
WARNING:
HIGHLY CLASSIFIED MATERIAL
ONLY THOSE WITH LEVEL ALPHA CLEARANCE
MAY VIEW THIS DOCUMENT.

To: Cyrus Krantz
    Special Operations Division
Fr: Special Agent Allan Johnson
Re: Special Subject Jessica Mastriani

What you have just read is the signed personal statement of Special Subject Jessica Mastriani. According to Miss Mastriani, her psychic powers ceased functioning on or about April 27—coincidentally, the morning after her escape from Crane. It is the opinion of this operative, however, that Miss Mastriani maintains full possession of her extraordinary powers, as illustrated by the following.

In the six weeks following Miss Mastriani's return to private life, 1-800-WHERE-R-YOU has received approximately one anonymous tip per week that has led to the successful recovery of a missing child. All of these calls have been received by Mrs. Rosemary Atkinson, a receptionist with whom Miss Mastriani seems to have developed a relationship during her initial contact with the NOMC. Mrs. Atkinson denies that the anonymous caller is Miss Mastriani. However, all of the calls have been made from pay phones within Indiana state lines.

Additionally, the day after the completion of the attached statement, Miss Mastriani received at her home a single postcard, bearing on it a photo of several dolphins. The postmark indicated that the card was mailed from Los Angeles. When questioned by her mother as to the identity of the anonymous sender, Miss Mastriani replied, within hearing of our positioned operative, "It's from Sean. He just wants to let me know where he is. Which is stupid, because I'll always know where he is."

It is the feeling of this operative that Miss Mastriani continues to maintain full possession of her psychic ability. I am hereby requesting authorization to continue monitoring Miss Mastriani, including tapping of her home telephone as well as the telephones of her father's restaurants. Should Miss Mastriani be proved to have been less than truthful in her submitted statement, this operative suggests utilizing her relationship with the mentally disturbed sibling as a form of persuasion in enlisting her aid on our behalf.

I look forward to your positive response to this request.

BOOK TWO
CODE NAME CASSANDRA

Many thanks to Beth Ader, Jennifer Brown,
John Henry Dreyfuss, Laura Langlie,
Ingrid van der Leeden,
David Walton, and especially Benjamin Egnatz

CHAPTER

1

I don't know why I'm doing this.

Writing this down, I mean. It's not like anybody is making me.

Not this time.

But it seems to me like *somebody* ought to be keeping track of this stuff. Somebody who actually knows what *really* happened.

And it isn't as if you can trust the Feds to do it. Oh, they'll write it down, of course. But they won't get it right.

I just think there needs to be one truthful account. A *factual* one.

So I'm writing it. It isn't a big deal, really. I just hope that someday somebody will actually read it, so I won't feel like it was a complete waste of time . . . not like the majority of my endeavors.

Take, for example, the sign. Now that's a classic example of a wasted endeavor if I ever saw one.

And if you think about it, that's really how it all started. With the sign.

Welcome to Camp Wawasee
Where Gifted Kids Come to Make Sweet Music
Together

That's what the sign said.

I know you don't believe me. I know you don't believe that in the history of time, there was ever a sign that said anything that stupid.

But I swear it's true. And I should know: I'm the one who'd painted it.

Don't get me wrong. I didn't *want* to. I mean, they totally made me do it. They handed me the paint and this giant white cotton sheet and told me what to write on it and everything. Their last sign, see, had met with this very tragic accident, in which someone had folded it up and stuck it in the pool house and some noxious chemical had dripped on it and eaten through the fabric.

So they made me make a new one.

It wasn't just that the sign was stupid. I mean, if you got a look at the kids standing under the sign, you'd have known right away that it was also probably libelous. Because if those kids were gifted, I was Jean-Pierre Rampal.

He was this famous flutist, by the way, for those of you who don't know.

Anyway, I had seriously never seen a whinier bunch of kids in my life. And I've been around a lot of kids, thanks to the nature of my, you know, unique gift and all.

But these kids . . . Let me tell you, they were something else. Every last one of them was all, "But I don't *want* to go to music camp," or "Why can't I just stay home with you?" Like the fact that they were going to get to spend six weeks away from their parents was some kind of hardship. If you had told me, at the age of ten or whatever, that I could go somewhere and be away from my parents for six weeks, I'd have been like, "Sign me up, dude."

But not these kids. I suppose on account of the fact they were gifted and all. Maybe gifted kids actually like their parents or something. I wouldn't know.

Still, I tried to believe in the sign. Especially, you know, since I'd made it. Well, with Ruth's help. If you can call Ruth's contribution help, which I wasn't so sure I would. It had consisted mostly of Ruth telling me that my lettering was crooked. Looking at the sign now, I saw that she was right. The letters *were* crooked. But I doubted anyone but me and Ruth had noticed.

"Aren't they cute?"

That was Ruth, sidling up beside me. She was gazing out at the children, looking all dewy-eyed. Apparently she hadn't noticed all the screaming and sniffling and cries of "But I wanna go *home*."

But I sure had. They were kind of making *me* want to go home, too.

Only, if I went home, I'd be stuck working the steam table. That's how you spend your summers when your parents own a restaurant: working the steam table. There was even less of a chance of escape for me, since my parents own *three* restaurants. It was the least fancy one, Joe Junior's, that offered the buffet of various pasta dishes, all of which were kept warm courtesy of a steam table.

And guess which kid traditionally gets put in charge of the steam table? That's right. The youngest one. Me. It was either that, or the salad bar. And believe me, I had had my fill of deep-sea diving into the ranch dressing tub for stray cherry tomatoes.

But the steam table wasn't the only thing back home that I was trying to avoid.

"I hope I get that one," Ruth gushed, pointing to a cherubic-faced blonde who was standing beneath my sign, clutching a pint-sized cello. "Isn't she sweet?"

"Yeah," I admitted grudgingly. "But what if you get *that* one?"

I pointed to a little boy who was screaming so loudly at the idea of being separated from Mommy and Daddy for a month and a half, he had gone into a full-blown asthma attack. Both of his frenzied-looking parents were thrusting inhalers at him.

"Aw," Ruth said tolerantly. "I was just like that the first year I came here as a camper. He'll be fine by suppertime."

I supposed I had to take her word for it. Ruth's parents had started shipping her off to Camp

Wawasee at the ripe old age of seven, so she had about nine years of experience to draw upon. I, on the other hand, had always spent my summers back at the steam table, bored out of my skull because my best (and pretty much only) friend was gone. In spite of the fact that my parents own three restaurants, in which my friends and I can dine any time we want, I have never exactly been Miss Popularity. This might be on account of the fact that, as my guidance counselor puts it, I have *issues.*

Which was why I wasn't so sure Ruth's idea—of me putting in an application to be a camp counselor—was such a good one. For one thing, despite my special talent, child care is not really my forte. And for another, well, like I said: I have these issues.

But apparently no one noticed my antisocial tendencies during the interview, since I got the job.

"Let me just make sure I got this right," I said to Ruth, as she continued to look longingly at the cellist. "It's Camp Wawasee, Box 40, State Road One, Wawasee, Indiana?"

Ruth wrenched her gaze from Goldilocks.

"For the last time," she said, with some exasperation. "Yes."

"Well," I said with a shrug, "I just wanted to make sure I told Rosemary the right address. It's been over a week since I last got something from her, and I'm a little worried."

"God." Ruth no longer spoke with just *some* exasperation. She was fed up. You could tell. "Would you stop?"

I stuck my chin out. "Stop what?"

"Stop *working*," she said. "You're allowed a vacation once in a while. Jeez."

I went, "I don't know what you're talking about," even though, of course, I did, and Ruth knew it.

"Look," she said. "Everything is going to be all right, okay? I know what to do."

I gave up trying to pretend that I didn't know what she was talking about, and said, "I just don't want to screw it up. Our system, I mean."

Ruth rolled her eyes. "Hello," she said. "What's to screw up? Rosemary sends the stuff to me, I pass it on to you. What, you think after three months of this, I don't have it down yet?"

Alarmed at the volume with which she'd announced this, I grabbed her arm.

"For God's sake, Ruth," I hissed. "Zip it, will you? Just because we're in the middle of nowhere doesn't mean there might not be you-know-whats around. Any one of those doting parents over there could be an F-E-D."

Ruth rolled her eyes again. "Please," was all she said.

She was right, of course: I was overreacting. But there was no denying the fact that Ruth had gotten seriously slack in the discretion department. Basically, since the whole camp thing had been decided, she'd been completely unable to keep anything else in her head. For weeks before we'd left for counselor training, Ruth had kept bubbling, "Aren't you *excited*? Aren't you *psyched*?" Like we were going to Paris with the French Club or something, and not to upstate Indiana to slave away as camp counselors for six weeks. I'd kept wanting to say to her, "Dude, it may not be the steam table, but it's still a *job*."

I mean, it's not like I don't also have my unofficial part-time career to contend with as well.

The problem was, Ruth's enthusiasm was totally catching. Like, she kept talking about how we were going to spend all of our afternoons on inner tubes, floating along the still waters of Lake Wawasee, getting tan. Or how some of the boy counselors were totally hot, and were going to fall madly in love with us, and offer us rides to the Michigan dunes in their convertibles.

Seriously.

And after a while, I don't know, I just sort of started to believe her.

And that was my second mistake. I mean, after putting in the application in the first place.

Ruth's descriptions of the campers, for instance. Child prodigies, she'd called them. And it's true, you have to audition even to be considered for a place at the camp, both as camper as well as counselor. Ruth's stories about the kids she'd looked after the year before—a cabin full of sensitive, creative, superintelligent little girls, who still wrote her sweet funny letters, a year later—totally impressed me. I don't have any sisters, so when Ruth started in about midnight gossip-and-hair-braiding sessions, I don't know, I began to think, Yeah, okay. This might be for me.

Seriously, I went from, "It's just a job," to "*I* want to escort adorable little girl violinists and flutists to the Polar Bear swim every morning. *I* want to make sure none of them are budding anorexics by monitoring their caloric intake at meals. *I* want to help them decide what to wear the night of the All-Camp Orchestral Concert."

It was like I went mental or something. I couldn't wait to take mastery over the cabin I'd been assigned—Frangipani Cottage. Eight little beds, plus mine in a separate room, in a tiny house (thankfully air-conditioned) that contained a mini-kitchen for snacks and its own private, multiple-showerhead and toilet-stalled bathroom. I had even gone so far as to hang up a sign (with crooked lettering) across the sweet little mosquito-netted front porch that said, *Welcome, Frangipanis!*

Look, I know how it sounds. But Ruth had me whipped up into some kind of camp-counselor frenzy.

But standing there, actually seeing the kids for whom I was going to be responsible for most of July and half of August, I began to have second thoughts. I mean, nobody wants to hang out next to a steam table when it's ninety degrees outside, but at least a steam table can't stick its finger up its nose, then try to hold your hand with that same finger.

It was as I was watching all these kids saying good-bye to their parents, wondering whether I'd just made the worst mistake of my life, that Pamela, the camp's assistant director, came up to me and, clipboard in hand, whispered in my ear, "Can we talk?"

I'll admit it: my heart sped up a little. I figured I was busted. . . .

Because, of course, there was a little something I'd left off of my application for the job. I just hadn't thought it would catch up with me this quickly.

"Uh, sure," I said. Pamela was, after all, my boss. What was I going to say, "Get lost"?

We moved away from Ruth, who was still gazing rapturously at what I would have to say were some very unhappy campers. I swear, I don't think Ruth even noticed how many of those kids were crying.

Then I noticed Ruth wasn't looking at the kids at all. She was staring at one of the counselors, a particularly hot-looking violinist named Todd, who was standing there chatting up some parents. That's when I realized that, in Ruth's head, she wasn't there underneath my crappy sign, watching a bunch of kids shriek, "Mommy, please don't leave me." Not at all. In Ruth's mind, she was in Todd's convertible, heading out toward the dunes for fried perch, a little tartar sauce, and some above-the-waist petting.

Lucky Ruth. She got Todd—at least in her mind's eye—while I was stuck with Pamela, a no-nonsense, khaki-clad woman in her late thirties who was probably about to fire me . . . which would explain why she'd draped an arm sympathetically across my shoulders as we strolled.

Poor Pamela. She was obviously not aware that one of my issues—at least according to Mr. Goodhart, my guidance counselor back at Ernest Pyle High School—is a total aversion to being touched. According to Mr. G, I am extremely sensitive about my personal space, and dislike having it invaded.

Which isn't technically true. There's one person I wouldn't mind invading my personal space.

The problem is, he doesn't do it anywhere near enough.

"Jess," Pamela was saying, as we walked along. She didn't seem to notice the fact that I'd broken into a sweat, on account of my nervousness that I was about to be fired—not to mention trying to restrain myself from flinging her arm off me. "I'm afraid there's been a bit of a change in plans."

A change in plans? That didn't sound, to me, like a prelude to dismissal. Was it possible my secret—which wasn't, actually, much of a secret anymore, but which had apparently not yet reached Pamela's ears—was still safe?

"It seems," Pamela went on, "that one of your fellow counselors, Andrew Shippinger, has come down with mono."

Relieved as I was that our conversation was definitely not going in the "I'm afraid we're going to have to let you go" direction, I have to admit I didn't know what I was supposed to do with this piece of information. The thing about Andrew, I mean. I knew Andrew from my week of counselor training. He played the French horn and was obsessed with

Tomb Raider. He was one of the counselors Ruth and I had rated Undo-able. We had three lists, see: the Undo-ables, like Andrew. The Do-ables, who were, you know, all right, but nothing to get your pulse going.

And then there were the Hotties. The Hotties were the guys like Todd who, like Joshua Bell, the famous violinist, had it all: looks, money, talent . . . and most important of all, a car.

Which was kind of weird. I mean, a car being a prerequisite for hotness. Especially since Ruth has her own car, and it's even a convertible.

But according to Ruth—who was the one who'd made up all these rules in the first place—going to the dunes in your own car simply doesn't count.

The thing is, the chances of a Hottie glancing twice in the direction of either Ruth or me are like nil. Not that we're dogs or anything, but we're no Gwyneth Paltrows.

And that whole Do-able/Undo-able thing? Yeah, need I point out that neither Ruth nor I have ever "done" anybody in our lives?

And I have to say, the way things are going, I don't think it's going to happen, either.

But *Andrew Shippinger?* So not Do-able. Why was Pamela talking to me about him? Did she think *I'd* given him mono? Why do I always get blamed for everything? The only way my lips would ever touch Andrew Shippinger's would be if he sucked down too much water in the pool and needed CPR.

And when was Pamela going to move her arm?

"Which leaves us," she went on, "with a shortage of male counselors. I have plenty of females on my waiting list, but absolutely no more men."

Again, I wondered what this had to do with me. It's true I have two brothers, but if Pamela was thinking either of them would make a good camp counselor, she'd been getting a little too much fresh air.

"So I was wondering," Pamela continued, "if it would upset you very much if we assigned you to the cottage Andrew was supposed to have."

At that point, if she'd asked me to kill her mother, I probably would have said yes. I was that relieved I wasn't being fired—and I'd have done anything, anything at all, to get that arm off me. It isn't just that I have a thing about people touching me. I mean, I do. If you don't know me, keep your damned mitts to yourself. What is the problem there?

But you'd be surprised how touchy-feely these camp people are. It's all trust falls and human pretzel twists to them.

But that wasn't my only problem with Pamela. On top of my other "issues," I have a thing about authority figures. It probably has something to do with the fact that, last spring, one of them tried to shoot me.

So I stood there, sweating copiously, the words "Sure, yeah, whatever, let go of me," already right there on my lips.

But before I could say any of that, Pamela must have noticed how uncomfortable I was with the whole arm thing—either that or she'd realized how damp she was getting from my copious sweating. In any case, she dropped her arm away from me, and suddenly I could breathe easily again.

I looked around, wondering where we were. I'd lost my bearings in my panic over Pamela's touching me. Beneath us lay the gravel path that led to various Camp Wawasee outbuildings. Close by was the dining hall, newly refinished with a twenty-foot ceiling. Next, the camp's administrative offices. Then the infirmary. Beside that, the music building, a modular structure built mostly underground in order to preserve the woodsy feel of the place, with a huge skylight that shone down on a tree-filled atrium from which extended hallways leading to the soundproof classrooms, practice rooms, and so on.

What I couldn't see was the Olympic-sized swimming pool, and the half dozen clay tennis courts. Not that the kids had much time for swimming and tennis, what with all the practicing they had to do for the end-of-session orchestral concert that took place in the outdoor amphitheater, with seating for nine hundred. But nothing was too good for these little budding geniuses. Not far from the amphitheater was the Pit, where campers gathered nightly to link arms and sing while roasting marshmallows around a sunken campfire.

From there the path curved to the various cabins—a dozen for the girls on one side of camp and a dozen for the boys on the other—until it finally sloped down to Camp Wawasee's private lake, in all its mirror-surfaced, tree-lined glory. In fact, the windows of Frangipani Cottage looked out over the lake. From my bed in my little private room, I could see the water without even raising my head.

Only, apparently, it wasn't my bed anymore. I could feel Frangipani Cottage, with its lake views, its angelic flutists, its midnight-gabfest-and-hair-braiding sessions, slipping away, like water down the drain of . . . well, a steam table.

"It's just that, of all our female counselors this year," Pamela was going on, "you really strike me as the one most capable of handling a cabinful of little boys. And you scored so well in your first aid and lifesaving courses—"

Great. I'm being persecuted because of my knowledge of the Heimlich maneuver—honed, of course, from years of working in food services.

"—that I know I can put these kids into your hands and not worry about them a second longer."

Pamela was really laying it on thick. Don't ask me why. I mean, she was my boss. She had every right to assign me to a different cabin if she wanted to. She was the one doling out my paychecks, after all.

Maybe in the past she'd switched a girl counselor to a boys' cabin and gotten flak for it. Like maybe the girl she'd assigned to the cabin had quit or something. I'm not much of a quitter. The fact is, boys would be more work and less fun, but hey, what was I going to do?

"Yeah," I said. The back of my neck still felt damp from where her arm had been. "Well, that's fine."

Pamela reached out to clutch me by the elbow,

looking intently down into my face. Being clutched by the elbow wasn't as bad as having her arm around my shoulders, so I was able to remain calm.

"Do you really mean that, Jess?" she asked me. "You'll really do it?"

What was I going to say, no? And risk being sent home, where I'd have to spend the rest of my summer sweating over trays of meatballs and manicotti at Joe Junior's? And when I wasn't at the restaurant, the only people I'd have to hang around with would be my parents (no thanks); my brother Mike, who was preparing to go away for his first year at Harvard and spent all the time on his computer e-mailing his new roommate, trying to determine who was bringing the minifridge and who was bringing the scanner; or my other brother, Douglas, who did nothing all day but read comic books in his room, coming out only for meals and *South Park*.

Not to mention the fact that for weeks now, there'd been a white van parked across the street from our house that didn't seem to belong to anyone in the neighborhood.

Um, no thanks. I'd stay here, if it was all the same.

"Um, yeah," I said. "Whatever. Just tell me what cabin I'm assigned to now, and I'll start moving my stuff."

Pamela actually hugged me. I can't say a whole lot for her management skills. One thing you would not catch my father doing is hugging one of his employees for agreeing to do what he'd asked her to do.

More like he'd have given her a big fat "so long" if she'd said anything but, "Yes, Mr. Mastriani."

"That's great!" Pamela cried. "That's just great. You are such a doll, Jess."

Yeah, that's me. A regular Barbie.

Pamela looked down at her clipboard. "You'll be in Birch Tree Cottage now."

Birch Tree Cottage. I was giving up frangipani for birch. Story of my damned life.

"Now I'll just have to make sure the alternate can make it tonight." Pamela was still looking down at her chart. "I think she's from your hometown. And she's a flutist, too. Maybe you know her. Karen Sue Hanky?"

I had to bite back a great big laugh. Karen Sue Hanky? Now, if Karen Sue had found out *she* was being reassigned to a boys' cabin, she *definitely* would have cried.

"Yeah, I know her," I said, noncommittally. *Boy, are you making a big mistake*, was what I thought to myself. But I didn't say it out loud, of course.

"She interviewed quite well," Pamela said, still looking down at her clipboard, "but she only scored a five on performance."

I raised my eyebrows. It wasn't news to me, of course, that Karen Sue couldn't play worth a hang. But it seemed kind of wrong for Pamela to be admitting it in front of me. I guess she thought we were friends and all, on account of me not crying when she told me she was moving me to a boys' cabin.

The thing is, though, I already have all the friends I can stand.

"And she's only fourth chair," Pamela murmured, looking down at her chart. Then she heaved this enormous sigh. "Oh, well," she said. "What else can we do?"

Pamela smiled down at me, then started back to the administrative offices. She had apparently forgotten the fact that I am only third chair, just one up from Karen Sue.

My performance audition score, however, for the camp had been ten. Out of ten.

Oh, yeah. I rock.

Well, at playing the flute, anyway. I don't actually rock at much else.

I figured I'd better get a move on, if I was going to gather my stuff before any of the Frangipanis showed up and got the wrong idea . . . like that Camp Wawasee was unorganized or something. Which, of course, they were, as both the disaster with the sign—the one I told you about earlier—and the fact that they'd hired me attested to. I mean, had they even run my name through Yahoo!, or anything? If they had, they might have gotten an unpleasant little surprise.

Skirting the pack of friendly—a little *too* friendly, if you ask me; you had to shove them out of your way with your knees to escape their long, hot tongues—dogs that roamed freely around the camp, I headed back to Frangipani Cottage, where I began throwing my stuff into the duffel bag I'd brought it all in. It burned me up a little to think that Karen Sue Hanky was the one who was going to get to enjoy that excellent view of Lake Wawasee from what had been my bed. I'd known Karen Sue since kindergarten, and if anyone had ever suffered from a case of the I'm-So-Greats, it was Karen Sue. Seriously. The girl totally thought she was all that, just because her dad owned the biggest car dealership in town, she happened to be blonde, and she played fourth chair flute in our school orchestra.

And yeah, you had to audition to make the Symphonic Orchestra, and yeah, it had won all these awards and was mostly made up of only juniors and seniors, and Karen and I had both made it as sophomores, but please. I ask you, in the vast spectrum of things, is fourth chair in Symphonic Orchestra anything? Anything at all? Not. So not.

Not to Karen it wasn't, though. She would never rest until she was first chair. But to get there, she had to challenge and beat the person in third chair.

Yeah. Me.

And I can tell you, that was so not going to happen. Not in this world. I wouldn't call making third chair of Ernest Pyle High School's Symphonic Orchestra a world-class accomplishment, or anything, but it wasn't something I was going to let Karen Sue take away from me. No way.

Not like she was taking Frangipani Cottage away from me.

Well, frangipani, I decided, was a stupid plant,

anyway. Smelly. A big smelly flower. Birch trees were way better.

That's what I told myself, anyway.

It wasn't until I actually got to Birch Tree Cottage that I changed my mind. Okay, first off, can I just tell you what a logistical nightmare it was going to be, supervising eight little boys? How was I even going to be able to take a shower without one of them barging in to use the john, or worse, spying on me, as young boys—and some not so young ones, as illustrated by my older brothers, who spend inordinate amounts of time gazing with binoculars at Claire Lippman, the girl next door—are wont to do?

Plus Birch Tree Cottage was the farthest cabin from everything—the pool, the amphitheater, the music building. It was practically in the *woods*. There was no lake view here. There was not even any light here, since the thickly leafed tree branches overhead let in not the slightest hint of sun. Everything was damp and smelled faintly of mildew. There *was* mildew in the showers.

Let me be the first to tell you: Birch Tree Cottage? Yeah, it sucked.

I missed Frangipani Cottage, and the little girls whose hair I could have been French braiding, already. If I knew how to French braid, that is.

Still, maybe they could have taught me. My little girl campers, I mean.

And when I'd stowed my stuff away and stepped outside the cabin and saw the first of my charges heading toward me, lugging their suitcases and instruments behind them, I missed Frangipani Cottage even more.

I'm serious. You never saw a scruffier, more sour-faced group of kids in your life. Ranging in age from ten to twelve years old, these were no mischievous-but-good-at-heart Harry Potters.

Oh, no.

Far from it.

These kids looked exactly like what they were: spoiled little music prodigies whose parents couldn't wait to take a six-week vacation from them.

The boys all stopped when they saw me and stood there, blinking through the lenses of their glasses, which were fogged up on account of the humidity. Their parents, who were helping them with their luggage, looked like they were longing to get as far from Camp Wawasee as they possibly could—preferably to a place where pitchers of margaritas were being served.

I hastened to say the speech I'd been taught at counselor training. I remembered to substitute the words *birch tree* for *frangipani.*

"Welcome to Birch Tree Cottage," I said. "I'm your counselor, Jess. We're going to have a lot of fun together."

The parents, you could tell, couldn't care less that I wasn't a boy. They seemed pleased by the fact that I clearly bathed regularly and could speak English.

The boys, however, looked shocked. Sullen and shocked.

One of them went, "Hey, you're a *girl.*"

Another one wanted to know, "What's a girl counselor doing in a boys' cabin?"

A third one said, "She's not a girl. Look at her hair," which I found highly insulting, considering the fact that my hair isn't *that* short.

Finally, the most sullen-looking boy of them all, the one with the mullet cut and the weight problem, went, "She is, too, a girl. She's that girl from TV. The lightning girl."

And with that, my cover was blown.

CHAPTER

2

That was me. Lightning Girl. The girl from TV.

Lucky me. Lucky, lucky, *lucky* me. Could there *be* a girl luckier than me? I don't think so. . . .

Oh, wait—I know. How about some girl who *hadn't* been struck by lightning and developed weird psychic powers overnight? Hey, yeah. *That* girl might be luckier than me. That girl might be *way* luckier than me. Don't you think?

I looked down at Mullet Head. Actually, not that much down, because he was about as tall as I was— which isn't saying much, understand.

Anyway, I looked down at him, and I went, "I don't know what you're talking about."

Just like that. Real smooth, you know? I'm telling you, I had it on.

But it didn't matter. It didn't matter at all.

One of the boys, a skinny one clutching a trumpet

case, said, "Hey, yeah, you *are* that girl. I remember you. You're the one who got hit by lightning and got all those special powers!"

The other boys exchanged excited glances. The glances clearly said, *Cool. Our counselor's a mutant.*

One of them, however, a dark, delicate-looking boy who had no parents with him and spoke with a slight accent, asked shyly, "What special powers?"

The chubby boy with the unfortunate haircut—a mullet, short in front and long in back—who'd outed me in the first place smacked the little dark boy in the shoulder, hard. The chubby boy's mother, from whom it appeared he'd inherited his current gravitationally challenged condition, did not even tell him to knock it off.

"What do you mean, what special powers?" Mullet Head demanded. "Where have you been, retard? On the little bus?"

All of the other boys chuckled at this witticism. The dark little boy looked stricken.

"No," he said, clearly puzzled by the little bus reference. "I come from French Guiana."

"Guiana?" Mullet Head seemed to find this hilarious. "Is that anywhere near Gonorrhea?"

Mrs. Mullet Head, to my astonishment, laughed at this witticism.

That's right. Laughed.

Mullet Head, I could see, was going to be what Pamela had referred to during counselor training as a challenge.

"I'm sorry," I said sweetly to him. "I know I look

like that girl who was on TV and all, but it wasn't me. Now, why don't you all go ahead and—"

Mullet Head interrupted me. "It was, *too*, you," he declared with a scowl.

Mrs. Mullet Head went, "Now, Shane," in this tone that showed she was proud of the fact that her son was no pushover. Which was true. Shane wasn't a pushover. What he was, clearly, was a huge pain in the—

"Um," another one of the parents said. "Hate to interrupt, but do you mind if we go ahead and go inside, miss? This tuba weighs a ton."

I stepped aside and allowed the boys and their parents to enter the cabin. Only one of them paused as he went by me, and that was the little French Guianese boy. He was lugging an enormous and very expensive-looking suitcase. I could see no sign of an instrument.

"I am Lionel," he said gravely.

Only he didn't pronounce it the way we would. He pronounced it Lee-Oh-Nell, with the emphasis on the *Nell*.

"Hey, Lionel," I said, making sure I pronounced it properly. We'd been warned at counselor training that there'd be a lot of kids from overseas, and that we should do all we could to show that Camp Wawasee was cultural-diversity aware. "Welcome to Birch Tree Cottage."

Lionel flashed me another glimpse of those pearly whites, then continued lugging his big heavy bag inside.

I decided to let the boys and their parents slug it out on their own, so I stayed where I was out on the mosquito-netted porch, listening to the ruckus inside as the kids tore around, choosing beds. Off in the distance, I saw someone else wearing the camp counselor uniform—white collared short-sleeve shirt with blue shorts—standing on his porch, looking in my direction. Whoever he was lifted a hand and waved.

I waved back, even though I didn't have any idea who it was. Hey, you never knew. He might have owned a convertible.

It took about two minutes for the first fight to break out.

"No, it's mine!" I heard someone inside the cabin shriek in anguish.

I stalked inside. All of the beds—thankfully, not bunks—had belongings strewn across them. The fight was evidently not territorial in nature. Little boys do not apparently care much about views, and thankfully know nothing about feng shui.

The fight was over a box of Fiddle Faddle, which Shane was holding and Lionel evidently wanted.

"It is *mine!*" Lionel insisted, making a leap for the box of candy. "Give it back to me!"

"If you don't have enough to share," Shane said primly, "you shouldn't have brought it in the first place."

Shane was so much bigger than Lionel that he didn't even have to hold the box very high in the air to keep it out of the smaller boy's reach. He just had to hold it at shoulder level. Lionel, even standing on his tiptoes, wasn't tall enough to grab it.

Meanwhile, Shane's mother was just standing there with a little smile on her face, carefully unpacking the contents of her boy's suitcase and placing each item in the drawers in the platform beneath her son's mattress.

The rest of the boys, however, and quite a few of the parents, were watching the little drama unfolding in Birch Tree Cottage with interest.

"Didn't they ever teach you," Shane asked Lionel, "about sharing back in Gonorrhea?"

I knew rapid and decisive action was necessary. I could not do what I'd have liked to do, which was whop Shane upside the head. Pamela and the rest of the administrative staff at Camp Wawasee had been very firm on the subject of corporal punishment—they were against it. That was why they'd spent four hours of one of our training days going over appropriate versus inappropriate disciplinary action. Whopping campers upside the head was expressly forbidden.

Instead, I stepped forward and snatched the box of Fiddle Faddle out of Shane's hand.

"There is no," I declared loudly, "outside food of any kind allowed in Birch Tree Cottage. The only food anyone may bring into this cabin is food from the dining hall. Is that understood?"

Everyone stood staring at me, some in consternation. Shane's mother looked particularly shocked.

"Well, that sure is a change from last year," she

said, in a voice that was too high-pitched and sugary to come from a woman who had produced, as she had, the spawn of Satan. "Last year, the boys could have all the candy and cookies from home they wanted. That's why I packed this."

Shane's mother hauled up another suitcase and flung it open to reveal what looked like the entire contents of a 7-Eleven candy rack. The other boys gathered around, their eyes goggling at the sight of so many Nestlé, Mars, and Hershey's products.

"Contraband," I said, pointing into the suitcase. "Take it home with you, please."

The boys let out a groan. Mrs. Shane's many chins began to tremble.

"But Shane gets hungry," she said, "in the middle of the night—"

"I will make sure," I said, "that there are plenty of healthful snacks for all the boys."

I was, of course, making up the rule about outside food. I just didn't want to have to be breaking up fights over Fiddle Faddle every five minutes.

As if sensing my thoughts, Shane's mother looked at the box in my hand.

"Well, what about that?" she demanded, pointing at it. "You can't send that home with *his* parents—" The accusing finger swung in Lionel's direction. "They didn't bother coming."

Uh, because they live in *French Guiana*, I wanted to say to her. Hello?

Instead, I found myself saying possibly the stupidest thing of all time: "This box of Fiddle Faddle will remain in my custody until camp is over, at which point, I will return it to its rightful owner."

"Well," Shane's mother sniffed. "If Shane can't have any candy, I don't think the other boys should be allowed any, either. I hope you intend to search their bags, as well."

Which was how, by the time supper rolled around, I had five boxes of Fiddle Faddle, two bags of Double-Stuff Oreo cookies, a ten-pack of Snickers bars, two bags of Fritos and one of Doritos, seven Gogurts in a variety of flavors, one bag of Chips Ahoy chocolate chip cookies, a box of Count Chocula, a two-pound bag of Skittles, and a six-pack of Yoo-Hoo locked in my room. The parents, thankfully, had left, chased off the property by the sound of the dinner gong. The good-byes were heartfelt but, except on the part of Shane's mother, not too tearful. Somewhere out there, a lot of champagne corks were popping.

As soon as the last parent had departed, I informed the boys that we were headed to the dining hall, but that before we went, I wanted to make sure I had all their names down. Once that was settled, I told them, I'd teach them the official Birch Tree Cottage song.

Shane and Lionel I was already well acquainted with. The skinny kid who played trumpet turned out to be called John. The tuba player was Arthur. We had two violinists, Sam and Doo Sun, and two pianists, Tony and Paul. They were pretty much all your typical gifted musician types—pasty-skinned, prone to allergies, and way too smart for their own good.

"How come," John wanted to know, "you told us you aren't that girl from TV, when you totally are?"

"Yeah," Sam said. "And how come you can only find missing kids with your psychic powers? How come you can't find cool stuff, like gold?"

"Or the remote control." Arthur, I could already tell, was going to make up for his unfortunate name by being the cabin comedian.

"Look," I said. "I told you. I don't know what you guys are talking about. I just look like that lightning girl, okay? It wasn't me. Now—" I felt a change of subject was in order. "Shane, you haven't told us yet what instrument you play."

"The skin flute," Shane said. All of the boys but Lionel cracked up.

"Really?" Lionel looked shyly pleased. "I play the flute, too."

Shane shrieked with laughter upon hearing this. "You would!" he cried. "Being from Gonorrhea!"

Now that his mother was gone, I felt free to walk over and flick the top of Shane's ear with my middle finger hard enough to produce a very satisfying snapping noise. One of my other issues, on which I'd promised Mr. Goodhart to work during my summer vacation, was a tendency to take out my frustrations with others in a highly physical manner—a fact because of which I had spent most of my sophomore year in detention.

"Ow!" Shane cried, shooting me an indignant look. "What'd you do *that* for?"

"While you are living in Birch Tree Cottage," I

302

informed him—as well as the rest of the boys, who were staring at us—"you will conduct yourself as a gentleman, which means you will refrain from making overtly sexual references within my hearing. Additionally, you will not insult other people's countries of origin."

Shane's face was a picture of confusion. "Huh?" he said.

"No sex talk," John translated for him.

"Aw." Shane looked disgusted. "Then how am I supposed to have any fun?"

"You will have good, clean fun," I informed him. "And that's where the official Birch Tree Cottage song comes in."

And then, while we undertook the long walk to the dining hall, I taught them the song.

> I met a miss,
> She had to pi—
> —ck a flower.
> Stepped in the grass,
> up to her a—
> —nkle tops.
> She saw a bird,
> stepped on a tur—
> —key feather.
> She broke her heart,
> and let a far—
> —mer carry her home.

"See?" I said as we walked. We had the longest walk of anyone to the dining hall, so by the time we'd reached it, the boys had the song entirely memorized. "No dirty words."

"Almost dirty," Doo Sun said with relish.

"That's the stupidest song I ever heard," Shane muttered. But I noticed he was singing it louder than anyone as we entered the dining hall. None of the other cabins, we soon learned, had official songs. The residents of Birch Tree Cottage sang theirs with undisguised gusto as they picked up their trays and got into the concession line.

I spied Ruth sitting with the girls from her cabin. She waved to me. I sauntered over.

"What is going on?" Ruth wanted to know. "What are you doing with all those boys?"

I explained the situation. When she had heard all, Ruth's mouth fell open and she went, her blue eyes flashing behind her glasses, "That is so unfair!"

"It'll be all right," I said.

"What will?" Shelley, a violinist and one of the other counselors, came by with a tray loaded down with chili fries and Jell-O.

Ruth told her what had happened. Shelley looked outraged.

"That is *bull*," she said. "A boys' cabin? How are you going to take a shower?"

Seeing everyone else so mad on my behalf, I started feeling less bad about the whole thing. I shrugged and said, "It won't be so bad. I'll manage."

"I know what you can do," Shelley said. "Just shower at the pool, in the girls' locker room."

"Or one of the guys from the cabins near yours can keep your campers occupied," Ruth said. "I mean, it wouldn't kill Scott or Dave to take on some extra kids for half an hour, here and there."

"What won't kill us?" Scott, an oboe player with thick glasses who'd nevertheless been judged Do-able thanks to his height (a little over six feet) and thighs (muscular) came over, followed closely by his shadow, a stocky Asian trumpet player named Dave . . . also rated Do-able, courtesy of a set of surprisingly washboard abs.

"They reassigned Jess to a boys' cabin," Shelley informed them.

"No kidding?" Scott looked interested. "Which one?"

"Birch," I said carefully.

Scott and Dave exchanged enthusiastic glances.

"Hey," Scott cried. "That's right near us! We're neighbors!"

"That was you?" Dave grinned down at me. "Who waved at me?"

"Yeah," I said. But you waved first.

I didn't say that part out loud, though. I wondered if either Dave or Scott had a convertible. I doubted it.

Not that I cared. I was taken, anyway. Well, in my opinion, at least.

"Don't worry, Jessica," Dave said, with a wink. "We'll look after you."

Just what I needed. To be looked after by Scott and Dave. Whoopee.

Ruth speared a piece of lettuce. She was eating a salad, as usual. Ruth would starve herself all summer in order to look good in a bikini she would never quite work up the courage to wear. If Scott or Dave or, well, anybody, for that matter, did ask her to go with him to the dunes, she would go dressed in a T-shirt and shorts that she would not remove, even in the event of heat stroke.

Ruth eyed me over a forkful of romaine. "What was with that dirty song you had those guys singing when you all came in?"

"It wasn't dirty," I said.

"It sounded dirty." Scott, who'd taken a seat on Ruth's other side, instead of sitting with his cabin, like he was supposed to, was eating spaghetti and meatballs. He was doing it wrong, too, cutting the pasta up into little bite-sized portions, instead of twirling it on his fork. My dad would have had an embolism.

Scott, I decided, must like Ruth. I knew Ruth liked Todd, the hot-looking violinist, but Scott wasn't such a bad guy. I hoped she'd give him a chance. Oboe players are generally better humored than violinists.

"Technically," I said, "that song wasn't a bit dirty."

"Oh, God," Ruth said, making a face at something she'd spotted over my shoulder. "What's *she* doing here?"

I looked around. Standing behind me was Karen Sue Hanky. I hadn't seen Karen Sue since school had let out for the summer, but she looked much the same as she always did—rat-faced and full of herself.

She was holding a tray laden with grains and legumes. Karen Sue is vegan.

Then I noticed that beside Karen Sue stood Pamela.

"Excuse me, Jess?" Pamela said. "Can I see you for a moment in my office, please?"

I shot Karen Sue a dirty look. She simpered back at me.

This was going to be, I realized, a long summer.

In more ways than one.

"It wasn't dirty," I said as I followed Pamela into her office.

"I know," Pamela said. She collapsed into the chair behind her desk. "But it sounds dirty. We've had complaints."

"Already?" I was shocked. "From who?"

But I knew. Karen Sue, on top of the whole vegan thing, is this total prude.

"Look," I said, "if it's that much of a problem, I'll tell them they can't sing it anymore."

"Fine. But to tell you the truth, Jess," Pamela said, "that's not really why I called you in here."

All of a sudden, it felt as if someone had poured the contents of a Big Gulp down my back.

She knew. Pamela *knew*.

And I hadn't even seen it coming.

"Look," I said. "I can explain."

"Oh, can you?" Pamela shook her head. "I suppose it's partly our fault. I mean, how the fact that you're *the* Jessica Mastriani slipped through our whole screening process, I cannot imagine. . . ."

Visions of steam tables danced in my head.

"Listen, Pamela." I said it low, and I said it fast. "That whole thing—the getting struck by lightning thing? Yeah, well, it's true. I mean I was struck by lightning and all. And for a while, I did have these special powers. Well, one, anyway. I mean, I could find lost kids and all. But that was it. And the thing is—well, as you probably know—it went away."

I said this last part very loudly, just in case my old friends, Special Agents Johnson and Smith, had the place bugged or whatever. I hadn't noticed any white vans parked around the campgrounds, but you never knew. . . .

"It went away?" Pamela was looking at me nervously. "Really?"

"Uh-huh," I said. "The doctors told me it probably would. You know, after the lightning was done rattling around in me and all." At least, that was how I liked to think about it. "And it turned out they were right. I am now totally without psychic power. So, um, there's really nothing for you to worry about, so far as negative publicity for the camp, or hordes of reporters descending on you, or anything like that. The whole thing is totally over."

Not even remotely true, of course, but what Pamela didn't know couldn't, I figured, hurt her.

"Don't get me wrong, Jess," she said. "We love

having you here—especially with you being so good about changing cabins—but Camp Wawasee has never known a single hint of controversy in the fifty years it's been in existence. I'd hate for . . . well, anything *untoward* to happen while you're here. . . ."

Untoward was, I guess, Pamela's way of referring to what had happened last spring, after I'd been struck by lightning and then got "invited" to stay at Crane Military for a few days, while some scientists studied my brain waves and tried to figure out how it was that, just by showing me a picture of a missing person, I could wake up the next morning knowing exactly where that person was.

Unfortunately, after they'd studied it for a while, the people at Crane had decided that my newfound talent might come in handy for tracking down so-called traitors and other unsavory individuals who really, as far as I knew, didn't want to be found. And while I'm as anxious as anybody to incarcerate serial killers and all, I just figured I'd stick to finding missing kids . . . specifically, kids who actually want to be found.

Only the people at Crane had turned out to be surprisingly unhappy to hear this.

But after some friends of mine and I had broken some windows and cut through some fencing and, oh, yeah, blown up a helicopter, they came around. Well, sort of. It helped, I guess, that I called the press and told them I couldn't do it anymore. Find missing people, I mean. That little special talent of mine just dried up and blew away. *Poof.*

That's what I told them, anyway.

But you could totally see where Pamela was coming from. On account of the fireball caused by the exploding helicopter and all. It *had* made a lot of papers. You don't get fireballs every day. At least, not in Indiana.

Pamela frowned a little. "The thing is, Jess," she said, "even though, as you say, you no longer have, um, any psychic powers, I have heard . . . well, I've heard missing kids across the country are still sort of, um, turning up. A lot more kids than ever turned up before . . . well, before your little weather-related accident. And thanks to some"—she cleared her throat—"anonymous tips."

My winning smile didn't waver.

"If that's true," I said, "it sure isn't because of me. No, ma'am. I am officially retired from the kid-finding business."

Pamela didn't exactly look relieved. She looked sort of like someone who wanted—really, really wanted—to believe something, but didn't think she should. Kind of like a kid whose friends had told her Santa Claus doesn't exist, but whose parents were still trying to maintain the myth.

Still, what could she do? She couldn't sit there and call me a liar to my face. What proof did she have?

Plenty, as it turned out. She just didn't know it.

"Well," she said. Her smile was as stiff as the Welcome to Camp Wawasee sign had been, in the places it hadn't been eaten away. "All right, then. I guess . . . I guess that's that."

I got up to go, feeling a little shaky. Well, you would have felt shaky, too, if you'd have come as close as I had to spending the rest of the summer stirring steaming platters of rigatoni bolognese.

"Oh," Pamela said, as if remembering something. "I almost forgot. You're friends with Ruth Abramowitz, aren't you? This came for her the other day. It didn't fit into her mailbox. Could you hand it to her? I saw you sitting with her at dinner just now. . . ."

Pamela took a large padded envelope out from behind her desk and handed it to me. I stood there, looking down at it, my throat dry.

"Um," I said. "Sure. Sure, I'll give it to her."

My voice sounded unusually hoarse. Well, and why not? Pamela didn't know it, of course, but what she'd just given me—its contents, anyway—could prove that every single thing I'd just told her was an out-and-out lie.

"Thanks," Pamela said with a tired smile. "Things have just been so hectic . . ."

The corners of my mouth started to ache on account of how hard I was still smiling, pretending like I wasn't upset or anything. I should, I knew, have taken that envelope and run. That's what I should have done. But something made me stay and go, still in that hoarse voice, "Can I ask you a question, Pamela?"

She looked surprised. "Of course you can, Jess."

I cleared my throat, and kept my gaze on the strong, loopy handwriting on the front of the envelope. "Who told you?"

Pamela knit her eyebrows. "Told me what?"

"You know. About me being the lightning girl." I looked up at her. "And that stuff about how kids are still being found, even though I'm retired."

Pamela didn't answer right away. But that was okay. I knew. And I hadn't needed any psychic powers to tell me, either. Karen Sue Hanky was dead meat.

It was right then there was a knock on Pamela's office door. She yelled, "Come in," looking way relieved at the interruption.

This old guy stuck his head in. I recognized him. He was Dr. Alistair, the camp director. He was kind of red in the face, and he had a lot of white hair that stuck out all around his shining bald head. He was supposedly this very famous conductor, but let me ask you: If he's so famous, what's he doing running what boils down to a glorified band camp in northern Indiana?

"Pamela," he said, looking irritated. "There's a young man on the phone looking for one of the counselors. I told him that we are not running an answering service here, and that if he wants to speak to one of our employees, he can leave a message like everybody else and we will post it on the message board. But he says it's an emergency, and—"

I moved so fast, I almost knocked over a chair.

"Is it for me? Jess Mastriani?"

It wasn't any psychic ability that told me that phone call was probably for me. It was the combination of the words "young man" and "emergency." All of the young men of my acquaintance, when confronted by someone like Dr. Alistair, would definitely go for the word "emergency" as soon as they heard about that stupid message board.

Dr. Alistair looked surprised . . . and not too pleased.

"Why, yes," he said. "If your name is Jessica, then it is for you. I hope Pamela has explained to you the fact that we are not running a message service here, and that the making or receiving of personal calls, except during Sunday afternoons, is expressly—"

"But it's an *emergency*," I reminded him.

He grimaced. "Down the hall. Phone at the reception desk. Press line one."

I was out of Pamela's office like a shot.

Who, I wondered, as I jogged down the hall, could it be? I knew who I *wanted* it to be. But the chances of Rob Wilkins calling me were slim to none. I mean, he never calls me at home. Why would he call me at camp?

Still, I couldn't help hoping Rob had overcome this totally ridiculous prejudice he's got against me because of my age. I mean, so what if he's eighteen and has graduated already, while I still have two years of high school left? It's not like he's leaving town to go to college in the fall, or something. Rob's not going to college. He has to work in his uncle's garage and support his mother, who recently got laid off from the factory she had worked in for like twenty years or something. Mrs. Wilkins was having trouble finding another job, until I suggested food services and gave her the number at Joe's. My dad, without even knowing Mrs. Wilkins and I were acquainted, hired her and put her on days at Mastriani's—which isn't a bad shift at all. He saves the totally crappy jobs and shifts for his kids. He believes strongly in teaching us what he calls a "work ethic."

But when I got to the phone and pushed line one, it wasn't Rob. Of course it wasn't Rob. It was my brother Douglas.

And that's how I *really* knew it wasn't an emergency. If it had been an emergency, it would have been *about* Douglas. The only emergencies in our family are because of Douglas. At least, they have been, ever since he got kicked out of college on account of these voices in his head that are always telling him to do stuff, like slit his wrists, or stick his hand in the barbecue coals. Stuff like that.

But so long as he takes his medicine, he's all right. Well, all right for Douglas, which is kind of relative.

"Jess," he said, after I went, "Hello?"

"Oh, hey." I hoped my disappointment that it was Douglas and not Rob didn't show in my voice.

"How's it going? Who was that freak who answered the phone? Is that your boss, or something?"

Douglas sounded good. Which meant he'd been taking his medication. Sometimes he thinks he's cured, so he stops. That's when the voices usually come back again.

"Yeah," I said. "That was Dr. Alistair. We aren't

supposed to get personal calls, except on Sunday afternoons. Then it's okay."

"So he explained to me." Douglas didn't sound in the least bit ruffled by his conversation with Dr. Alistair, world-famous orchestra conductor. "And you prefer working for him over Dad? At least Dad would let you get phone calls at work."

"Yeah, but Dad would withhold my pay for the time I spent on the phone."

Douglas laughed. It was good to hear him laugh. He doesn't do it very often anymore.

"He would, too," he said. "It's good to hear your voice, Jess."

"I've only been gone a week," I reminded him.

"Well, a week's a long time. It's seven days. Which is one hundred and sixty-eight hours. Which is ten thousand, eighty minutes. Which is six hundred thousand, four hundred seconds."

It wasn't the medication that was making Douglas talk like this. It wasn't even his illness. Douglas has always gone around saying stuff like this. That's why, in school, he'd been known as The Spaz, and Dorkus, and other, even worse names. If I'd asked him to, Douglas could tell me exactly how many seconds it would be before I got back home. He could do it without even thinking about it.

But go to college? Drive a car? Talk to a girl to whom he wasn't related? No way. Not Douglas.

"Is that why you called me, Doug?" I asked. "To tell me how long I've been gone?"

"No." Douglas sounded offended. Weird as he is,

he doesn't think he's the least unusual. Seriously. To Douglas, he's just, you know, average.

Yeah. Like your average twenty-year-old guy just sits around in his bedroom reading comic books all day long. Sure.

And my parents let him! Well, my mom, anyway. My dad's all for making Doug work the steam table in my absence, but Mom keeps going, "But Joe, he's still *recovering. . . .*"

"I called," Douglas said, "to tell you it's gone."

I blinked. "What's gone, Douglas?"

"You know," he said. "That van. The white one. That's been parked in front of the house. It's gone."

"Oh," I said, blinking some more. "*Oh.*"

"Yeah," Douglas said. "It left the day after you did. And you know what that means."

"I do?"

"Yeah." And then, I guess because it was clear to him that I wasn't getting it, he elaborated. "It proves that you weren't being paranoid. They really *are* still spying on you."

"Oh," I said. "Wow."

"Yeah," Douglas said. "And that's not all. Remember how you told me to let you know if anyone we didn't know came around, asking about you?"

I perked up. I was sitting at the receptionist's desk in the camp's administrative offices. The receptionist had gone home for the day, but she'd left behind all her family photos, which were pinned up all around her little cubicle. She must have really liked NASCAR racing, because there were a lot of photos of guys in these junky-looking race cars.

"Yeah? Who was it?"

"I don't know. He just called."

Now I really perked up. Rob. It had to have been Rob. My family didn't know about him, on account of how I never really told them we were going out. Because we aren't, technically. Going out. For the reasons I already told you. So what's to tell?

Plus my mom would so kill me if she knew I was seeing a guy who wasn't, you know, college-bound. And had a police record.

"Yeah?" I said eagerly. "Did he leave a message?"

"Naw. Just asked if you were home, is all."

"Oh." Now that I thought about it, it probably hadn't been Rob at all. I mean, I'd made this total effort to let Rob know I was leaving for the rest of the summer. I had even gone to his uncle's garage, you know, where Rob works, and had this long conversation with his feet while he'd been underneath a Volvo station wagon, about how I was going away for seven weeks and this was his last chance to say good-bye to me, et cetera.

But had he looked the least bit choked up? Had he begged me not to go? Had he given me his class ring or an ID bracelet or something to remember him by? Not. So not. He'd come out from under that Volvo and said, "Oh, yeah? Well, that'll be good for you, to get away for a while. Hand me that wrench right there, will you?"

I tell you, romance is dead.

"Was it a Fed?" I asked Douglas.

Douglas went, "I don't know, Jess. How am I supposed to know that? He sounded like a guy. You know. Just a guy."

I grunted. That's the thing about Feds, see. They can sound just like normal people. When they aren't wearing their trench coats and earpieces, they look just like anybody else. They're not like the Feds on TV—you know, like Mulder and Scully, or whatever. Like, they aren't really handsome, or pretty, or anything. They just look . . . average. Like the kind of people you wouldn't actually notice, if they were following you—or even if they were standing right next to you.

They're tricky that way.

"That was it?" I noticed that there was this one guy who kept reappearing in the photographs on the secretary's bulletin board. He was probably her boyfriend or something. A NASCAR-driver boyfriend. I felt jealous of the secretary. The guy she liked liked her back. You could tell by the way he smiled into the camera. I wondered what it would be like to have the boy you like like you back. Probably pretty good.

"Well, not really," Douglas said. He said it in this way that—well, I could just tell I wasn't going to like the rest of this story.

"What," I said flatly.

"Look," Douglas said. "He sounded . . . well, he seemed to really want to talk to you. He said it was really important. He kept asking when you'd be back."

"You didn't," I said, just as flatly.

"He kept asking and asking," Douglas said. "Finally I had to say you wouldn't be back for six weeks, on account of you were up at Lake Wawasee. Look, Jess, I know I screwed up. Don't be mad. Please don't be mad."

I wasn't mad. How could I be mad? I mean, it was Douglas. It would be like being mad at the wind. The wind can't help blowing. Douglas can't help being a complete and utter moron sometimes.

Well, not just Douglas, either. A lot of boys can't, I've noticed.

"Great," I said with a sigh.

"I'm really sorry, Jess," Douglas said.

He really sounded it, too.

"Oh, don't worry about it," I said. "I'm not so sure I'm cut out for this camp counselor stuff anyway."

Now sounding surprised, Douglas said, "Jess, I can't think of a job more perfect for you."

I was shocked to hear this. "Really?"

"Really. I mean, you don't—what's the word?—condescend to kids like a lot of people do. You treat them like you treat everybody else. You know. Shitty."

"Gee," I said. "Thanks."

"You're welcome," Douglas said. "Oh, and Dad says anytime you want to quit and come on back home, the steam table's waiting for you."

"Ha-ha," I said. "How's Mikey?"

"Mike? He's trying to get as many glimpses of Claire Lippman in her underwear as he can before he leaves for Harvard at the end of August."

"It's good to have a hobby," I said.

"And Mom's making you a dress." You could tell Douglas was totally enjoying himself, now that he'd gotten over giving me the bad news. "She's got this idea that you're going to be nominated for homecoming queen this year, so you'd better have a dress for the occasion."

Of course. Because thirty years ago, my mom had been nominated homecoming queen of the very same high school I was currently going to. Why shouldn't I follow in her footsteps?

Um, how about because I am a mutated freak? But my mom stubbornly refuses to believe this. We mostly just let her live in her fantasy world, since it's easier than trying to drag her into the real one.

"And that's about it," Douglas said. "Got any messages for anybody? Want me to tell Rosemary anything?"

"*Douglas,*" I hissed in a warning tone.

"Oops," he said. "Sorry."

"I better go," I said. I could hear someone coming down the hall. "Thanks for the heads up and all. I guess."

"Well," Douglas said. "I just thought you should know. About the guy, I mean. In case he shows up, or whatever."

Great. Just what I needed. Some reporter showing up at Lake Wawasee to interview Lightning Girl. Pamela wouldn't freak too much about that.

"Okay," I said. "Well, bye, Catbreath." I used my pet name for Douglas from when we were small.

He returned the favor. "See ya, Buttface."

I hung up. Down the hall, I heard keys rattle. Pamela was just locking up her office. She came out into the main reception area.

"Everything all right at home?" she asked me, sounding as if she actually cared.

I thought about the question. *Was* everything all right at home? Had everything *ever* been all right at home? No. Of course not.

And I didn't think it'd be too much of a stretch to say that everything would never be all right at home.

But that's not what I told Pamela.

"Sure," I said, hugging the padded envelope to my chest. "Everything's great."

CHAPTER

4

I was forced to eat those words a second later, however, when I stepped outside the camp's administrative offices, into the sticky twilight, and heard it.

Someone screaming. Someone screaming my name.

Pamela heard it, too. She looked at me curiously. I didn't have time for questions, though. I took off running in the direction the screams were coming from. Pamela followed me. I could hear her office keys and loose change jangling in the pockets of her khaki shorts.

Dinner was over. The kids were streaming out of the dining hall and heading over toward the Pit for their first campfire. I saw kids of all sizes and colors, but the two to whom my gaze was instantly drawn were, of course, Shane and Lionel. This time, Shane had Lionel in a headlock. He wasn't choking him, or anything. He just wouldn't let go.

"It's okay, Lionel," Shane was saying. He pronounced it the American way, LIE-oh-nell. "They're just dogs. They're not going to hurt you."

The camp dogs, barking and wagging their tails delightedly, were leaping around, trying to lick Lionel and just about any other kid they could catch. Lionel, being so short, was getting most of these licks in the face.

"See, I know in Gonorrhea, you eat dogs," Shane was saying, "but here in America, see, we keep dogs as pets. . . ."

"Jess!" Lionel screamed. His thin voice broke with a sob. "Jess!"

There was a group of kids gathered around, watching Shane torture the smaller boy. Have you ever noticed how this always happens? I have. I mean, I know whenever I take a swing at somebody, people immediately come flocking to the area, eager to watch the fight. No one ever tries to break it up. No one ever goes, "Hey, Jess, why don't you just let the guy go?" No way. It's like why people go to car races: They want to see someone crash.

I waded through the kids and dogs until I reached Shane. I couldn't do what I wanted to, since I knew Pamela was right behind me. Instead, I said, "Shane, let him go."

Shane looked up at me, his eyes—which were already small—going even smaller.

"Whadduya mean?" he demanded. "I'm just showing him how the dogs aren't gonna hurt him.

See, he's afraid of them. I'm doing him a favor. I'm trying to help him overcome his phobia—"

Lionel, by this time, was openly sobbing. The dogs licked away his tears before they had a chance to trickle down his face very far.

I could hear Pamela's keys still jangling behind me. She wasn't, I realized, on the scene quite yet. Clutching my envelope in one hand, I reached out with the other and, placing my thumb and middle finger just above Shane's elbow, squeezed as hard as I could.

Shane let out a shriek and let go of Lionel just as Pamela broke through the crowd that had gathered around us.

"What—" she demanded, bewilderedly, "is going on here?"

Lionel, free at last, hurled himself at me, flinging his arms around my waist and burying his face in my stomach so the dogs couldn't get at his tears.

"They try to kill me!" he was screaming. "Jess, Jess, those dogs are try to kill me."

Shane, meanwhile, was massaging his funny bone. "Whaddidja have to go and do that for?" he demanded. "You know, if it turns out I can't play anymore on account of you, my dad's going to sue you—"

"Shane." I put one hand on Lionel's shaking shoulders and, with the envelope, pointed toward the Pit. "You've got one strike. Now go."

"A strike?" Shane looked up at me incredulously. "A *strike?* What's a *strike?* What'd I get a *strike* for?"

"You know what you got it for," I said, answering his last question first. The truth was, I hadn't figured out the answer to his first question. But one thing I did know: "Two more, and you're out, buddy. Now go sit with the others at the campfire and keep your hands to yourself."

Shane stamped a sneakered foot. "Out? You can't do that. You can't throw me out."

"Watch me."

Shane turned his accusing stare toward Pamela. Unlike when he was looking at me, he actually had to tilt his chin a little to see her eyes.

"Can she do that?" he demanded.

Pamela, to my relief, said, "Of course she can. Now all of you, go to the Pit."

Nobody moved. Pamela said, "I said, *go.*"

Something in her voice made them do what she said. Now *that*'s an ability I wouldn't mind having: making people do what I told them, without having to resort to doing them bodily harm.

Lionel continued to cling to me, still sobbing. The dogs had not gone away. In the usual manner of animals, they had realized that Lionel wanted nothing to do with them, and so they remained stubbornly at his side, looking at him with great interest, their tongues ready and waiting for him to turn around so they could continue lapping up his tears.

"Lionel," I said, giving the little boy's shoulder a shake. "The dogs really won't hurt you. They're good dogs. I mean, if any of them had ever hurt anyone, do you think they would be allowed to stay? No way. It would open the camp up to all sorts of law-suits. You know how litigious the parents of gifted children can be." Shane being example numero uno.

Pamela raised her eyebrows at this but said nothing, letting me handle the situation in my own way. Eventually, Lionel took his head out of my midriff and blinked up at me tearfully. The dogs, though they stirred eagerly at this motion, stayed where they were.

"I don't know what this means, this 'litigious,' " Lionel said. "But I thank you for helping me, Jess."

I reached out and patted his springy hair. "Don't mention it. Now, watch."

I stuck my hand out. The dogs, recognizing some sort of weird human/dog signal, rushed forward and began licking my fingers.

"See?" I said as Lionel watched, wide-eyed. "They're just interested in making friends." Or in the smell of all the Fiddle Faddle I'd handled earlier, but whatever.

"I see." Lionel regarded the dogs with wide dark eyes. "I will not be afraid, then. But . . . is it permissible for me not to touch them?"

"Sure," I said. I withdrew my hand, which felt as if I'd just dipped it into a vat of hot mayonnaise. I wiped it off on my shorts. "Why don't you go join the rest of the Birch Trees?"

Lionel gave me a tremulous smile, then hurried toward the Pit, with many furtive glances over his shoulder at the dogs. I don't think he noticed that Pamela and I had as many by the collar as we could hold.

"Well," Pamela said when Lionel was out of earshot. "You certainly handled that . . . interestingly."

"That Shane," I said. "He's a pill."

"He is a challenge," Pamela corrected me. "He does seem to get worse every year."

I shook my head. "Tell me about it." I was beginning to wonder if Andrew, whose cabin I'd inherited, had heard through the grapevine that Shane had been assigned to it, and then lied about having mono to get out of having to spend his summer dealing with that particular "challenge." Andrew was a "returner." He'd worked at the camp the summer before as well.

"Why do you let him come back?" I asked.

Pamela sighed. "I realize you wouldn't know it to look at him, but Shane's actually extremely gifted."

"*Shane* is?"

My astonishment must have shown in my voice, since Pamela nodded vigorously as she said, "Oh, yes, it's true. The boy is a musical genius. Perfect pitch, you know."

I just shook my head. "Get out of town."

"I'm serious. Not to mention the fact that . . . well, his parents are very . . . generous with their support."

Well. That pretty much said it all, didn't it?

I joined my fellow Birch Trees—and the rest of the camp—around the fire. The first night's campfire was devoted almost entirely to staff introductions and acquainting the campers with Camp Wawasee's many rules. All of the musical instructors were paraded out, along with the rest of the camp staff—the counselors, the administrators, the lifeguards, the handymen, the nurse, the cafeteria workers, and so on.

Then we went over the list of rules and regulations: no running; no littering; no one allowed out of the cottages after 10:00 P.M.; no cabin raids; no diving into the lake; no playing of musical instruments outside of the practice rooms (this was a crucial rule, because if everyone tried to practice outside of the soundproof rooms provided for that purpose, the camp would soon sound worse than a traffic jam at rush hour). We learned about how Camp Wawasee was smack in the middle of five hundred acres of federally protected forest, and how, if any one of us went wandering off into this forest, we should pretty much expect never to be heard from again.

On this encouraging note, we were reminded that the mandatory Polar Bear swim commenced at seven in the morning. Then, after a few rounds of *Dona Nobis Pacem* (hey, it was orchestra camp, after all), we were dismissed for the night.

Shane was at my side the minute I stood up.

"Hey," he said, tugging on my shirt. "What happens if I get three strikes?"

"You're out," I informed him.

"But you can't throw me out of the camp." Shane's freckles—he had quite a lot of them—stood out in the firelight. "You try to do that, my dad'll sue you."

See what I meant, about gifted kids' parents being litigious?

"I'm not going to throw you out of camp," I said. "But I might throw you out of the cabin."

Shane glared at me. "Whadduya mean?"

"Make you sleep on the porch," I said. "Without benefit of air-conditioning."

Shane laughed. He actually laughed and went, "That's my punishment? Sleep without air-conditioning?"

He cackled all the way back to the cottage, and accrued another strike when, along the way, he threw a rock—supposedly at a firefly, or so he claimed—which just happened to miss Lionel by only about an inch and ended up hitting Arthur—who took out his feelings on the matter with prompt assertiveness. I, relieved to see that at least one member of Birch Tree Cottage could defend himself against Shane, did nothing to stop the fight.

"Jeez," Scott said. He and Dave, their own campers having obediently gone on ahead to their cabins—and probably brushed their teeth and tucked themselves in already—paused beside me to observe Shane and Arthur's wrestling match, which was happening off the lighted path, and in what appeared to be a dense patch of poison ivy. "What'd you ever do to deserve *that* kid?"

Watching the fight, I shrugged. "Born under an unlucky star, I guess."

"That kid," Dave said, watching as Shane tried, unsuccessfully, to grind Arthur's face into some tree roots, "is just destined to take an Uzi to his home-room teacher someday."

"Maybe I should stop this—" Scott started to step off the path.

I grabbed his arm. "Oh, no," I said. "Let's let them get it out of their systems." Arthur had just gotten the upper hand, and was seated on Shane's chest.

"Say you're sorry," Arthur commanded Shane, "or I'll bounce up and down until your ribs break."

Scott and Dave and I, impressed by this threat, looked at one another with raised eyebrows.

"Jess!" Shane wailed.

"Shane," I said, "if you're going to throw rocks, you have to be prepared to pay the consequences."

"But he's going to kill me!"

"Just like you could have killed him with that rock."

"He wouldn't have died from that rock," Shane howled. "It was a little itty-bitty rock."

"It could have put his eye out," I said in my prissi-est voice. Scott and Dave both had to turn away, lest the boys catch them laughing.

"When you break a rib," Arthur informed his quarry, "you can't breathe from your diaphragm. You know, when you play. Because it hurts so much. Don't know how you're going to sustain those whole notes when—"

"GET OFFA ME!" Shane roared.

Arthur scooped up a handful of dirt, apparently with the intention of shoveling it into Shane's mouth.

"All right, all right," Shane bellowed. "I'm sorry."

Arthur let him up. Shane, following him back to the path, gave me a dirty look and said, "Wait until my dad finds out what a sucky counselor you are. He'll get you fired for sure."

"Gosh," I said. "You mean I might have to leave here and never listen to your whining voice again? What a punishment."

Furious, Shane stormed off toward Birch Tree Cottage. Arthur, chuckling, followed him.

"Jeez," Scott said again. "You want help putting those guys to bed?"

I knit my brow. "What are you talking about? They're almost twelve years old. They don't need to be put to bed."

He just shook his head.

About half an hour later, I realized what he'd been talking about. It was close to ten, but none of the residents of Birch Tree Cottage were in bed. None of them were even in their pajamas. In fact, they were doing everything *but* getting ready for bed. Some of them were jumping on the beds. Others were racing around the beds. A few had climbed under their beds, into the cubbies where they were supposed to stash their clothes.

But none of them were actually in the beds.

Somehow, I couldn't see any of this happening in Frangipani Cottage. Karen Sue Hanky, I was willing to bet, was probably braiding somebody's hair right now, while somebody else told ghost stories and they all enjoyed a big bowl of buttered popcorn from the utility kitchen.

Popcorn. My stomach rumbled at the thought. I hadn't had any dinner. I was starving. I was starving, Birch Tree Cottage was out of control, and I still hadn't had a chance to open that envelope Pamela had given to me to give to Ruth.

Except, of course, that what was inside the envelope was really for me.

It was the idea of the ghost stories that did it, I guess. I couldn't shriek over the screaming, and I couldn't catch any of the kids who were racing around, but I could make it a lot harder for them to see. I stalked over to the fuse box and, one by one, threw the switches.

The cottage was plunged into blackness. It's amazing how dark things can get out in the country. They had switched off the lights along the paths through camp, since everyone was supposed to be in bed, so there wasn't even any light from outdoors to creep in through the windows—especially since the area we were in was so thickly wooded, not even moonbeams could penetrate the canopy of leaves overhead. I couldn't see my own hand in front of my face.

And the other residents of Birch Tree Cottage were suffering from a similar difficulty. I heard several thumps as the runners collided with pieces of furniture, and a number of people shrieked as the lights went out.

Then frightened voices began to call out my name.

"Oops," I said. "Power outage. There must be a storm somewhere."

More frightened whimpering.

"I guess," I said, "we'll all just have to go to sleep. Because we can't do anything in the dark."

It was Shane's voice that rang out scathingly, "There's no power outage. You turned out the lights."

Little brat.

"I didn't," I said. "Come over here, and try the switch." I illustrated for them, flicking the switch on and off. The sound was unmistakable. "I guess everybody better get into their pajamas and get into bed."

There was a good deal of moaning and groaning about how were they supposed to find their pajamas in the dark. There was also some bickering about the fact that they couldn't brush their teeth in the dark, and what if they got cavities, et cetera. I ignored it. I had found, in the utility kitchen, a flashlight, for use in the event of a real blackout, and I offered to escort whoever wanted to go to the bathroom.

Shane said, "Just give me the flashlight, and I'll escort everyone," but I wasn't falling for that one.

After everyone had done what he needed to do, ablution-wise, I reminded them all about the early morning Polar Bear swim, and that they had better get plenty of sleep, since their first music lessons would begin right after breakfast. The only time they wouldn't be playing their instruments, in fact, would be at the Polar Bear swim, meals, and a two-hour period from three to five, when lake swims, tennis, baseball, and arts and crafts were allowed. There were nature walks, for those who were so inclined. There even used to be trips to Wolf Cave, a semi-famous cave near the lake—semi-famous because up so far north, caves are almost unheard of, the glaciers having flattened most of upstate Indiana. But of course some stupid camper had gotten himself whacked on the head by a falling stalactite, or something, so now spelunking was no longer listed as one of the activities allowed during the kids' few short hours of free time.

It seemed to me that for kids, the campers at Lake Wawasee weren't allowed a whole lot of time to be . . . well, just kids.

When they were all in their beds, and had sweetly sang out good night to me, I took the flashlight with me into my own room. No sense adjusting the fuse box so that my own light would turn on: they'd just see it, shining out from under the crack in the door, and know I'd lied to them about the power outage. I took off my counselor shirt and shorts, and, in a pair of boxers I'd stolen from Douglas and a tank top, I consumed most of a box of Fiddle Faddle while perusing, by flashlight beam, the contents of the envelope Pamela had given me to give to Ruth.

Dear Jess,
I hope this finds you well. Your camp counselor job sounds like a lot of fun.

Yeah, right, I grunted to myself. Of course it sounded like fun . . . to people who'd never had the displeasure of meeting Shane, anyway. The very feminine cursive went on.

Enclosed please find a photo of Taylor Monroe.

I shined the beam from the flashlight into the envelope and found a color studio portrait—like the kind you would get at Sears, with Sesame Street in the background—of a curly-headed toddler in overalls. OshKosh B'gosh.

Taylor disappeared from a shopping mall two years ago, when he was three years old. His parents are desperate to get him back. The police have no suspects or leads.

Good. A neat and simple kidnapping. Rosemary had done a lot of homework to make sure of this. She only sent me the cases in which she was certain the kid in question actually wanted to be found. It was my only condition for finding the kids: that they really wanted to be found.

Well, that, and maintaining my anonymity, of course.

As always, call if you find him. You know the number.

The letter was signed, *Love, Rosemary.*

I studied the photo in the beam from my flashlight. Taylor Monroe, I said to myself. Taylor Monroe, where are you?

The door to my room banged open, and I dropped the photo—and the flashlight—in my surprise.

"Hey," Shane said with interest. "What's that stuff?"

"Jeez," I said, scrambling to hide the photo and letter in my sheets. "Ever heard of knocking?"

"Who's the kid?" Shane wanted to know.

"None of your business." I found the flashlight and shined it on him. "What do you want?"

Shane's eyes narrowed, but not just because there was a bright light shining into them. They narrowed with suspicion.

"Hey," he said. "That's a picture of a missing kid, isn't it?"

Well, Pamela had been right about one thing, anyway. Shane was gifted. And not just musically, either, it appeared. The kid was sharp.

"Don't be ridiculous," I said.

"Oh, yeah? Well, what are you hiding it for, then?"

"Shane." I couldn't believe this. "What do you want?"

Shane ignored my question, however.

"You lied," he said, sounding indignant. "You totally lied. You *do* still have those powers."

"Yeah, that's right, Shane," I said. "That's why I'm working here at Camp Wawasee for five bucks an hour. I have psychic powers and all, and could be raking in the bucks finding missing people for the government, but I prefer to hang around here."

Shane's only response to my sarcasm was to blink a few times.

"Come off it," I said sourly. "Okay? Now why are you out of bed?"

The look of dark suspicion didn't leave Shane's face, but he did manage to remember his fake excuse for barging in on me, undoubtedly in an effort to catch me sans apparel. He whined, "I want a drink of water."

"So go get one," I said, not very nicely.

"I can't see my way to the bathroom," he whined some more.

"You found your way here," I pointed out to him.

"But—"

"Get out, Shane."

He left, still whining. I fished out Taylor's photo and Rosemary's letter. I didn't feel bad about lying to Shane. Not at all. I'd done it as much to protect Rosemary as myself. After my run-in last spring with the U.S. government, whose ideas about the best way to use my psychic ability had sort of differed from mine, Rosemary, a receptionist who worked at a foundation that helped find missing children, had very generously agreed to help me . . . um, well, privatize. And we had been working together, undiscovered, ever since.

And I wanted things to stay that way between us: undiscovered. I would not risk revealing our secret even to a whiny almost-twelve-year-old musical genius like Shane.

To be on the safe side, I put away Rosemary's letter and picked up a copy of *Cosmo* Ruth had lent me. "10 Ways to Tell He Thinks of You as More Than Just a Friend." Ooh. Good stuff. I read eagerly, wondering if I'd realize, just from reading this article, that Rob really did like me, only I had simply been too stupid to read the signs.

1. He cooks you dinner on your birthday.

Well, Rob certainly hadn't done that. But my birthday was in April. He and I hadn't really started . . . well, whatever it was we were doing . . . until May. So that one was no good.

2. He makes an attempt to get along with your girl-friends.

I only have one real friend, and that's Ruth. She's barely even met Rob. Well, not really. See, Rob's from what you might call the wrong side of the tracks. Ruth isn't a snob . . . at least, not really . . . but she definitely wouldn't approve of me going out with someone who didn't have college and a career as a professional in his sights.

So much for Number 2.

3. He listens to you when—

I was interrupted by a thump. It was followed immediately by a wail.

Gripping my flashlight, I stalked out of my room.

"All right," I said, shining the flashlight into one face after another—all of which were very much awake. "What gives?"

When the light from my flashlight reached Lionel's face, it picked up the tear tracks down his cheeks.

"Why are you crying?" I demanded. But I knew. That thump I heard. Shane was in his bed, some feet away, but his face looked too sweetly innocent for him to not be guilty of something.

But all Lionel would say was, "I am not crying."

I was sick of it. I really was. All I wanted to do was read my magazine and go to bed, so I could find Taylor Monroe. Was that so much to ask, after such a long day?

"Fine," I said, sitting down on the floor, my flashlight shining against the ceiling.

Arthur went, "Uh, Jess? What are you doing?"

"I am going to sit here," I said, "until you all fall asleep."

This caused some excited giggling. Don't ask me why.

There was silence for maybe ten seconds. Then Doo Sun went, "Jess? Do you have any brothers?"

Guardedly, I replied in the affirmative.

"I thought so," Doo Sun said.

Instantly suspicious, I asked, "Why?"

"You're wearing boys' underpants," Paul pointed out.

I looked down. I'd forgotten about Douglas's boxers.

"So I am," I said.

"Jess," Shane said, in a voice so sugary, I knew he was up to no good.

"What," I said flatly.

"Are you a lesbian?"

I closed my eyes. I counted to ten. I tried to ignore the giggling from the other beds.

I opened my eyes and said, "No, I am not a lesbian. As a matter of fact, I have a boyfriend."

"Who?" Arthur wanted to know. "One of those guys I saw you with on the path? One of those other counselors?"

This caused a certain amount of suggestive hooting. I said, "No. My boyfriend would never do anything as geeky as be a camp counselor. My boyfriend rides a Harley and is a car mechanic."

This caused some appreciative murmuring. Eleven-year-old boys are much more impressed by car mechanics than people like . . . well, my best friend, Ruth, for instance.

Then . . . don't ask me why—maybe I was still thinking about Karen Sue over there in Frangipani Cottage. But suddenly, I launched into this story about Rob, and about how once this guy had brought a car into Wilkins's Auto that turned out to have a skeleton in the trunk.

It was, of course, a complete fabrication. As I went on about Rob and this car, which turned out to be haunted, on account of the woman who'd been left to suffocate in its trunk, I borrowed liberally from Stephen King, incorporating aspects from both

Maximum Overdrive and *Christine*. These kids were too young, of course, to have read the books, and I doubted their parents had ever let them see the movies.

And I was right. I held them enthralled all the way until the fiery cataclysm at the end, in which Rob saved our entire town by bravely pointing a grenade launcher at the renegade automobile and blowing it into a thousand pieces.

Stunned silence followed this pronouncement. I had, I could tell, greatly disturbed them. But I was not done.

"And sometimes," I whispered, "on nights like this, when a storm somewhere far away douses the power, blanketing us in darkness, you can still see the headlights of that killer car, way off on the horizon"—I flicked off the flashlight—"way off in the distance . . . coming closer . . . and closer . . . and closer . . ."

Not a sound. They were hardly breathing.

"Good night," I said, and went back into my room.

Where I fell asleep a few minutes later, after finishing the box of Fiddle Faddle.

And I didn't hear another peep out of my fellow residents of Birch Tree Cottage until after reveille the next morning. . . .

By which time, of course, I knew precisely where Taylor Monroe was.

CHAPTER

5

"I was so scared, I almost wet the bed," said John.

"Yeah? Well, I was so scared, I couldn't get out of bed, not even to go to the bathroom." Sam had a towel slung around his neck. His chest was so thin, it was practically concave. "I just held it," he said. "I didn't want to run the risk, you know, of seeing those headlights out the window."

"I saw them," Tony declared.

There were general noises of derision at this.

"No, really," Tony said. "Through the window. I swear. It looked like they were floating over the lake."

A heated discussion followed about whether or not Rob's killer car could float, or if it had merely hovered over the lake.

Standing in line for the Polar Bear swim, I began to feel that things were not nearly so bleak as they'd seemed yesterday. For one thing, I'd had a good night's sleep.

Really. I know that sounds surprising, considering that while I'd slept, my brain waves had apparently been bombarded with all this information about a five-year-old kid I had never met. On TV and in books and stuff, psychics always get this tortured look on their faces when they get a vision, like someone is jabbing them with a toothpick, or whatever. But that's never happened to me. Maybe it's because I only get my psychic visions while I sleep, but none of them have ever hurt.

The way I see it, it's exactly like all those times you've been sitting there thinking to yourself, Gee, So-and-So hasn't called in a while, and all of a sudden the phone rings, and it's So-and-So. And you're all, "Dude, I was just thinking about you," and you laugh because it's a big coincidence.

Only it's not. It's not a coincidence. That was the psychic part of your brain working, the part hardly any of us ever listens to, the part people call "intuition" or "gut feeling" or "instinct." That's the part of my brain that the lightning, when it struck me, sent all haywire. And that's why I'm a receiver now for all sorts of information I shouldn't have—like the fact that Taylor Monroe, who'd disappeared from a shopping center in Des Moines two years ago, was now living in Gainesville, Florida, with some people to whom he wasn't even remotely related.

See, ordinary people—most everyone, really, even

smart people, like Einstein and Madonna—use only three percent of their brain. Three percent! That's all it takes to learn to walk and talk and make change and parallel park and decide which flavor of yogurt is your favorite.

But some people—people like me, who've been hit by lightning, or put into a sensory deprivation tank, or whatever—use more than their three percent. For whatever reason, we've tapped into the other ninety-seven percent of our brain.

And that's the part, apparently, where all the good stuff is. . . .

Except that the only stuff I seem to have access to is the current address of just about every missing person in the universe.

Well, it was better than nothing, I guess.

But yeah, okay? In spite of the psychic vision thing, I'd slept great.

I don't think the same could be said for my fellow campers—and their counselors. Ruth in particular looked bleary-eyed.

"My God," she said. "They kept me up all night. They just kept yakking. . . ." Her blue eyes widened behind her glasses as she got a better look at me. I was in my bathing suit, just like my boys, with a towel slung around my own neck. "God, you're not actually going *in*, are you?"

I shrugged. "Sure." What else was I supposed to do? I was going to have to call Rosemary, as soon as I could get my hands on a phone. But that, I was pretty sure, wasn't going to be for hours.

"You don't have to," Ruth said. "I mean, it's just for the kids. . . ."

"Well, it's not like I could take a shower this morning," I reminded her. "Not with eight budding little sex maniacs around."

Ruth looked from me to the bright blue water, sparkling in the morning sun. "Suit yourself," she said. "But you're going to smell like chlorine all day."

"Yeah," I said. "And who's going to get close enough to smell me?"

We both looked over at Todd. He, too, was in a bathing suit. And looking very impressive in it, as well, I might add.

"Not him," I said.

Ruth sighed. "No, I guess not."

I noticed that while Todd might be ignoring us, Scott and Dave definitely weren't. They both looked away when I glanced in their direction, but there was no question about it: they'd been scoping.

Ruth, however, only had eyes for Todd.

"And you have your tutorial today," she was pointing out. "I thought that flute guy was pretty hot. You don't want to smell chlorine-y for *him*, do you?"

"That flute guy" was the wind instructor, a French dude name Jean-Paul something or other. He was kind of hot, in a scruffy-looking French kind of way. But he was a little old for me. I mean, I like my men older, and all, but I think thirty might be pushing it a little. How weird would *that* look at prom?

"I don't know," I said as our line moved closer to the water. "He's Do-able, I guess. But no Hottie."

I hadn't realized Karen Sue Hanky was eavesdropping until she spun around and, with flashing but deeply circled eyes, snarled, "I hope you aren't speaking of Professor Le Blanc. He happens to be a musical genius, you know."

I rolled my eyes. "Who *isn't* a musical genius around here?" I wanted to know. "Except you, of course, Karen."

Ruth, who'd been chewing gum, swallowed it in her effort not to laugh.

"I resent that," Karen said, slowly turning as red as the letters on the lifeguard's T-shirt. "I will have you know that I have been practicing for four hours a day, and that my dad's paying thirty dollars an hour to a professor who's been giving me private lessons over at the university."

"Yeah?" I raised my eyebrows. "Gosh, maybe you'll be able to keep up with the rest of us now."

Karen narrowed her eyes at me.

But whatever she'd been going to say was drowned out when the lifeguard—who was also pretty cute: definitely Do-able—blew a whistle and yelled, "Birch Tree!"

My fellow birches and I made a run for the water and jumped in simultaneously, with much shrieking and splashing. Some of us were better swimmers than others, and there was much choking and sputtering, and at least one attempted drowning, which the lifeguard spotted. Shane was forced to sit out for twenty minutes. But, otherwise, we had a good time.

I was teaching them a new song—since Pamela had put the kibosh on "I Met a Miss"—when Scott and Dave and Ruth and Karen strolled by with their campers. All of them, I noticed, looked a little bleary around the edges.

"I don't understand how you can be so wide awake," Scott said. "Didn't they keep you up all night?"

"No," I said. "Not at all."

"What's your secret?" Dave wanted to know. "Mine were bouncing off the walls. I had to sleep with a pillow over my head."

Ruth shook her head. "Their first night away from home," she said knowingly. "It's always the toughest. They usually settle down by the third or fourth night, out of sheer exhaustion."

Karen Sue exhaled gustily. "Not mine, I'll bet." She glared at some passing Frangipanis, who giggled and tore off along the path, causing all of us to chime, in unison, "*Walk, don't run!*"

"They are little monsters," Karen muttered, under her breath. "Won't do a thing I say, and the mouths on them! I never heard such language in all my life! And all night long, it was giggle, giggle, giggle."

"Me, too," Ruth said tiredly. "They didn't nod off until around five, I think."

"Five-thirty for me," Scott said. He looked at me. "I can't believe that Shane of yours just slipped off to Slumberland without a fight."

"Yeah," Dave said. "What's your secret?"

I honestly didn't know any better. I said, cheerfully, "Oh, I just told them all this really long story, and they nodded off right away. We all slept like stones. Didn't wake up until reveille."

Ruth, astonished, said, "Really?"

"What was the story about?" Dave wanted to know.

Laughingly, I told them. Not about Rob, of course, but about the killer car, and the appropriating of some of Mr. King's works.

They listened in stunned silence. Then Karen said vehemently, "I don't believe in frightening children with ghost stories."

I snorted. Karen, of course, didn't know what she was talking about. What kid didn't love a ghost story? Ghost stories weren't the problem. But the fact that a three-year-old could be kidnapped from a mall and not be found until two years later?

Now *that* was scary.

Which was why, instead of joining my fellow Birch Trees for breakfast that morning—even though I was starving, of course, after my swim and my Fiddle Faddle dinner of the night before—I snuck back into the camp's administrative offices, in the hopes of finding a phone I could use.

I scored one without a lot of trouble. The secretary with the NASCAR-driving boyfriend wasn't in yet. I slipped into her chair and, dialing nine first to get out, dialed the number to the National Organization for Missing Children.

Rosemary didn't pick up. Some other lady did.

"1-800-WHERE-R-YOU," she said. "How may I direct your call?"

I had to whisper, of course, so I wouldn't be overheard. I also assumed my best Spanish accent, just in case the line was being monitored. "Rosemary, *por favor.*"

The lady went, "Excuse me?"

I whispered, *"Rosemary."*

"Oh," the lady said. "Um. One moment."

Jeez! I didn't have a moment! I could be busted any *second*. All I needed was for Pamela to walk in and find that not only had I abandoned my charges, but I was also making personal use of camp property. . . .

"This is Rosemary," a voice said, cautiously, into my ear.

"Hey," I said, dropping the Spanish accent. There was no need to say who was calling. Rosemary knew my voice. "Taylor Monroe. Gainesville, Florida." I rattled off the street address. Because that's how it comes. The information, I mean. It's like there's a search engine inside of my brain: insert name and photo image of missing child, and out comes full address, often with zip code attached, of where child can be located.

Seriously. It's bizarre, especially considering I've never even heard of most of these places.

"Thank you," Rosemary said, careful not to say my name within hearing of her supervisor, who'd sicced the Feds on me once before. "They're going to be so happy. You don't know—"

It was at this point that Pamela, looking troubled, came striding down the hall, heading straight toward the secretary's desk.

I whispered, "Sorry, Rosemary, gotta go," and hung up the phone. Then I ducked beneath the desk.

It didn't do any good, though. I was busted. Way busted.

Pamela went, "Jess?"

I curled into a tight ball underneath the secretary's desk. Maybe, if I didn't move, didn't even breathe, Pamela would think she had seen a mirage or something, and go away.

"Jessica," Pamela said, in the kind of voice you probably wouldn't use if you were talking to a mirage. "Come out. I saw you."

Sheepishly, I crawled out from beneath the desk.

"Look," I said. "I can explain. It's my grandma's ninetieth birthday today, and if I didn't call first thing, well, there'd be H to pay—"

I thought I'd get brownie points for saying H instead of hell, but it didn't work out that way. For one thing, Pamela had looked as if she'd already been in a bad mood before she saw me. Now she was even more upset.

"Jess," she said in a weird voice. "You know you aren't supposed to be using camp property—"

"—for personal calls," I finished for her. "Yes, I know. And I'm really sorry. Like I said, it was an emergency."

Pamela looked way more upset than the situation warranted. I knew something else was up. But I figured it was some kind of orchestra camp emergency or something. You know, like they'd run out of clarinet reeds.

But of course that wasn't it. Of course it turned out to have something to do with me after all.

"Jess," Pamela said. "I was just going to look for you."

"You were?" I blinked at her. There was only one reason for Pamela to have been looking for me, and that was that I was in trouble. Again.

And the only thing I'd done recently—besides make a personal call from a camp phone—was the whole ghost story thing. Had Karen Sue ratted me out for that? If so, it had to be a record. I had left her barely five minutes ago. What did the girl have, bionic feet?

It was clear that Pamela was on Karen Sue's side about the whole not frightening little children thing. I could see I was going to have to do some fast talking.

"Look," I said. "I can explain. Shane was completely out of control last night, and the only way I could get him to stop picking on the littler kids was to—"

"Jessica," Pamela interrupted, sort of sharply. "I don't know what you're talking about. There's . . . there's actually someone here to see you."

I shut up and just stared at her. "Someone here?" I echoed lamely. "To see *me?*"

A thousand things went through my head. The first thing I thought was . . . Douglas. Douglas's phone call the night before. He hadn't just been calling to say he missed me. He'd been calling to say good-bye. He'd finally done it. The voices had told him to, and so he had. Douglas had killed himself, and my dad—my mother—my other brother—one of them was here to break the news to me.

A roaring sound started in my ears. I felt as if the bottom had dropped out of my stomach.

"Where?" I asked, through lips that felt like they were made of ice.

Pamela nodded, her expression grave, toward her office door. I moved toward it slowly, with Pamela following close behind. Let it be Michael, I prayed. Let them have sent Mikey to break the news to me. Michael I could take. If it was my mother, or even my father, I was bound to start crying. And I didn't want to cry in front of Pamela.

It wasn't Mikey, though. It wasn't my father, either, or even my mother. It was a man I'd never seen before.

He was older than me, but younger than my parents. He looked to be about Pamela's age. Still, he was definitely Do-able. He may have even qualified for Hottie. Clean-shaven, with dark, slightly longish hair, he had on a tie and sports coat. When my gaze fell upon him, he climbed hastily to his feet, and I saw that he was quite tall—well, everyone is, to me—and not very graceful.

"M-Miss Mastriani?" he asked in a shy voice.

Social worker? I wondered, taking in the fact that his shoes were well-worn, and the cuffs of his sports coat a bit frayed. Definitely not a Fed. He was too good-looking to be a Fed. He'd have drawn too much attention.

Schoolteacher, maybe. Yeah. Math or science. But why on earth would a math or science teacher be here to break the news about my brother Douglas's suicide?

"I'm Jonathan Herzberg," the man said, thrusting his right hand toward me. "I really hope you won't resent the intrusion. I understand that it is highly unusual, and a gross infringement on your rights to personal privacy and all of that . . . but the fact is, Miss Mastriani, I'm desperate." His brown-eyed gaze bore into mine. "Really, really desperate."

I took a step backward, away from the hand. I moved back so fast, I ended up with my butt against the edge of Pamela's desk.

A reporter. I should have known. The tie should have been a dead giveaway.

"Look," I said.

The icy feeling had left my lips. The roaring in my ears had stopped. The feeling that the bottom of my stomach had dropped out? Yeah, that had disappeared. Instead, I just felt anger.

Cold, hard anger.

"I don't know what paper you're from," I said stonily. "Or magazine or news show or whatever. But I have had just about enough of you guys. You all practically ruined my life this past spring, following me around, bugging my family. Well, it's over, okay?

Get it through your heads: lightning girl has hung up her bolts. I am not in the missing person business anymore."

Jonathan Herzberg looked more than a little taken aback. He glanced from me to Pamela and then back again.

"M-Miss Mastriani," he stammered. "I'm not . . . I mean, I don't—"

"Mr. Herzberg isn't a reporter, Jess." Pamela's voice was, for her, uncharacteristically soft. That, more than anything, got my attention. "We never allow reporters—and we have had our share of illustrious guests in the past—onto our property. Surely you know that."

I suppose I did know that, somewhere deep in the recesses of my mind. Lake Wawasee was private property. You had to be on a list of invited guests even to be let through the gates. They took security very seriously at Camp Wawasee, due to the number of expensive instruments lying around. Oh, and the kids, and all.

I looked from Pamela to Mr. Herzberg and then back again. They both looked . . . well, flushed. There was no other way to put it.

"Do you two know each other or something?" I asked.

Pamela, who was by no means what you'd call a shrinking violet kind of gal, actually blushed.

"No, no," she said. "I mean . . . well, we just met. Mr. Herzberg . . . well, Jess, Mr. Herzberg—"

I could see I was going to get nothing rational out of Miss J Crew. I decided to tackle Mr. L.L. Bean, instead.

"All right," I said, eyeing him. "I'll bite. If you're not a reporter, what do you want with me?"

Jonathan Herzberg wiped his hands on his khaki pants. He must have been sweating a lot or something, since he left damp spots on the cotton.

"I was hoping," he said softly, "that you could help me find my little girl."

CHAPTER

6

I looked quickly at Pamela. She hadn't taken her eyes off Jonathan Herzberg.

Great. Just great. Mary Ann was in love with the Professor.

"Maybe you didn't hear me the first time," I said. "I don't do that anymore."

A lie, of course. But he didn't know that.

Or maybe he did.

Mr. Herzberg said, "I know that's what you told everyone. Last spring, I mean. But I . . . well, I was hoping you only said that because the press and everything . . . well, it got a little intense."

I just looked at him. *Intense?* He called being chased by government goons with guns *intense?*

I'd show him intense.

"Hello?" I said. "What part of 'I can't help you' don't you understand? It doesn't work anymore. The psychic thing is played out. The batteries have run dry—"

As I'd been speaking, Mr. Herzberg had been digging around in his briefcase. When he stood up again, he was holding a photograph.

"This is her," he said, thrusting the photo into my hands. "This is Keely. She's only five—"

I backed away with about as much horror as if he'd put a snake, and not a photo of a little girl, into my fingers.

"I'm not looking at this," I said, practically heaving the photo back at him. "I *won't* look at this."

"Jess!" Pamela sounded a little horrified herself. "Jess, please, just listen—"

"No," I said. "No, I won't. You can't do this. I'm out of here."

Look, I know how it sounds. I mean, here was this guy, and he seemed sincere. He seemed like a genuinely distraught father. How could I be so cold, so unfeeling, not to want to help him?

Try looking at it from my point of view: It is one thing to get a package in the mail with all the details of a missing child's case laid neatly out in front of one . . . to wake the next morning and make a single phone call, the origins of which the person on the receiving end of that call has promised to erase. Easy.

More than just easy, though: Anonymous.

But it is another thing entirely to have the missing kid's parent in front of one, desperately begging for help. There is nothing easy about that.

And nothing in the least anonymous.

And I have to maintain my anonymity. I have to.

I turned and headed for the door. I was going to say, I staggered blindly for the door, because that sounds all dramatic and stuff, but it isn't true, exactly. I mean, I wasn't exactly staggering—I was walking just fine. And I could see and all. The way I know I could see just fine was that the photo, which I thought I'd gotten rid of, came fluttering down from the air where I'd thrown it. Just fluttered right down, and landed at my feet. Landed at my feet, right in front of the door, like a leaf or a feather or something that had fallen from the sky, and just randomly picked me to land in front of.

And I looked. It landed faceup. How could I help but look?

I'm not going to say anything dorky like she was the cutest kid I'd ever seen or something like that. That wasn't it. It was just that, until I saw the photo, she wasn't a real kid. Not to me. She was just something somebody was using to try to get me to admit something I didn't want to.

Then I saw her.

Look, I was not trying to be a bitch with this whole not-wanting-to-help-this-guy thing. Really. You just have to understand that since that day, that day I'd been struck by lightning, a lot of things had gotten very screwed up. I mean, really, really screwed up. My brother Douglas had had to be hospitalized again on account of me. I had practically ruined this other kid's life, just because I'd found him. *He hadn't wanted to be found.* I had had to do a lot of really tricky stuff to make everything right again.

And I'm not even going to go into the stuff about the Feds and the guns and the exploding helicopter and all.

It was like that day the lightning struck me, it caused this chain reaction that just kept getting more and more out of control, and all these people, all of these people I cared about, got hurt.

And I didn't want that to happen again. Not ever.

I had a pretty good system in the works, too, for seeing that it didn't. If everyone just played along the way they were supposed to, things went fine. Lost kids, kids who wanted to be found, got found. Nobody hassled me or my family. And things ran along pretty damn smoothly.

Then Jonathan Herzberg had to come along and thrust his daughter's photo under my nose.

And I knew. I knew it was happening all over again.

And there wasn't anything I could do to stop it.

Jonathan Herzberg was no dope. He saw the photo land. And he saw me look down.

And he went in for the kill.

"She's in kindergarten," he said. "Or at least, she would be starting in September, if . . . if she wasn't gone. She likes dogs and horses. She wants to be a veterinarian when she grows up. She's not afraid of anything."

I just stood there, looking down at the photo.

"Her mother has always been . . . troubled. After

Keely's birth, she got worse. I thought it was post-partum depression. Only it never went away. The doctors prescribed antidepressants. Sometimes she took them. Mostly, though, she didn't."

Jonathan Herzberg's voice was even and low. He wasn't crying or anything. It was like he was telling a story about someone else's wife, not his own.

"She started drinking. I came home from work one day, and she wasn't there. But Keely was. My wife had left a three-year-old child home, by herself, all day. She didn't come home until around midnight, and when she did, she was drunk. The next day, Keely and I moved out. I let her have the house, the car, everything . . . but not Keely." Now his voice started to sound a little shaky. "Since we left, she—my ex-wife—has just gotten worse. She's fallen in with this guy . . . well, he's not what you'd call a real savory character. And last week the two of them took Keely from the day care center I put her in. I think they're somewhere in the Chicago area—he has family around there—but the police haven't been able to find them. I just . . . I remembered about you, and I . . . I'm desperate. I called your house, and the person who answered the phone said—"

I bent down and picked the photo up. Up close, the kid looked no different than she had from the floor. She was a five-year-old little girl who wanted to be a veterinarian when she grew up, who lived with a father who obviously had as much of a clue as I did about how to braid hair, since Keely's was all over the place.

"He's got the custody papers," Pamela said to me softly. "I've seen them. When he first showed up . . . well, I didn't know what to do. You know our policy. But he . . . well, he . . ."

I knew what he had done. It was right there on Pamela's face. He had played on her natural affection for children, and on the fact that he was a single dad who was passably good-looking, and she was a woman in her thirties who wasn't married yet. It was as clear as the whistle around her neck.

I don't know what made me do it. Decide to help Jonathan Herzberg, I mean, in spite of my suspicion that he was an undercover agent, sent to prove I'd lied when I'd said I no longer had any psychic powers. Maybe it was the frayed condition of his cuffs. Maybe it was the messiness of his daughter's braids. In any case, I decided. I decided to risk it.

It was a decision that I'd live to regret, but how was I to know that then?

I guess what I did next must have startled them both, but to me, it was perfectly natural. Well, at least to someone who's seen *Point of No Return* as many times as I have.

I walked over to the radio I'd spied next to Pamela's desk, turned it on very loud, then yelled over the strains of John Mellencamp's latest, "Shirts up."

Pamela and Jonathan Herzberg exchanged wide-eyed glances. "What?" Pamela asked, raising her voice to be heard over the music.

"You heard me," I yelled back at her. "You want my help? I need to make sure you're legit."

Jonathan Herzberg must have been a pretty desperate man, since, without another word, he peeled off his sports coat. Pamela was slower to untuck her Camp Wawasee oxford T.

"I don't understand," she said as I went around the office, feeling under countertops and lifting up plants and the phone and stuff and looking underneath them. "What's going on?"

Jonathan was a little swifter. He'd completely unbuttoned his shirt, and now he held it open, to show me that nothing was taped to his surprisingly hairless chest.

"She wants to make sure we're not wearing wires," he explained to Pamela.

She continued to look bewildered, but she finally lifted her shirt up enough for me to get a peek underneath. She kept her back to Mr. Herzberg while she did this, and after I'd gotten a look at her bra, I could see why. It was kind of see-through, quite sexy-looking for a camp director and all. I don't know much about bras, not having much of a need for one myself, but couldn't help being impressed by Pamela's.

When they had both proved they weren't wearing transmitters, and I had determined that the place wasn't bugged, I switched the radio off. Then, holding up Keely's photo, I said, "I have to keep this awhile."

"Does this mean you're going to help?" Mr. Herzberg asked eagerly, as he buttoned up again. "Find Keely, I mean?"

"Just give your digits to Pamela," I said, putting Keely's photo in my pocket. "You'll be hearing from me."

Pamela, looking kind of moist-eyed, went, "Oh, Jess. Jess, I'm so glad. Thank you. Thank you so much."

I'm not one for the mushy stuff, and I could feel a big wave of it coming on—mostly from Pamela's direction, but Keely's dad didn't look exactly stone-faced—so I got out of there, and fast.

I would say I'd gotten approximately five or six steps down the hall before I began to have some serious misgivings about what I'd just done. I mean, okay, Pamela had seen some papers giving the guy custody, but that didn't really mean anything. Courts award custody to bad parents all the time. How was I supposed to know whether the story he'd told me about his wife was true?

Simple. I was going to have to check it out.

Great. Not like I didn't have enough to do. Like, for instance, look out for a cabinful of little boys, and, oh yeah, practice for my private lesson with Professor Le Blanc, flutist extraordinaire.

I was wondering how on earth I was going to accomplish all of this—find Keely Herzberg and make sure she really wanted to go back to living with her dad, keep Shane from killing Lionel, and brush up on my fingering for Professor Le Blanc—when I noticed that the secretary whose phone I'd borrowed was in her seat.

And oh, my God, she looked just like John Wayne!

I'm not joking! She looked like a man, and *she* had a boyfriend. Not just any boyfriend, either, but one who raced cars for a living.

I ask you, what is wrong with this picture? Not like unattractive people don't deserve to have boyfriends, but hello, I have been told by several people—and not just by my mother, either—that I am fairly attractive. But do *I* have a boyfriend?

That would be a big N-O.

But Ms. John Wayne over here, she not only has a boyfriend, but a totally hot one, who drives race cars.

Okay. There is so not a God. That's all I have to say about that.

"Hey." I put my tray down next to Ruth's. "I need to talk to you."

Ruth was sitting with the girls of Tulip Tree Cottage. They were all eating the same thing for lunch: a large salad, dressing on the side; chicken breasts with the skin removed; cottage cheese; melon slices; and raspberry sherbet for dessert. I am not even joking.

Not that the boys of Birch Tree Cottage were any different. They were following their counselor's example, too. Only their trays were loaded down with pizza, Tater Tots, coleslaw, baked beans, peanut butter bars, macaroni and cheese, ice cream sandwiches, and chocolate chip cookies.

Hey, I'd missed dinner and breakfast. I was hungry, all right?

Ruth looked down at my tray and then glanced quickly away, with a shudder.

"Is it about your saturated fat intake?" she wanted to know. "Because if you keep eating like that, your heart is going to explode."

"You know I have a high metabolism," I said. "Now, listen, this is serious. I might need to borrow your car."

Ruth had been delicately sipping her glass of Diet Coke. When I said the words "your car," she sprayed what was in her mouth all over the little girl sitting opposite her.

"Oh, my God," Ruth said as she leaned across the table to mop up the soda from the little girl's face. "Oh, Shawanda, I am so sorry—"

Shawanda went, "That's okay, Ruth," in this worshipful voice. Like getting sprayed in your face by your counselor was this big honor or something.

"Jeez." Ruth turned to me. "Are you high? You think I'm going to let you borrow my car? You don't even have a license!"

I know it sounds hard to believe, but Ruth was telling the truth. I don't have a driver's license. I am probably the only sixteen-year-old in the state of Indiana without one.

And it's not because I can't drive. I am a good driver, I really am. Better, probably, than Ruth, when it comes down to it.

I just have this one little problem.

Not even a problem, really. More like a need.

A need for speed.

"Absolutely not," Ruth said, spearing a melon wedge and stuffing it into her mouth. Ruth and I have been best friends since kindergarten, so it's not like we ever bother being polite around one another. Ruth spoke around the food in her mouth. "If you think for one minute I would ever let you touch my car, Miss But-I-Was-Only-Going-Eighty-in-a-Thirty-Five-Mile-an-Hour-Zone, you must be on crack."

"I am not," I hissed at her, conscious that the gazes of all the little residents of Tulip Tree Cottage were upon us, "on crack. I just might need a car tomorrow, is all."

"What for?" Ruth demanded.

I didn't want to just come right out and tell her. Not in front of all those inquisitive little faces. So I said, "A situation might arise."

"Jessica," Ruth said. She only calls me by my full name when she is well and truly disgusted with me. "You know we aren't allowed to leave the campgrounds except on Sunday afternoons, which we get off. Tomorrow, I shouldn't need to remind you, is Tuesday. You can't go anywhere. Not without losing your job. Now what's so all-fired important that you are willing to risk losing your job over it?"

I said, "I think I have management's okay on this one. Come on, Ruth, it will only be for a couple of hours."

Ruth's eyes, behind the lenses of her glasses, widened. "Wait a minute. This isn't . . . this isn't about that, you know, *thing,* is it?"

"That, you know, *thing"* is how Ruth often refers

to my newfound talent. The fact that "you know, *thing*" is pretty much all her fault has never seemed to occur to her. I mean, she was, after all, the person who made me walk home the day of the lightning storm. But whatever.

"Yes," I said. "It is about that, you know, *thing*. Now are you going to let me borrow your car, or not?"

Ruth looked thoughtful. "I'll tell you what. If you can promise we won't get into trouble, I'll take you wherever it is you want to go."

Great. Just what I needed.

Don't get me wrong. Ruth's my best friend, and all. But Ruth isn't what you'd ever call good in a crisis. For example, once Ruth's twin brother, Skip, who is allergic to bees, got stung by one, and Ruth responded by clapping her hands over her ears and running out of the room. Seriously. And she'd been fourteen at the time, fully capable of dialing 911 or whatever.

I tell you, it's enough to make you question the judgment of Camp Wawasee's hiring staff, isn't it?

I went, carefully, "Um, you know what? Just forget about it, okay?" Maybe Pamela would let me borrow her car.

But what if Pamela was in on it? I mean, what if, despite the fact she and Jonathan Herzberg hadn't been wearing wires, the two of them were in cahoots with the Feds? What if this whole thing was an elaborately orchestrated sting set up by my good friends with the FBI?

Which was why I needed a car. I needed to check out the situation for myself first.

And not just because there was a chance this might be a setup, but because, well, Keely had rights, too. One thing I had learned last spring—one thing that had been taught to me, and very emphatically, by a boy named Sean who I'd thought was missing, but who, when I found him, turned out to be exactly where he wanted to be—is that when you are in the missing person business, it is a good idea to make sure the person you are looking for actually wants to be found before you go dragging him or her back to where he or she came from. It just makes sense, you know?

Not that I imagined Jonathan Herzberg was lying. If he wasn't in cahoots with the Feds, I mean.

Still, I sort of wanted to hear Keely's mom's side of the story before turning her over to the cops or whatever. And if she really was in Chicago, well, that was only like an hour north of Lake Wawasee. I could make it there and back in the time it took the kids to finish Handel's *Messiah*. Well, almost, anyway.

I wanted to explain all this to Ruth. I wanted to say, "Ruth, look, Pamela isn't going to fire me if I leave the campgrounds because Pamela's the person who is responsible for this in the first place . . . well, sort of."

But another thing I'd learned last spring is that the less people who know about stuff, the better. Really. Even people like your best friend.

"So what I hear you saying"—I tried talking to Ruth the way we'd learned during counselor training to talk to troubled kids—"is that you would feel uncomfortable loaning me your car."

Ruth said, "You hear me correctly. But I'll be glad to go with you, wherever it is. That is, if you can promise we won't get into trouble."

I ate some mac and cheese and pondered how to get out of this without hurting her feelings.

"No guarantees," I finally said, with a shrug.

"Well," Ruth said. "Then you're going to have to find some other boob to loan you their car. What about Dave? I saw him giving you the eye at the pool this morning."

I straightened up. "You did?" I thought he'd been giving *Ruth* the eye.

"I sure did. You should go for it." Ruth nibbled on a piece of chicken. "Hey, maybe we could double. You know, you and Dave, and me and—" I saw her gaze dart over toward Scott's table, then skitter back toward me. She swallowed. "Well, you know," she said, looking embarrassed. "If things work out."

If things worked out between her and Scott, she meant. She took it for granted things would work out between me and Dave. Ruth seemed to forget that I already liked someone, and it wasn't Dave.

Or maybe she wasn't forgetting. Ruth did not exactly approve of my relationship—such as it was—with Rob Wilkins.

Dave Chen, however, was acceptable. In a big

way. I'd overheard him telling someone he'd gotten a near perfect score on his math PSATs.

I was sitting there, wondering why it felt wrong, somehow, to drag a guy like Dave into my problematic existence, when I had never thought twice about dragging Rob, whom I like a whole lot better than I like Dave, into it, when Ruth suddenly went, "Don't you have your first tutorial this afternoon? Shouldn't you be, oh, I don't know, practicing, or something?"

I took a bite of my pizza. Not bad. Not as good as my dad's, of course, but certainly better than that sorry excuse for pizza they serve at the Hut.

"I prefer for Monsieur Le Blanc to hear me at my worst," I explained. "I mean, you can't improve on perfection."

Ruth just waved at me irritably. "Go sit with your little hellions. They're calling you, you know."

My little hellions were, indeed, calling to me. I picked my tray up and joined the rest of the Birch Trees.

"Jess," Tony said. "Get a load of this."

He belched. The rest of the Birch Trees tittered appreciatively.

"That's nothing. Listen to this." Sam took a long swallow of Coke. He then let out a burp of such length and volume, diners at nearby tables glanced over in admiration. Although pleased by this, Sam modestly refused to take total credit for his accomplishment. "Having a deviated septum helps," he informed us.

Seeing that Dr. Alistair, the camp director, had

glanced our way, I quickly steered the conversation in another direction—toward the new Birch Tree Cottage theme song, which I soon had all of them singing heartily:

> *Oh, they built the ship* Titanic
> *To sail the ocean blue.*
> *They thought it was a ship*
> *No water could get through.*
> *But on its maiden voyage*
> *An iceberg hit that ship.*
> *Oh it was sad when the great ship went down.*
>
> *Chorus:*
> *Oh it was sad*
> *So sad*
> *It was sad*
> *It was sad when the great ship went down*
> *To the bottom of the—*
> *Husbands and wives, little children lost their lives*
> *It was sad when the great ship went down*
> *Kerplunk*
> *She sunk*
> *Like junk*
> *Cha-cha-cha*

Everything was going along swimmingly until I caught Shane, between verses, shoveling down all of Lionel's ice cream—the one food item of which there were no second helpings served at Camp Wawasee, for the obvious reason that, without this restriction, the campers would eat nothing but mint chocolate chip.

"Shane!" I bellowed. He was so surprised, he dropped the spoon.

"Aw, hell," Shane said, looking down at his ice cream–spattered shirt. "Look what the lesbo made me do."

"That's three, Shane," I informed him calmly.

He looked up at me bewilderedly. "Three what? What are you talking about?"

"Three strikes. You're sleeping on the porch tonight, buddy."

Shane sneered. "Big deal."

Arthur said, "Shane, you dink, that means you're going to miss out on the story."

Shane narrowed his eyes at me. "I am not missing out on the story," he said evenly.

I blinked at Arthur. "What story?"

"You're going to tell us another story tonight, aren't you, Jess?"

All the residents of Birch Tree Cottage swiveled their heads around to stare at me. I said, "Sure. Sure, there'll be another story."

Tony poked Shane. "Ha, ha," he teased. "You're gonna miss it."

Shane was furious.

"You can't do that," he sputtered at me. "If you do that, I'll—I'll—"

"You'll do what, Shane?" I asked in a bored voice.

He narrowed his eyes at me. "I'll tell," he said menacingly.

"Tell what?" Arthur, his mouth full of fries, wanted to know.

"Yeah," I said. "Tell what?"

Because of course I'd forgotten. About Shane barging into my room the night before, and catching me with Taylor's photo. I'd forgotten all about it.

But he wasted no time reminding me.

"You know," he said, his eyes slitted with malice. "*Lightning* girl."

I swallowed the mouthful of pizza I'd been chewing. It was like cardboard going down my throat. And not just because it was cafeteria food.

"Hey," I said, attempting to sound as if I didn't care. "Tell whoever you want. Be my guest."

It was a feint, of course, but it worked, taking the wind right out of his sails. His shoulders slumped and he studied his empty plate meditatively, as if hoping an appropriate reply would appear upon it.

I didn't feel the least bit sorry for him. Little bully. But I wasn't just mad at Shane. I was peeved at Lionel, too. How could he just sit there and let people pick on him like that? Granted Shane outweighed him by fifty pounds or so, but I had bested far bigger adversaries when I'd been Lionel's same age and size.

After lunch, as we were walking toward the music building, where the kids would continue their lessons until free play at three, I tried to impress upon Lionel the fact that, if he didn't stand up for himself, Shane was just going to keep on torturing him.

"But, Jess," Lionel said. He pronounced my name as if it were spelled Jace. "He will pound on me."

"Look, Lionel," I said. "He might pound on you. But you just pound him back, only harder. And go for the nose. Big guys are total babies when it comes to their noses."

Lionel looked dubious. "In my country," he said, trilling his *r*'s musically, "violence is looked upon with disfavor."

"Well, you're in America now," I told him. The other Birch Trees had disappeared into their various practice rooms. Only Lionel and I remained in the atrium, along with a few other people.

"Look," I said to him. "Make a fist."

Lionel did so, making the fatal error of folding his thumb inside his fingers.

"No, no, no," I said. "Hold your thumb outside your fingers, or you'll break it, see, when you smash your knuckles into Shane's face."

Lionel moved his thumb, but said, "I do not think I want to smash Shane's face."

"Sure, you do," I said. "And when you do, you don't want to break your thumb. And remember what I said. Go for the nose. Nasal cartilage breaks easily, and you won't hurt your knuckles as much as if you went for, say, the mouth. Never go for the mouth."

"I do not think," Lionel said, "we have to worry about that."

"Good." I patted him on the shoulder. "Now go to class, before you're late."

Lionel took off, clutching his flute case and looking down, a little warily, at his own fist. From the other side of the atrium, I heard applause. Ruth,

Scott, and Dave were standing there with, of all people, Karen Sue Hanky.

"Way to discharge that volatile situation, Jess," Ruth commented sarcastically.

"Yeah," Scott said with a snicker. "By teaching the kid to throw a punch."

Dave was feigning thoughtfulness. "Funny, I don't remember them teaching us that particular method of conflict resolution in counselor training."

They were joking, of course. But Karen Sue, as usual, was deadly serious.

"I think it's disgraceful," she said. "You teaching a little boy to settle his problems with violence. You should be ashamed of yourself."

I stared at her. "You," I said, "have obviously never been the victim of a bully."

Karen Sue stuck out her chin. "No, because I was taught to resolve my differences with others peacefully, without use of force."

"So in other words," I said, "you've never been the victim of a bully."

Ruth laughed outright, but Scott and Dave both put their hands over their mouths, trying to hide their grins. Karen Sue wasn't fooled, though. She said, "Maybe that's because I don't go around *aggravating* people like you do, Jess."

"Oh, that's nice," I said. "Blame the victim, why don't you?"

Now Scott and Dave had to turn toward the wall, they were laughing so hard. Ruth, of course, didn't bother.

The tips of Karen Sue's ears started turning pink. The way I noticed this is that she was wearing this blue headband—which matched her blue shorts, which matched her blue flute case—and the headband pulled her hair back over her ears, so that it fell into these perfect curls just above her shoulders. Oh, and it also showed off her pearl earrings.

Have I mentioned that Karen Sue Hanky is kind of a girlie-girl?

"Well," she said primly. "If you'll excuse me, I'm going back to my cottage now to put my flute away. I hope you enjoy your tutorial with Professor Le Blanc, Jess. He told me that I play exceptionally."

"Yeah," I muttered. "Exceptionally crappy."

Ruth elbowed me.

"Oh, please," I said. "Her flute isn't even open hole. How good can she be?" Besides, Karen Sue had already flounced out. No way she'd overheard me.

Scott, still chuckling, said, "Listen, Jess. Dave and I had an idea. About this ghost story thing of yours. What do you say to teaming up?"

I eyed them. "What are you talking about?"

"Like our cabins could get together after Pit tonight, and you could tell them all another one of those ghost stories. You know, like the one you told last night, that had your little guys so scared, they wouldn't get out of bed afterwards."

"We could bring our guys over," Dave said, "around nine-thirty."

"Yeah," Scott said, glancing shyly in Ruth's direction. "And maybe your girls would want to come, Ruth."

Ruth looked surprised—and pleased—at the suggestion. But reluctance to subject her girls to the likes of Shane overcame her desire to spend quality time with Scott.

"No way," she said. "I'm not letting any of my girls around that little nightmare."

"Maybe Shane'd behave himself," I ventured, "if we threw some estrogen into the mix." It was an experiment they'd tried during detention back at Ernest Pyle High, with somewhat mixed results.

"Nuh-uh," Ruth said. "You know what that kid did during all-camp rehearsal this morning?"

This I hadn't heard. "What?"

"He opened a trumpet's spit valve all over some Frangipanis."

I winced. Not as bad as I'd feared . . . but not exactly good, either.

"And it wasn't," Ruth went on, "even his instrument. He'd *stolen* it. If you think I'm letting my girls near him, you're nuts."

I figured it was just as well. It wasn't like I had a ghost story on hand that I could tell in the presence of a couple of guys like Scott and Dave. They'd know I was plagiarizing Stephen King right away. And how embarrassing, to be sitting there telling some story with my would-be boyfriend Rob as the hero, in front of those guys.

Dave must have noticed my reluctance, since he said, "We'll bring popcorn."

I could see there was no way of getting out of it. And free popcorn is never anything to be sneered at. So I said, "Well, all right. I guess."

"Awesome." Scott and Dave gave each other high fives.

I winced again, but this time it had nothing to do with Shane. Dave had jostled me so that a sharp corner of Keely Herzberg's photo, tucked into the back pocket of my shorts, jabbed me into remembering that I had a little something else to do tonight, too.

CHAPTER

8

"Paul Huck was a guy who lived down the road from me."

I had figured out a way to not embarrass myself in front of Scott and Dave. I'd abandoned the rehashing of an old Stephen King story and opted for a ghost story my dad used to tell, back when my brothers and I had been little and he'd taken us on camping trips to the Indiana backwoods—trips my mother never went on, since she claimed to be allergic to nature, and most particularly to backwoods.

"He wasn't a very bright guy," I explained to the dozens of rapt little faces in front of me. "In fact, he was kind of dim. He only made it to about the fourth grade before school got too hard for him, so his parents let him stay home after that, since they didn't put much stock in education anyway, on account of none of the Hucks ever amounting to anything with or without having gone to school—"

"Hey." A small, high-pitched voice sounded from behind the closed porch door. "Can I come in now?"

"No," I shouted back. "Now, where was I?"

I went on to relate how Paul Huck had grown into a massive individual, stupid as a corncob, but good at heart.

But really, I wasn't thinking about Paul Huck. I wasn't thinking about Paul Huck at all. I was thinking about what had happened right after I'd agreed to allow Scott and Dave have their cabins stage a mini-invasion on mine. What had happened was, I had gone for my tutorial with Professor Le Blanc.

And I had ended up nearly getting fired.

Again.

And this time, it hadn't been because I'd been making personal use of camp property, or teaching the kids risqué songs.

Then why, you ask? Why would the famous classical flutist Jean-Paul Le Blanc attempt to fire a totally hip—not to mention talented—individual like myself?

Because he had discovered my deepest secret, the one I hold closest to my heart. . . .

No, not that one. Not the fact that I am still very much in possession of my psychic gift. My *other* secret.

What happened was this.

Right after Scott and Dave and Ruth took off, I sauntered over to the practice room where I was supposed to have my lesson with Professor Le Blanc. He was in there, all right. I could tell by the pure, sweet tones emanating from the tiny room. The practice rooms are supposed to be soundproof, and they are . . . but only if you're in one of the rooms. From the hallway, you can hear what's going on behind the door.

And let me tell you, what was going on behind that door was some fine, fine Bach. We're talking flute-playing so elegant, so assured, so . . . well, passionate, it almost brought tears to my eyes. You don't hear that kind of playing in the Ernest Pyle High School Symphonic Orchestra, you get what I'm saying? I was so entranced, I didn't even think to knock on the door to let the professor know I'd arrived. I never wanted that sweet music to end.

But it did end. And then the next thing I knew, the door to the practice room was opening, and Professor Le Blanc emerged. He was saying, "You have a gift. An extraordinary gift. Not to use it would be a crime."

"Yes, Professor," replied a bored voice that, oddly, I recognized.

I looked down, shocked that such lovely music had been coming from the flute of a student, and not the master.

And my jaw sagged.

"Hey, lesbo," Shane said. "Shut the barn door, you're lettin' the flies in."

"Ah," Professor Le Blanc said, spying me. "You two know one another? Oh, yes, of course, Jessica, you are his counselor, I'd forgotten. Then you can do me a very great favor."

I was still staring at Shane. I couldn't help it. That music? That beautiful music? That had been coming from *Shane?*

"Make certain," Professor Le Blanc said, resting his hands on Shane's pudgy shoulders, "that this young man understands how rare a talent like his is. He insists that his mother made him come to Wawasee this summer. That in fact he'd have much preferred to attend baseball camp instead."

"*Football* camp," Shane burst out bitterly. "I don't *want* to play the flute. *Girls* play the flute." He glared at me very fiercely as he said this, as if daring me to contradict him.

I did not. I could not. I was still transfixed. All I could think was *Shane? Shane* played the *flute?* I mean, he'd said he played the *skin* flute. I didn't know he'd been telling the truth . . . well, partially, anyway.

But an actual *flute? Shane* had been the one making that gorgeous—no, not just gorgeous—*magnificent* music on *my* instrument of choice? Shane? *My* Shane?

Professor Le Blanc was shaking his head. "Don't be ridiculous," he said to Shane. "Most of the greatest flutists in the world have been men. And with talent like yours, young man, you might one day be amongst them—"

"Not if I get recruited by the Bears," Shane pointed out.

"Well," Professor Le Blanc said, looking a little taken aback. "Er, maybe not then . . ."

"Is my lesson over?" Shane demanded, craning his neck to get a look at the professor's face.

"Er," Professor Le Blanc said. "Yes, actually, it is."

"Good," Shane said, tucking his flute case beneath his arm. "Then I'm outta here."

And with that, he stalked away.

Professor Le Blanc and I stared after him for a minute or two. Then the instructor seemed to shake himself, and, holding open the door to the practice room for me, said with forced jocularity, "Well, now, let's see what you can do, then, Jessica. Why don't you play something for me?" Professor Le Blanc went to the piano that stood in one corner of the walk-in-closet-sized room, sat down on the bench, and picked up a Palm Pilot. "Anything you like," he said, punching the buttons of the Palm Pilot. "I like to assess my pupil's skill level before I begin teaching."

I opened my flute case and began assembling my instrument, but my mind wasn't on what I was doing. I just couldn't get what I'd heard out of my head. It didn't make sense. It didn't make sense that Shane could play like that. It just didn't seem possible. The kid had played beautifully, movingly, as if he'd been swept away by the notes, each one of which had rung out with angelic—almost aching—purity. The same Shane who had stuck an entire hamburger in his mouth at lunch—I'd sat there and watched him do it—bun and all, then swallowed it, practically whole, just because Arthur had dared him to. That same Shane. That Shane could play like *that*.

And he didn't even care. He'd wanted to go to football camp.

He'd been lying. He cared. No one could play like that and not care. No one.

I put my own flute to my lips, and began to play. Nothing special. Green Day. "Time of Our Lives." I jazzed it up a little, since it's a relatively simple little song. But all I could think about was Shane. There had to be depths, *wells* of untapped emotion in that boy, to make him capable of producing such music.

And all he wanted to do was play football.

Professor Le Blanc looked up from his Palm Pilot at some point during my recital. When I was through, he said, "Play something else, please."

I launched into an old standby. "Fascinating Rhythm." Always a crowd-pleaser. At least it pleased my dad, when I was practicing at home. I usually played it at double time, to get it over with. I did so now.

The question was, how could a kid who could play like that be such a total and complete pain in the butt? I mean, how was it possible that the person who'd played such hauntingly beautiful music, and the person who this morning had told Lionel he'd dipped his toothbrush in the toilet—after, of course, Lionel had started using it—be one and the same individual?

Professor Le Blanc was rooting through his briefcase, which he'd left on top of the piano.

"Here," he said. "Now this." He dropped a book of sheet music onto the stand in front of my chair.

Brahms. Symphony Number 1. What was he trying to do, put me to sleep? It was an insult. We'd
played that my freshman year, for God's sake. My
fingers flew over the key holes. Open, of course. My
instrument was practically an antique, handed down
from some obscure member of the Mastriani clan
who'd gotten it under questionable circumstances.
Yeah, okay, so my flute was probably hot.

The thing I couldn't figure out was what was
God—and I'm not saying I'm so all-fired sure there is
one, but for argument's sake, let's say there is—
thinking, giving a kid like Shane talent like that?
Seriously. Why had he been given this incredible gift
of music, when clearly, he'd have been happier tearing down a field with a ball in his arms?

I tell you, if that's not proof there is a God, and
that he or she has one heck of a wacked-out sense of
humor, I don't know what is.

"Stop." Professor Le Blanc took the Brahms away
and put another music book in front of me.

Beethoven. Symphony Number 3.

I don't know how long I sat there looking at it.
Maybe a full minute before I was able to rouse myself
from my Shane-induced stupor and go, "Um, Professor? Yeah, look, I don't know this piece."

Professor Le Blanc was still sitting on the piano
bench, his arms folded across his chest. He had put
away the Palm Pilot, and was now watching me
intently. The fact that he was, in fact, a bit of a hottie,
did not make this any pleasanter than it sounds. He
looked a little like a hawk, one of those hawks you

see all the time, wheeling in tighter and tighter circles above something in a cornfield, making you wonder what the stupid bird is looking at down there. Is it a field mouse, or the decomposing body of a coed?

Professor Le Blanc said, enunciating carefully, "I know you don't know this piece, Jess. I want to see if you can play it."

I just stared at it.

"Well," I said after a while. "I probably could. If you would maybe just hum my part first?"

He didn't look surprised by my request. He shook his head so that his kind of longish, curly brown hair—definitely longer than mine, anyway—swung around.

"No," he said. "I do not hum. Begin, please."

I squirmed uncomfortably in my seat. "It's just," I explained, "usually, back home, my orchestra teacher, he kind of hums the whole thing out for us first, and I really—"

"Aha!"

Professor Le Blanc yelled so loud, I almost dropped my flute. He pointed a long, accusing finger at me.

"*You*," he said, in tones of mingled triumph and horror, "*cannot read music.*"

I felt my own ears turning as pink as Karen Sue's had out in the atrium. Only not just pink. Red. My ears were burning. My face was burning. It was air-conditioned enough in that practice room that you practically needed a winter parka, but me, I was on fire.

"That isn't true," I said, trying to appear casual. Yeah, real easy to do with a face that was turning fire-engine red. "That note right there, for instance." I pointed at the music. "That's an eighth note. And over here, that's a whole note."

"But what note," Professor Le Blanc demanded, "is it?"

My shoulders slumped. I was so busted.

"Look," I said. "I don't *need* to read music. I just have to hear the piece once, and I—"

"—and you know how to play it. Yes, yes, I know. I know all about you people. You I-hear-it-once-and-I-know-it people." He shook his head disgustedly at me. "Does Dr. Alistair know about this?"

I felt my feet beginning to sweat inside my Pumas, that's how freaked out he had me.

"No," I said. "You aren't going to tell him, are you?"

"Not going to tell him?" Professor Le Blanc leaped up from the piano bench. "Not going to tell Dr. Alistair that one of his counselors is musically *illiterate?*"

He bellowed the last word. Anyone passing outside the door could have heard. I went, in a small voice, "Please, Professor Le Blanc. Don't turn me in. I'll learn to read this piece. I promise."

"I do not want you to learn to read this piece." Professor Le Blanc was on his feet now, and pacing the length of the practice room. Which, only being about six feet by six feet, wasn't very far. "You should be able to read *all* pieces. How can you be so lazy? Simply because you can hear a piece once and then play it, you use this as an excuse never to learn to read music? You ought to be ashamed. You ought to be sent back to where you came from and made to work there at the IG of A as a sack girl."

I licked my lips. I couldn't help it. My mouth had gone completely dry.

"Um, Professor?" I said.

He was still pacing and breathing kind of hard. In school, they made us read this book about this guy named Heathcliff who liked this loser chick named Cathy, who didn't like him back, and I swear to God, Professor Le Blanc kind of reminded me of old Heathcliff, the way he was huffing and puffing about something that really boiled down to nothing.

"*What?*" he yelled at me.

I swallowed. "It's bag girl." When he only gazed at me uncomprehendingly, I said, "You said I'd have to work as a sack girl. But it's called a bag girl."

Professor Le Blanc pointed toward the door. "*Out,*" he roared.

I was shocked. The whole thing was totally unfair. In the movies, when somebody finds out the other person can't read, they're always filled with all this compassion and try to help the poor guy. Like Jane Fonda helped Robert De Niro when she found out he couldn't read in this really boring movie my mom made me watch with her once. I couldn't believe Professor Le Blanc was being so unfeeling. My case, if you thought about it, was really quite tragic.

I figured I'd make a play for his heartstrings . . . if he had any, which I doubted.

"Professor," I said. "Look. I know I deserve to get thrown out of here and all, but really, that's partly why I took this gig. I mean, I completely realize my inability to read music is hampering my growth as an artist, and I was really hoping this was my big chance to, you know, rectify that."

I totally did not believe he would go for this crap, but to my never-ending relief, he did. I don't know why. Maybe it was because I was trembling. Not because I was nervous or anything. I was, but not that much. I mean, it wasn't like the steam table held that much horror for me. It was just because it was about thirty degrees in there.

But I guess Professor Le Blanc thought I was suitably cowed or whatever, since he finally said he wouldn't turn me in to Dr. Alistair. Although he wasn't very gracious about it, I must say. He told me that, since his class schedule was completely filled, he didn't have the time to teach me to read music *and* prepare my piece for the concert at the end of the summer. I was like, fine, I don't want to be in the stupid concert anyway, but he got all offended, because the concert's supposed to be, you know, what all of us are working toward for the six weeks we're here.

Finally, we agreed I'd meet him three times a week at seven A.M.—yes, that would be seven in the morning—so he could teach me what I needed to know. I tried to point out that seven A.M. was the

Polar Bear swim, which also happened to be the only time I could realistically bathe, but he so didn't care.

God. Musicians. So temperamental.

While I was sitting there back in Birch Tree Cottage, thinking about how close I'd been to getting fired, and talking about Paul Huck, I looked out at all the kids in front of me and wondered how many of them were going to grow up to be Professor Le Blancs. Probably all of them. And that saddened me. Because it seemed like they were never even going to get the chance to be anything else, if they only got two hours of free time a day to play.

Except Shane, of course. Shane, the only one of the kids at Camp Wawasee for Gifted Child Musicians who probably could make a living as a musician one day if he wanted to, clearly didn't. Want to, I mean. He wanted to be a football player.

And you know, I could sort of relate to that. I knew what a pain it was to have a gift you'd never, ever asked for.

"—so Paul Huck got jobs around the neighborhood," I went on, "mowing lawns and doing people's yardwork in the summer, and chopping firewood in the winter. And pretty much nobody noticed him, but when they did, they thought he was, you know, a pretty nice guy. Not a whole lot upstairs, though."

I glanced at Scott and Dave. They were sitting on the windowsill. In a few minutes, I would give the signal, and one of them would sneak into the kitchen to say his line.

"But there was actually a lot going on upstairs in Paul Huck's head," I said. "Because Paul Huck, while he was in people's yards, digging up their tree stumps or whatever, he was watching them. And the person he liked to watch most of all was a girl named Claire Lippman, who, every day during the summer, liked to climb out onto her porch roof and sunbathe in this little bitty bikini."

It was kind of disturbing the way real people crept into my made-up stories. In my dad's version, the girl was named Debbie. But Claire, who'd be a senior at Ernie Pyle this year, just seemed to fit somehow.

"Paul fell for Claire," I went on. "And Paul fell hard. He thought about Claire while he ate breakfast every morning. He thought about Claire while he was riding his tractor mower every afternoon. He thought about Claire when he was eating his dinner at night. He thought about Claire while he was lying in bed after a long day's work. Paul Huck thought about Claire Lippman *all* the time.

"But." I looked out at all the little faces turned toward me. "Claire Lippman didn't think about Paul Huck at breakfast. She didn't think about him while she was sunning herself on her porch roof every afternoon. She didn't think about him while she ate her dinner, and she certainly never thought about him before she fell asleep at night. Claire Lippman never thought about Paul Huck at all, because she barely even knew Paul Huck existed. To Claire, Paul was just the handyman who knocked squirrels' nests out of her chimney every spring, and who scooped the dead opossums out of this decorative little well she had in her backyard. And that was it."

I could feel the crowd getting restless. It was time to start getting to the gore.

Eventually, I told them, Paul got desperate. He knew if he was ever going to win Claire's heart, he had to act. So one spring day when he was cleaning out Claire's gutters, he got an idea. He decided he was going to tell Claire how he felt.

"Just as this occurred to Paul, Claire appeared in the window right where he was cleaning out the gutter. This seemed to Paul like the perfect time to say what he was going to say. But just as he was about to tap on the window, Claire started taking her clothes off." This caused some tittering that I ignored. "See, the room she was in was the bathroom, and she was getting ready to take a shower. She didn't notice Paul there in the window . . . at first. And Paul, well, he didn't know what to do. He had never seen a naked woman before, let alone the love of his life, Claire. So he just froze there on the ladder, totally incapable of moving.

"So when Claire happened to glance at the window, just as she was about to get in the shower, and saw Paul there, she was so startled, she let out a scream so loud, it almost made Paul fall off the ladder he was on.

"But Claire didn't stop with one scream. She was so startled, she kept right on screaming. People outside heard the screaming, and they looked up, and they saw Paul Huck looking through Claire Lippman's bathroom window, and, well, they didn't know he was there to clean the gutters. He had always been a weird guy, who lived at home with his parents even though he was in his twenties, and who talked like a nine-year-old. Maybe he'd flipped out or something. So they started yelling, too, and Paul was so scared, with all the yelling and everything going on, he jumped down from the ladder and ran for all he was worth.

"Paul didn't know what he'd done, but he figured it had to be pretty bad, if it had made so many people mad at him. All he knew was that, whatever it was he'd done, it was probably bad enough that someone had called the police, and if the police came, they'd put him in jail. So Paul didn't go home, because he figured that'd be the first place people would look for him. Instead, he ran to the outskirts of town, where there was this cave. Everyone was scared to go into this cave, because bats and stuff lived in there. But Paul was more afraid of the police than he was of bats, so he ducked into that cave, and he stayed there, all the way until it got dark.

"Now, once Claire got over being startled, she realized what had happened, and she felt pretty bad about it. But she didn't want to admit to anyone that it had been her mistake—that she'd asked Paul to clean her gutters, and that's what he'd been doing on that ladder. Because then she'd look like a big idiot. So she kept that information to herself, and let everyone think Paul was a Peeping Tom."

I went on to describe how Paul, scared for his life,

stayed in that cave. He stayed there all night, and all the next day, and the next night, too. I explained how by then, Paul's parents were really worried. They had called the police to help them look, but that just made things worse, because one time Paul came out of the cave, to see if people were still looking for him, and he saw a sheriff's cruiser go by. That just drove him deeper back into the cave, where when he was thirsty, he drank cave water.

"But there was no food in the cave," I said. "And Paul couldn't come out to buy any, because he might get caught. Eventually, he got so hungry, well, he just lost his mind. He saw a bat, and he grabbed it, ripped its head off, and ate it raw."

This elicited some groans of disgust.

And that, I told the boys, was the beginning of Paul's descent into madness. Very soon, he was living on nothing but cave water and bat meat. He lost all this weight, and started growing this long, matted beard. He couldn't wash his hair because he didn't have any shampoo, so it started getting all filled with twigs and dirt. His clothes became tattered and hung off him like rags. But still, he wouldn't come out of the cave, because he couldn't face the shame of whatever it was he'd done to Claire.

Time went by. Winter came. Soon Paul ran out of bats to eat. He had no choice but to leave the cave at night, and root through people's garbage for old chicken bones and rotten milk, so he wouldn't starve. Sometimes, little children would wake up in the night and see him, and they'd tell their parents the next morning about the strange, long-haired man they'd seen in the backyard, and their parents would say, "Stop telling lies."

But the children knew what they'd seen.

More time went by. One night, Paul Huck was going through someone's garbage when he came across a newspaper. Newspapers didn't interest Paul much, on account of his not being able to read. But this one had a picture on it. He squinted at the picture in the moonlight and realized it was a picture of his old love, Claire Lippman. He didn't need to know how to read in order to figure out why Claire's picture was in the paper. In the photo, she was dressed in a wedding gown and veil. Claire Lippman had gotten married.

Paul, crazy as he was now, couldn't think like a normal person—not that he'd ever been able to before. But after a steady diet of bats and garbage, which was all he'd had to eat for the past few years, he'd gotten much worse. So what seemed to Paul like a really good idea—he ought to give Claire a wedding present, to show there were no hard feelings—well, that just wouldn't have occurred to a normal person.

"What was worse," I said, "Paul's idea of a wedding present was to go through all the yards in the town and pick every rose he could find. He did this, of course, in the middle of the night, and all over town children woke up and looked out the window and said, 'There's Paul Huck again,' and they wondered what he was going to do with all the roses.

"What Paul did with all the roses was, he piled

them up on Claire Lippman's front porch, so she'd see them first thing when she came out of her house to go to work."

And there, I told the kids, for the first time ever, an adult woke up and heard Paul Huck. It was Claire's new husband, Simon, who was a stranger to the town. He didn't know who Paul Huck was. All Simon knew was, when he came downstairs into the kitchen to get a glass of milk before going back to sleep, he saw this gigantic, shaggy-haired man, covered in dirt and blood—because the roses' thorns had cut Paul everywhere he touched them—standing on his front porch. Simon didn't even think about what he was doing. Since he was in the kitchen, he grabbed the first thing he saw that he could use as a weapon—a carving knife—and went to the front door, threw it open, and said, "Who the hell are you?"

"Paul was so surprised that someone was speaking to him—no one had said a word to him, not in five long years—that he spun around, just as he'd been about to leave the porch. Simon didn't understand that Paul was just startled. He thought this giant, hairy, bloody guy was coming after him. So Simon swung the carving knife, and it caught Paul just beneath the chin, and *whoosh* . . . it cut off his head. Paul Huck," I said, "was dead."

Silence followed this.

I went on to describe how Claire's husband, in a panic after seeing what he had done, ran inside the house to call the police. Hearing all the commotion,

Claire woke up and came downstairs. She went out onto the porch. The first thing she saw was all the roses. The second thing she saw was this great big bloody body laying on top of them. The last thing she saw was a head, almost buried in the roses.

And even though the head had this long beard, and the eyes were all rolled back, Claire recognized Paul Huck. And she put together the roses and the fact that it was Paul and she knew that her husband had just killed the man that, because of her, had been living like an animal for five long years.

Claire wouldn't let Simon call the police. He had killed, she insisted, an innocent man. Paul had never meant to hurt either of them. If word got out about this, Claire and her new husband—who was this very important surgeon—were going to be socially ruined in town, and she knew it. She explained all this to Simon. They had, she said, to hide the body, and pretend like nothing had happened.

Simon was disgusted, but like Claire, he enjoyed his status high at the top of the town's social ladder. So he made a deal with her: he'd get rid of Paul's body, if Claire got rid of the head.

Claire agreed. So while Simon wrapped Paul's body in sheets—so he wouldn't bleed all over the back of his new car while Simon drove over to the lake, where he intended to dump the body—Claire lifted up the head and threw it in the first place she thought of: down the well in her backyard.

When Simon got back from the lake, the two of them

cleaned up all the blood and roses. Then, exhausted, they went back to bed.

Everything seemed to go okay at first. Nobody except the children of the town had ever believed Paul Huck was still alive anyway, so nobody noticed that he was gone. Little by little, Claire and Simon were able to put from their minds what they had done. Their lives went back to normal.

Until the first full moon after Paul's murder. That night, Claire and Simon were awakened from their sleep by a moaning they heard coming from the backyard. At first they thought it was the wind. But it seemed to be moaning words. And those words were, "Where's . . . my . . . head?"

They thought they must have been hearing things. But then, sounding even closer than the first moan, they heard the words, "Down . . . in . . . the . . . well."

Claire and Simon put on their bathrobes and hurried downstairs. Looking out into their backyard, they got the shock of their lives. For there, in the moonlight, they saw a horrifying sight: Paul Huck's headless body, all covered with lake weeds and dripping wet, moaning, "Where's . . . my . . . head?"

And, from deep inside the well, the echoing reply: "Down . . . in . . . the . . . well!"

Claire and her husband both went instantly insane. They ran from the house that night, and they never went back, not even to move out their stuff. They hired a moving company to do it for them. They put the house up for sale.

"But you know what?" I looked at all the faces

gazing at me in the soft glow of my single flashlight. "No one ever bought the house. It was like everyone could sense that there was something wrong with it. No one ever bought it, and little by little, it began to fall apart. Vandals threw rocks through its windows, and rats moved in, and bats, just like the ones Paul used to eat, lived in the attic. It is still empty, to this day. And on nights when the moon is full, if you go into the backyard, you can still hear the wind moaning, just like Paul Huck: 'Where's . . . my . . . head?'"

From the dark kitchen came a deep, ghostly wail: "Down . . . in . . . the . . . well!"

Several things happened at once. The boys all screamed. Scott, grinning, emerged from the kitchen. And the front door burst open, and Shane, panting and white-faced, cried, "Did you hear that? Did you hear that? It's him, it's Paul Huck! He's coming to get us! Please don't make me sleep outside, I promise I'll be good from now on, I promise!"

And with that, I began to see a little—just a little—more clearly how it might be possible for a kid like Shane to make that beautiful music.

CHAPTER

9

When I woke up the next morning, I knew where Keely Herzberg was.

Not that there was much I could do with the information. I mean, it wasn't like I was going to run over to Pamela's office and tell her what I knew. Not yet, anyway. I needed to check the situation out, make sure Keely wanted to be found.

And, thanks to Paul Huck, I knew exactly how I was going to do it.

Well, not thanks to Paul Huck, exactly. But thanks to the fact that I'd had Scott and Dave and their kids over the night before, I was a lot more savvy to the whole phone situation than I'd been before. It turns out all the counselors have cell phones. Seriously. Everyone except Ruth and me . . . and Karen Sue Hanky, I suppose, since she'd never do anything that might be construed as breaking the rules.

I don't know why Ruth and I are so out of it. We're like the only two sixteen-year-old girls in Indiana without cell phones. What is wrong with our parents? You would think they would want us to have cell phones, so that we could call them when we're going to be out late, or whatever.

But then, we're never out late, because we never really get invited anywhere. That would be on account of our being orchestra nerds. Oh, and on account of my *issues*, too, I guess.

But everybody else on the camp counseling staff had cell phones. They'd been making and receiving calls all week, just keeping them on vibrate and picking up out of Pamela's and Dr. Alistair's sight.

So now, thanks to my scaring their charges so thoroughly the night before that they apparently did everything their counselors asked them to afterward—like go to sleep—both Scott and Dave were eager, when I asked them at breakfast, to lend me their phones.

I took Dave's, since it had less buttons and looked less intimidating. Then I ducked out of the dining hall and went to the Pit, which was empty this time of day. I figured reception there was bound to be good. . . .

And it didn't seem likely that if the Feds were still monitoring my activities they'd be able to sneak up on me without me noticing.

Rob's phone rang about five times before he picked up.

"Hey, it's me," I said. And then since, for all I

knew, there might be dozens of girls calling him before nine in the morning, I added, "Jess."

"I know it's you," Rob said. He didn't sound sleepy or anything. He usually opened the garage for his uncle, so he gets up pretty early. "What's up? How are things up there at band camp?"

"It's orchestra camp."

"Whatever. How's it going?"

What is it about Rob's voice that makes me feel all shivery, the way I'd felt in the super air-conditioned practice room the day before . . . only inside, not outside? I don't know. But I strongly suspect it had something to do with the *L* word.

Though it was just plain wrong, my having fallen so hard for a guy who so clearly wanted to have nothing to do with me. Why couldn't he see we were made for each other? I mean, we'd met in detention, for God's sake. Need I say more?

"Things are okay," I said. "Except I sort of have this problem."

"Oh, yeah? What's that?"

I tried to picture what Rob looked like, sitting there in his kitchen—he and his mom only have one phone, and it's in the kitchen. I figured he was probably wearing jeans. I'd never seen him in anything but jeans. Which was just as well, because he looks extraordinarily fine in them. It was like his butt had been designed to be molded by a pair of Levi's, his broad shoulders contoured specifically to fill out that leather jacket he always wore when he rode his motorcycle.

And the rest of him wasn't that bad, either.

"Well," I said, trying not to think about the way his curly dark hair, which was usually in need of a trim, had felt against my cheek the last time he'd let me kiss him. It had been a long time ago. Too long. Oh, God, why couldn't I be just a couple years older?

"Look," I said. "Here's the thing." And I told him, briefly, about Jonathan Herzberg.

"So," I concluded, "I just need a ride into Chicago to sort of check out the situation, and I know you have work and all, but I was kind of wondering if, when you get a day off, or whatever, you wouldn't mind—"

"Mastriani," he said. He didn't sound mad or anything, even though I was trying to use him . . . and pretty blatantly, too. "You're *four hours* away."

I winced. I'd been hoping he wouldn't remember that until after he'd said yes. See, in my imagination, when I'd rehearsed this call, Rob had been so excited to hear from me, he'd hopped right onto his bike and come over, no questions asked.

In real life, however, guys ask questions.

"I know it's far," I said. You dope. What did you expect? He said he doesn't want to go out with you. When are you going to get that through your thick skull?

"You know what?" I said. "Never mind. I can just get somebody else—"

"I don't like it," Rob said. I thought he meant he didn't like my asking somebody else to drive me, and I got kind of excited for a minute, but then he went, "Why the hell did your brother tell this guy where you were in the first place?"

I sighed. Rob had never met Douglas. Or anybody in my family, for that matter, except my dad, and that was just for a minute once. I don't think any of them would be that thrilled by the fact that I was in love with a guy I'd met in detention.

Or that the reason—at least the one that he gives me—that we aren't going out is that he's on probation, and doesn't want to screw it up by dating a minor.

My life has gotten seriously complicated, I swear.

"How do you know," Rob demanded, "that this isn't a setup by those agents who were after you last spring? I mean, it very well could be a trap, Mastriani. They might have arranged this whole thing as a way to prove you lied when you said you didn't have your powers anymore."

"I know," I said. "That's why I want to check it out first. But I'll just get someone else to take me. It's no big deal."

"What about Ruth?" Rob had only met Ruth once or twice. He had called her the fat chick the first time he'd ever referred to her, but he'd quickly learned I don't let people dis my best friend that way. Nor do I let Ruth call Rob what she calls everybody in our town who lives outside the city limits: a Grit. If Rob and I ever did start going out, there'd definitely be a little friction between the two of them. So much for me being able to tell he secretly loves me by the way he treats my friends. "Can't Ruth take you?"

"No," I said. I didn't want to get into the whole Ruth-being-no-good-in-a-crisis thing. "Look, don't worry about it. I'll find someone. It's no big deal."

"What do you mean, you'll find someone?" Rob sounded exasperated with me, which he didn't have any right to be. It's not like he's my boyfriend, or anything. "Who are you going to find?"

"There are a couple people," I said, "with cars. I'll just have to see if I can get any of them to take me, that's all."

Dave appeared suddenly at the top of the stairs down into the Pit. He called, "Hey, Jess, you almost through? I gotta take my crew on over to the music building now."

"Oh," I said. "Yeah, just a minute." Into the phone, I said, "Look, I gotta go. This guy loaned me his phone, and I have to give it back now, because he's leaving."

"What guy?" Rob demanded. "There's guys there? I thought it was a camp for kids."

"Well, it is," I said. Was it my imagination, or did he sound . . . well, unsettled? "But there's guy counselors and all."

"What's a *guy* doing," Rob wanted to know, "working at a band camp for little kids? They let *guys* do that?"

"Well, sure," I said. "Why not? Hey, wait a minute." I squinted up at Dave. Even though it wasn't quite nine yet, you could tell from the way the sun was beating down that it was going to be a scorcher. "Hey, Dave," I called. "You got a car, right?"

"Yeah," Dave said. "Why? You planning on staging a breakout?"

Into the phone, I said, "You know what, Rob? I think I—"

But Rob was already talking. And what he was saying, I was surprised to hear, was, "I'll pick you up at one."

I went, totally confused, "You'll what? What are you talking about?"

"I'll be there at one," Rob said again. "Where will you be? Give me directions."

Bemused, I gave Rob directions, and agreed to meet him at a bend in the road just past the main gates into the camp. Then I hung up, still wondering what had made him change his mind.

I trudged up the steps to where Dave stood, and handed him back his phone.

"Thanks," I said. "You're a lifesaver."

Dave shrugged. "You really need a ride somewhere?"

"Not anymore," I said. "I—"

And that's when it hit me. Why Rob had been so blasé about my going away for seven weeks, and why, just now on the phone, he'd changed his mind about coming up:

He hadn't thought there'd be guys here.

Seriously. He'd thought it was just going to be me and Ruth and about two hundred little kids, and that was it. It had never occurred to him there might be guys my own age hanging around.

That was the only explanation I could think of, anyway, for his peculiar behavior.

Except, of course, that explanation made no sense whatsoever. Because for it to be true, it would mean Rob would have to like me, you know, *that way*, and I was pretty sure he didn't. Otherwise, he wouldn't care so much about his stupid probation officer, and what he has to say on the matter.

Then again, the prospect of jail *is* a pretty daunting one. . . .

"Jess? Are you all right?"

I shook myself. Dave was staring at me. I had drifted off into Rob Wilkins dreamland right in front of him.

"Oh," I said. "Yeah. Fine. Thanks. No, I don't need a ride anymore. I'm good."

He slipped his cell phone back into his pocket. "Oh. Okay."

"You know what I do need, though, Dave?" I asked.

Dave shook his head. "No. What?"

I took a deep breath. "I need someone to keep an eye on my kids this afternoon," I said, in a rush. "Just for a little while. I, um, might be tied up with something."

Dave, unlike Ruth, didn't give me a hard time. He just shrugged and went, "Sure."

My jaw sagged. "Really? You don't mind?"

He shrugged again. "No. Why should I mind?"

We started back toward the dining hall. As we approached it, I noticed most of the residents of Birch

Tree Cottage had finished breakfast and were outside, gathered around one of the campground dogs.

"It's a grape," Shane was saying, conversationally,
to Lionel. "Go ahead and eat it."

"I do not believe it is a grape," Lionel replied. "So
I do not think I will, thank you."

"No, really." Shane pointed at something just
beneath the dog's ear. "In America, that's where
grapes grow."

When I got close enough, of course, I saw what it
was they were talking about. Hanging off one of the
dog's ears was a huge, blood-engorged tick. It did
look a bit like a grape, but not enough, I thought, to
fool even the most gullible foreigner.

"Shane," I said, loudly enough to make him jump.

"What?" Shane widened his baby blues at me
innocently. "I wasn't doing anything, Jess. Honest."

Even I was shocked at this bold-faced lie. "You
were so," I said. "You were trying to make Lionel eat
a tick."

The other boys giggled. In spite of the fright Shane
had gotten the night before—and I had ended up letting him sleep inside; even I wasn't mean enough to
make him sleep on the porch after the whole Paul
Huck thing—he was back to his old tricks.

Next time, I was going to make him spend the
night on a raft in the middle of the lake, I swear to
God.

"Apologize," I commanded him.

Shane said, "I don't see why I should have to
apologize for something I didn't do."

"Apologize," I said, again. "And then get that tick off that poor dog."

This was my first mistake. I should have removed the tick myself.

My second mistake was in turning my back on the boys to roll my eyes at Dave, who'd been watching the entire interaction with this great big grin on his face. Last night, he and Scott had confided to me that all the other counselors had placed bets on who was going to win in the battle of wills between Shane and me. The odds were running two to one in Shane's favor.

"Sorry, Lie-oh-nell," I heard Shane say.

"Make sure you mention this," I said, to Dave, "to your—"

The morning air was pierced by a scream.

I spun around just in time to see Lionel, his white shirt now splattered with blood, haul back his fist and plunge it, with all the force of his sixty-five pounds or so, into Shane's eye. He'd been aiming, I guess, for the nose, but missed.

Shane staggered back, clearly more startled by the blow than actually hurt by it. Nevertheless, he immediately burst into loud, babyish sobs, and, both hands pressed to the injured side of his face, wailed in a voice filled with shock and outrage, "He *hit* me! Jess, he *hit* me!"

"Because he make the tick explode on me!" Lionel declared, holding out his shirt for me to see.

"All right," I said, trying to keep my breakfast down. "That's enough. Get to class, both of you."

Lionel, horrified, said, "I cannot go to class like this!"

"I'll bring you a new shirt," I said. "I'll go back to the cabin and get one and bring it to you while you're in music theory."

Mollified, the boy picked up his flute case and, with a final glare in Shane's direction, stomped off to class.

Shane, however, was not so easily calmed.

"He should get a strike!" he shouted. "He should get a strike, Jess, for hitting me!"

I looked at Shane like he was crazy. I actually think that at that moment, he *was* crazy.

"Shane," I said. "You sprayed him with tick blood. He had every right to hit you."

"That's not fair," Shane shouted, his voice catching on a sob. "That's not *fair!*"

"For God's sake, Shane," I said, with some amusement. "It's a good thing you went to orchestra camp instead of football camp this summer, if you're gonna cry every time someone pokes you in the eye."

This had not, perhaps, been the wisest thing to say, under the circumstances. Shane's face twisted with emotion, but I couldn't tell if it was embarrassment or pain. I was a little shocked that I'd managed to hurt his feelings. It was actually kind of hard to believe a kid like Shane *had* feelings.

"I didn't *choose* to come to this stupid camp," Shane roared at me. "My mother *made* me! She wouldn't *let* me go to football camp. She was afraid I'd hurt my stupid hands and not be able to play the stupid flute anymore."

I dried up, hearing this. Because suddenly, I could see Shane's mother's point of view. I mean, the kid could play.

"Shane," I said gently. "Your mom's right. Professor Le Blanc, too. You have an incredible gift. It would be a shame to let it go to waste."

"Like you, you mean?" Shane asked acidly.

"What do you mean?" I shook my head. "I'm not wasting my gift for music. That's one of the reasons I'm here."

"I'm not talking," Shane said, "about your gift for *music*."

I stared at him. His meaning was suddenly clear. *Too* clear. There were still people, of course, standing nearby, watching, listening. Thanks to his theatrics, we'd attracted quite a little crowd. Some of the kids who hadn't made it to the music building yet, and quite a few of the counselors, had gathered around to watch the little drama unfolding in front of the dining hall. They wouldn't, I'm sure, know what he was referring to. But I did. I knew.

"Shane," I said. "That's not fair."

"Yeah?" He snorted. "Well, you know what else isn't fair, Jess? My mom, making me come here. And you, not giving Lionel a strike!"

And with that, he took off without another word.

"Shane," I called after him. "Come back here. I swear, if you don't come back here, it's the porch with Paul Huck for you tonight—"

Shane stopped, but not because I'd intimidated him with my threat. Oh, no. He stopped because he'd run smack into Dr. Alistair, the camp director, who—having apparently heard the commotion from inside the dining hall, where he often sat after all the campers were gone and enjoyed a quiet cup of coffee—had come outside to investigate.

"*Oof*," Dr. Alistair said, as Shane's mullet head sank into his midriff. He reached down to grasp the boy by the shoulders in an attempt to keep them both from toppling over. Shane was no lightweight, you know.

"What," Dr. Alistair asked, as he steered Shane back around toward me, "is the meaning of all this caterwauling?"

Before I could say a word, Shane lifted his head and, staring up at Dr. Alistair with a face that was perfectly devoid of tears—but upon which there was an unmistakable bruise growing under one eye—said, "A boy hit me and my counselor didn't do anything, Dr. Alistair." He added, with a hiccupy sob, "If my dad finds out about this, he's going to be plenty mad, boy."

Dr. Alistair glared at me from behind the lenses of his glasses. "Is this true, young lady?" he demanded. He only called me young lady, I'm sure, because he couldn't remember my name.

"Only partially," I said. "I mean, another boy did hit him, but only after—"

Before I could finish my explanation, however, Dr. Alistair was taking charge of the situation.

"You," he said to Dave, who'd been standing close by, watching the proceedings with open-mouthed wonder. "Take this boy here to the nurse to have his eye looked at."

Dave sprang to attention. "Yes, sir," he said and, throwing me an apologetic look, he put a hand on Shane's shoulder and began steering him toward the infirmary. "Come on, big guy," he said.

Shane, sniffling, went with him . . . after pausing to throw me a triumphant look.

"You," Dr. Alistair said, jabbing his index finger at me. "You and I are going to meet in my office to discuss this matter."

My ears, I could tell, were redder than ever. "Yes, sir," I murmured. It was only then that I noticed that there among the onlookers stood Karen Sue Hanky, her mouth forming a little *V* of delight. How I longed to ram my fist, as Lionel had his, into her rat face.

"But not," Dr. Alistair continued, pausing to look down at his watch, "until one o'clock. I have a seminar until then."

And without another word, he turned around and headed back into the dining hall.

My shoulders slumped. One o'clock? Well, that was it. I was fired for sure.

Because of course there was no way I was making my meeting with Dr. Alistair. Not when I had an appointment at the same time to check out the situation with Keely Herzberg. I mean, my job was important, I guess. But not as important as a little girl who may or may not have been stolen from her custodial parent.

Remember what I was saying about how compli-cated my life had gotten lately? Yeah. That about summed it up.

"I told you," Karen Sue said as soon as Dr. Alistair was out of earshot, "that violence is never the answer."

I glanced at her sourly. "Hey, Karen Sue," I said.

She looked at me warily. "What?"

I made a gesture with my finger that caused her to gasp and go stalking off.

I noticed that a lot of the other counselors who were still standing there seemed to find it quite amusing, however.

10

He was late.

I stood on the side of the road, trying not to notice the sweat that was prickling the back of my neck. Not just the back of my neck, either. There was a pool of it between my boobs. I'm serious.

And I wasn't too comfortable in my jeans, either.

But what choice did I have? I'd learned the hard way never to ride a motorcycle in shorts. The scar was gone, but not the memory of the way the skin of my calf, sizzling against the exhaust pipe, had smelled.

Still, it had to be a hundred degrees on that long, narrow road. There were plenty of trees, of course, to offer shade. Hell, Camp Wawasee was nothing but trees, except where it was lake.

But if I stood in the trees, Rob might not see me when he came roaring up, and he might whiz right on past, and precious moments might be lost. . . .

Not that it mattered. I was going to be fired anyway, on account of missing my one o'clock meeting with Dr. Alistair. I was willing to bet that by the time I got back, all my stuff would be packed up and waiting for me by the front gates. Kerplunk, she sunk, like junk, cha, cha, cha.

Sweat was beginning to drip from the crown of my head, beneath my hair and into my eyes, when I finally heard the far off sound of a motorcycle engine. Rob isn't the type to let a muffler go, so his Indian didn't have one of those annoyingly loud engines you can hear from miles away. I simply became aware of a sound other than the shrill whine of the cicadas that were in the tall grass along the side of the road, and then I saw him, clipping along at no mean pace.

I didn't have to—we were the only two people on the road for miles, Lake Wawasee being about as isolated, I was becoming convinced, as Ice Station Zebra—but I put my arm out, to make sure he saw me. I mean, he could have thought I was a mirage or something. It was one of those kind of blazingly hot sunny days when you looked down a long straight road and saw pools of water across it, even though, when you finally got to the pool, it had evaporated as if it had never been there . . . because, of course, it hadn't been. It had just been one of those optical illusions they talk about, you know, in human bio.

Rob came cruising up to me and then put out a booted foot to balance himself when he came to a stop. He looked, as always, impressively large, like a lumberjack or something, only more stylishly dressed.

And when he took off his helmet and squinted at me in the sunlight with those eyes—so pale blue, they were practically the same color gray as his bike's exhaust—and I drank in his sexily messed-up hair and his darkly tanned forearms, all I could think was that, bad as it had been, that whole thing with the lightning and Colonel Jenkins and all, it had actually been worth it, because it had brought me the hottest Hottie of them all, Rob.

Well, sort of, anyway.

"Hey, sailor," I said. "Give a girl a ride?"

Rob just gave me his trademark don't-mess-with-me frown, then popped open the box on the back of his bike where he keeps the spare helmet.

"Get on," was all he said, as he held the helmet out to me.

Like I needed an invitation. I snatched up the helmet, jammed it into place (trying not to think about my sweaty hair), then wrapped my arms around his waist and said, "Put the pedal to the metal, dude."

He gave me one last, half-disgusted, half-amused look, then put his own helmet back on.

And we were off.

Hey, it wasn't a big, wet one or anything, but "Get on" isn't bad. I mean, Rob may not be completely in love with me yet or anything, but he'd shown up, right? That had to count for something. I mean, I'd called him that morning, and said I needed him to drive for four hours, cross-country, to pick me up.

And he'd shown up. He'd have had to find someone to cover for him at work, and explain to his uncle why he couldn't be there. He'd have had to buy gas, both for the trip to Chicago and then back again. He'd be spending a total of ten hours or so on the road. Tomorrow, he'd probably be exhausted.

But he'd shown up.

And I didn't think he was doing it because it was such a worthy cause, either. I mean, it *was*, and all, but he wasn't doing it for Keely.

At least . . . God, I *hope* not.

By two-thirty, we were cruising along Lake Shore Drive. The city looked bright and clean, the windows of the skyscrapers sparkling in the sunlight. The beaches were crowded. The songs playing from the car radios of the traffic we passed made it seem like we were a couple in a music video, or on a TV commercial or something. For Levi's, maybe. I mean, here we were, two total Hotties—well, okay, one total Hottie. I'm probably only Do-able—tooling around on the back of a completely cherried-out Indian on a sunny summer day. How much cooler could you get?

I guess if we'd noticed from the beginning we were being followed, that might have been cooler. But we didn't.

I didn't because I was busy experiencing one of those epiphanies they always talk about in English class.

Only my epiphany, instead of being some kind of spiritual enlightenment or whatever, was just this gush of total happiness because I had my arms around this totally buff guy I'd had a crush on since what seemed like forever, and he smelled really good, like Coast deodorant soap and whatever laundry detergent his mother uses on his T-shirts, and he had to think that I was at least somewhat cute, or he wouldn't have come all that way to pick me up. I was thinking, if only this was how I could spend the rest of my life: riding around the country on the back of Rob's bike, listening to music out of other people's car radios, and maybe stopping every once in a while for some nachos or whatever.

I don't know what was occupying Rob's thoughts so much that he didn't see the white van on our tail. Maybe he was having an epiphany of his own. Hey, it could happen.

But anyway, what happened was, eventually we had to pull off Lake Shore Drive in order to get where Keely was, and little by little, the traffic thinned out, and we still didn't notice the van purring along behind us. I don't know for sure, of course, because we weren't paying attention, but I like to think it stayed at least a couple car lengths away. Otherwise, well, there's no other explanation for it. We're just idiots. Or at least I am.

Anyway, finally we pulled onto this tree-lined street that was one hundred percent residential. I knew exactly which one Keely was in, of course, but I made Rob park about three houses away, just to be on the safe side. I mean, *that* much I knew. *That* much I was paying attention to.

We stood in front of the place where Keely was staying. It was just a house. A city house, so it was kind of narrow. On one side of it ran a skinny alley. The other side was attached to the house next door. Keely's house hadn't been painted as recently as the one next to it. What paint was left on it was kind of peeling off in a sad way. I would call the neighborhood sketchy, at best. The small yards had an untended look to them. Grass grows fast in a humid climate like the one in northern Illinois, and needs constant attention. No one on this street seemed to care, particularly, how high their grass grew, or what kind of garbage lay in their yards for that grass to swallow.

Maybe that was the purpose of the high grass. To hide the garbage.

Rob, standing next to me as I gazed up at the house, said, "Nice-looking crack den."

I winced. "It's not that bad," I said.

"Yeah, it is," he said.

"Well." I squared my shoulders. I wasn't sweaty anymore, after having so much wind blown on me, but I soon would be, if I stood on that hot sidewalk much longer. "Here goes nothing."

I opened the gate in the low chain-link fence that surrounded the house, and strode up the cement steps to the front door. I didn't realize Rob had followed me until I'd reached out to ring the bell.

"So what exactly," he said, as we listened to the hollow ringing deep inside the house, "is the plan here?"

I said, "There's no plan."

"Great." Rob's expression didn't change. "My favorite kind."

"Who is it?" demanded a woman's voice from behind the closed door. She didn't sound very happy about having been disturbed.

"Hello, ma'am?" I called. "Hi, my name is Ginger Silverman, and this is my friend, Nate. We're seniors at Chicago Central High School, and we're doing a research project on parental attitudes toward children's television programming. We were wondering if we could ask you a few questions about the kinds of television programs your children like to watch. It will only take a minute, and will be of invaluable help to us."

Rob looked at me like I was insane. "Ginger Silverman?"

I shrugged. "I like that name."

He shook his head. "*Nate?*"

"I like that name, too."

Inside the house, locks were being undone. When the door was thrown back, I saw, through the screen door, a tall, skinny woman in cutoffs and a halter top. You could tell she'd once taken care to color her hair, but that that had sort of fallen by the wayside. Now the ends of her hair were blonde, but the two inches of it at the top were dark brown. On her forehead, not quite hidden by her two-tone hair, was a dark, crescent-moon-shaped scab, about an inch and a half long. Out of one corner of her mouth, which was as flat and skinny as the rest of her, dangled a cigarette.

She looked at Rob and me as if we had dropped down from another planet and asked her to join the Galaxian Federation, or something.

"*What?*" she said.

I repeated my spiel about Chicago Central High School—who even knew if there was such a place?—and our thesis on children's television programming. As I spoke, a small child appeared from the shadows behind Mrs. Herzberg—if, indeed, this was Mrs. Herzberg, though I suspected it was—and, wrapping her arms around the woman's leg, blinked up at us with big brown eyes.

I recognized her instantly. Keely Herzberg.

"Mommy," Keely said curiously, "who are they?"

"Just some kids," Mrs. Herzberg said. She took her cigarette out of her mouth and I noticed that her fingernails were very bleedy-looking. "Look," she said to us. "We aren't interested. Okay?"

She was starting to close the door when I added, "There's a ten-dollar remuneration to all participants. . . ."

The door instantly froze. Then it swung open again.

"Ten bucks?" Mrs. Herzberg said. Her tired eyes, under that crescent-shaped scab, looked suddenly brighter.

"Uh-huh," I said. "In cash. Just for answering a few questions."

Mrs. Herzberg shrugged her skinny shoulders, and then, exhaling a plume of blue smoke at us through the screen door, she went, "Shoot."

"Okay," I said eagerly. "Um, what's your daughter's—this is your daughter, isn't it?"

The woman nodded without looking down. "Yeah."

"Okay. What is your daughter's favorite television show?"

"*Sesame Street*," said Mrs. Herzberg, while her daughter said, "*Rugrats*," at the same time.

"No, Mommy," Keely said, tugging on her mother's shorts. "*Rugrats*."

"*Sesame Street*," Mrs. Herzberg said. "My daughter is only allowed to watch public television."

Keely shrieked, "*Rugrats!*"

Mrs. Herzberg looked down at her daughter and said, "If you don't quit it, I'm sending you out back to play."

Keely's lower lip was trembling. "But you know I like *Rugrats* best, Mommy."

"Sweetheart," Mrs. Herzberg said. "Mommy is trying to answer these people's questions. Please do not interrupt."

"Um," I said. "Maybe we should move on. Do you and your husband discuss with one another the kinds of television shows your daughter is allowed to watch?"

"No," Mrs. Herzberg said shortly. "And I don't let her watch junk, like that *Rugrats*."

"But, Mommy," Keely said, her eyes filled with tears, "I love them."

"That's it," Mrs. Herzberg said. She pointed with her cigarette toward the back of the house. "Outside. Now."

"But, Mommy—"

"No," Mrs. Herzberg said. "That's it. I told you once. Now go outside and play, and let Mommy talk to these people."

Keely, letting out a hiccuppy little sob, disappeared. I heard a screen door slam somewhere in the house.

"Go on," Mrs. Herzberg said to me. Then her eyebrows knit. "Shouldn't you be writing my answers down?"

I reached up to smack myself on the forehead. "The clipboard!" I said to Rob. "I forgot the clipboard!"

"Well," Rob says. "Then I guess that's the end of that. Sorry to trouble you, ma'am—"

"No," I said, grabbing him by the arm and steering him closer to the screen door. "That's okay. It's in the car. I'll just go get it. You keep asking questions while I *go and get the clipboard.*"

Rob's pale blue eyes, as he looked down at me, definitely had ice chips in them, but what was I supposed to do? I went, "Ask her about the kind of programming *she* likes, Nate. And don't forget the ten bucks," and then I bounded down the steps, through the overgrown yard, out the gate . . .

And then, when I was sure Rob had Mrs. Herzberg distracted, I darted down the alley alongside her house, until I came to a high wooden fence that separated her backyard from the street.

It only took me a minute to climb up onto a Dumpster that was sitting there, and then look over that fence into the backyard.

Keely was there. She was sitting in one of those green plastic turtles people fill with sand. In her hand was a very dirty, very naked Barbie doll. She was singing softly to it.

Perfect, I thought. If Rob could just keep Mrs. Herzberg busy for a few minutes . . .

I clambered over the fence, then dropped over the other side into Keely's yard. Somehow, in spite of my gymnast-like grace and James Bondian stealthiness, Keely heard me, and squinted at me through the strong sunlight.

"Hey," I said as I ambled over to her sandbox. "What's up?"

Keely stared at me with those enormous brown eyes. "You aren't supposed to be back here," she informed me gravely.

"Yeah," I said, sitting down on the edge of the sandbox beside her. I'd have sat in the grass, but like in the front yard, it was long and straggly-looking, and after my recent tick experience, I wasn't too anxious to encounter any more bloodsucking parasites.

"I know I'm not supposed to be back here," I said to Keely. "But I wanted to ask you a couple of questions. Is that okay?"

Keely shrugged and looked down at her doll. "I guess," she said.

I looked down at the doll, too. "What happened to Barbie's clothes?"

"She lost them," Keely said.

"Whoa," I said. "Too bad. Think your mom will buy her some more?"

Keely shrugged again, and began dipping Barbie's head into the sandbox, stirring the sand like it was cake batter, and Barbie was a mixer. The sand in the sandbox didn't smell too fresh, if you know what I mean. I had a feeling some of the neighborhood cats had been there a few times.

"What about your dad?" I asked her. "Could your dad buy you some more Barbie clothes?"

Keely said, lifting Barbie from the sand and then smoothing her hair back, "My daddy's in heaven."

Well. That settled that, didn't it?

"Who told you that your daddy is in heaven, Keely?" I asked her.

Keely shrugged, her gaze riveted to the plastic doll in her hands. "My mommy," she said. Then she added, "I have a new daddy now." She wrenched her gaze from the Barbie and looked up at me, her dark eyes huge. "But I don't like him as much as my old daddy."

My mouth had gone dry . . . as dry as the sand beneath our feet. Somehow I managed to croak, "Really? Why not?"

Keely shrugged and looked away from me again. "He throws things," she said. "He threw a bottle, and it hit my mommy in the head, and blood came out, and she started crying."

I thought about the crescent-shaped scab on Mrs. Herzberg's forehead. It was exactly the size and shape a bottle, flying at a high velocity, would make.

And that, I knew, was that.

I guess I could have gotten out of there, called the

cops, and let them handle it. But did I really want to put the poor kid through all that? Armed men knocking her mother's door down, guns drawn, and all of that? Who knew what the mother's bottle-throwing boyfriend was like? Maybe he'd try to shoot it out with the cops. Innocent people might get hurt. You don't know. You can't predict these things. I know *I* can't, and I'm the one with the psychic powers.

And yeah, Keely's mother seemed like kind of a freak, protesting that her kid only watches public television while standing there filling that same kid's lungs with carcinogens. But hey, there are worse things a parent could do. That didn't make her an unfit mother. I mean, it wasn't like she was taking that cigarette and putting it out on Keely's arm, like some parents I've seen on the news.

But telling the kid her father was dead? And shacking up with a guy who throws bottles?

Not so nice.

So even though I felt like a complete jerk about it, I knew what I had to do.

I think you'd have done the same thing, too, in my place. I mean, really, what else could anybody have done?

I stood up and said, "Keely, your dad's not in heaven. If you come with me right now, I'll take you to him."

Keely had to crane her neck to look up at me. The sun was so bright, she had to do some pretty serious squinting, too.

"My daddy's not in heaven?" she asked. "Where is he, then?"

That was when I heard it: the sound of Rob's motorcycle engine. I could tell the sound of that bike's engine from every single other motorcycle in my entire town.

I know it's stupid. It's more than stupid. It's pathetic, is what it is. But can you really blame me? I mean, I really did harbor this hope that Rob was pining for me, and satisfied his carnal longing for me by riding by my house late at night.

He never actually did this, but my ears had become so accustomed to straining for the sound of his bike's engine, I could have picked it out in a traffic jam.

The real question, of course, was why Rob had left Mrs. Herzberg's front porch when he had to know I wasn't finished with my business in her backyard.

Something was wrong. Something was very wrong.

Which was why I didn't suffer too much twinging of my conscience when I looked down at Keely and said, "Your daddy's at McDonald's. If we hurry, we can catch him there, and he'll buy you a Happy Meal."

Did I feel bad, invoking the *M* word in order to lure a kid out of her own backyard? Sure. I felt like a worm. Worse than a worm. I felt like I was Karen Sue Hanky, or someone equally as creepy.

But I also felt like I had no other choice. Rob's bike roaring to life just then meant one thing, and one thing only:

We had to get going. And now.

It worked. Thank God, it worked. Because Keely Herzberg, bless her five-year-old heart, stood up and, looking up into my face, shrugged and said, "Okay."

It was at that moment I realized why Rob had taken off. The screen door that led to the backyard burst open, and a man in a pair of fairly tight-fitting jeans and some heavy-looking work boots—and who was clutching a beer bottle—came out onto the back porch and roared, "Who the hell are you?"

I grabbed Keely by the hand. I knew, of course, who this was. And I could only pray that his aim, when it came to moving targets, left something to be desired.

The sound of Rob's motorcycle engine had been getting closer. I knew now what he was doing.

"Come on," I said to Keely.

And then we were running.

I didn't really think about what I was doing. If I had stopped and thought about it, of course, I would have been able to see that there was no way that we could run faster than Mrs. Herzberg's boyfriend. All he had to do was leap down from the back porch and he'd be on us.

Fortunately, I was too scared of getting whacked with a beer bottle to do much thinking.

Instead, what I did was, while we ran, I shifted my grip on Keely from her hand to her arm, until I had scooped her up in both hands and she was being swept through the air. And when we reached the part of the fence I'd jumped down from, I swung her, with all my strength, toward the top of the fence. . . .

And she went sailing over it, just like those sacks of produce Professor Le Blanc had predicted I was going to be spending the rest of my life bagging.

Professor Le Blanc was right. I was a bag girl, in a way. Only what I bagged wasn't groceries, but other people's mistreated kids.

I heard Keely land with a scrape of plastic sandals on metal. She had made it onto the lid of the Dumpster, where, I could only hope, Rob would grab her. Now it was my turn.

Only Keely's new bottle-throwing dad was right behind me. He had let out a shocked, *"Hey!"* when I'd thrown Keely over the fence. The next thing I knew, the ground was shaking—I swear I felt it shudder beneath my feet—as he leaped from the porch and thundered toward me. Behind us a screen door banged open, and I heard Mrs. Herzberg yell, "Clay! Where's Keely, Clay?"

"Not me," I heard Clay grunt. *"Her!"*

That was it. I was dead.

But I wasn't giving up. Not until that bottle was beating my skull into pulp. Instead, I jumped, grabbing for the top of the fence.

I got it, but not without incurring some splinters. I didn't care about my hands, though. I was halfway there. All I had to do was swing my leg over, and—

He had hold of my foot. My left foot. He had grabbed it, and was trying to drag me down.

"Oh, no, you don't, girlie," Clay growled at me.

With his other hand, he grabbed the back of my jeans. He had apparently dropped the beer bottle, with was something of a relief.

Except that in a second, he was going to lift me off that fence, throw me to the ground, and step on me with one of those giant, work-booted feet.

"Jess!" I heard Rob calling to me. "Jess, come *on!*"

Oh, okay. I'll just hurry up now. Sorry about the delay, I'm just putting on a little lipstick—

"You," Clay said, as he tugged on me, "are in big trouble, girlie—"

Which was when I launched my free foot in the direction of his face. It connected solidly with the bridge of his nose, making a crunching sound that was quite satisfying, to my ears.

Well, I've never liked being called girlie.

Clay let go of both my foot and my waistband with an outraged cry of pain. And the second I was free, I swung myself over that fence, landed with a thump on the roof of the Dumpster, then jumped straight from the Dumpster onto the back of Rob's bike, which was waiting beneath it.

"Go!" I shrieked, throwing my arms around him and Keely, who was huddled, wide-eyed, on the seat in front of him.

Rob didn't waste another second. He didn't sit around and argue about how neither Keely nor I were wearing helmets, or how I'd probably ruined his shocks, jumping from the Dumpster onto his bike, like a cowboy onto the back of a horse.

Instead, he lifted up his foot and we were off, tearing down that alley like something NASA had launched.

Even with the noise of Rob's engine, I could still hear the anguished shriek behind us.

"Keely!"

It was Mrs. Herzberg. She didn't know it, of course, but I wasn't stealing her daughter. I was saving her.

But as for Keely's mother . . .

Well, she was a grown-up. She was just going to have to save herself.

11

I don't know what your feelings on McDonald's are. I mean, I know McDonald's is at least partly responsible for the destruction of the South American rain forest, which they have apparently razed large sections of in order to make grazing pastures for all the cattle they need to slaughter each year in order to make enough Big Macs to satisfy the demand, and all.

And I know that there's been some criticism over the fact that every seven miles, in America, there is at least one McDonald's. Not a hospital, mind you, or a police station, but a McDonald's, every seven miles.

I mean, that's sort of scary, if you think about it.

On the other hand, if you've been going to McDonald's since you were a little kid, like most of us have, it's sort of comforting to see those golden arches. I mean, they represent something more than just high-fat, high-cholesterol fast food. They mean that wherever you are, well, you're actually not that far from home.

And those fries are killer.

Fortunately, there was a Mickey D's just a few blocks away from Keely's house. Thank God, or I think Rob would have had an embolism. I could tell Rob was pretty unhappy about having to transport Keely and me, both helmetless, on the back of his Indian . . . even though it was completely safe, with me holding onto her and all. And it wasn't like he ever went more than fifteen miles per hour the whole time.

Well, except when we'd been racing down that alley to get away from Clay.

But let me tell you, when we pulled into the parking lot of that McDonald's, I could tell Rob was plenty relieved.

And when we stepped into the icy air-conditioning, I was relieved. I was sweating like a pig. I don't mind the crime-fighting stuff so much. It's the humidity that bugs me.

Anyway, once we were inside, and Keely was enjoying her Happy Meal while I thirstily sucked down a Coke, Rob explained how he'd been listening attentively to Mrs. Herzberg's description of her television-viewing habits, when her boyfriend appeared as if from nowhere, preemptively ending their little interview with a fist against the door frame. Sensing trouble, Rob hastily excused himself—though he did fork over the promised ten-dollar bill—and came looking for me.

Thank God he had, too, or I'd be the one with a footprint across my face, as opposed to Clay.

I tried to pay him back the ten he'd given to Mrs. Herzberg. He wouldn't take my money though. Also, he insisted on paying for Keely's Happy Meal and my giant Coke. I let him, thinking if I were lucky, he might expect me to put out for it.

Ha. I wish.

Then, once we'd compared notes on our adventures with Clay, I left Rob sitting with Keely while I got on the pay phone and dialed Jonathan Herzberg's office.

A woman answered. She said Mr. Herzberg couldn't come to the phone right now, on account of being in a meeting.

I said, "Well, tell him to get out of it. I have his kid here, and I don't know what I'm supposed to do with her."

I didn't realize until after the woman had put me on hold that I'd probably sounded like a kidnapper, or something. I wondered if she was running around the office, telling the other secretaries to call the police and have the call traced or something.

But I doubt she had time. Mr. Herzberg picked up again almost right away.

"Hey," I said. "It's me, Jess. I'm at a McDonald's—" I gave him the address. "I have Keely here. Can you come pick her up? I'd bring her to you, but we're on a motorcycle."

"Fifteen m-minutes." Mr. Herzberg was stammering with excitement.

"Good." I started to hang up, but I heard him say something else. I brought the phone back to my ear. "What was that?"

"God bless you," Mr. Herzberg said. He sounded kind of choked up.

"Uh," I said. "Yeah. Okay. Just hurry."

I hung up. I guess that's the only good part about this whole thing. You know, that sometimes, I can reunite kids with the parents who love them.

Still, I wish they didn't have to get so mushy about it.

It was after I'd hung up and felt around in the change dispenser to see if anybody had left anything behind—hey, you never know—that I noticed the van.

I walked over to where Rob and Keely were sitting.

"Hey," I said. "We got visitors."

Rob looked around the restaurant. "Oh, yeah?"

"Outside," I said. "The white van. Don't look. I'll take care of it. You stay here with Keely."

Rob shrugged, and dipped a fry into some ketchup. "No problem," he said.

To Keely, I said, "Your dad's on his way."

Keely grinned happily and sucked on the straw in her milk shake.

I went up to the counter and ordered two cheeseburger meals to go. Then I took the two bags and the little cardboard drink holder and went out the door opposite the one where the van was sitting. Then I walked all the way around the outside of the restaurant, past the drive-through window and the Dumpsters out back, until I came up behind the van.

Then I opened the side door and climbed on in.

"Ooh," I said appreciatively. "Nice air you got in here. But you'll wear out the battery if you sit here and idle for too long."

Special Agents Johnson and Smith turned around and looked at me. They both had sunglasses on. Special Agent Smith lifted hers up and looked at me with her pretty blue eyes.

"Hi, Jessica," she said, in a resigned sort of way.

"Hi," I said. "I figured you guys might be getting hungry, so I brought you this." I passed her the drinks and the bags with the cheeseburgers and fries in them. "I super-sized it for you."

Special Agent Smith opened her bag and looked inside it. "Thanks, Jess," she said, sounding pleasantly surprised. "That was very thoughtful."

"Yes," Special Agent Johnson said. "Thank you, Jessica."

But he said it in this certain way that you could just tell he was kind of, you know. Unhappy.

"So how long have you guys been following me?" I asked.

Special Agent Johnson—who hadn't even touched his food—said, "Since shortly after you left the camp."

"Really?" I thought about this. "All the way from there? I didn't notice you."

"We *are* professionals," Special Agent Smith pointed out, nibbling on a fry.

"We're *supposed* to be, anyway," Special Agent

Johnson said, in this meaningful way that made his partner put down the fry she was eating and look guilty. "How'd you know we were here, anyway?" he asked me.

"Come on," I said. "There's been a white van sitting on my street back home for months now. You think I wouldn't notice?"

"Ah," Special Agent Johnson said.

We sat there, all three of us, basking in the air-conditioning and inhaling the delicious scent of fries. There was a lot of stuff in the back of the van, stuff with blinking red and green buttons. It looked like surveillance equipment to me, but I could have been wrong. Nice to know the government wasn't wasting the taxpayers' money on frivolous things like the monitoring of teen psychics.

Finally, the luscious odor of Mickey D's proved too much for Special Agent Smith. She reached into her bag again and this time pulled out one of the cheeseburgers, then began unwrapping it. When she noticed Special Agent Johnson glaring at her disapprovingly, she went, "Well, it's just going to get cold, Allan," and took a big bite.

"So," I said. "How you two been?"

"Fine," Special Agent Smith said, with her mouth full.

"We're doing all right," Special Agent Johnson said. "We'd like to talk to you, though."

"If you wanted to talk to me," I said, "you could have just stopped by. I mean, you obviously know where to find me."

"Who's the little girl?" Special Agent Johnson said, nodding toward the window, where Rob and Keely were sitting.

"Oh, her?" I leaned forward and, since he obviously didn't want them, dug my hand into Special Agent Johnson's fries and pulled out a bunch for myself. "She's my cousin," I said.

"You don't have any cousins that age," Special Agent Smith said, after taking a sip from the soda I'd bought her.

"I don't?"

"No," she said. "You don't."

"Well," I said. "She's Rob's cousin, then."

"Really?" Special Agent Johnson took out a notepad and a pen. "And what's Rob's last name?"

"Ha," I said, with my mouth full of fry. "Like I'd tell you."

"He's kind of cute," Special Agent Smith observed.

"I know," I said, with a sigh.

The sigh must have been telling, since Special Agent Smith went, "Is he your boyfriend?"

"Not yet," I said. "But he will be."

"Really? When?"

"When I turn eighteen. Or when he is no longer able to resist the overwhelming attraction he feels for me and jumps my bones. Whichever comes first."

Special Agent Smith burst out laughing. Her partner didn't look so amused though.

"Jessica," he said. "Would you like to tell us about Taylor Monroe?"

I cocked my head innocently to one side. "Who?"

"Taylor Monroe," Special Agent Johnson said. "Disappeared two years ago. An anonymous call was placed yesterday to 1-800-WHERE-R-YOU, giving an address in Gainesville, Florida, where the boy could be found."

"Oh, yeah?" I picked at a loose thread on my jeans. "And was he there?"

"He was." Special Agent Johnson's gaze, reflected in the rearview mirror, did not waver from mine. "You wouldn't know anything about that, would you, Jess?"

"Me?" I screwed up my face. "No way. That's great, though. His parents must be pretty happy, huh?"

"They're ecstatic," Special Agent Smith said, taking a sip from her Coke. "The couple who took him—they apparently couldn't have children of their own—are in jail, and Taylor's already been returned to his folks. You never saw a more joyous reunion."

"Aw," I said, genuinely pleased. "That's sweet."

Special Agent Johnson adjusted the rearview mirror so he could see my reflection more clearly. "Very nicely done," he said drily. "I almost believed you had nothing to do with it."

"Well," I said. "I didn't."

"Jessica." Special Agent Johnson shook his head. "When are you finally going to admit that you lied to us last spring?"

"I don't know," I said. "Maybe when you admit

that you made a big mistake marrying Mrs. Johnson and that your heart really belongs to Jill here."

Special Agent Smith choked on a mouthful of cheeseburger. Special Agent Johnson had to ram her on the back a couple of times before she could breathe again.

"Oh," I said. "That go down the wrong pipe? I hate when that happens."

"Jessica." Special Agent Johnson spun around in his seat—well, as much as he could with the steering wheel in the way—and eyed me wrathfully. Really. *Wrathful* is about the only way I can describe it. Hey, I took the PSATs. I know what I'm talking about.

"You may think you got away with something last spring," he growled, "with that whole going-to-the-press thing. But I am warning you, missy. We are on to you. We know what you've been up to. And it's just a matter of time—"

Over Special Agent Johnson's shoulder, I saw a Passat come barreling through the intersection. Brakes squealing, it pulled into the McDonald's parking lot and came to a stop a few spaces down from the van. Jonathan Herzberg popped out from the driver's seat, so anxious to see his daughter he forgot to take off his seat belt. It strangled him, and he had to sit back down and unsnap it before he could get up again.

"—before Jill or I or someone catches you at it, and—"

"And what?" I asked. "What are you going to do to me, Allan? Put me in jail? For what? I haven't done anything illegal. Just because I won't help you find your little murderers and your drug lords and your escaped convicts, you think I'm doing something wrong? Well, excuse me for not wanting to do your job for you."

Special Agent Smith laid a hand on her partner's shoulder. "Allan," she said, in a warning voice.

Special Agent Johnson just kept glaring at me. He'd been so upset, he'd knocked over his fries, and now they lay all over the floor beneath his feet. He had already squashed one into the blue carpeting beneath the gas pedal. Behind him, Jonathan Herzberg was hurrying into the restaurant, having already spotted his daughter through the window.

"One thing you can do for me, though," I said, amiably enough. "You can tell me who tipped you off that I'd left the campgrounds."

I saw them exchange glances.

"Tipped us off?" Special Agent Smith ran her fingertips through her light brown hair, which was cut into a stylish—but not too stylish—bob. "What are you talking about, Jess?"

"Oh, what?" I rolled my eyes. "You expect me to believe the two of you have been sitting in this van outside of Camp Wawasee for the past nine days, waiting to see when I'd leave? I don't think so. For one thing, there aren't nearly enough food wrappers on the floor."

"Jessica," Special Agent Smith said, "we haven't been spying on you."

"No," I said. "You've just been paying somebody else to do it."

"Jess—"

"Don't bother to deny it. How else would you have known I was leaving the camp?" I shook my head. "Who is it, anyway? Pamela? That secretary who looks like John Wayne? Oh, wait, I know." I snapped my fingers. "It's Karen Sue Hanky, isn't it? No, wait, she's too much of a crybaby to be a narc."

"You," Special Agent Johnson said, "are being ridiculous."

Ridiculous. Yeah. That's right.

I watched through the plate glass window as Jonathan Herzberg snatched up his daughter and gave her a hug that came close to strangling her. She didn't seem to mind, though. Her grin was broader than I'd ever seen it—way bigger than it had been over the Happy Meal.

Another joyous reunion, brought about by me.

And I was missing it.

Ridiculous. They were the ones going around spying on a sixteen-year-old girl. And they said *I* was being ridiculous.

"Well," I said. "It's been fun, you guys, but I gotta motor. Bye."

I got out of the van. Behind me, I heard Special Agent Johnson call my name.

But I didn't bother turning around.

I don't like being called missy any more than I liked being called girlie. I was proud that I'd at least managed to restrain myself from slamming my foot into Special Agent Johnson's face.

Mr. Goodhart was really going to be pleased by the progress I'd made so far this summer.

CHAPTER

12

"So," Rob said. "Was it worth it?"

"I don't know," I said with a shrug. "I mean, her mom didn't seem that bad. She might have gotten out on her own, eventually."

"Yeah," Rob said. "After enough stitches."

I didn't say anything. Rob was the one who came from the broken home, not me. I figured he knew what he was talking about.

"She claims her favorite TV show is *Masterpiece Theater*," Rob informed me.

"Well," I said. "That doesn't prove anything. Except, you know, that she wanted to impress us."

"Impress Ginger and Nate," he said, with one raised eyebrow, "from Chicago Central High? Yeah, that's important."

"Well," I said. I rested my elbows on my knees. We were sitting on a picnic table, gazing out over

Lake Wawasee. Well, the edge of Lake Wawasee, anyway. We were about two miles from the actual camp. Somehow, I just couldn't bring myself to go back there. Maybe it was the fact that when I set foot through those gates, I was going to be fired.

Then again, maybe it was because when I set foot through those gates, I'd have to say good-bye to Rob.

Look, I'll admit it: I'm warm for the guy's form. Anybody here have a problem with that?

And it was really nice, sitting there in the shade with him, listening to the shrill *whirr* of the cicadas and the birdsong from the treetops. It seemed as if there wasn't another human being for miles and miles. Above the trees, clouds were gathering. Soon it was going to rain, but it looked as if it would hold off for a little while longer—besides, we were somewhat protected by the canopy of leaves over our heads.

If it had been dark enough, it would have been a perfect make-out spot.

Well, if Rob didn't have this total prejudice against making out with girls sixteen and under.

It was as I was sadly counting the months until I turned seventeen—all eight and a half of them; Douglas could have told me exactly how many days, and even minutes, I had left—that Rob reached out and put his arm around me.

And unlike when Pamela had done the exact same thing, I did not mind. I did not mind at all.

"Hey," Rob said. I could feel his heart thudding against my side, where his chest pressed against me.

"Stop beating yourself up. You did the right thing. You always do."

For a minute, I couldn't figure out what he was talking about. Then I remembered. Oh, yeah. Keely Herzberg. Rob thought I'd been mulling over her, when really, I'd just been trying to figure out a way to get him to make a pass at me.

Oh, well. I figured what I was doing was working so far, if the arm around me was any indication. I sighed and tried to look sad . . . which was difficult, because I was sort of having another one of those epiphanies, what with the breeze off the lake and the birds and Rob's Coast deodorant soap smell and the nice, heavy weight of his arm and everything.

"I guess," I said, managing to sound uncertain even to my own ears.

"Are you kidding?" Rob gave me a friendly squeeze. "That woman told her kid that her father was dead. *Dead!* You think she was playing with a full deck?"

"I know," I said. Maybe if I looked sad enough, he'd stick his tongue in my mouth.

"And look how happy Keely was. And Mr. Herzberg. My God, did you see how stoked he was to have his kid back? I think if you'd have let him, he'd have written you a check for five grand, right there and then."

Jonathan Herzberg had been somewhat eager to offer me compensation for the trouble I'd taken, returning his daughter to him . . . a substantial monetary reward I had politely turned down, telling him that if he absolutely had to fork his money over to somebody, he should donate it to 1-800-WHERE-R-YOU.

Because, I mean, let's face it: you can't go around taking rewards for being human, now can you?

Even if it does get you fired.

"I guess," I said again, still sounding all sad.

But if I'd thought Rob was going to fall for my whole poor-little-me routine, it turned out I had another think coming.

"You can forget it, Mastriani," he said, suddenly removing his arm. "I'm not going to kiss you."

Jeez! What's a girl have to do around here to get felt up?

"Why not?" I demanded.

"We've been over this before," he said, looking bored.

This was true.

"You *used* to kiss me," I pointed out to him.

"That was before I knew you were jailbait."

This was also true.

Rob leaned back, propping himself up on his elbows and gazing out at the trees across the water. In a month or two, all the green leaves he was looking at now would be blazing red and orange. I would be starting my junior year at Ernest Pyle High School, and Rob would still be working in his uncle's garage, helping his mother with the mortgage on their farmhouse (his father had split, as Rob put it, when he was just a little kid, and hadn't been heard from since), and fiddling around with the Harley he was rebuilding in their barn.

But really, if you thought about it, we weren't so different, Rob and I. We both liked going fast, and we both hated liars. Our clothing ensemble of preference was jeans and a T-shirt, and we both had short dark hair . . . mine was even shorter than Rob's. We both loved motorcycles, and neither of us had aspirations for college. At least, I didn't think I did. And I know my grades didn't exactly leave a whole lot of hope for it.

Our similarities completely outweighed our differences. So what if Rob has no curfew, and I have to be home every night by eleven? So what if Rob has a probation officer, and I have a mother who makes me dresses for homecoming dances I'll never go to? People really shouldn't let those things get in the way of true love.

I pointed this out to him, but he didn't look very impressed.

"Look." I flopped down on top of the picnic table, turned toward him on one elbow, holding my head in one hand. "I don't see what the problem is. I mean, I'm going to be seventeen in eight and a half months. Eight and a half months! That's nothing. I don't see why we can't—"

I was lying in just such a way that Rob's face was only a couple of inches from mine. When he turned to look at me, our noses almost bumped into one another.

"Didn't your mother ever tell you," Rob asked, "that you're supposed to play hard to get?"

I looked at his lips. I probably don't need to tell you that they're really nice lips, kind of full and strong-looking. "What," I wanted to know, "is *that* going to get me?"

I swear to you, he was a second away from kissing me then.

I know he said he wasn't going to. But let's face it, he always says that, and then he always does—well, almost always, anyway. I swear that's why he avoids me half the time . . . because he knows that for all he says he isn't going to kiss me, he usually ends up doing it anyway. Who knows why? I'd like to think it's because I'm so damned irresistible, and because he's secretly in love with me, in spite of what it says in the *Cosmo* quiz.

But I wasn't destined to find out. Not just then, anyway. Because just as he was leaning over in the direction of my mouth, this unearthly siren started to wail . . .

. . . and we were both so startled, we wrenched apart.

I swear I thought a tornado alarm was going off. Rob said later he thought it was my dad, with one of those klaxon things old ladies set off when a mugger is attacking them.

But it wasn't either of those things. It was a Wawasee County police cruiser. And it whizzed by the campground we were parked at like a bullet. . . .

Only to be followed by another.

And another.

And then another.

Four squad cars, all headed at breakneck speed in the direction of Camp Wawasee.

I should have known, of course. I should have guessed what was wrong.

But my psychic abilities are limited to finding people, not predicting the future. All I knew was that something was definitely wrong back at the camp . . . and it wasn't my psychic powers telling me that, either. It was just plain common sense.

"What," Rob wanted to know, "have you done now?"

What *had* I done? I wasn't sure.

"I have," I said, "a very bad feeling about this."

"Come on." Rob sighed tiredly. "Let's go find out."

They didn't want to let us in at the gate, of course. Rob had no visitor's pass, and the security guard looked down his nose at my employee ID and went, "Only time counselors are allowed to leave the camp is Sunday afternoons."

I looked at him like he was crazy. "I know that," I said. "I snuck out. Now are you going to let me back in, or not?"

You could totally tell the guy, who couldn't have been more than nineteen or twenty, had tried for the local police force and hadn't made it. So he'd opted to become a security guard, thinking that would give him the authority and respect he'd always yearned for. He sucked on his two overlarge front teeth and, peering at Rob and me, went, " 'Fraid not. There's a bit of a problem up at the camp, you know, and—"

I put down the face shield of my helmet and said to Rob, "Let's go."

Rob said to the security guard, "Nice talkin' to ya."

Then he gunned the engine, and we went around the red-and-white barrier arm, churning up quite a bit of dust and gravel as we did so. What did it matter? I couldn't get more fired than I already was.

The security guard came out of his little house and started yelling, but there wasn't much he could do to make us turn around. It wasn't like he had a gun, or anything.

Not that guns had ever stopped us before, of course.

As we drove up the long gravel road to the camp, I noticed how still and cool the woods were, especially with the coming rainstorm. The sky above us was clouding up more with every passing moment. You could smell the rain in the air, fresh and sweet.

Of course it wasn't until I was about to be kicked out of there that I'd finally begun to appreciate Camp Wawasee. It was too bad, really. I'd never even gotten a chance to float around the lake on an inner tube.

When we pulled up to the administrative offices, I was surprised at how many people were milling around. The squad cars were parked kind of haphazardly, and there was no sign of the cops who'd been driving them. They must, I figured, be inside, talking to Dr. Alistair, Pamela, and Ms. John Wayne.

But there were campers and counselors aplenty, which I thought was a little weird. If there'd been some sort of accident or crisis, you'd have thought they'd have tried to keep it from the kids. . . .

. . . And that's when I realized that they couldn't have kept it from the kids, even if they'd wanted to. It was five-thirty, and the kids and their counselors were streaming into the dining hall for supper. The dining staff prepared meals at exactly the same time every day, crisis or no crisis.

All of the kids were staring curiously at the squad cars. When they noticed Rob and me, they looked even more curious, and began whispering to one another. Oddly enough, I saw no members of Birch Tree Cottage in the crowds. . . .

But I saw a lot of other people I knew, including Ruth and Scott, who made no move whatsoever to approach me.

That's when I realized I still had my helmet on. Of course no one was saying hi. No one recognized me. As soon as I'd dragged the heavy thing off, Ruth came right over, and, as Rob pulled his helmet off as well, said, very sarcastically, "Well, I see you managed to find that ride you were looking for."

I shot her a warning look. Ruth can really be very snotty when she puts her mind to it.

"Ruth," I said. "I don't think I've ever formally introduced you to my friend, Rob. Ruth Abramowitz, this is Rob Wilkins. Rob, Ruth."

Rob nodded curtly to Ruth. "How you doing," he said.

Ruth smiled at him. It was not her best effort, by any means.

"I'm doing very well, thank you," she said primly. "And you?"

Rob, his eyebrows raised, said, "I'm good."

"Ruth." One of the residents of Tulip Tree Cottage pulled on Ruth's T-shirt. "I'm *hungry*. Can we go in now?"

Ruth turned and said to her campers, "You all go in now, and save a place for me. I'll be there in a minute."

The kids went away, with many glances not only at me and Rob, but at the squad cars. "What are the *police* doing here?" more than one of them asked loudly of no one in particular.

"Good question," I said to Ruth. "What *are* the police doing here?"

"I don't know." Ruth was still looking at Rob. She had seen him before, of course, back when he and I had had detention together. Ruth used to come pick me up, so my parents wouldn't find out about my somewhat checkered disciplinary record.

But I guess this was the first time she'd ever seen Rob from close up, and I could tell she was memorizing the details for later analysis. Ruth's like that.

"What do you mean, you don't know?" I

demanded. "The place is crawling with cops, and you don't know why?"

Ruth finally wrenched her gaze from Rob and fastened it onto me instead.

"No," she said. "I don't know. All I know is, we were down at the lake, having free swim and all, and the lifeguard blew his whistle and made us all go back inside."

"We thought it was on account of the storm," Scott said, nodding toward the still-darkening sky above us.

It was at this point that Karen Sue Hanky strolled up to us. I could tell by the expression on her pointy rat face that she had something important to tell us . . . and by the unnatural glitter in her baby-blue eyes, I knew it was something I wasn't going to like.

"Oh," she said, pretending she had only just noticed me. "I see you've decided to join us again." She glanced flirtatiously at Rob. "And brought along a friend, I see."

Even though Karen Sue had gone to school with Rob, she didn't recognize him. Girls like Karen Sue simply don't notice guys like Rob. I suppose she thought he was just some random local I'd picked up off the highway and brought back to camp for some recreational groping.

"Karen Sue," I said, "you better hurry and get into the dining hall. I heard a rumor they were running low on wheatgrass juice."

She just smiled at me, which wasn't a very good sign.

"Aren't you funny," Karen Sue said. "But then I suppose it's very amusing to you, what's going on. On account of it all being because of you telling that one little boy to hit that other little boy." Karen Sue flicked some of her hair back over her shoulder and sighed. "Well, I guess it just goes to show, violence doesn't pay."

Overhead, the clouds had gotten so thick, the sun was blocked out almost entirely. Inside the dining hall, the lights had come on, though this usually didn't happen until seven or eight o'clock, when the cleaning crew was at work. In the distance, thunder rumbled. The smell of ozone was heavy in the air.

I stepped forward until Karen Sue's upturned nose was just an inch from mine, and she stumbled back a step, tripping over a root and nearly falling flat on her face.

When she straightened, I asked her just what the heck she was talking about.

Only I didn't say heck.

Karen Sue started talking very quickly, and in a voice that was higher in pitch than usual.

"Well, I just went into the administrative offices for a second because I had to make sure the fax from Amber's doctor had come—about how her chronic ear infections prevent her from taking part in the Polar Bear swim—and I just happened to overhear the police talking to Dr. Alistair about how one of the boys from Birch Tree Cottage went to the lake, but no one saw him come out of it—"

I reached out and grabbed a handful of Karen

Sue's shirt, on account of how she was slowly backing farther and farther away from me.

"Who?" I demanded. Even though it was still about seventy-five degrees, in spite of the coming rainstorm, my skin was prickly with goose bumps. "Who went into the lake and didn't come out of it?"

"That one you were always yelling at," Karen Sue said. "Shane. Jessica, while you were gone"—she shook her head—"Shane *drowned.*"

CHAPTER

13

Thunder rumbled again, much closer this time. Now the hair on my arms was standing up not because I was cold, but because of all the electricity in the air.

I grabbed hold of Karen Sue's shirt with my other hand as well, and dragged her toward me. "What do you mean, *drowned?*"

"Just what I said." Karen Sue's voice was higher than ever. "Jess, he went into the lake and he never came out—"

"Bull," I said. "That's bull, Karen. Shane's a good swimmer."

"Well, when they blew the whistle for everyone to get out," Karen Sue said, her tone starting to sound a little hysterical, "Shane never came onto shore."

"Then he never went into the water in the first place," I hissed from between gritted teeth.

"Maybe," Karen Sue said. "And maybe if you'd been here, doing your job, and hadn't gone off with your boyfriend"—she sneered in Rob's direction—"you'd know."

Everything, the trees, the cloudy sky, the path, everything, seemed to be spinning around. It was like that scene in the *Wizard of Oz* when Dorothy wakes up in the tornado. Except that I was the only thing standing still.

"I don't believe you," I said again. I shook Karen Sue hard enough to make her pink headband snap off and go flying through the air. "You're lying. I ought to smash your face in, you—"

"All right." Suddenly, the world stopped spinning, and Rob was there, prying my fingers off Karen Sue's shirt. "All right, Mastriani, that's enough."

"You're lying," I said to Karen Sue. "You're a liar, and everyone knows it."

Karen Sue, white-faced and shaking, bent down, picked up her headband, and pushed it shakily back into place. There were some dead leaves stuck to it, but she apparently didn't notice.

I really wanted to jump her, knock her to the ground, and grind her rat face into the dirt. Only I couldn't get at her, because Rob had me around the waist, and wouldn't let go, no matter how hard I struggled to get away. If Mr. Goodhart had been there, he'd have been way disappointed in me. I seemed to have forgotten all the anger-management skills he'd taught me.

"You know what else, Karen Sue?" I shouted.

"You can't play flute for squat! They weren't even going to let you in here, with your lousy five out of ten on your performance score, except that Andrew Shippinger came down with mono, and they were *desperate*—"

"Okay," Rob said, lifting me up off my feet. "That's enough of that."

"That was supposed to be *my* cabin," I yelled at her, from over Rob's shoulder. "The Frangipanis were supposed to be *mine!*"

Rob had turned me around so that I was facing Ruth. She took one look at me and went, "Jess. Cool it."

I said fiercely, "He's *not* dead. He's *not.*"

Ruth blinked, then looked from me to Scott and back again. I looked at them, too, and realized from the way they were staring at me that something weird was going on with my face. I reached up to touch it, and felt wetness.

Great. I was crying. I was crying, and I hadn't even noticed.

"She's lying," I said one last time, but not very loudly.

Rob must have decided the fight had gone out of me, since he put me down—though he kept one hand glued to the back of my neck—and said, "There's one way to find out, isn't there?"

He nodded toward the administrative offices. I wiped my cheeks with the backs of my hands and said, "Okay."

Ruth insisted on following Rob and me, and Scott,

to my surprise, insisted on coming with her. It sunk into my numbed consciousness that there was something going on there, but I was too worried about Shane to figure it out just then. I'd think about it later. When we stepped into the building, the John Wayne look-alike secretary stood up and said, "Kids, they still don't know anything yet. I know you're worried, but if you could just stay with your campers—"

"Shane *is* my camper," I said.

The woman's thick eyebrows went up. She stared at me, apparently uncertain as to how best to reply.

I helped her out.

"Where are they?" I demanded, striding past her and down the hall. "Dr. Alistair's office?"

The secretary, scrambling out from behind her desk, went, "Oh, wait. You can't go back there—"

But it was too late. I'd already turned the corner and reached the door marked "Camp Director." I threw it open. Behind a wide desk sat the white-haired, red-faced Dr. Alistair. In various chairs and couches around his office sat Pamela, two state troopers, a sheriff's deputy, and the sheriff of Wawasee County himself.

"Jess." Pamela jumped to her feet. "There you are. Oh, thank God. We couldn't find you anywhere. And Dr. Alistair said you didn't show up for a meeting with him this afternoon—"

I looked at Pamela. What was she playing at? She, of all people, should have known where I was. Hadn't Jonathan Herzberg called and told her all about my returning his daughter to him?

I didn't think this was an appropriate time to bring that up, however. I said, "I was unavoidably detained. Can someone please tell me what's going on?"

Dr. Alistair stood up. He didn't look like a world-famous conductor anymore, or even a camp director. Instead, he looked like a frail old man, though he couldn't have been more than sixty years old.

"What's going on?" he echoed. "What's going on? You mean to say you don't know? Aren't you the famous psychic? How could you not know, with your special, magic powers? Hmm, Miss Mastriani?"

I glanced from Dr. Alistair to Pamela and back again. Had she told him? I supposed she must have.

But the astonished look on her face implied that she had not.

"I'll tell you what's going on, young lady," Dr. Alistair said, "since your psychic powers seem to be failing you at the moment. One of our campers is missing. Not just any camper, but one of the boys assigned to *your* care. Ostensibly, he's drowned. For the first time in our fifty-year history, we've had a death here at the camp."

I flinched as if he'd hit me. Not because of what he'd said, though that was bad enough. No, it was what he hadn't said, the thing that was implied in his tone:

That it was all my fault.

"But I'm surprised you didn't know that already." Dr. Alistair's tone was mocking. "Lightning Girl."

"Now, Hal," the sheriff said in a gruff voice. "Why

don't we just calm down here? We don't know that for sure. We don't have a body yet."

"The last time anyone saw him alive, he was on the way to the lake with the rest of his cabin. He isn't anywhere on the campgrounds. The boy's dead, I tell you. And it's entirely our fault! If his *counselor* had been there to keep an eye on him, it wouldn't have happened."

My throat was dry. I tried to swallow, but couldn't. Outside, lightning flashed, followed almost immediately by a long roll of thunder.

Then the heavens unloosed. Rain beat against the windows behind Dr. Alistair's desk. One of the state troopers, looking out at the downpour, said, in a morose voice, "Gonna be hard to drag that lake now."

Drag the lake? *Drag the lake?*

"Wasn't there a lifeguard?"

Rob. Rob was trying to help. Rob was trying to deflect some of the blame from me. Sweet of him, of course, but a useless effort. It was my fault. If I'd been there, Shane never would have drowned. I wouldn't have let him.

"It seems to me," Rob said reasonably, "if the kid was swimming, there ought to have been a lifeguard. Wouldn't the lifeguard have noticed someone drowning on his watch?"

Dr. Alistair squinted at him through the lenses of his bifocals. "Who," he demanded, "are you?" Then he spied Ruth and Scott in the doorway. "What is this?" he demanded. "Who are you people? This is my private office. Get out."

None of them moved, although Ruth looked like she really wanted to run somewhere far away. Somewhere where there weren't any sheriff deputies or angry camp directors. It was just like the time her brother Skip had been stung by the bee, only instead of someone going into anaphylactic shock, some-one—namely me—was dying a slower death . . . of guilt.

"Well," Rob said. "Wasn't there a lifeguard?"

The sheriff said, "There was. He didn't notice anything unusual."

"That's because," I said, more to myself than anyone else, "Shane never went into the water." It wasn't something I knew with any certainty. Just something I suspected.

But that didn't stop Dr. Alistair from looking at me from behind his wire-rimmed glasses and demanding, "And I suppose, since you weren't there, you're able to tell that using your special powers?"

It was at this point that Rob took a step toward Dr. Alistair's desk. The sheriff put out a hand, however, and said, "Easy, son." Then, to Dr. Alistair, he said, "Just what are you talking about, Hal?"

"Oh, you don't recognize her?" Dr. Alistair looked prim. I wondered if maybe losing a camper had sent him around the bend. He'd never been one of the most stable people, anyway, if his erratic behavior during all-camp rehearsal had been any indication: Dr. Alistair frequently became so enraged with the horn section, he threw his conducting baton at them, only missing because they'd learned to duck.

"Jessica Mastriani," he went on, "the girl with the psychic power to find missing people. Of course it's a little late for her help now, isn't it? Considering the fact that the boy's already dead."

"Oh, Hal." Pamela stood up. "We don't know that. He might just have run away." She looked at me. "Wasn't there some altercation earlier today?"

I nodded, remembering the tick incident, and the fact that I had refused to give Lionel a strike for punching Shane.

More than that, however, I remembered the look Shane had given me when I'd lied to him about that photo of Taylor Monroe. He hadn't believed me. He hadn't believed a word I'd said.

Was this his way of getting back at me for lying to him?

If only, I thought, I could go to sleep right now. If I went to sleep right now, I'd be able to find out exactly where Shane was. Maybe if I could get Dr. Alistair really mad, he'd clock me with his baton, the way he was always trying to clock the horn players. Could I find missing kids while unconscious? Was that the same as being asleep?

Probably not. And I doubted the sheriff would let Dr. Alistair clock me, anyway. Rob definitely wouldn't. I wondered if protectiveness was listed as one of the "10 Ways to Tell He Thinks of You as More Than Just a Friend."

Like it mattered now. Now that it looked as if I might have killed a kid. Well, indirectly, anyway.

"What about the other boys from Birch Tree

Cottage?" I asked. "Did anybody talk to them? Ask them if they'd seen Shane?" Dave? Where was Dave? He'd promised to look after them. . . .

"We've got some officers interviewing them now," the sheriff said to me. "In their cabin. But so far . . . nothing."

"He was last seen on his way to the lake with the others," Dr. Alistair insisted stubbornly.

"Doesn't mean he drowned," Rob pointed out.

Dr. Alistair looked at him. "Who," he wanted to know, "are you? You're not one of the counselors." He looked at Pamela. "He's not one of the counselors, is he, Pamela?"

Pamela reached up to run a hand through her short blond hair. "No, Hal," she said tiredly. "He's not."

"He's my friend," I said. I didn't say Rob was my boyfriend because, well, he's not. Plus I thought it might look even worse than it already did, me being gone for hours, then showing up with some random guy in tow. "And we were just leaving."

But my efforts to cover up the truth about my feelings for Rob proved to be for nothing as Dr. Alistair said, pretty nastily, "Leaving? Oh, well, isn't that special. You seem to have a knack, Miss Mastriani, for being unavailable when you're needed most."

My mouth fell open. What *was* this? I wondered. If he was going to fire me, why didn't he just get it over with? I had to hurry up and get to sleep if we were ever going to find Shane.

"What about those special powers of yours?" Dr.

Alistair went on. "Don't you feel the slightest obligation to help us find this boy?"

Even then, I still didn't get what was going on. I just thought Dr. Alistair was crazy, or something.

I think Rob must have felt the same thing, because he reached out and grabbed one of my arms, just above the elbow, like he was going to pull me out of the way if Dr. Alistair whipped out that baton and started firing.

I went, "I don't have special powers anymore, Dr. Alistair."

"Oh?" Dr. Alistair's shaggy white eyebrows went up. "Is that so? *Then where were you all afternoon?*"

I felt my stomach drop, as if I'd been on an elevator. Except, of course, that I wasn't. How had he known? *How had he known?*

"Okay," Rob said, steering me toward the door—I guess because I was so stunned, I wasn't moving. "We're going now."

"You can't go anywhere!" Dr. Alistair thumped on his desk with his fist. "You are an employee of Lake Wawasee Camp for Gifted Child Musicians, and you—"

Something finally got through the haze of confusion his question about where I'd been all afternoon had cast around me. And that something was the fact that he was still speaking to me as if I worked for him.

"Not anymore," I interrupted. "I mean, I'm fired, aren't I?"

Dr. Alistair looked alarmed. "Fired?" at the same

time as Pamela said, "Oh, Jess, of course not. None of this is your fault."

Not fired? *Not fired?* How could I be not fired? I had taken off for hours, without offering a single explanation as to where I'd been. And while I'd been gone, one of the kids in my charge had disappeared. And I *wasn't fired?*

The uncomfortable feeling that had been creeping over me since I'd set foot in Dr. Alistair's office got stronger than ever. And suddenly I knew what I had to do.

"If I'm not fired," I said, "then I quit. Come on, Rob."

Pamela looked stricken. "Oh, Jess. You can't—"

"You can't quit," Dr. Alistair cried. "You signed a contract!"

He said a bunch of other things, but I didn't wait to hear them. I left. I just walked out.

Rob and the others followed me out into the waiting area. The John-Waynish secretary was there, talking on the phone. She lowered her voice when she saw us, but didn't hang up.

"Are you crazy, Jess?" Ruth wanted to know. "Quitting, when you didn't have to? They weren't going to fire you, you know."

"I know," I said. "That's why I had to quit. Who would want to hang on to an employee like me? I'll tell you who: someone with ulterior motives."

"I don't really understand any of this." Scott, speaking for the first time, looked concerned. "And it probably isn't any of my business. But it seems to me if you really do have psychic powers and all of that, and people want you to use them, shouldn't you, I don't know, do it? I mean, you could probably make a lot of money at it."

Rob and I just stared at him incredulously. Ruth's look was more pitying.

"Oh," she said. "You poor thing."

It was right then that the double glass doors to the administrative building blew open. We all backed out of the way as two people, holding dripping umbrellas, stepped into the office waiting room.

It wasn't until they shook the umbrellas closed that I recognized them. And when I did, I groaned.

"Oh, jeez," I said. "Not you again."

CHAPTER

14

"Jess." Special Agent Smith shook rainwater from her hair. "We need to talk."

I couldn't believe it. I really couldn't. I mean, it is one thing to have the FBI following you wherever you go.

But it is quite another to have the people who are supposed to be anonymous tails come up and start talking to you. It simply isn't done. Everyone knows *that*. I mean, how uncool can you get?

"Look," I said, holding up my right hand. "I really don't have time for this right now. I am having a personal crisis, and—"

"It's going to become really personal," Special Agent Johnson said—his lips, I noticed, looked thinner than usual—"if Clay Larsson gets his hands on you."

"Clay Larsson?" I tried to think who they were

talking about. Then it dawned on me. "You mean Keely's new dad?"

"Right." Special Agent Johnson threw Rob a look. "His cousin's mother's boyfriend."

Rob screwed up his face and went, "My what?"

I didn't blame him. I was confused, too.

"After you left him this afternoon," Special Agent Johnson explained, "Mr. Larsson rightly guessed that the person who had kidnapped his girlfriend's daughter was someone who'd been hired by the child's father. He therefore paid a little visit to your friend Mr. Herzberg, who returned to his office after his rendezvous with you at the McDonald's."

"Oh." God, I'm a moron sometimes. "Is he . . . I mean, he's all right and everything, right?"

"He's got a broken jaw." Special Agent Johnson referred to the notepad he always carries around. "Three fractured ribs, a concussion, a dislocated knee, and a severely contused hip bone."

"Oh, my God." I was shocked. "Keely—"

"Keely is fine." Special Agent Smith's voice was soothing. "We have her in protective custody, where she'll remain while Mr. Larsson is still at large."

I raised my eyebrows. "You guys didn't catch him?"

"We might have," Special Agent Johnson pointed out—rather nastily, if you ask me, "if certain people had been a bit more forthcoming about their activities earlier today."

"Whoa," I said. "You are *not* pinning this on me. It

doesn't have anything to do with me. I'm just an innocent bystander in this one—"

"Jess." Special Agent Johnson frowned down at me. "We know. Jonathan Herzberg told us everything."

My mouth fell open. I couldn't believe it. That rat! That dirty rat!

It was Rob who asked suspiciously, "He told you everything, did he? With a broken jaw?"

Special Agent Johnson flipped back a few pages in his notepad, then showed it to us. There, in shaky handwriting I didn't recognize—it certainly wasn't Allan Johnson's precise script—was Jonathan Herzberg's version of the events leading up to his assault by his ex-wife's boyfriend. My name appeared frequently.

The louse. The louse had ratted me out. I couldn't believe it. After everything I'd done for him . . .

"Jess." Special Agent Smith, in her powder blue suit, looked more like a real estate broker than she did an FBI agent. I guess that was the point. "Clay Larsson is not a particularly stable individual. He has an arrest record a mile long. Assault and battery, resisting arrest, assaulting a police officer . . . He is a very dangerous and volatile person, and from what Mr. Herzberg tells us, we have reason to believe that, at this point in time, he has a particular grudge against . . . well, against you, Jess."

Considering the foot I'd smashed into his face, I could readily believe this. Still, it wasn't as if Clay Larsson knew who I was, much less where I lived.

"Well, that's just the thing," Special Agent Smith said, when I voiced these thoughts. "He *does* know, Jess. You see, he . . . well, he pretty much tortured Keely's father until he told him."

Rob said, "Okay. That's it. Let's go get your stuff, Mastriani. We're out of here."

It took me longer than it had taken Rob to digest what I'd just heard, though. Clay Larsson, who clearly had even worse anger-management issues than I did, knew who I was and where I lived, and was coming after me to exact revenge for (a) kicking him in the face, and (b) kidnapping his girlfriend's daughter, whom she, in turn, had kidnapped from her ex-husband?

How did I ever get to be so lucky? Really. I want to know. I mean, have you ever, in your life, met anyone with worse luck than mine?

"Well," I said. "That's great. That's just great. And I suppose you two are here to protect me?"

Special Agent Johnson put his notepad away, and when he did, I saw that his pistol was in its shoulder holster, ready for action.

"That's one way of putting it," he said. "It is in the national interest to keep you alive, Jess, despite your assertions that you no longer possess the, er, talent that originally brought you to the attention of our superiors. We're just going to hang around here and make sure that, if Mr. Larsson makes it onto Camp Wawasee property, you are protected."

"The best way to protect Jess," Rob said, "would be to get her out of here."

"Precisely," Agent Johnson said. He looked Rob up and down, like he was seeing him for the first time—which I guess he was, up close, anyway. The two of them were about the same size—a fact which seemed to surprise Agent Johnson a little. For some-body who was supposed to be inconspicuous, the agent was pretty tall.

"We're planning on taking her to a safe house until Mr. Larsson has been captured," he said to Rob.

"I don't think so," Rob said at the same time that Ruth, standing behind him, went, "Oh, no. Not again."

"Excuse me," I said to Special Agent Johnson. "But don't you remember the last time you guys took me somewhere I was supposed to be safe?"

Special Agents Johnson and Smith exchanged glances. Agent Smith said, "Jess, this time, I promise you—"

"No way," I said. "I'm not going anywhere with you two. Besides"—I looked out the double glass doors at the rain which was still streaming down—"I've got some unfinished business here."

"Jess," Special Agent Smith began.

"No, Jill," I said. Don't ask me when my relation-ship with Special Agents Johnson and Smith had graduated to a first-name basis. I think it was around the time I'd bought them their first double cheese-burger meal. "I'm not going anywhere. I have things to do here. Responsibilities."

"Jessica," Special Agent Smith said. "This really isn't the time to—"

"I mean it," I said. "I have to go."

And I went. I walked right out of there, right out into the rain. It was still coming down—not as hard as before, maybe, but there was plenty of it. It only took a few seconds for my shirt and jeans to get soaked.

I didn't care. I hadn't lied to them. I had things to do. Finding Shane, wherever he was, was first and foremost on my list. Was he out, I wondered, as I stalked with my head bent in the direction of Birch Tree Cottage, in this storm? Had he found shelter somewhere? Was he dry? Was he warm? Did I even care? As many times as I'd wanted to wring his stupid neck—and I'd thought about it, fairly seriously, several times a day—did I really care what happened to him?

Yeah, I did. And not just because that oversized Mullet Head was capable of making such beautiful music. But because, well, I sort of liked him. Surprising, but true. I liked the annoying little freak.

Thunder rumbled overhead, though it was farther away than before. Then Rob came jogging up behind me.

"That was some dramatic exit," he said. His shirt and jeans, I noted, were also quickly becoming soaked.

"My specialty," I said.

"You're going the wrong way."

I stopped in the middle of the path and looked around, forgetting for a second that Rob had never been to Camp Wawasee, and so would have no way of knowing which way was the right way to Birch Tree Cottage.

"No, I'm not," I said.

"Yes, you are." He jerked a thumb over his shoulder. "The bike's that way."

I realized what he meant, then shook my head. "Rob," I said. "I can't leave."

"Jess."

Rob hardly ever calls me by my first name. More often than not, he refers to me the way he used to in detention, where we were, basically, nothing but discipline files, badly in need of sorting—by last name only.

So when he does call me by my first name, it usually means he's being very serious about something. In this case, it appeared to be my personal safety.

Unfortunately, I had no choice but to disappoint him.

"No," I said. "No, Rob. I'm not going."

He didn't say anything right away. I squinted up at him, the rain making it hard to see. He was looking down at me, his pale blue eyes filled with something I couldn't quite put my finger on. Not love, certainly.

"Jess," he said in a low, even voice. "You know I think you're a pretty down girl. You know that, don't you?"

I blinked. It wasn't easy to look up at him, with all that rain coming down in my eyes. Plus it was pretty dark. The only way I could see him was in the light from one of the lamps along the pathways, and that was pretty dim.

But he certainly looked serious.

I nodded. "Okay," I said. "We'll call that one a given, if you want."

"Good," he said. The rain had plastered his dark hair to his face and scalp, but he didn't seem to notice. "Then maybe when I say this next part, you'll understand where I'm coming from. I did not drive all the way up here to watch you get your brains hacked out by some psycho, okay? Now you get that ass"—he pointed to the one in question—"on my bike, or I swear to God, I'm going to put it there for you."

Now I knew what was in his eyes. And it wasn't love. Oh, definitely not.

It was anger.

I wiped rainwater from my eyes.

And then I said the only thing I could say: "No."

He made that half-disgusted, half-amused smile he seems to wear fifty percent of the time he's with me, then looked off into the distance for a second . . . though what he saw out there, I couldn't say. All I could see was rain.

"I have to find Shane," I shouted above a rumble of thunder.

"Yeah?" He looked down at me, still smiling. "I don't give a crap about Shane."

Anger bubbled, hot and dark, inside me. I tried to tamp it down. Count to ten, I told myself. Mr. Goodhart had suggested a long time ago that I count to ten when I felt like slugging someone. Sometimes it even worked.

"Well, I do," I said. "And I'm not leaving here until I know he's safe."

He stopped smiling.

I should have guessed what was coming next. Rob's not the kind of guy who goes around saying stuff just to hear himself talk.

Still, he's never gotten physical with me before. Not the way he did then.

I like to think that, if it had come down to it, I could have gotten away. I really think I could have. Okay, yeah, he had me upside down, which is pretty disorienting. Also, my arms were pinned, which certainly puts a girl at a disadvantage.

But I am thoroughly convinced that, with a few well-placed head-butts—if I could have gotten my head near his, which I am convinced I could have, given enough time—I could have gotten away.

Unfortunately, our tender interlude in the woods was interrupted before I was able to bring it to any sort of head-butting climax.

"Son." Special Agent Johnson's voice rang out through the rain and mist. "Put the girl down."

Rob was already striding purposefully toward his bike. He did not even slow down.

"I don't think so," was all he said.

Then Special Agent Johnson stepped out from between the trees. Even though I was upside down, I could still see he had his gun drawn—which surprised me, I must say.

It seemed to surprise Rob, too, since he froze, and stood there for a second or two. Now that I was upside down, I began to realize that my previous assumption—you know, that I was soaked—had actually been erroneous. I was not soaked. There had been no rainwater, for instance, on my stomach.

But now that I was upside down, there certainly was.

And might I add that this was not a pleasant sensation?

"You," Rob said to Special Agent Johnson, "are not going to shoot me. What if you hit her?"

"It would be unfortunate," Special Agent Johnson said, "but since she has been a thorn in my side since the day we met, it wouldn't upset me too much."

"Allan!" I was shocked. "What would Mrs. Johnson say if she could hear you now?"

"Put her down, son."

Rob flipped me over, and put me back on my feet. While this was happening, Special Agent Johnson came up and took my arm. He still had his gun out, to my surprise. But he was pointing it into the air.

"Now get on your motorcycle, Mr. Wilkins," he said to Rob, "and go home."

"Hey." Now that some of the blood was receding from my head, I could think straight. "How did you know his last name? I never told you that."

Special Agent Johnson looked bored. "License plate."

"Oh," I said.

I glanced back at Rob, standing in the rain, with

his T-shirt all sticking to him. You could see his abs through the drenched material. It occurred to me that this, too, was like a scene from a music video. You know, the totally hot guy standing in the rain after his girlfriend dumps him?

Except that I so totally was not dumping him. I was just trying to find a kid. That was all.

Only nobody was letting me.

Then something else occurred to me: If Rob's T-shirt was that wet, then what about mine?

I looked down, and promptly folded my arms across my chest.

It was better this way, I thought. I mean, not about our wet T-shirts, but the fact that they were making him go away. Because I knew it would be a lot easier to ditch the Wonder Twins than it would Rob. FBI agents I didn't mind head-butting. But when it came down to it, I think hurting Rob would have been hard.

"I'll call you," I said to Rob over my shoulder, as Special Agent Johnson started to pull me back toward the center of the camp.

"Do me a favor, Mastriani," Rob said.

"Sure," I said. It was hard to walk backward through the rain, but Special Agent Johnson was pulling so hard on me, I didn't have much choice. "What?"

"Don't."

And then Rob turned and started walking away. It didn't take long for the rain and mist to swallow him up. A minute later, I heard the engine of his Indian rev up.

And then he was gone.

I looked up at Special Agent Johnson, who, unlike Rob, did not look sexy drenched in rainwater.

"I hope you're happy now," I said to him. "That guy might have been my boyfriend someday, if you hadn't come along and ruined it."

Special Agent Johnson was busy dialing some numbers on his cell phone. He said, "Do your parents know about you and Mr. Wilkins, Jess?"

"Of course they do," I said very indignantly. "Though I have my own life, you know. My parents do not dictate whom I see or do not see socially."

This was such an outrageous string of lies, I'm surprised my tongue didn't shrivel up and fall off.

Special Agent Johnson didn't look like he believed any of them, either.

"Do your parents know," he went on, as if our conversation hadn't been interrupted, "that Mr. Wilkins has an arrest record? And is currently on probation?"

"Yes," I said, as sassily as I could. Then, because I couldn't resist, I went, "Although they aren't too clear on just what he's on probation for. . . ."

Special Agent Johnson just looked down at me, frowning a little. He went, "That information is, of course, confidential. If Mr. Wilkins has not chosen to share it with . . . your parents, I don't see that I can."

Jeez! Shot down again! How was I *ever* going to find out what Rob had done to land him in the cinderblock jungle? Rob wouldn't tell me, and, not surprisingly, I couldn't get a straight answer out of the

Feds, either. It couldn't have been that bad, or he'd have served time and not just gotten probation. But what *was* it?

It didn't look like I'd ever find out now. No, I'd managed to ruin that little relationship, hadn't I?

But what was I supposed to do? I mean, really?

Whoever was on the other end of Special Agent Johnson's cell phone must have picked up, since he said into it, "Cassie secured. Repeat, Cassie secured."

Then he hung up.

"Who," I demanded, "is Cassie?"

"I beg your pardon," Special Agent Johnson said, putting his phone away. "I ought to have said Cassandra."

"And who's Cassandra?"

"No one you need to worry about."

I glared at him. Now that I'd been out in the rain so long, I didn't even care how wet I was. I mean, it wasn't like I couldn't get any wetter.

Or more miserable.

"Wait a minute," I said. "I remember now. Seventh grade. We did mythology. Cassandra was like a psychic, or something."

"She had a talent," Special Agent Johnson admitted, "for prophecy."

"Yeah," I said. "Only she was under this curse, and—" I shook my head in disbelief. "*That's* my code name? *Cassandra?*"

"You'd have preferred something else?"

"Yeah," I said. "How about no code name?"

I was having, I decided, a pretty bad day. First a

psycho wife-beater tries to kill me, then my boyfriend walks out on me. Now I find out I have a code
name with the FBI. What next?

Special Agent Smith appeared from the shadows,
sheltered under a big black umbrella.

"Look at you two," she said when she saw us.
"You're soaked." She moved until the umbrella was
covering all three of us. Well, more or less.

"I managed to secure some rooms," she said, "at a
Holiday Inn a few miles away. I don't think Mr.
Larsson will think to look for Jess there."

"Do I get my own room?" I asked hopefully.

"Of course not." Special Agent Smith smiled at
me. "We're roomies."

Great. "I'm a remote hog," I informed her.

"I'll live," she said.

This was horrible. This was terrible. I couldn't go
stay in a cushy Holiday Inn while Shane was out in
the wilderness somewhere . . . or worse, dead. I had
to find him.

Only how was I going to do that? How was I
going to find him, and not let Allan and Jill know
what I was up to?

"I have to," I said, my throat dry, "get my stuff."

"Of course." Special Agent Johnson looked at his
watch. It was one of those ones that light up. "We'll
escort you back to your cabin to gather your belongings."

Jeez!

Still, I think Special Agents Johnson and Smith
began to regret their assignment to Project Cassandra

more than ever when we stepped into Birch Tree Cottage and observed the level of chaos there. The kids were off the wall. When we walked in, we narrowly escaped being hit by a flying chunk of bow rosin. Arthur was playing his tuba, in spite of the no-practicing-outside-of-the-music-building rule; Lionel was screaming for silence at the top of his lungs; Doo Sun and Tony were sword-fighting with a pair of violin bows . . .

And in the middle of it all, a lady police officer was standing with her hands over her ears, pleading ineffectively with her charges: "Please! Please listen to me, we're going to find your friend—"

I strode into the kitchen, opened the fuse box, and threw the switches.

Plunged into semi-darkness, the boys froze. All noise ceased.

Then I stepped out from the kitchen—

—and instantly became part of a Jessica sandwich as all of the boys surrounded me, clinging to various parts of my body and crying my name.

"All right," I yelled, after a while. "Simmer down. Simmer down!"

I disentangled myself from their embrace, then sank down onto a bed—Shane's empty bed, I saw, when lightning again lit the now darkened room. The bed was haphazardly made, with musical note sheets. Shane would have preferred, I was fairly certain, bedding emblazoned with football paraphernalia. Nevertheless, the sheets gave off a Shane-like odor that, for once, I found comforting.

"All right," I said, interrupting the cries of "Jess, where have you been?" and "Didja hear about Shane?"

"Yes, I heard about Shane," I said. "Now I want to hear your version of what happened."

The boys looked at one another blankly, then shrugged, more or less in unity.

"He was with us on the way to the lake," Sam volunteered.

Lionel's accent worsened, I realized, when he was stressed. It took me a minute to figure out his next words: "But I think he did not go in the water."

"Really, Lionel?" I peered down at the little boy. "Why do you think that?"

"If Shane had gone into the water," Lionel said thoughtfully, "he would have tried to push my head under. But he did not."

"So he didn't actually make it into the lake?" I asked.

The boys shrugged again. Only Lionel nodded with anything like assurance.

"I think," Lionel said, "that Shane ran away. He was very angry with you, Jess, for not giving me the strike."

As usual, he pronounced my name Jace. And, as usual, Lionel was right. At least I thought so. I think Shane had been angry with me . . . angry enough that maybe—just maybe—he wanted to teach me a lesson.

Shane, I thought to myself. Where are you? And what are you up to?

Suddenly, the lights came back on. Special Agent Smith came out of the kitchen, then nodded toward my room. "Are those your belongings in there?"

I nodded.

"I'll pack them for you," she said, and disappeared into my room, while her partner leaned against the front doorjamb and looked at his watch again.

"Who's that guy?" Tony wanted to know.

"Is that your *boyfriend?*" Doo Sun asked.

"Is that *Rob?*" Arthur started to ask, but I slapped a hand over his mouth . . . probably as much to my own surprise as his.

"Shhh," I said. "That's not Rob. That's just a, um, friend of mine."

"Oh," Arthur said, when I'd removed my hand. "Have you been eating McDonald's?"

I picked up Shane's pillow and lowered my face into it. Oh, Lord, I prayed. Give me the strength not to kill any more little boys today. One is really enough, I think.

Special Agent Smith came out of my room, holding a duffel bag.

"I think I've got everything," she said. "Are these Gogurts yours, or should I leave them for the children?"

Arthur, his eyes very bright, swiveled his head toward me.

"Hey," he said. "What is she doing? Is that your stuff?"

"Are you leaving?" Lionel's chin began to tremble. "Are *you* going, Jace?"

Exasperated—this was *not* how I'd wanted to break the news to the boys that I was leaving—I said to Special Agent Smith, "The Gogurts and the cookies and the chips and stuff aren't mine. Don't pack them."

Special Agent Smith looked confused. "There are no cookies, Jess. Just these Gogurt things."

"No cookies?" I stared at her. "There should be. There should be cookies and chips and Fiddle Faddle."

"Fiddle *what?*" Special Agent Smith looked more confused than ever.

"Fiddle Faddle," the boys shouted at her.

"No." Special Agent Smith blinked. "None of that. Just these Gogurts."

Still clutching Shane's pillow, I stood up and looked down at the boys.

"Did you guys eat all that candy and stuff I confiscated from you the other day?"

They looked at one another. I could have sworn they had no idea what I was talking about.

"No," they said, shaking their heads.

"I tried," Arthur confessed. "But I couldn't reach it. You put it up too high."

Too high for Arthur.

But not, I realized, for the largest resident of Birch Tree Cottage . . . besides me, of course.

I became aware of several things all at once. One, that Ruth and Scott—followed by Dave—were stepping up onto the front porch . . . come to say goodbye, I guessed.

Two, the rain outside had suddenly stopped. There was only the most distant rumbling from the sky now, as the storm moved out toward Lake Michigan.

And three, the smell from Shane's pillow, which I still clutched, had become overwhelming.

And that was because all at once, I knew where he was.

And it wasn't at the bottom of Lake Wawasee.

CHAPTER

15

Look, what do you want me to say? I don't understand this psychic stuff any more than you do. Back when I'd been a special guest at Crane Military Base, they'd run a bunch of tests on me, and basically what they'd found out was that when I slip into REM-stage sleep, something happens to me. It's like the webmaster of my brain suddenly downloads some information that wasn't there before. That's how, when I wake up, I know stuff.

Only this time, it had happened while I was awake. Really. Right while I was standing there clutching Shane's stinky pillow.

And I hadn't felt a thing. In the comic books my brother Douglas is always reading, whenever one of the characters gets a psychic vision—and they do, frequently—he scrunches up his face and goes, *"Uhnnnn..."*

Seriously. *Uhnnn*. Like it hurts.

But I am telling you, downloading a psychic vision—or however they come—doesn't hurt. It's like one second the information is not there, and a second later, it is.

Like an e-mail.

Which was why, when I looked up from that pillow, it was really hard to contain myself. I mean, I didn't want to shout out what I knew for Special Agents Johnson and Smith to hear. I wasn't exactly anxious to let them in on this new development, considering all the time and effort I'd spent, assuring them I'd lost all psychic power entirely.

Still, when I finally did get a chance to impart what seemed, to me, like some pretty miraculous stuff, no one was very impressed.

"A *cave?*" Ruth's voice rose to a panic-stricken pitch. "You want me to go into a *cave* to look for that miserable kid? No, thanks."

I shushed her. I mean, it wasn't like the Feds weren't in the next room, or anything.

"Not you," I said. "I'll do the actual, um, cave entering." I didn't want to offend her by telling her the truth, which was that Ruth was the last person I'd ever pick to go spelunking with.

"But a *cave?*" Ruth still looked skeptical. "Why would he run off and hide in a cave?"

"Two words," I said. "Paul Huck."

"Who," Ruth whispered, "or should I say, *what* is a Paul Huck?"

"He's a guy who ran away to a cave," I explained quietly, "when he felt he was being persecuted."

We had to talk in whispers, because we were sequestered in my tiny cubicle of a bedroom, while outside, Special Agents Johnson and Smith sat guarding the perimeter. I was supposed to be saying good-bye to the boys and my friends. The Feds had very generously allotted me ten minutes to do this. I suppose their line of thinking was, Well, she can't get up to much trouble in that tiny room, now can she?

What they did not know, however, was that (a) the window in my tiny room actually opened wide enough for just about any size body to slip through, (b) two bodies had already slipped through it, in order to perform a small favor for me, and (c) instead of saying good-bye, like I was supposed to be doing, to Ruth and Scott and Dave, I was waiting for an opportunity to sneak out and find Shane, whom I knew now was not only not dead, but still on Camp Wawasee property.

"Remember," I whispered to Ruth, "at the first Pit, when they read off the rules and regulations? One of them was that Wolf Cave was off-limits. What kid, hearing about Paul Huck and feeling persecuted himself, isn't going to make a beeline for that cave? Plus he took all the junk food, *and* my flashlight is missing."

Ruth went, in this very meaningful tone, "Do you have any *other* reason to suspect he might be there, Jess?"

The surprising answer was, "Yes."

Ruth raised her eyebrows. "Really? What about all

that stuff about how you need to enter REM-stage sleep in order to achieve . . . you know?"

"I don't know," I said. "Maybe I don't need it, if I'm worked up enough. . . ."

I didn't know how to put into words what had happened when I'd hugged Shane's pillow. How the smell of his shampoo had filled my head with an image of him, huddled in the glow of a flashlight, and stuffing his face with Fiddle Faddle.

I don't know how it had happened, or if it would ever happen again. But I had had a vision, while wide-awake, of a missing person. . . .

And I was going to act on that vision, and right what I'd made wrong.

"If you ask me," Ruth said, "the stupid kid isn't worth the trouble."

"Ruth." I shook my head at her. "What kind of Camp Wawasee attitude is that?"

"He's a pill," Ruth said.

"You wouldn't say that," I assured her, "if you'd ever heard him play."

"He can't be that good."

"He is. Believe me." The memory of the hauntingly beautiful music Shane had played was as sharp in my head as the vision I'd had of him, shoveling Doritos into his mouth by flashlight.

Ruth sighed. "If you say so. Still, if I were you, I'd let him stay out there and rot. He'll come back on his own when the food runs out."

"Ruth, a kid got lost in that cave and died, remember? That's why it's off-limits. For all I know, Shane might not be able to find his way out, and that's why he's still in there."

Ruth looked skeptical. "And what makes you think you'll be able to find your way out, if he can't?"

I tapped my head. "My built-in guidance system."

"Oh, right," Ruth said. "I forgot. You and my dad's Mercedes."

Suddenly, the stillness that had fallen over the camp after the heavy rainstorm was ripped apart by an explosion so loud it made thunder sound like a finger-snap. Ruth clapped her hands over her ears.

"Whoa," I said, impressed. "Right on cue. That boyfriend of yours sure knows how to create a diversion."

Ruth lowered her hands and went primly, "Scott isn't my boyfriend." Then she added, "Yet. And he should know about diversions. He was an Eagle Scout, after all."

The door to my bedroom flew open. Special Agent Smith stood there, gun drawn.

"Thank God you're all right," she said when she saw me. Her blue eyes were wide with anxiety. "That can only be him. Clay Larsson, I mean. Stay here while Agent Johnson and I go to investigate, all right? We're leaving Officer Deckard and one of the sheriff's deputies, too—"

"Sure," I said calmly. "You go on."

Special Agent Smith gave me a nervous smile I suppose she meant to be reassuring. Then she shut the door.

I stood up. "Let's get out of here," I said, and headed for the window.

"I hope you know what you're doing," Ruth muttered unhappily as she followed me. "You know, they're probably overreacting with this whole Clay Larsson thing, but what if he really is, you know, out there, looking for you?"

I gave her a disgusted look over my shoulder before I dropped out the window. "Ruth," I said. "It's me you're talking to. You think I can't handle one little old wife-beater?"

"Well," Ruth said. "If you're going to put it *that* way . . ."

We slithered out the window as quietly as we could. Outside, except for a mysterious bright orange glow from the parking lot, it was dark. It wasn't as hot as it had been, thanks to the rain.

But everything, everything was wet. My sneakers, and the cuffs of my jeans, which had only just started to dry off, were soon soaked again. Drops of water fell down from the treetops every time a breeze stirred the leaves overhead. It was quite unpleasant . . . as Ruth did not hesitate to point out, at her first opportunity.

"My ankles itch," she whispered.

"No one said you had to come," I whispered back.

"Oh, sure," Ruth hissed. "Leave me behind to deal with the cops. Thanks a lot."

"If you're going to come with me, you have to quit complaining."

"Okay. Except that all of this rain is making my allergies act up."

I swear to you, sometimes I think it would be easier if I just didn't have a best friend.

We'd only gone about a dozen yards when we heard it—footsteps swiftly approaching us. I hissed at Ruth to put out her flashlight, but it turned out our caution had been for nothing, since it was only Scott and Dave, hurrying to join us.

"Hey," I said to them as they came trotting up. "Good job, you guys. They totally fell for it."

Scott ducked his head modestly. "You were right, Jess," he said. "Tampons do make good fuses."

I glanced at Ruth. "And you said detention was a waste of my time."

Ruth only shook her head. "The American public education system," she said, "was clearly not designed with ingrates like you in mind."

Dave glanced over his shoulder at the thick black smoke pouring from the parking lot into the night sky.

"Oh, I don't know," he said. He was panting, smudged with dirt, and covered in dead leaves and clearly exhilarated. I knew what he was thinking: Never, in his seventeen years of trumpet-playing, Dungeons-&-Dragon-dice-throwing geekdom, had he ever done anything so dangerous . . . and fun. "I was going to see if I could get extra credit for this from my chemistry teacher next semester. Lighting a van on fire with a Molotov cocktail has to be good for at least ten bonus points."

"You guys," Ruth said, "are insane."

Scott looked wounded. "Hey," he said. "We used

appropriate caution. No children or animals were harmed in the execution of this prank."

"No law enforcement officials, either," Dave added.

"I am surrounded," Ruth murmured, "by lunatics."

"Enough already," I whispered. "Let's go."

We ended up not actually needing our flashlights to see our way around the lake. The storm had passed, leaving behind a sky that was mostly clear. A shiny new moon shone down on us—just a sliver, but it shed enough of a glow for us to see by, at least while there were no trees overhead to block its light—along with a light dusting of stars.

If I hadn't realized it before, from the allergy remark, I knew by the time we were halfway around the lake that bringing Ruth along had been a big mistake. She simply would not shut up . . . and not because she wanted the whole world to know about her itching, watery eyes, but because she wanted Scott to know how big and brave she thought he was, taking on the FBI all by himself . . . well, okay, with Dave's help, but still. I sincerely hoped I didn't sound like that when I talked to Rob—you know, all sugary sweet and babyish. I think if I did, Rob would have told me to knock it off already. I hoped so, anyway.

I don't know what Dave was thinking as we made our way along the shore. He was pretty quiet. It had been, I reflected, a big day for both him and Scott. I mean, they had gotten to meet a real live psychic, thwart some FBI agents, and blow up a van, all in one day. No wonder he wasn't very talkative. It was a lot to process.

I was having trouble processing some stuff of my own. The Rob thing, if you want the truth, bothered me a lot more than the whole thing where I managed to find a kid without catching forty winks first—especially considering the fact that I am a vital, independent woman who has no need of a man to make her feel whole. I mean, I said I'd call him, and he'd said *don't?* What kind of baloney was that? Is it my fault I have this very important career, and that sometimes I am forced to think first not of my own personal safety, but about the children? Couldn't he see that this wasn't about him, or even me, but a missing twelve-year-old, who, it's true, couldn't stop making fart jokes, but nevertheless didn't deserve to perish in the wilds of northern Indiana?

Of course, there was also the small matter of my having dragged poor Rob into all of this in the first place. I mean, he'd come all the way up here, and driven me all around Chicago, and helped me deal with Keely, just because I'd asked him to. And he hadn't expected anything at all in return. Not even a single lousy kiss.

And all he'd gotten for it was a pistol brandished at him by a member of the FBI.

I guess, when you took into account all of these facts, it wasn't any wonder he didn't want me to call him anymore.

But while this was perhaps the most personally troubling of the problems that were on my mind as we trudged toward Wolf Cave, it was by no means the only one. There was also, of course, the puzzling little matter of just how Dr. Alistair had found out about me. I didn't believe Pamela had told him. It was strange that he had known where I was that afternoon, when Pamela hadn't even known. I mean, I'm sure she suspected, but I hadn't discussed my plans concerning Keely Herzberg with her. I figured the less people who knew about it, the better.

So how had Dr. Alistair known?

Then the moonlight vanished as we moved from the lake's shore to the deeply wooded embankment where Wolf Cave was located. If I had thought the wet grass was bad, this was about ten times worse. The incline was really steep, and since it was mostly unused, there was no path to follow . . . just slick, wet ground cover, mostly mud and dead leaves. The others had no choice but to turn on their flashlights now, if we didn't want to break our necks tripping over some root, or something.

In spite of our efforts to approach the cave quietly, we must have made a considerable amount of noise—especially considering the fact that Ruth would *not* shut up about her stupid ankles. It was pretty quiet, that deep in the woods. There were crickets chirping, but for the first time since I'd arrived at the camp, no cicadas screamed. Maybe the rain had drowned them all.

So it couldn't have been all that hard for Shane to hear our approach.

Which might have explained why, when we

finally reached the mouth of Wolf Cave—just a dark spot under an outcropping of boulders, jutting from the side of the steep hill we'd just climbed—there was no sign of Shane. . . .

Well, unless you count the candy wrappers and empty boxes of Fiddle Faddle that lined the narrow entrance.

I borrowed Ruth's flashlight and shined it into the cave—really, the mouth was surprisingly small . . . only three feet high and maybe two feet wide. I did not relish squeezing through it, let me tell you.

"Shane," I called. "Shane, come out of there. It's me, Jess. Shane, I know you're in there. You left all this Fiddle Faddle out here."

There was a sound from within the cave. It was the sound of someone crawling.

Only the sound was going away from us, not coming closer.

"Let's just leave him in there," Ruth suggested. "The little jerk completely deserves it."

Scott seemed sort of shocked by her callousness. "We can't do that," he said. "What if he gets lost in there?"

Ruth's eyelashes fluttered behind the lenses of her glasses. "Oh, Scott," she cooed in that unnaturally sweet voice. "You're so right. I never thought of that."

Yuck.

"Maybe," Dave said, "there's another way in. You know, a wider side entrance. Most caves have more than one."

"Shane," I called into the cave. "Look, I'm sorry, okay? I'm sorry I didn't give Lionel a strike. I swear he's got one now, okay?"

No response. I tried again.

"Shane, everybody is really worried about you," I called. "Even Lionel missed you. Even the girls from Frangipani Cottage miss you. In fact, they miss you the most. They're holding a candlelight vigil for you right now. If you come out, we can panty-raid them while they're praying for you. Seriously. I'll even donate a pair of my own panties to the cause."

Nothing. I straightened up.

"I'm going to have to go in there after him," I said softly.

"I'll go with you," Dave volunteered. Which was pretty gallant of him, if you think about it. But I suppose he was only doing it because he felt guilty over letting Shane slip away from him in the first place.

My gaze flicked over him. "You'll never fit."

Which was true. The only person small enough, of the four of us, to fit through that hole was me, and they all knew it.

"Besides," I said. "This is between me and Shane. I better go on my own. You guys stay here and make sure he doesn't sneak out any of those side entrances you were talking about."

Nobody needed to tell Ruth twice to stay put. She plunked down onto a nearby boulder and immediately began rubbing her chigger-ravaged ankles.

Scott and Dave offered me a couple of caving tips from their days as Cub Scouts—if you shine your flashlight into a hole, and can't see the bottom of it, that's a hole you should avoid.

Armed with this piece of information, I dropped down to my knees and began to crawl. It was no easy task, crawling on all fours and trying to see where I was going at the same time. Still, I managed not to fall down any bottomless holes. At least, not right away. Instead, I found myself inching along a narrow—but dry, at least—tunnel. There were, much to my gratification, no bats and nothing slimy. Just a lot of dried leaves, and the occasional scrunched Dorito.

One thing you had to hand to Shane: if it was attention he was after, he sure knew how to get it. His camp counselor was crawling through a hole in the ground after him, following his trail of Snicker bar wrappers and cookie crumbs. What more could a kid ask?

Still, the deeper I went, the more I thought he might be taking things a little far. I called out to Shane a few times, but the only response I heard was more scraping of jeans against rock. For a chubby kid, Shane sure could crawl fast.

There was no way to tell how deep we'd gone—a quarter of a mile? half?—into the earth before I noticed the cave was starting to widen a bit. Now I glimpsed stalactites, and what I knew from sixth grade bio were stalagmites—stalactites point down from the ceiling, while stalagmites shot up from the ground (stalactite, ceiling; stalagmite, ground. That's how Mr. Hudson explained it, anyway). Both, I remembered, were formed by the precipitation of calcite, whatever that was. Which meant, of course, that the cave wasn't as snug and dry as it seemed.

Not that I minded. That meant there'd be less chance of encountering any woodland creatures who might otherwise have chosen to make their home here, which suited me fine.

Soon the cave started widening. Eventually, it was big enough for me actually to stand up. As the way widened, I found myself in a cavern about the size of my room back home.

Only, unlike my room back home, it was filled with creepy shadows, and a floor that seemed to slope up toward the ceiling at the sides. Pointy stalactites loomed everywhere, and even when you shined your flashlight on them, you couldn't tell if they were hiding some bats, or if the stuff growing at their base was just a fungus or what.

I learned something that night. I really don't like caves too much. And I don't think I'll be telling the story of Paul Huck again to young and impressionable children when there happens to be a cave nearby.

Fortunately, Shane seemed as creeped out by the shadowy room as I was, since, even though there were several other tunnels opening out from it, he hadn't budged. The beam from my flashlight soon crossed his, and I studied him as he sat in his

Wranglers and his blue- and red-striped shirt, glaring at me.

"You're a damned liar," was the first thing he said to me.

"Oh, yeah?" There was an eerie echo in the cavern. Somewhere water was dripping, a steady *plink, plink, plink.* It appeared to be coming from one of the wider tunnels off the chamber we were in. "That's a nice thing to say to somebody who just crawled into the bowels of the earth to find you."

"How'd you know where to look?" Shane demanded. "Huh? How'd you know I'd be in the cave?"

"Easy," I said, sauntering over to him. "Everyone knows you took that Paul Huck story way too seriously."

"Bullshit!" Shane's voice bounced off the walls of the cave, his *bullshit* repeating itself over and over until it finally faded away.

I blinked at him. "Excuse me?"

"You used your powers to find me," Shane hollered. "Your psychic powers! You still have them. Admit it!"

I stopped coming toward him. Instead, I shined my flashlight on his face, picking up cookie crumbs and a Dorito-orange mouth.

"Shane," I said. "Is that what this was about? Getting me to prove I still have ESP?"

"Of course." Shane wiggled his butt against the hard cave floor, his lip curled disgustedly. "Why else? I knew you were lying about it. I knew the minute I saw that kid's picture in your hand, that first night. You're a liar, Jess. You know that? You can give me all the strikes you want, but the truth is, you're no better than me. Worse, maybe. Because you're a liar."

I narrowed my eyes at him. The kid was a piece of work.

"Oh, yeah," I said. "And you're one to talk. Do you have any idea how many people are out there looking for you? They all think you drowned in the lake."

"Too bad they didn't ask you, huh, Jess?" Shane's eyes were very bright in my flashlight's beam. "You could have set them straight, huh?"

"Your mom," I went on. "Your dad. They're probably worried sick."

"Serve them right," Shane said in a sullen tone. "Making me come to this stinking camp in the first place."

I crossed the rest of the distance between us, then sank down beside Shane, leaning my back against the hard stone wall.

"You know what, Shane?" I said. "I think you're a liar, too."

Shane made an offended sound. Before he could say anything else, I went on, not looking at him, but at the weird shadows across the way.

"You know what I think?" I said. "I think you like playing the flute. I don't think you'd be able to play that well if you didn't like it. You may have perfect pitch and all of that, but playing like that, that takes practice."

Shane started to say something, but I just kept on going.

"And if you really hated it that much, you wouldn't practice. So that makes you as big a liar as I am."

Shane protested, quite colorfully, that this was untrue. His use of four-letter words was really very creative.

"You want to know why I tell people I can't do the psychic thing anymore, Shane?" I asked him, when I got tired of listening to him sputter invectives. "Because I didn't like my life too much back when they all thought I could still do it. You know? It was too . . . complicated. All I wanted was to be a normal girl again. So that's why I started lying."

"I'm not a liar," Shane insisted.

"Okay," I said. "Let's say you aren't. My question to you would be, why aren't you?"

He just stared at me. "W-what?"

"Why aren't you lying? If you hate coming here to Lake Wawasee so much, why don't you just tell everyone you can't play anymore, same way I told everyone I can't find people anymore?"

Shane blinked a few times. Then he laughed uncertainly. "Yeah, right," he said. "That'd never work."

I shrugged. "Why not? It worked for me. You're

the only one who knows—outside of a few close friends—that I've still got this 'gift' of mine. Why can't you do the same thing? Just play bad."

Shane stared at me. "Play bad?"

"Sure. It's easy. I do it every year when our orchestra teacher holds chair auditions. I play badly—just a little badly—on purpose, so I don't get first chair."

Shane did a surprising thing then. He looked down at his hands. Really. Like they weren't attached to him. He looked down at them as if he were seeing them for the first time.

"Play bad," he whispered.

"Yeah," I said. "And then go out for football. If that's what you really want. Personally, I think giving up the flute for football is stupid. I mean, you can probably do both. But hey, it's your life."

"Play bad," he murmured again.

"Yeah," I said again. "It's easy. Just say to them, Yes, I *had* a gift. But then I lost it. Just like that." I snapped my fingers.

Shane was still gazing down at his hands. May I add that those hands—those hands that had made that achingly sweet music—were not too clean? They were grimy with dirt and potato chip crumbs.

But Shane didn't seem to care. "I had a gift," he murmured. "But then I lost it."

"That's it," I said. "You're getting the hang of it."

"I *had* a gift," Shane said, looking up at me, his eyes bright. "But then I lost it."

"Right," I said. "It will, of course, be a blow to

music-lovers everywhere. But I'm sure you'll make a very excellent receiver."

Shane's look of appreciative wonder turned to one of disgust. "Lineman," he said.

"I beg your pardon. Lineman."

Shane continued to stare at me. "Jess," he said. "Why did you come looking for me? I thought you hated me."

"I do not hate you, Shane," I said. "I wish you would stop picking on people who are smaller than you are, and I would appreciate it if you would stop calling me a lesbian. And I can guarantee, if you keep it up, someday someone is going to do something a lot worse to you than what Lionel did."

Shane just stared at me some more.

"But I do not," I concluded, "hate you. In fact, I decided on my way over here that I actually like you. You can be pretty funny, and I really do think you'll be a good football player. I think you'd be good at anything you set your mind to being."

He blinked at me, his chubby, freckled cheeks smudged with dirt and chocolate.

"Really?" he asked. "You really think that?"

"I do," I said. "Although I also think you need to get a new haircut."

He pulled on the back of his mullet and looked defensive. "I like my hair," he said.

"You look like Rod Stewart," I informed him.

"Who's Rod Stewart?" he wanted to know.

But this seemed beyond even my descriptive ability at that particular moment. So I just said, "You know what? Never mind. Let's just go back to the cabin. This place is giving me the major creeps."

We turned back toward the way we'd come. Which was when I noticed something.

And that's that we were not alone.

"Well, lookie what we have here," said Clay Larsson.

I would just like to take this opportunity to say that I, for one, had not believed Special Agents Johnson and Smith when they'd announced that Mrs. Herzberg's boyfriend was on some kind of killing rampage, and that I was his next intended victim. I think I was pretty much under the impression that they were just trying to scare me, to get me alone with them somewhere so that they could make their observations of me without interruption.

For instance, had I gone with them to the Holiday Inn, Special Agent Smith would have undoubtedly gotten up very early and then sat there, with pen poised on notepad, at my bedside, to see if I'd wake up babbling about where Shane was, thus proving that I had lied about having lost my telekinetic powers, or whatever.

That's what a part of me had thought. I had

never—unlike Rob—taken very seriously the idea that there might be a man unhappy enough with my recent behavior to want me, you know. Dead.

At least, I didn't believe it until he was standing in front of me, with one of those long, security-guard-type flashlights in his hands. . . .

One of those flashlights that would actually make a really handy weapon. Like if you wanted to conk somebody over the head with it. Someone who, for example, had kicked you in the face earlier that day.

"Thought you'd seen the last of me, dincha, girlie?" Clay Larsson leered down at Shane and me. He was what you'd call a large man, though I couldn't say much for his fashion sense. He looked no prettier now, in the glow of my flashlight, than he'd looked in broad daylight.

And he was even less appealing now that he had the imprint of the bottom of my Puma tattooed across the bridge of his nose. There were deep purple and yellow scars around his eyes—bruising from the nasal cartilage I'd crushed with my kick—and his nostrils were crusted over with blood.

These were, of course, the unavoidable consequences of being kicked in the face. I couldn't really hold the contusions against him, fashion-wise. It was the razor stubble and the halitosis that he really could have done something about.

"Look," I said, stepping in front of Shane. "Mr. Larsson, I can appreciate that you might be upset with me."

It might interest you to know that, at this point,

my heart wasn't beating fast or anything. I mean, I guess I was scared, but usually, in situations like this, I don't tend to realize it until the whole thing is over. Then, if I'm still conscious, I usually throw up, or whatever.

"But you have to understand"—as I spoke, I was backing up, pushing Shane slowly toward one of the other tunnels that branched out from the cavern we were in—"I was only doing my job. I mean, you have a job, right?"

Looking at him, of course, I couldn't think what kind of moron might have hired him for any job. I mean, who would willingly employ anybody who gave so little thought to his personal grooming and hygiene? Look at his shirt, for Pete's sake: it was stained. Stained with what I really hoped was chili or barbecue sauce. It was certainly red, whatever it was.

But whatever: Clearly, a complete lack of adequate forethought had gone into Clay's ensemble, and I, for one, considered it a crying shame, since he was not, technically, an unattractive man. Maybe not a Hottie, but certainly Do-able, if you got him cleaned up.

"I mean, people call me up," I said, continuing to back up, "and they say their kid is missing or whatever, and I, well, what am I supposed to do? I mean, I have to go and get the kid. That's my job. What happened today was, I was just doing my job. You're not really going to hold that against me now, are you?"

He was moving slowly toward me, the beam from his flashlight trained on my face. This made it kind of hard for me to see what he was doing, other than inexorably coming at me. I had to shield my eyes with one hand, while, with the other, I kept pushing Shane back.

"You made Darla cry," Clay Larsson said in his deep, really quite menacing voice.

Darla? Who the heck was Darla?

Then it hit me.

"Yes," I said. "Well, I'm sure Mrs. Herzberg was quite upset." I wanted to point out to him that I had it on pretty good authority that he, in fact, had probably made Keely's mother cry a lot more often than I had—throwing bottles at people tends to do that—but I felt at this juncture in our conversation, it might not be the wisest thing to bring up.

"But the fact is," I said instead, "you two shouldn't have taken Keely away from her father. The court awarded him custody for a reason, and you didn't have any right to—"

"And"—Clay didn't seem to have heard my pretty speech—"you broke my nose."

"Well," I said. "Yes. I did do that. And you know, I'm really sorry about it. But you did have hold of my leg, remember? And you wouldn't let go of it, and I guess, well, I got scared. You aren't going to hold a grudge against me for that, are you?"

Evidently, he had every intention of doing so, since he said, "When I'm through with you, girlie, you're gonna have a new definition for scared."

Definition. Wow. A four-syllable word. I was impressed.

"Now, Mr. Larsson," I said. "Let's not do anything you might regret. I think you should know, this place is crawling with Feds. . . ."

"I saw 'em." I couldn't see his expression because of the light shining in my eyes, but I could hear his tone. It was mildly ironic. "Runnin' toward that burning van. Right before I saw you and your friends outside." He seemed to be grinning. "I was glad when I saw you were the one who went in."

"Oh, yeah?" I didn't know what else to say. Keep him talking, was all I could think to do. Maybe Ruth or one of the boys would hear him, and run for help. . . .

That is, if we weren't too deep underground for them to hear us.

"I like caves," Clay Larsson informed me. "This is a real nice one. Lots of different ways in. But only one way out . . . for you, anyway."

I did not like the sound of that.

"Now, Mr. Larsson," I said. "Let's talk this over, okay? I—"

"Couldn't have picked a better place for what I got planned if you'd tried," Clay Larsson finished for me.

"Oh," I said, gulping. My throat, which had been having a tendency lately, I noticed, to run a little on the dry side, felt like the Sahara. Oh, yeah, and remember how I said my heart wasn't beating fast?

Well, it was. Fast and hard.

"Um," I said. "Okay." I tried to remember what I'd learned in counselor training about conflict resolution. "So what I hear you saying, Mr. Larsson, is that you are unhappy with the way I took Keely from you—"

"And kicked me in the face."

"Right, and kicked you in the face. I hear you saying that you are somewhat dissatisfied with this turn of events—"

"You hear that correctly," Clay Larsson assured me.

"And what *I* would like to say to you"—I tried to keep my voice pleasant, like they'd said to in counselor training, but it was hard on account of how hard I was shaking—"is that this disagreement seems to be between you and me. Shane here really had nothing to do with it. So if it's all right with you, maybe Shane could just slip on out—"

"And run for those Fed friends of yours?" Clay Larsson's tone was as disgusted as mine had been pleasant. "Yeah. Right. No witnesses."

I swallowed hard. Behind me, I could feel Shane's breath, hot and fast, on the back of my arm. He was clinging to the belt loops of my jeans, strangely silent, for him. I wouldn't have minded a reassuring belch, but none seemed forthcoming. Under the circumstances, I regretted the crack I'd made about his hair.

Could I stall long enough to get Shane into a position so he could make it through one of those tunnels and escape? The opening I'd followed him through was way too narrow for Clay Larsson to fit into. If I could just distract him long enough . . .

"This isn't," I pointed out, "the way to go about ensuring that Mrs. Herzberg gets visitation rights, you know. I mean, a court of law would probably look askance at her sharing a household with a guy who had, um, attempted murder."

Clay Larsson asked, "Who said anything about attempted?"

And suddenly, the light that had been in my eyes danced crazily against the ceiling as Clay Larsson lifted the flashlight, with the intention, I supposed, of bringing it down on my head.

I screamed, "Run!" to Shane, who wasted no time doing so. He popped through the narrow tunnel behind us quicker than anybody in *Alice in Wonderland* had ever plunged down a rabbit hole. One minute he was there, and the next he was gone.

It seemed to me like following him would be pretty smart. . . .

But first I had to deal with this heavy flashlight coming at me.

Being small has its compensations. One of them is that I'm fast. Also, I can compress myself into spaces otherwise unfit for human occupation. In this case, I ducked behind this stalactite/stalagmite combo that had made a sort of calcite pillar to one side of the hole Shane had slipped through. As a result, Clay Larsson's flashlight connected solidly with the rock formation, instead of with my head.

There was an explosion of stone shards, and Clay Larsson said a very bad word. The calcite formation split in half, the stalactite plunging from the ceiling like an icicle off the gutter. It fell to the floor with a clatter.

As for me, well, I kept going.

Only along the way, somehow, I dropped my flashlight.

Considering what happened next, this might have been for the best. Clay, seeing the bright white beam, swung his own flashlight—with enough force for it to make a whistling noise as it sailed through the air—in the direction he thought I was standing. There was another loud clatter, this one from his heavy metal flashlight as it connected with the cavern wall.

He hadn't been kidding about the attempted murder thing. If that had been my head, I thought, with a touch of queasiness, I'd have a handy space near my brain stem right about now to keep loose change.

"Nice trick," Clay grunted, as he squatted down to retrieve my flashlight. "Only now you can't see to get out of here, can you, girlie?"

Good point. On the other hand, I could see what mattered most, and that was him.

And, more to the purpose, he couldn't see me. I figured I'd better press that advantage while I still had it.

The question was, how? I figured I had several options. I could simply stay where I was, until the inevitable moment I was once again caught in the sweeping arc of his flashlight . . . and now he had two flashlights, so make that two sweeping arcs.

My second option was to attempt to follow, as

quickly as I could, Shane down his rabbit hole. The only problem with this plan was that any rock I happened to kick loose on my way there would give me away. Could I really outcrawl a guy that size? I didn't think so.

My third alternative was the one I liked the least, but which seemed to be the one I was stuck with. So long as the guy had me to worry about, he wasn't going to mess with Shane. The longer I could keep him from trying to go after the kid, the better Shane's chances of somehow escaping.

And so it was, with great regret, that I made a sound to distract Clay, luring him toward where I hid, and away from Shane.

What I had not counted on was Clay Larsson being smart enough—and let's face it, sober enough—to fake me out. Which was exactly what he did. I'd thrown a pebble one way, thinking he'd follow the sound, and immediately darted in the opposite direction. . . .

Only to find, to my great surprise, that Mr. Larsson had whipped around and, fast as a cat, blocked my path.

I threw on the brakes, of course, but it was too late.

Next thing I knew, he'd tackled me.

As I went flying through the air, narrowly missing several stalactites, I had time to reflect that really, Professor Le Blanc was right: I *had* been lazy, never learning to read music. And I swore to myself that if I got out of Wolf Cave alive, I would dedicate the rest of my life to combating musical illiteracy.

I hit the floor of the cave with considerable force, but it was Clay Larsson's heavy body, slamming into mine, that drove all the wind from me. It also convinced me that moving again would probably be excessively painful—quite possibly even fatal, due to the massive internal injuries I was pretty sure I'd just incurred. As I lay there, dazed from the blow—which felt as if it had broken every bone in my body—I had time to wonder if they would ever find our skeletal remains, or if Shane and I would just be left to rot in Wolf Cave until the next camper, some other Paul Huck wannabe, stumbled across us.

This was a depressing thought. Because, you know, there were a lot of things I'd wanted to do that I'd never gotten a chance to. Buy my own Harley. Get a mermaid tattoo. Go to prom with Rob Wilkins (I know it's geeky, but I don't care: I think he'd look hot in a tux). That kind of stuff.

And now I was never going to get to.

So when Clay Larsson went, "Nightie-night, girlie," and raised his steel flashlight high in the air, I was more or less resigned to my death. Dying, I felt, would actually be a relief, as it would make the mind-numbing pain I felt in every inch of my body go away.

But then something happened that didn't make any sense at all. There was a thud, accompanied by a sickening, crunching noise—which I, as a veteran fistfighter, knew only too well was the sound of breaking bone—and then Clay Larsson's heavy body came slamming into mine again. . . .

Only this time, it appeared to be because the man was unconscious.

Suddenly recovering my mobility, I reached for his flashlight, which had fallen harmlessly to one side of my head, and shined it in the direction from which I'd heard the thudding sound. . . .

And there stood Shane, holding on to one end of the stalactite that had broken off from the cave ceiling, which he had clearly just swung, baseball-bat style, at Clay Larsson's head. . . .

And hit it out of the park.

Shane, looking down at Clay's limp, still form sprawled across my legs, dropped the stalactite, then glanced toward me.

I went, "Way to go, slugger."

Shane burst into tears.

"Well," I said. "What was I supposed to think? I mean, after that whole don't-call-me thing."

Rob, sounding—as usual—half-amused and half-disgusted with me, said, "I knew what you were after, Mastriani. You wanted to get rid of me so you could ditch the Feds and go after the little guy."

Shane—who was tucked into the bed beside mine in the Camp Wawasee infirmary, a thermometer in his mouth—made a noise that I suppose was meant to signal his objection to being called a little guy.

"Sorry," Rob said. "I meant little dude."

"Thank you," Shane said sarcastically.

"No talking," the nurse admonished him.

"And you were okay with that?" I asked Rob. "I mean, letting me ditch the Feds, and you, in order to go after Shane?"

I suppose it was kind of weird, the two of us

working out our recent relationship difficulties while the camp nurse fussed over me and Shane. But what else were we supposed to talk about? My recent brush with death? The expressions Ruth, Scott, and Dave had worn when Shane and I, bruised and battered, crawled out of Wolf Cave and asked them to call the police? The look on Rob's face when he'd roared up a minute or so later and heard what had happened in his absence?

"Of course I wasn't okay with that." Rob paused while the nurse butted in to take my pulse. Seemingly pleased by the steadiness of its beat, she moved away to do the same to Shane.

"But what was I supposed to do, Mastriani?" Rob went on. "The guy pulled a gun on me. Not like I thought he'd shoot me, but it was clear nobody—most specifically you—wanted me around."

I said defensively, "That isn't true. I always want you around."

"Yeah, but only if I'll go along with whatever harebrained idea you've come up with. And let me tell you, going into a cave in the middle of the night with a killer on the loose? Not one I'd probably go for."

I said, "Well, it all turned out okay."

Rob snorted. "Oh, yeah. Shane?" He turned around and looked at the chubby-cheeked boy in the bed next door. "You agree with that? You think it all turned out okay?"

Shane nodded vigorously. Then, when the nurse reached down and took the thermometer from his mouth, he said, "I think it turned out great."

Rob snorted. "You didn't seem to think so when you first got out of that cave."

Well, that much was true, anyway. Shane had pretty much been in hysterics up until Special Agents Smith and Johnson arrived, along with the sheriff and his deputies, and put a still unconscious Clay Larsson under arrest. They had a hard time dragging him out of that cave, believe me, even using the wider side entrance he'd discovered.

"Yeah," Shane admitted. "But that was before the cops got there. I was afraid he was going to wake up and come after us again."

"After that whack you gave him?" Rob raised his eyebrows. "Never mind football, kid. You've got batting in your blood."

Shane flushed with pleasure at this praise. He had nothing but admiration for Rob, having recognized him as the guy from the story I'd told that first night, the one about the murdering car.

What's more, Rob had pretty much been the only one who'd kept his head in the wake of our crawling out of Wolf Cave. That week's worth of counselor training hadn't prepared Ruth, Scott, or Dave for dealing with a couple of victims of an attempted murder.

"You know, Mastriani," Rob went on, "you have more than just an anger-management problem. You are also the stubbornest damned person I've ever met. Once you get an idea into your head, nothing can make you change your mind. Not your friends. Not the FBI. And certainly not me." He added, "I used to have a dog a lot like you."

This seemed to me to be neither flattering nor very romantic, but Shane found it hilarious. He giggled.

"What happened?" Shane wanted to know. "To the dog that was like Jess?"

"Oh," Rob said. "He was convinced he could stop moving cars with his teeth, if he could just sink them into their tires. Eventually, he got run over."

"I am not," I declared, "a car-chasing dog. Okay? There is absolutely no parallel between me and a dog that's stupid enough to—"

I broke off, realizing with indignation that Rob was chuckling to himself. He was in a much better mood now than he'd been earlier, when he hadn't been sure I wasn't seriously injured. He'd had a lot to say, let me tell you, on the subject of my insisting on staying at Camp Wawasee in order to find Shane, and thus endangering not only my life, but, as it had ended up, a lot of other people's as well.

And, of course, he was right. I'd screwed up. I was willing to admit it.

But, hey, things had turned out all right in the end.

Well, for everybody but Clay Larsson.

"So," I couldn't help asking, "you're not mad at me?"

All he said in reply was, "I think I'll be able to get over it."

But for Rob, that was like admitting—I don't know. His undying love for me, or something. So while I lay there, waiting for the inevitable moment when the nurse was going to decide I was well enough for questioning, I perked up. Why, I thought to myself, I'm going into my junior year! Juniors at Ernie Pyle High are allowed to go to the prom. I could invite Rob, and then I'd get to see him in a tux after all . . . that is, if he'd go with me. It *is* kind of weird, I'll admit, to go to prom with a guy who's already graduated, and who knows, maybe if I ask him, he'll refuse. . . .

But by the time prom rolls around, I'll finally be seventeen, so how *can* he refuse? I mean, really? Resist me? I don't think so.

These happy thoughts were somewhat dampened by the fact that Shane was in the next bed making gagging noises over what he deemed our "mushiness"—though if you ask me, there'd been nothing mushy at all going on . . . at least, not by *Cosmo* standards. Or any other standards, really, that I could see.

It was at that moment that the nurse went, "Well, from the sound of it, you two are well enough to take on a few more visitors. And there are a lot of them out there. . . ."

And then the evening became a blur of relieved faces and pointed questions, which we answered according to the story we'd so carefully prepared, Rob and Ruth and Scott and Dave and me, while we'd been waiting for the cops to show up.

"So," Special Agent Johnson said, sinking into a seat close to the one Rob occupied. "Anything you'd like to add to your somewhat sketchy account of just what, exactly, happened out there tonight, Miss Mastriani?"

I pretended to think about it. "Well," I said. "Let me see. I remembered a ghost story I'd told about a cave, so I figured I'd check the one on the camp property for Shane, just in case, and while we were in there, that crazy Larsson guy tried to kill us, and Shane whacked him in the head with a stalactite. That's about it, I think."

Special Agent Johnson didn't look very surprised. He looked over at Shane, who was sitting up in bed, fingering a plastic sheriff's badge one of the deputies had given him for his bravery.

"That sound right to you?"

Shane shrugged. "Yeah."

"I see." Special Agent Johnson closed his notebook, then exchanged a significant look with his partner, who was sitting on the end of my bed. "A hero. And just how, precisely, did you happen upon the scene, Mr. Wilkins? It was my impression that you left the camp some hours ago."

"Well," Rob said. "That's true. I did. But I came back."

"Uh-huh," Special Agent Johnson said. "Yes, I can see that. Any particular reason you came back?"

Rob did something very surprising then. He reached out, took hold of my hand, and said, "Well, I couldn't leave things the way they were with my girl, could I? I had to come back and apologize."

His girl? He had called me his girl! He had taken my hand and called me his girl!

I was grinning so happily, I was afraid my lips might break. Special Agent Johnson, noticing this, looked pointedly toward the ceiling, clearly sickened by my adolescent enthusiasm. But how could I help it? Rob had called me *his girl!* So what if he'd done it to throw off a federal investigation into my affairs that evening? Prom had never seemed so likely a prospect as it did at that moment.

"Um," Special Agent Johnson said. "I see. Please forgive me if I sound unconvinced. The fact is, Special Agent Smith and I feel that it is a bit of a co-incidence, Jess, that you went looking for young Master Shane in Wolf Cave. You certainly didn't mention that he might have been in this cave to anyone when you first learned of his disappearance."

"Excuse me, sir." The nurse appeared and stuck a mug of extremely hot, extremely sugary tea in my hands. "For the shock," she said in an explanatory manner to the agents, even though they hadn't asked, before she handed a similar mug to Shane.

I took a sip. It was surprisingly restorative, in spite of the fact that I was trying to look like someone whose only recent shock had been finding her boyfriend's tongue in her mouth.

Yeah, I know. Wishful thinking, right?

"Jess," Special Agent Smith said. "Why don't you tell us what really happened?"

I sat there, enjoying the warm tea flowing down my insides, and the warm arm flung across my out-sides. Talk about a happy camper.

"I already told it," I said, "exactly like it was."

At their raised eyebrows, I added, "No, really. That's it."

"Yes," Shane said. "She's telling the truth, sir."

We all looked over at Shane, who, like me, was downing his own mug of tea. He had, through it all, clung to his bag of Chips Ahoy cookies, and now he slipped one from the bag, and dunked it into his tea.

Special Agent Johnson looked back at me.

"Nice try," he said. "But I don't think so."

"I highly doubt, for instance," Special Agent Smith said, "that that little boy was the one who set off a Molotov cocktail beneath our van."

I rolled my eyes. "Well, obviously," I said, "that could only have been Mr. Larsson."

Both Special Agents Johnson and Smith stared down at me.

"No, really," I said. "To distract you. I mean, come on. The guy's a real psycho. I hope they put him away for a long, long time. Going after a little kid like that? Why, it's unconscionable."

"Unconscionable," Special Agent Johnson repeated.

"Sure," I said defensively. "That's a word. I took the PSATs. I should know."

"Funny how," Special Agent Johnson said, "Clay Larsson happened to know exactly which vehicle was ours."

"Yeah," I said, swallowing a sip of tea. "Well, you know. Criminal genius and all."

"And strange," Special Agent Smith said, "that he would pick our vehicle, out of all the other ones parked in that lot, to set on fire, when he doesn't even know us."

"One of the hardest things to accept," Rob remarked, "about violent crime is its seeming randomness."

They both looked at Rob, and I felt a moment of pride that I was, as he'd so matter-of-factly put it, his girl.

Then Dr. Alistair appeared at the end of my cot, wringing his hands.

"Jessica," he said, glancing worriedly from me to Special Agents Johnson and Smith and then back again. "You're all right?"

I looked at him like he was crazy. Which I was pretty sure he was.

"Oh, thank goodness," he cried, even though I hadn't said anything in reply to his question. "Thank goodness. I do hope, Jessica, that you'll forgive me for my outburst earlier this evening—"

I said, "You mean when you asked me why I didn't get my psychic friends to help me find Shane?"

He swallowed, and darted another nervous look at the agents.

"Yes," he said. "About that. I didn't mean—"

"Yes, you did," I said. "You meant every word." I looked hard at Special Agents Johnson and Smith. "How much did you guys pay him, anyway, to report my every move to you?"

Jill and Allan exchanged nervous glances.

"Jessica," Special Agent Smith said. "What are you talking about?"

"It's so obvious," I said, "that he was your narc. I

mean, he scheduled that one o'clock appointment with me, and then when I didn't show up, he called you. That's how you knew I'd left the camp. You didn't have to sit outside by the gates and wait to see if I'd leave. You had someone working on the inside to spare you the trouble."

"That," Special Agent Johnson said, "is patently—"

"Oh, come on." I rolled my eyes. "When are you guys going to get it through your heads that you're going to have to find yourselves a new Cassandra? Because the truth is, this one's retired."

"Jessica," Dr. Alistair cried. "I would never in a million years compromise the integrity of this camp by accepting money for—"

"Aw, shut up," Shane snapped. I could see that his campaign to be kicked out of music camp had now entered high gear. I hadn't any doubt that the traumatic event in Wolf Cave was going to—for the time being, anyway—have a detrimental effect on his ability to play the flute.

Dr. Alistair, looking startled, did shut up, to everyone's surprise.

Special Agent Johnson leaned forward and said, in a low, rapid voice, "Jessica, we know perfectly well that Jonathan Herzberg asked you to find his daughter, and that you, in fact, did so. We also know that this evening, you again used your psychic powers to find Shane Taggerty. You can't go on with this ridiculous charade that you've lost your psychic powers any longer. We *know* it isn't true. We *know* the truth." He leaned back and regarded me menacingly.

"And it's only a matter of time," Special Agent Smith added, "before you'll be forced to admit it, Jess."

I digested this for a moment. And then I said, "Jill?"

Special Agent Smith looked at me questioningly. "Yes, Jess?"

"Are you a lesbian?"

After that, the nurse made everyone leave, on account of the fact she was worried Shane was going to make himself sick from laughing so hard.

CHAPTER

18

"Doug," I said, trailing one hand through the cool, silver water.

Ruth, sprawled across an inner tube a few feet from mine, gazed through the dark lenses of her sunglasses into the clear blue sky overhead. "Do-able," she said, after a moment.

"Agreed," I said. "What about Jeff?"

Ruth adjusted a strap on her bikini. After six weeks of salads, she had finally deemed herself svelte enough for a two-piece. "Do-able," she said.

"Agreed." I leaned my head back and felt the sun beat down on my throat. It was beating down on other places, as well. After several weeks of spending my afternoons floating across the mirrored surface of Lake Wawasee, I was the color of Pocahontas. I would look, I knew, exceptionally good at tonight's all-camp concert, at which I was playing the piece

Professor Le Blanc had despaired of me ever learning, except by imitation.

I didn't have to imitate anyone, though. I could read each and every note.

A shout wasn't enough to break the trance-like daze the sun had sent Ruth and me into, but it got our attention. We lifted our heads and looked toward shore. Scott and Dave were playing Frisbee with some of the campers. Scott waved at us, and Dave, distracted, missed a catch, and landed in the sand.

"Dave," I said.

"Do-able," Ruth said.

"Agreed. Scott," I said, watching as he dove to make a catch.

"Hottie," Ruth said. "Of course."

I raised my sunglasses and looked at her from beneath the lenses in surprise.

"Really? He used to be Do-able."

"He's *my* summer fling," she informed me. "If I say he's hot, he's hot."

I lowered my sunglasses. "Okay," I said.

"Besides," she said. "That whole thing with lighting the Feds' van on fire? That was kind of cool. You might have something with the whole dangerous-guy thing."

"Rob," I said, "is not dangerous."

"Please," Ruth said. "Any guy who drives a motorcycle as his main form of transportation is dangerous."

"Really? Is that better than a guy with a convertible?"

Ruth shrugged. "Sure."

Wow. I leaned back, digesting this. My dangerous boyfriend was driving up to watch me perform at the concert that night. So was my family. I wondered what would happen if I introduced Rob to my mother. Frankly, I couldn't picture my mother and Rob in the same room. It was going to be very—

I felt something brush against the hand I was trailing in the water. I screamed and yanked my fingers away, just as Ruth did the same thing.

Two snorkel-fitted heads popped up from beneath the water and promptly began laughing at us.

"Ha-ha," Arthur cried, pointing at me as he treaded water. "You screamed just like a girl!"

"Like a girl," Lionel echoed incoherently. He was laughing too hysterically to speak.

"Very funny," I said to them. "Why don't you two swim over to the deep area and get a cramp?"

"Yeah," Ruth said. "And don't bother calling for us, because we won't come fish you out."

"Come on, Lionel," Arthur said. "Let's go. These two are no fun."

The two heads promptly disappeared. I watched the ends of their snorkels slice the water's surface as they headed back to shore. The two had become fast friends, once Shane was out of the picture and Lionel no longer spent every waking moment in fear of being tortured.

As I'd predicted, Shane's ability to play the flute had mysteriously disappeared shortly after the Wolf Cave incident, and though it was too late to get him into any self-respecting football camp, several had offered him scholarships, based on his size alone, for the following summer. Mr. and Mrs. Taggerty were not, it was rumored, happy about this, but what could they do? The boy was, according to more than one coach, a natural.

Off over in the direction of Wolf Cave, a cicada began its shrill call—one of the last ones I'd hear, I knew, before they all sank back into the ground to hibernate until next summer.

"So did Dr. Alistair ask you to come back next year?" Ruth wanted to know.

"Yeah," I said, with some disgust. "I suppose so he can supplement his income again by ratting me out to the Feds."

"How'd you know it was him, anyway?" Ruth asked.

I shrugged. "I don't know. I just did. Same way I know they're still monitoring me."

Ruth nearly lost her balance in the inner tube. "They *are?*" she sputtered. "How do you know?"

I pointed out toward the trees on the side of the lake closest to us. "See that thing over there, glinting in the sun?"

Ruth looked where I was pointing. "No. Wait. Yeah. I guess. What is that?"

"Telephoto lens," I said, lowering my arm. "Watch. Now that he knows we spotted him, he'll drive to some other spot and try again."

Sure enough, the glint disappeared, and far off, we heard the sound of a car engine.

"Ew," Ruth cried. "How creepy! Jess, how can you stand it?"

I shrugged. "What can I do? That's just the way it is, I guess."

Ruth chewed her lower lip. "But aren't you . . . I mean, aren't you worried they're going to catch you one of these days? In a lie, I mean?"

"Not really." I tilted my head back, letting the sun warm my neck again. "The trick, I guess, is just never to stop."

"Never stop what?"

"Lying," I said.

"Isn't that going to be hard," Ruth asked, "now that . . . well, you know? Now that your powers are getting stronger?"

I shrugged. "Probably." It wasn't something I liked to think about.

"Hey," I said, to change the subject. "Isn't that Karen Sue over there, on that pink inflatable raft?"

Ruth looked, then made a face. "I can't believe she's wearing one of those headbands in the water. And is that Todd she's with? He is so not Do-able. Did you hear him rehearsing that piece he's playing tonight? Bartok. What a show-off."

"Let's go tip them over," I suggested.

"You've got to be kidding," Ruth said. "That's so . . ."

I raised my eyebrows. "So what?"

"So childish," Ruth said. Then she grinned. "Let's do it."

And so we did.